The
Lost Queen

By Lynde Leatherwood

iyunadilpress.wordpress.com

iyuandilpress@gmail.com

Iyuandil Press ISBN 978-1-7325837-1-9

Cover Design by Ross Funderburk
Edited by Hillary Buchanan

For my brothers, Jack, Steven, and Daniel. Thanks for all the adventures in Contaria, Sky Land, the Backwards Islands, Underground World, and beyond.

Map of Iyuandil

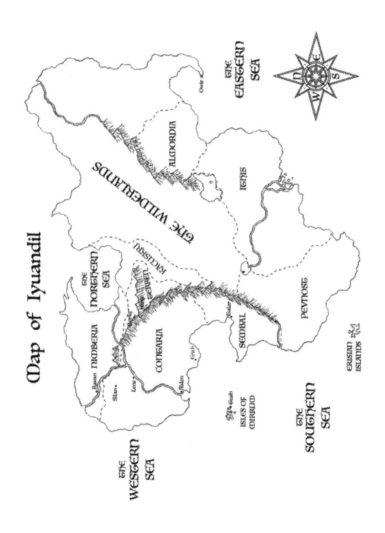

THE WILDERLANDS

ALDORDIA

SIGHI

THE
EASTERN
SEA

N
E
W
S

THE
NORTHERN
SEA

NIOBERIA

CONGARIA

NACUSSIRU

SEGOBAL

PEVLOSE

THE
WESTERN
SEA

ISLES OF DIRRUD

THE
SOUTHERN
SEA

ERUSIND
ISLANDS

Table of Contents

The
Lost Queen

Prologue

A young man with golden-blonde hair and electric blue eyes paced back and forth across the hall, his palms sweaty and his hands trembling. He was dressed in cardinal-red robes embroidered with gold thread. On his finger was a silver ring with the insignia of a magnificent dragon, and on his head rested a golden crown. His anxious gaze was drawn to the large, wooden door that stood intimidatingly at the end of the hall. The rhythmic treading of his boots against the stone floor was all that kept the night's silence at bay.

Suddenly, a high-pitched cry pierced the dull silence of the castle passageways. The young man's heart leapt inside his chest. It felt like an eternity before the door at the end of the hall finally creaked open and the midwife's head peeked out.

"Your Majesty," said the midwife, "you're welcome to come in now." The young king ran to the door in his excitement. He slowed his pace when he reached it and peeked through the crack in the door. A grand bed sat at the other side of the room. Its dark, mahogany posts reached for the ceiling, its golden curtains open. The sheets were made of fine silk imported across the kingdoms from Kacuskri.

Sitting in the bed was a beautiful lady, about the same age as the young man. She had long, wavy, auburn hair and emerald green eyes that shimmered in the candlelight. In her arms rested a small bundle of crimson cloth, richly embroidered like the king's own robes. The young king walked slowly to her bedside, his heart beating out of his chest.

"Darius," said the woman endearingly.

"How are you, Genevieve, my love?" Darius asked her.

"Tired," replied Genevieve, smiling softly. Darius's eyes moved to the bundle. Genevieve's smile broadened as she lifted the bundle upwards to Darius. The king gently took the bundle and looked down at the tiny, sleeping face surrounded by the cloths. The babe began to coo softly in Darius's arms.

"It's a girl," Genevieve said. "What shall we name her?"

"I'm not sure," Darius said. He looked lovingly upon his first born's shining face. The baby girl's eyes struggled to open, blinking in the candlelight. "You are so beautiful," Darius muttered to the baby. Darius caught a glimpse of electric blue eyes before they fluttered shut again.

"I know exactly what we can name her," Genevieve said. She leaned over to her husband and whispered the name in his ear. Darius smiled.

"That is a beautiful name," Darius proclaimed. Then he pulled from his pocket a golden medallion. Engraved in the medallion was a mighty dragon with outstretched wings on either side of its body. It was the royal family crest. "This is a gift from a friend, my darling. And one day, you will proudly wear it. I know you are going to be the greatest, most beautiful queen that Contaria has ever seen."

Chapter 1
A New King

The night was cold and as dark as the deed that took place on it. The crescent moon shone dimly over Castle Galador, the towering palace at Alden. Faint moonbeams crept silently over the turrets and towers, barely lighting the large courtyard garden in which stood a man.

The man was tall and handsome. He had dark, curly hair, beautiful dark brown eyes, and a small goatee that curled slightly at the tip. He was clad in a thick fur robe trimmed with silver that shimmered in the faint moonlight. He had a regal air about him.

His foot tapped anxiously on the cobblestone path, his hands fidgeting behind his back. The frustration and annoyance in his heart seemed to seep into every fiber of his being. Patience might be a virtue, but this man hadn't an ounce of it. *It's been too long,* he thought. *He should have been back by now.*

"My lord," said a voice. The man spun to face the entrance to the garden. Another man had walked in. He wore a black tunic with a black, leather belt, to which a small sheath for a dagger was tied. On his back was a quiver, with the fletchings of eleven black arrows sticking out. In his hand was a black recurve bow.

"Is it done, Acillion?" asked the first man in a deep, yet quiet voice.

"Yes, sire," Acillion said. "He's dead." The first man slowly turned away from Acillion and stared at the stars with a smile on his face as if he had just conquered the heavens.

"I shall tell the nobles of the king's tragic demise," the man said. "In the morning, they shall crown me King of all Contaria."

"But, Prince Alexander—"

"It's *King* Alexander to you now!" he interrupted.

"But, *King* Alexander," Acillion corrected himself, "what of the princess, your niece?"

"What of her?" asked Alexander. "Getting rid of that nuisance was part of your job." Acillion hesitated to respond. "Well?"

"When I went to find the girl in the nursery, she wasn't there," said Acillion. "She's disappeared. She and her nursemaid." The two men stood in silence for a moment.

"You are one of the greatest assassins under my command," Alexander started quietly. "And yet, you let a five-year-old girl slip under your nose? Now how could that have happened?"

"My lord, I—" Alexander smacked Acillion across the face.

"You idiot!" shouted the angered prince. "How could you let her get away? This could ruin my plans!" Acillion only glared back, his right cheek bright red.

Before either of them could say another word, panicked voices and thundering footsteps from inside the palace filled the courtyard, growing ever nearer. Suddenly, two armed guards and two knights ran into the garden. One knight wore black armor and obviously led the party. The other wore chainmail under a yellow tunic embroidered with a great black bear.

"Prince Alexander!" the knight in black said. "King Darius, your brother, is dead. We found him in his bed with an arrow through his heart and blood staining the sheets."

15

"He's been killed?" Alexander asked, feigning shock. "Then I know who killed him. It was the man who stands before you: Acillion."

"My lord?" Acillion asked, confused.

"The princess is also missing," said the second knight. "We could not find her anywhere in the palace."

"He is responsible for that as well," Alexander explained. "He stole the princess, shot her through the heart, and then threw her body into the river. I was taking a moonlit walk and saw the whole vile act. But I was too far to reach them before it was too late. I followed him here to the garden. His actions have caused many a tragedy this night. He must be punished."

"My prince, please," Acillion begged as he began to back away from the soldiers.

"Apprehend that villain!" Alexander shouted. The guards grabbed Acillion by his arms. Surprise and horror washed over Acillion's face. "I wouldn't be surprised if I were next on your list to be murdered! Take him to the dungeon!"

"No! Please!" shouted Acillion. He turned suddenly to the knight in yellow. "Marcus! You know me. Please. My family." He looked longingly at his fellow soldier. But Marcus only looked away.

The two guards dragged the struggling Acillion off to the dungeons. Sir Marcus gently picked Acillion's bow from the ground before following the guards and the prisoner out of the garden. But the knight in black did not follow. Instead, he approached Alexander and gave a low bow.

"Speak, Sir Wallace," said Alexander.

"You realize, my lord, what all these assassinations in the royal family mean?" said Sir Wallace.

"I do but with a... *heavy* heart," replied Alexander.

"On the morrow, the nobles of the Council of Contaria will insist you be crowned king."

"Yes I know." Alexander turned from Sir Wallace. In turn, the knight left the garden, following after the guards and their new prisoner. A smirk crept onto the prince's face.

Chapter 2
Eleven Years Later

E vening was coming fast as the great golden sun began to set on the distant western horizon. A teenaged boy sat on the lower branches of an old oak tree whose once bright green leaves were beginning to show signs of the coming autumn. He was tall and handsome, but you wouldn't be able to tell at this time as he was crouching in the shadows of the tree. His hair, dirty blonde and in need of a trim, was hidden underneath his cloak hood. He tightly gripped a bow in his hand, and a quiver full of homemade arrows swung on the tree branch on which he crouched. A small hunting knife was in a leather sheath tied to the his belt. In that great oak, he crouched, waiting. *It's so silent,* he thought. *So still.*

His thoughts wandered to that morning. He and Henry Smith had been doing their chores at the blacksmith's shop when they had had an interesting conversation.

"When I'm old enough," Henry had said, "I'm going to leave this little village."

"Leave?" he had said. "I thought you wanted to be a blacksmith like your father."

"Not really," Henry had said. "Nothing ever happens here."

"The merchants come at every spring and autumn equinox," he had replied.

"You know what I meant, Jonathan," Henry had said. Henry had always been one to seek adventure. When they were kids, Henry had always dragged Jonathan out on some adventure in the nearby forest. Jonathan loved the forest. It was where he hunted in the summer and autumn. It was where he had his own space to think. But going and searching for dragons or gnomes was Henry's idea of an adventure in the woods, not Jonathan's.

"You should come with me," Henry had said.

"What? Me?" Jonathan had said in astonishment. The idea excited him and frightened him at the same time. Then reality kicked in. "You know I can't. I have to take care of my brother and my mum."

"I guess you're right," Henry had said. His red hair looked like fire in the light of the sunrise.

"Jonathan? Jonathan? Where are you?" a voice shouted in the forest, abruptly interrupting Jonathan's thoughts.

A younger boy was calling through the woods. His head of shaggy, dirty-blonde hair, very much the same as Jonathan's, was somewhat matted, and his clothes were ragged and dirty. As he obliviously passed under the tree, Jonathan grabbed hold of the boy's cloak and pulled him into the oak.

"Aahhhhh! Let me go!" he shouted as he was set on a branch.

"Shhhh," Jonathan shushed.

"Jonathan! There you are!" said the boy.

"Be quiet, Micah," Jonathan said.

"What are you doing?" Micah whispered.

"*Trying* to hunt," replied Jonathan, also whispering.

"Oh," said Micah. "Can I help?"

"Just tell me if you see anything moving. And stay quiet." Micah nodded. For a few minutes, they sat in the still silence of the woods. Until–

Snap.

Jonathan drew an arrow and aimed into the underbrush.
Snap.

The twang of the bowstring echoed through the tree branches. Jonathan jumped down from the branch and laid his bow in the grass beneath the tree, running towards his prey. He lifted the plump, brown rabbit from the forest floor, pulling the bloody arrow out of it. He held it up for Micah to see as he too leapt from the tree.

"I'll name it Dinner," said Micah, grinning at his joke.

"Come on. We should get back," said Jonathan. The two returned to the tree that Jonathan had crouched in all afternoon. Micah climbed back into the tree and grabbed his brother's quiver and satchel, into which they put the rabbit. Meanwhile, Jonathan unstrung his bow and cleaned off the arrow that had just shot their dinner. Then the brothers walked through the Endale Woods, the satchel swaying back and forth at Jonathan's side.

"So, when we get back to Silan, can I try out Father's bow?" Micah asked.

"I don't know," Jonathan replied.

"But it's *our* father's bow," Micah begged.

"I don't think you're ready yet," Jonathan said.

"That's what you say every time I ask," Micah mumbled. "You know, you could just make me a bow like the one you made Henry Smith."

"That took weeks," Jonathan said, remembering the early mornings and late nights he had worked in secret three years ago to complete the gift for his friend's thirteenth birthday.

"I know. But I'm twelve now. I think I'm old enough to go hunting with you," Micah said. "And a second bow would give us more of a chance of getting a rabbit, or, even better, venison." Micah loudly smacked his lips.

"What would we do with an entire deer?" Jonathan asked. Micah only shrugged. "Fine. I'll see what I can do, Micah."

"Thank you!" Micah cried. It wasn't long before the two brothers reached the outskirts of their home, the little village called Silan.

Silan was a small village. Its inhabitants mostly consisted of farmers. However, there was a blacksmith, Henry Smith's father, to whom Jonathan was apprenticed. Mr. Daniels was the local carpenter, the Scotts family kept the very small inn that bore their name, and Mr. Mooreson ran the Old Elbow, the local tavern and most popular place in the village. And on the other side of town was the small chapel the size of a shack where the people of the village could worship the Creator and receive teachings and blessings from Cleric Aaron. Hardly anyone ever left Silan and hardly anyone came to Silan, except for a few merchants at the spring and autumn equinoxes.

As Jonathan, leading Micah, walked over the last small hill that blocked their view of Silan, he saw a sight that he would never have expected in all his days. A heavily armed knight in black armor sat on a proud horse as black as a moonless night. A page stood next to the knight holding a black banner with a blood-red dragon embroidered on it. Soldiers marched from house to house on the main road, pounding on the doors until they opened. They flooded into the homes and dragged out men and boys alike.

"Why are they doing that?" Micah whispered. Then, as if to answer his question, the page stepped forward in the town and unrolled a scroll of parchment.

"By order of King Alexander," the page cried. "All men able to carry a sword is hereby conscripted to His Majesty's armies. Failure to comply will result in corporal punishment or execution."

When the page's proclamation ended, Jonathan's eyes were drawn to three soldiers as they marched into the blacksmith's shop. A moment later, two guards emerged, dragging a struggling Henry between them. The third followed behind them, his gaze drifting towards the hill behind which the two brothers were hiding. Instinctively, Jonathan ducked behind the hill and pulled Micah down with him.

"They took Henry!" Jonathan exclaimed in hushed tones. He peeked over the hill for another look at the village. From a distance he saw the soldiers lead Henry to a large group of other boys and men who were closely guarded by a dozen fully armed soldiers with broadswords and spears.

"What do we do?" Micah asked.

"I have to help him somehow," Jonathan whispered to Micah. He began to get up and nock an arrow. He saw Henry's terrified green eyes locked onto Jonathan. Jonathan lifted his bow. But Henry shook his head. Jonathan saw his friend begin to mouth words and was barely able to figure out what he was saying: *Get out of here.*

"Jonathan!" Micah said, grabbing hold of his older brother's arm. Jonathan looked away from Henry. Micah pointed towards their small cottage, which was far to the left of the soldiers. Jonathan saw what Micah was pointing out. It was their mother. She was frantically waving, trying to get her sons' attentions. She looked frightened.

"We need to go down there," Micah said. "Mum's probably terrified." Jonathan hesitated before nodding and reluctantly returning the arrow to his quiver. Running as fast, but as low to the ground, as they could, the boys hurried to the other side of Silan and their mother.

As Jonathan approached Mum, he inspected her to see what was the matter. She still stood with her head high and her hair in two long braids that she tied together at the back of her head with a length of leather. And she still had the signs of wearing from the many long years of raising two sons alone.

However, Jonathan noticed something different, something that worried him very much: her smile. Usually, Mum's gentle smile remained unwavering. She always tried to stay positive for the sake of her sons. But now she was not smiling. This wasn't a good sign. Mum didn't smile only when something was wrong. Very wrong. She beckoned them to hurry inside the small thatch-roofed house that Jonathan and Micah called home.

"Mum, are you alright?" asked Micah.

"I'm fine," she said, gathering her younger son in a great hug. "But there are soldiers in town."

"We know, Mum, we saw," Jonathan said, setting his bow and hunting knife on the table. "They're conscripting men for the king's army. They already took Henry."

"I was afraid they had taken you two, too!" cried Mum. Tears streamed down her cheeks. A mix of fear and relief glinted in her dim, hazel eyes. Suddenly, a fist pounded on the door, followed by a shout.

"Open this door!" bellowed the rough voice of a soldier. "Open up or we'll open it by force."

"I can't let them take you two," whispered Mum. "You're all I have left." She was trembling. Jonathan wrapped his arms around her and hugged her tightly.

"I won't let take us, or hurt us," Jonathan promised her. But he wasn't just promising her; he was promising himself. He wouldn't let this family fall apart. He had to be the man of the house. Jonathan pulled away from his mother's embrace.

"If we hurry we can escape through the back door. We could make it to the woods." Jonathan could hear the soldiers trying to kick down the door. "We have to go now." Mum opened her mouth to say something. But nothing came out. Instead, she stared at Jonathan and smiled, tears trickling from the corners of her eyes.

"You look so much like him," Mum finally muttered. Jonathan knew the *him* she was talking about: his father.

"Alright," she said. "Run. Run to the woods. Go to Alden. You might find refuge with my brother there. Don't come back until it's safe." She kissed Jonathan on the forehead, and then Micah. "I love you both so much."

Those were the last words Jonathan would hear from his mother for a long time, for at that moment, the soldiers made a hole in the wooden door. With one hand Jonathan grabbed Micah's hand. With the other he scooped his knife and bow from the table and ran. He ran as fast as he could. He thought he could outrun the king's fastest horses at that moment. He wouldn't slow down. He couldn't slow down.

While running towards the woods, clutching Micah's hand, Jonathan made another promise to himself. He promised himself that no matter what happened and no matter how long it took, he would return home to this little village. Then, hearing the soldiers running behind him, Jonathan ran straight into the woods, dragging Micah behind him.

Chapter 3
A Stranger in the Night

B y the time the two brothers stopped running, the horizon had almost completely swallowed the sun. Jonathan could no longer hear the shouts of the pursuing soldiers. Micah stood a few paces away catching his breath. Jonathan's heart pounded so loudly he could hardly think.

Mum had said to go to Alden, the capital city of Contaria, to find her brother. Jonathan knew of this uncle. His name was Elijah Beckett, but they had always called him Uncle Eli. He used to live in Silan when Jonathan was little. But, desperate for a different life from that of a simple farmer, Uncle Eli had left for Alden to become a sailor. He reminded Jonathan of Henry Smith.

Jonathan hadn't seen Uncle Eli since he'd left nearly twelve years ago, and he hardly remembered what he looked like. Micah wasn't even a year old when Uncle Eli had left. But Jonathan knew that if his mother thought it best for them to take refuge with Uncle Eli, then that was what they must do.

There was one problem though: Jonathan had no idea where he was or where Alden was. He knew it was to the south and near the mouth of the Anafract River. But he had no map, and even the sun had almost disappeared from the sky. After resting a brief moment, Jonathan looked up. He could see signs of neither villages nor houses.

"We're lost, aren't we?" asked Micah.

"We're not lost," said Jonathan. "We're just… not going the right way." *Which is true,* Jonathan thought, *to an extent.* He just didn't know which way was the right way.

"Should we head back to Silan?" Micah asked. "The soldiers might be gone by now."

"But they might not be," replied Jonathan. "Besides, Mum told us to go to Alden."

"But that's miles away," Micah said. "It'll take us days to walk there!"

"Listen, we'll stay here for the night," Jonathan said. "There's not enough daylight to go anywhere else today. We can figure out what we're going to do and where we're going to go in the morning."

"Fine," Micah sighed. "Do you still have that rabbit with you?"

"Yeah," said Jonathan. A grin spread across Micah's face.

"Good," he said. "I'm starving."

It didn't take the brother long to gather enough dry twigs and logs for a fire. Jonathan was able to get a spark by knocking the blunt side of his knife against one of the flint arrowheads. Then he skinned the rabbit, skewered it, and set it to roast over the fire.

Soon, the moon peeked through the boughs of the trees. The rabbit was still cooking over the fire, but Micah had fallen asleep. An owl began hooting in the distance. The trees whispered to each other as a gentle, yet chilling, breeze began to stir.

Jonathan pulled his cloak around himself and tried to warm his fingers by holding them up to the fire's heat. He moved closer to the dancing flames. Waves of warmth spread throughout his body. The heat of the fire lulled Jonathan closer and closer towards sleep. He shook himself and rubbed his eyes to keep awake. But it didn't seem to help. His eyes didn't want to stay open.

Snap.

Jonathan's eyes shot open. He must have dozed off, for now the fire was dying out. Thankfully for Jonathan, the rabbit hadn't burned.

Snap.

What was that? Jonathan wondered. Had it been his imagination?

Snap.

No, there it was again. A branch snapping just a few yards away. And it wasn't a rabbit. The snaps were too loud for an animal that small.

Snap.

There was only one thing it could be: a human.

Snap.

Jonathan jumped from where he'd nodded off.

Snap.

He grabbed his bow and nocked an arrow. *No soldier is going to take us tonight*, Jonathan thought.

Snap.

Slowly, he crept towards the place that the sound was coming from.

Snap.

A second later, Jonathan's arrow zipped through the air towards the place where he had heard the noise. Jonathan raced after it and arrived to find... nothing. He had shot nothing. Jonathan pulled the arrow out of the leaf-covered forest floor and brushed off the dirt from the tip.

He was just about to head back to their makeshift camp when, like a ghost, a hooded figure emerged from behind an enormous tree. Jonathan's heart nearly stopped. The cloaked stranger drew his sword. Jonathan grabbed his bow and ran back towards the camp.

"Micah! Micah, wake up!" shouted Jonathan as he ran. Micah groggily sat up.

"What?" Micah called in an irritated manner, rubbing his eyes. "Is the rabbit done?"

"No time to explain," continued Jonathan. "Run!" At that moment, the hooded stranger walked into the camp. "*Run!*" Jonathan repeated.

Micah's eyes widened as he saw the attacker. He got to his feet and ran. The stranger pursued. Jonathan nocked another arrow as he ran for his life, Micah at his heels. He let the arrow fly towards the cloaked figure. But Jonathan didn't watch to see where the arrow landed. He just kept running. He nocked another and let it fly. Suddenly, Jonathan heard a piercing scream, like no man he had ever heard. He glanced back to look at the stranger. The stranger pulled an arrow from his side and sank to his knees.

Jonathan came to a halt, adrenaline still pumping through his veins. He wanted to know who this stranger was. Turning around, Jonathan, with his bow still in hand, ran back to the cloaked stranger. The hooded figure backed away, frightened, leaving his sword on the ground next to the bloody arrow. He tried to run, but Jonathan was determined to see whom this cloaked stranger was. He nocked an arrow and aimed at the figure. Then he shot it. The arrow pinned the stranger's cloak to a large tree. The stranger tried to pull free, but Jonathan was too fast. Like a bolt of lightning, Jonathan ran to the hooded figure, pinned him to the tree with one hand, and pulled another arrow from his quiver with the other. Once he placed the arrow's point at the stranger's throat, the hooded figure stopped trying to free himself and raised his hands over his head in surrender.

"Who are you?" Jonathan asked fiercely. The hooded stranger didn't reply. Instead, he slowly moved his hands towards his hood, lifted it, and revealed his face. Standing before Jonathan was a girl. A girl! She wasn't even sixteen by the looks of her. She was tall with long blonde hair and fierce, electric blue eyes, which were puffy from crying.

"You're— you're a girl!" Jonathan exclaimed. At that moment, the girl kicked Jonathan in the chest, knocking the breath out of him. Jonathan took a knee to catch his breath. He gasped for air as he watched the girl pull his arrow out of the tree. Before Jonathan could get back on his feet, the girl had the tip of the arrow against *his* throat.

"Jonathan!" shouted Micah from a distance. The girl looked up. "What happened?" Micah was running towards Jonathan, but stopped dead in his tracks when he saw his brother at the girl's mercy. "What are you doing?" Micah whimpered. The girl looked from Jonathan to Micah and back to Jonathan. Then Micah asked the question Jonathan was still wondering: "Who are you?"

"This is who attacked us," replied Jonathan, frightened but trying his best not to show it.

"I wasn't attacking you," said the girl.

"What do you call this, then?" Jonathan asked, nodding to the arrow tip she still held to his neck. She quickly lowered the arrow.

"You attacked *me*," she said. "I merely defended myself."

"By attacking us?" Micah said. "What kind of logic is that?" The girl ignored the question.

"I assume you have a name," Jonathan said.

"You assume correctly." She extended her arm to Jonathan.

"Well, what is it?" Jonathan asked. The girl stared at Jonathan as though trying to look into his soul.

"It's Melony," she finally said. Jonathan stared at her in suspicion. Then he took her still extended arm and heaved himself off the forest floor.

"Melony what?" Jonathan asked as he brushed dead leaves from his pants and cloak.

"Uh... Wilson," Melony replied. "Melony Wilson."

"Well, Melony Wilson," began Jonathan, "I'd like to know why in Iyuandil you attacked me and chased my brother and me through the woods in the dead of night!"

"First of all, as I just said, you attacked me," Melony responded calmly. "I was defending myself. Second, I thought that you were some of King Alexander's men."

"Why would you think that?" Jonathan asked.

"There were some soldiers not far from here," Melony said. "So when I saw your fire, I assumed you were more soldiers."

"That doesn't change the fact that you attacked us," Micah muttered.

"Can we end this useless argument?" Melony exclaimed.

"Fine," Jonathan said. "Where are you from?"

"Ravan," Melony replied.

"Ravan?" Jonathan repeated. "I've never heard of that place."

"It's a small village in Nimberia," said Melony.

"You're Nimberian?" exclaimed Micah.

"No, I'm Contarian," Melony said. "But I did live in Nimberia for a long time."

"I thought Nimberians were barbarians," Jonathan said. "Why would you go and live there?" But Melony wasn't able to answer Jonathan's question before Micah interrupted with another.

"If you're coming all the way from Nimberia, why are you traveling alone?" Micah asked. Melony's eyes shifted to the ground. Jonathan thought he could see tears glistening in them.

"I told you my name," Melony said, changing the subject. "Are you going to tell me *yours*?"

"Oh yeah!" said Micah. "I'm Micah Fletcher."

"Nice to meet you, Micah," Melony said. Then she turned to Jonathan. Jonathan just looked back at her and didn't say a word.

"His name's Jonathan," Micah said in Jonathan's stead. "He's my older brother."

"It's nice to meet you too, Jonathan," Melony said, handing him back his arrow. "I suppose I will be off then."

"Off where?" Micah asked.

"Um…" Melony stuttered. "I've just gotta go."

"It's not safe out there alone," Jonathan said.

"It's urgent that I leave," said Melony.

"Fine," Jonathan said. "But when you're alone and surrounded by wolves in the middle of the night, don't come crying to us for help."

"You think I can't handle a couple of wolves?" Melony said. "You were at my mercy only moments ago."

"But can you handle twenty wolves?" Jonathan asked testingly.

"You'd be surprised by what I can handle," Melony said. She leaned over to grab her sword from the forest floor. But as she did so, she winced in pain, clutching her side. Jonathan could see the blood covering her hand and dripping to the forest floor.

"Are you alright?" Micah asked.

"I'm fine," Melony muttered in reply.

"Maybe you should stay with us tonight," Micah suggested. "We've got some roast rabbit to share."

"No, it's alright," Melony said. "I'll head off."

"But it's the least we can do," Micah said. "I mean, Jonathan *did* shoot you with an arrow."

"Hey!" Jonathan exclaimed.

"It's true," Micah muttered. Jonathan stared at his younger brother. He had to admit that a pang of guilt burned in his chest. But he didn't exactly fancy the idea of having a complete stranger stay with them. Though, he *had* shot her. And she needed a safe place to heal. Jonathan sighed.

"Micah's right," Jonathan said. "You should stay with us tonight. But only the one night. In the morning, we part ways." Melony hesitated a moment, as if she wasn't sure whether or not to trust him.

"Fine," she finally said, returning her sword to its sheath. The three of them walked back to the campfire silently. Jonathan sat next to the fire and stirred the flames with a stick. They took the roasted rabbit off the skewer, and the three of them ate the entire hare, with merely a small pile of bones to prove that there had ever been a rabbit. When they were done, they all sat with their backs to different trees. Jonathan noticed Melony glance down at her side and furrow her brow in concern.

"You may want to have someone look at that," Jonathan suggested. "Silan isn't far from here, and there are people there who could help stitch it up."

"It's not bad," Melony said "It just grazed me. It should be fine by morning." Jonathan knew she was lying. That arrow had not grazed her; he had seen her pull it from her side. But Jonathan let it be. He laid his head against the tree and shut his eyes.

The next thing Jonathan knew, he could hear the chirping of the morning birds and see the bright beams of the rising sun shining in his eyes. He sat up and stretched his arms. His back ached from sleeping against the tree the whole night so he soon got to his feet. Micah and Melony were still sleeping soundly. But when Jonathan looked closer, he noticed that Melony was as pale as a freshly fallen snow.

"Melony?" Jonathan whispered. Melony stirred slightly.

"What?" she asked groggily.

"You're deathly pale," Jonathan said. "You have to let me help you. I can probably make some bandages or–"

"I said no," Melony said, standing up shakily. "Now that it's morning, I'll be off."

"Where are you going?" Micah asked, rubbing the sleep from his eyes.

"South," Melony said, tying her sword sheath to her belt, "to Alden."

"You're heading to Alden?" Micah exclaimed.

"Micah," Jonathan said.

"Yes," Melony replied.

"What a coincidence! That's where we're headed!" Micah said.

"Micah," Jonathan said again.

"Really?" Melony asked.

"Yeah!" Micah said. "You know what would be a great idea?"

"Micah," Jonathan interrupted.

"We should all travel together!" Micah said.

"Micah, can I talk to you?" Jonathan said. He pulled his younger brother to the side, turning their backs away from Melony so she couldn't hear them.

"What's wrong?" Micah asked.

"Listen. She's injured, and not ready for travel. I say we leave her with some food so she can rest and heal before she starts on her journey again."

"You're the one who shot her, though," Micah pointed out.

"Don't remind me," Jonathan said.

"So you don't want to take responsibility for shooting her?" Micah said.

"No, I mean–" Jonathan started. He sighed. "Look, I don't really like the idea of going to Alden anyway. But Mum told us to, so we're going. And protecting you from bandits and soldiers on the way is one thing. You're my brother. But she is a stranger. I don't want to be responsible for protecting her too."

"Just like you don't want to be responsible for shooting her?" Micah asked.

"That's not what I —"

"You know I can still hear you, right?" Melony said loudly. "And I can protect myself, thank you very much."

"See, Jonathan," Micah said. "It'll be fine." Jonathan glanced at Melony. Her blood-stained dress was visible under her blue cloak. The pang of guilt returned, stronger than last night.

"Fine," Jonathan sighed. "She can come."

"Great!" Micah said.

"Thank you, Jonathan," Melony said.

"So, why are you heading to Alden?" asked Micah.

"Because," Melony replied.

"Oh, come on. You can tell us," Micah said. Melony didn't reply. Micah quickly gave up on trying to get the answer out of Melony, but in the back of his mind, Jonathan still wondered about the answer. When the morning's fire had reduced to only black chunks of burnt wood, the trio began heading south.

Chapter 4

The Mystery Camp

Mid-morning came, and the sun shone through the lofty leaves of the woods. The crunch of leaves under their feet echoed in the woods, harmonizing with the squeaks of squirrels and the songs of birds and the whisperings of the trees. Suddenly, Jonathan smelled a quite familiar scent.

"Smoke," Jonathan said to the others. "Do you smell it?"

"There must be a village around here," said Melony.

"But there aren't any settlements this deep in the forest," Jonathan replied. "Besides, we'd have seen a path or a road by now."

"Then what could it be?" asked Micah.

Cautiously, the trio continued walking through the woods, the smell of smoke growing stronger with each step. A few minutes later, they stumbled upon a large group of tents and firepits. They crept closer, hiding behind a rather large log that was covered with mushrooms and bright green moss.

Sitting on a small three-legged stool near the fire in front of one of the tents was a greatly aged man. He wore a deep forest green cloak, which was fastened by a small silver object. He had a long, white beard that was speckled with silver hairs. He carried no weapons of which Jonathan could see.

"Could they be Wanderers?" Micah asked.

"So far west? I don't think so," said Jonathan.

"What about bandits?" asked Micah.

"Possibly," Jonathan said. At that moment, a boy emerged from the woods only a few feet away from their hiding place and approached the older man. He looked about fourteen and wore the same green cloak as the older man. And his jet black hair nearly covered his eyes despite his frequent attempts to brush it away. As he ran to the man, his leather satchel swayed at his side.

"Fraxinus," the boy said to the man. "Ytaluyuat vaskien shelos. Nasel bebianu shnan nataliscon. Yip e discuvu nabas ydiomycota.[1]" Then the boy pulled something from his bag and handed it to the older man, but Jonathan couldn't see it from his hiding spot.

"Do you have any idea what he's saying?" Jonathan whispered to Melony. She shook her head.

"Benac,[2]" said the man with a voice that croaked, almost like an old bullfrog. "E cogu ub eb trit nahumoc piso illac kotsuroc. Ia yip vidu.[3]" Then the man pointed in the direction of their hiding spot. The boy began to walk in their direction. Jonathan got as low to the forest floor as he could. Micah and Melony followed his example. Jonathan prayed to the Creator that the boy would not spot them. He wanted to be absolutely sure who these people were before they found him. The boy took something from the log, a mushroom Jonathan thought, and then returned to the old man.

"Did you see the symbol on that boy's cloak clasp?" Melony asked in excitement. Micah and Jonathan shook their heads. "It was a druid symbol!" Melony unsteadily stood up.

---

[1] The hunt is going well. They've brought down two does. And I found some mushrooms.

[2] Good

[3] I think there are three people behind that log. Go and see.

"Are you crazy?" Jonathan whispered in protest.

"I know what I'm doing," said Melony. Slowly, she approached the man and the boy with shaky footsteps. They turned towards her.

"Come on," Jonathan whispered to Micah. "Let's get out of here." Jonathan began to back away into the woods, but Micah grabbed his arm.

"We can't leave her," Micah whispered back.

"Uchninan, ami,[4]" the old man called to Melony.

"Good morning," said Melony. "My name is Melony."

"I am Fraxinus, the chief of the Tetwes druid clan," croaked the man. "Why do you and your companions hide from us in the shadows, Melony?"

"We were afraid you were bandits."

"We are no bandits. You need not fear any longer."

"We're not afraid," Melony assured him. Fraxinus's gaze shifted from Melony directly to the spot where Jonathan and Micah were hiding. Jonathan could have sworn the man could see through the log and foliage blocking the two of them from his view.

"Why do your friends still hide in the trees?" Fraxinus asked Melony.

"I don't think they trust you."

"Come, friends. You are welcome here." But Jonathan was determined to remain in his hiding spot, the only thing that separated him from these strangers. He feared this man was not who he said he was.

"Shouldn't we get up?" asked Micah. Jonathan shook his head.

Suddenly, Jonathan felt a hand on his shoulder and jumped from his hiding place, startled. It was the druid boy. His ivory

---

[4] Greetings, friend.

skin looked as pale as death itself against Jonathan's dirty, dark brown traveling cloak. His black hair had been pushed out of his face, but, even then, Jonathan could see it creeping back down towards his dark brown eyes.

"Qui eb nateachn nateetieg, naami?[5]" said the boy.

"What?" asked Jonathan, confused.

"Sel dinu Contarian,[6]" Fraxinus told the boy

"Oh!" the boy said nodding. "Sorry. What are your names, friends?" he said in Contarian. His accent was distinctly druidic. Even Jonathan, who had never met a druid in his life, could recognize the rolled r's and the tapped consonants of the accent.

"I'm Micah," Micah said proudly.

"My name's Jonathan," Jonathan said cautiously.

"I am Belnor Yuovech," said the boy.

"Belnor is my grandson and apprentice," said Fraxinus.

"So, you *are* druids?" Jonathan asked. Fraxinus nodded. Jonathan's grip on his bow relaxed.

"Isn't the Tetwes clan a southern druid clan?" Melony asked. "Why are you so far north?" These words came out very shaky and weak.

"It is because of King Alexander," replied Fraxinus. "He has decreed that all men strong enough to hold a sword must join his growing army for the war on Nimberia. But my people do not wish to fight in this war. So we are travelling north to Erukial, the great druid library, where we might find the peace we seek."

"That's why the Black Knight was in our village," Micah exclaimed. "And that's why we're heading south to Alden."

"You're going south?" Belnor asked.

"Yes," Micah said.

"Micah," Jonathan scolded. Belnor turned to Fraxinus.

---

[5] What are your names, friends?

[6] He speaks Contarian.

"Naillet manda habitu co nae weven,[7]" Belnor said to Fraxinus in their druid tongue.

"Quite right, Belnor," said Fraxinus. Turning to them, he said, "You must stay with us this night. You look weary and travel worn. Do my people the honor of being our guests for this evening."

"That's a great idea," Micah exclaimed. Jonathan, however, didn't like the proposition.

"Can I talk to you, Micah," Jonathan whispered in his brother's ear. He pulled him aside by the arm, out of earshot of the druids. "Listen, Micah. We just met these people. How can we trust them? They could be lying and just waiting to rob us blind."

"Or they could be exactly who they say they are," Micah said. "They could be trying to help."

"And if they are druids?" Jonathan said. "Druids use magic. They could put us under a spell or–"

"You're determined not to trust these people, aren't you?" Micah said. Jonathan sighed, shaking his head. Micah just didn't understand how dangerous the world could be. Jonathan was about to step forward to refuse the offer. But suddenly, Melony fell to her knees on the forest floor, hissing in pain. Her face was deathly pale; her skin was as cold as ice.

"Melony!" Jonathan exclaimed. He rushed to Melony to see what was wrong. She was clutching her side again. Jonathan could see a mixture of blood and some yellow fluid slipping between Melony's fingers.

"What's going on?" Fraxinus asked.

"She's injured," Jonathan replied. "An arrow wound to her side last night." Jonathan carefully removed Melony's trembling hands to inspect the wound. The small, one-inch wide hole in

---

[7] They should stay with us tonight.

Melony's side was bright red and oozing a yellowish puss. "I think it's infected." Fraxinus rushed to join Jonathan next to Melony. He too began to carefully inspect the wound.

"You are correct, Jonathan," Fraxinus said. "The wound is infected. And the infection is spreading quickly. She has also lost quite a lot of blood." Then he called to Belnor, saying, "Belnor! Ia yip luisae axinak![8]" Belnor ran further into the camp, his cloak billowing behind him. "We must take her back to my tent in the center of camp. I will do what I can to help. If the Creator is willing, we will be able to heal her by morning."

"And if he's not willing?" Jonathan asked. Fraxinus gave Jonathan a grave look.

At that moment, Belnor returned with two men and three women running behind him. The women gently helped Melony to her feet and helped her walk towards the other tents. Jonathan and Micah followed the druids further into the center of the camp.

As they walked, Jonathan looked around the camp. The more he looked around, the more he realized that this was no bandits' camp. There were tents of many different shapes, colors, and sizes. Jonathan tried to count how many there were, but he lost track at about thirty-seven. Jonathan peeked through the tents entrances and saw that each tent had a number of small mats inside. Tall poles stood in front of each tent, with charm necklaces hanging from the poles. At the very heart of the camp was a large cleared area with a huge pile of firewood in the center.

Jonathan noticed that more and more druids were coming into the camp, some with baskets of foraged greens, others with jugs of water, and even a group of young men dragging a freshly killed deer with them. A large group of children, maybe Micah's

---

[8] Belnor! Go and get help!

age and younger, were playing some sort of game with a ball as they walked into the camp.

The druids led Melony into one of the tents lining the central cleared area. But Fraxinus and Belnor stayed outside to speak with the boys.

"You are welcome to stay here for now," Fraxinus said. "If we can heal Melony, it will take most of the night." With that, he followed Melony and the other druids into the tent. But Belnor remained and called in the druid tongue to the children playing nearby.

"Naami! Nae tenu naaminarik,[9]" said Belnor. The children began to greet Jonathan and Micah. Then Belnor turned to Micah. "They want to know if you'll play with them."

"Yes!" Micah said. Before Jonathan could say anything, Belnor began to speak again.

"Illis eb Micah,[10]" Belnor said to the druid children. "Ytalu sel li utinu quen.[11]" They smiled and nodded. Belnor signaled one of the boys. This boy had black hair like Belnor and looked about Micah's age. Then Belnor turned back to Micah. "This is my cousin, Naru. He only speaks a little of your language, but he is very smart. He will make sure you don't get lost, Micah."

"Nice to meet you," Micah said. And before Jonathan could stop him, Micah ran off with the group of druid children. They went back into the woods with Jonathan's brother among them. Belnor turned back to Jonathan. But before Belnor or Jonathan could speak, Fraxinus poked his head out of the tent.

"Belnor, nae necu te,[12]" the old druid said. Belnor ran into the tent. For a minute, Jonathan stood outside, wondering what

---

[9] Friends! We have guests.

[10] This is Micah.

[11] Make sure he doesn't get lost.

[12] Belnor, we need you.

he should do. Finally, he slipped into the tent and saw Melony lying on a mat in the corner of the tent. Druids were bustling about, preparing different herbs in stone mortars and pestles. Unnoticed by the druids, Jonathan knelt down next to Melony. Her blue cloak had been removed and thrown aside. The elegance of Melony's white dress glowing in the soft candlelight was diminished by the numerous tears and the bloody stains on the fabric. The hem of the dress was stained with mud and torn in several places, and one of the long sleeves had been completely torn from the dress, revealing a brand on her shoulder shaped like an eagle.

"You can't be in here, right now," Belnor said, finally noticing Jonathan's presence.

"I just wanted to help," said Jonathan. But Belnor ushered him out of the tent. Jonathan looked back through the entrance to see Fraxinus muttering something over Melony just before Belnor pulled the tent entrance closed.

Evening arrived. Druid women were tending a great bonfire that had been built from the large pile of wood Jonathan had seen earlier. Waves of delicious smells wafted through the air. But he couldn't eat. Melony still lay inside Fraxinus's tent. And Jonathan had gotten no word of the druids' progress.

Finally, Belnor exited Fraxinus's tent, the first person to do so in hours. But he didn't even look at Jonathan as he walked towards the central bonfire. When he returned to where Jonathan was, his face still red from the great heat of the flames, he was holding two bowls, both full of the stew that the druid women had been making. Belnor sat himself on the ground next to Jonathan and offered him the food in the bowl.

"No, thank you," Jonathan said. "I'm not hungry right now."

"Do you not like my people's cooking?" Belnor asked, looking offended.

"It's not that," said Jonathan, eyeing the entrance of Fraxinus's tent.

"Ah, I see," Belnor said. "You're worried for Melony's life. You must love your sister dearly."

"My sister?" Jonathan exclaimed. "She's not my sister!"

"Sorry!" said Belnor. "I just thought, since you were traveling together—"

"Oh no," Jonathan said quickly. "We just crossed paths last night."

"I see," Belnor said. "Well, she is healing very well. She's very strong. Many might have died from the wounds she'd sustained by the time she came to us. The Creator must have great plans for her."

"Wounds?" Jonathan asked. "More than one wound?"

"Well yes," replied Belnor. "There was the arrow wound as well as several sword wounds along her arms, legs, and chest."

"How did you all do it?" Jonathan asked.

"Do what?" Belnor said.

"Heal her, of course."

"Oh, I—" But at that moment, one of the druids from inside the tent poked his head out and gestured to Belnor. "I have to go. They need my help again." Then Belnor quickly got up and ran back into the tent. As soon as Belnor left, Jonathan began to wonder about Micah. *Where could he be?* he thought. It was getting late and, more importantly, dark.

At that moment, a group of children passed in front of Jonathan. He scoured the group, looking for his younger brother's patched, dirt-colored cloak. A boy with shaggy, dirty-blonde hair passed close by Jonathan. *Micah,* Jonathan thought.

But he wasn't wearing the same clothing Jonathan had seen his brother leave in. He wore a small, dark green cloak, and around his neck must have been half a dozen necklaces and charms. Another boy wore Micah's worn traveling cloak, but he had bright red hair that went to his shoulders, with several small braids and beads scattered throughout it. Micah and the redhead druid boy had switched cloaks.

"Micah!" Jonathan called over the noise of the playing children. Micah, his borrowed green cloak flying behind him, ran to Jonathan's side, laughing and shouting from excitement.

"Jonathan! I've had such a great time!" Micah said, laughing. "Vulpus, the red-headed boy there wearing my cloak, taught me how to make a whistle from a willow branch. And Callidus, the boy with the short brown hair, made me a necklace with a crystal on it. And Naru, he's wearing the reddish cloak, taught me a bunch of words in the druid tongue. And Yuend–"

"It sounds like fun," Jonathan interrupted him. "Why did you and Viper–"

"Vulpus," Micah corrected him.

"Why did you switch cloaks?" Jonathan asked.

"Vulpus liked the patches on my cloak.," Micah explained quickly. "He thought that it looked colorful. And if you get to know Vulpus, you know he *really* likes color. So we switched and he said I could keep his if he could keep mine." Jonathan couldn't find a reason to object to this trade. The new green cloak Micah now wore was almost new and was much less worn or patched than the brown cloak he had worn from Silan. "Do you want to see me do a butterfly call?" Micah continued.

"Not now," Jonathan said as he sat back down on his spot by Fraxinus's tent. Micah sat himself next to Jonathan. There they sat together in silence, watching the flaming tongues of the bonfire try to lick the stars in the high heavens.

"Are you worried?" Micah asked quietly.

"About what?" Jonathan responded.

"Mum. Silan." He paused. "Melony."

"Why should I be worried about Melony?" said Jonathan, forcing a chuckle.

"You know, Jonathan, you've never been very good at lying," Micah said.

"You should get some rest," Jonathan said.

"Where are we sleeping?" asked Micah.

"I was thinking by those trees over there," Jonathan replied. So he started towards the edge of the woods to find an adequate place to sleep, Micah following behind him, rambling on about all the things he'd done that day.

"Jonathan?" Jonathan heard someone call from behind. He turned and saw Belnor, his green cloak billowing behind him as he ran towards them. "Where are you two going?"

"To find somewhere to sleep," Jonathan replied.

"Why do you head for the woods?" the druid asked. "You're welcome to sleep in one of our camp's tents. You will find them much more comfortable than sleeping on the forest floor."

"Thanks!" Micah said, accepting Belnor's offer before Jonathan could say anything.

"Um, right. Thank you," said Jonathan. Belnor waved to them to follow him back towards the camp.

The druid led them to a small tent near the camp's southern edge. On the tall pole in front of it, there were three charms. The first was a small white crystal, the second a large dragon, and the third a small vial with a tiny plant growing inside. Inside the tent, there were two sleeping mats with pillows, quilts, and fur blankets. Jonathan found that the mats were very comfortable. He and Micah wrapped in the fur blankets that were sitting in the tent. And after settling into the small tent fit for two, Jonathan turned to face Micah.

"You know this is only for a few nights, right, Micah?"

"What do you mean?" Micah asked.

"Soon, Melony will be well, and we'll be on our way again," Jonathan said.

"Why don't we just stay here?" asked Micah. "We could get back home faster when we need to get back."

Jonathan hesitated. Why shouldn't they just stay here? There was plenty of food and shelter and they would be safe: safe from King Alexander's armies. But Mum had specifically told him to go to Alden. Also, Melony would be heading to Alden alone if they stayed here. He couldn't let her go by herself while she was still recovering, especially since her injury was his fault.

"We can't stay," Jonathan said. "We need to keep moving so we can find Uncle Eli."

Chapter 5
Birdbrains

Bright morning light peering through the crack of the tent's entrance gently woke Jonathan as it fell directly into his eyes. He squinted as he sat up and saw Micah still fast asleep, drool running down one side of his open mouth. So he silently slipped on his boots and his leather hunting jerkin and crept out of the tent. The fresh scent of morning filled the air. The dew that covered the grass darkened Jonathan's boots with every step he took. He walked directly to Fraxinus's tent.

"Hello?" Jonathan whispered outside the entrance of the tent. There was no response. "Melony?" But again, no one answered. Jonathan opened the tent's entrance only a crack and peeked inside. But it was empty. Bandages and herbs were scattered across the floor, and the mat where Melony had lain the night before was empty except for the sheets and blankets that had been thrown about on the mat.

"Are you looking for me?" Melony said behind him. Jonathan whipped around. Melony's cheeks had a rosy tint, leaving no evidence of her pale complexion from the day before. Her blood-stained, white dress had been replaced by a crimson traveling dress, and her torn blue cloak had been replaced by a dark forest green one. And her hair was twisted into a flower-adorned braid.

"You're alive!" Jonathan exclaimed. "And awake!"

"Yes, I've been up awhile now," she replied.

"How is your– how do– how are you?" Jonathan stammered.

"Honestly, better than I've been in a while," Melony said. Then Jonathan heard the pitter-patter of feet running in his direction.

"Jonathan! You left the tent without me!" Micah said, jumping on one foot towards Jonathan as he tried to pull on his boots. Not until he had finally pulled on the boot did he catch sight of Melony. "Melony! You're alive! Jonathan was worried sick. He even talked in his sleep. He said, 'Melony. Melony, don't die. Melony. Melony, I won't let you–' " Jonathan grabbed Micah and put his hand over Micah's mouth. He could feel himself blushing. Had he really said those things in his sleep?

All of a sudden, Jonathan felt something warm and wet on his hand. He yanked his hand away from Micah's mouth to find that Micah had licked his hand and it was now wet with spit. Micah bolted away from him. Jonathan wiped his hand on his pants.

"Micah! You little…" Jonathan yelled, running after his brother. He could barely keep up as Micah weaved between the druid tents. But he'd nearly caught up to his younger brother when their chase was interrupted by Fraxinus walking right into Jonathan's path.

"I see you slept well," Fraxinus said as Jonathan came to a halt in front of him.

"Yes sir," Jonathan said quickly. Melony came behind him.

"Fraxinus," she said, "I'd like to thank you for your kindness and hospitality. I would be dead now if it weren't for your people."

"You are quite welcome, Melony," Fraxinus said with a warm smile. Many of the druids who had been working nearby stopped what they were doing and gathered around Melony, Jonathan, and Fraxinus to listen to what they were saying. Many were smiling, others had curious expressions, but all were staring at Melony.

"Unfortunately, my friends and I must continue our journey," Melony said. Jonathan was surprised. Melony had called him and Micah her friends. He didn't know if he was glad or not. "We must make haste to the city of Alden," Melony continued. A murmur rippled through the crowd of druids when Melony mentioned the capital city.

"I understand," Fraxinus said. "My people and I will help you prepare for your journey. We will have you ready to leave by tomorrow morning."

"Thank you," Melony said. Jonathan could see her nervously eyeing the crowd. Just then Micah broke through the crowd of druids.

"Are you going to chase me or what?" Micah said. Then he bolted away from the crowd once again. Jonathan smiled but didn't follow.

"Melony," Jonathan started. He noticed the druids eyeing them and felt their uncomfortable stares. He lowered his voice. "Do you know how they healed you?"

"Why do you ask?" Melony asked.

"I just need to know," Jonathan said cautiously. "Did they use magic?"

"Well of course they used magic," Melony said. "They're druids. What did you expect them to do?" Jonathan didn't answer. He'd expected that answer, however much he'd dreaded it.

"Is there something wrong?" Melony asked.

"Be up early tomorrow morning," he said, ignoring her question. "We should leave before dawn."

"Why so early?" Melony asked.

"I just don't think we need to stay here much longer," Jonathan said. And before she could say anything else, he slipped through the crowd and away from Melony.

The next morning, Jonathan woke before the sunrise. The faint, grey light of dawn crept into the tent and allowed Jonathan to begin getting ready for the day's journey. He slipped on his cotton shirt and trousers, his jerkin, his worn leather boots, and his dull, brown, patched traveling cloak. He woke Micah and waited for him to get dressed. When Micah emerged from the tent, he was wearing the green druid cloak he had been given by the druid boy.

The two brothers made their way to the center of the camp, where Melony, Fraxinus, and half the druid clan waited for them. Belnor was nowhere in sight. Two packs had been carefully laid on the forest floor, each with a bedroll and food enough to last several days. The larger of the two packs had a quiver of newly made arrows. As Jonathan picked up the larger of the packs and Micah picked up the other, Jonathan saw Melony also had an identical pack. He stood beside her, eyeing the crowd of druids.

"Are you ready?" Jonathan asked quietly.

"As I'll ever be," Melony replied.

"Melony," Fraxinus said. Melony took a step towards the druid. The old man pulled a roll of dry, yellowed parchment out of his bag and handed it to Melony. "This is a map of all the lands of Iyuandil. May it serve as your guide and find you safely to Alden."

"Thank you," Melony said softly, carefully taking the map.

"Micah," said Fraxinus. Micah looked up eagerly. Fraxinus pulled a slingshot out of his bag and handed it to Micah. His eyes lit up with excitement. "May this sling hit its mark when it is in your hands."

"Thank you," Micah said, his eyes fixed on the slingshot.

"And finally, Jonathan," Fraxinus said, taking a shortsword from the extended arms of one of the druid men. The sword surprised Jonathan. He had always been told that the druids were a peaceful people. But when he looked around, he saw that each man there had a sword or dagger tied to his belt. All except Fraxinus. "May this sword protect you and your friends from any evil that may come."

"Thank you, sir," Jonathan said, carefully taking the sword. It was lighter than he had expected. The hilt was simple, but it fit Jonathan's grip perfectly. The sword itself fit snugly in its leather sheath, which was adorned with depictions of leaves and vines.

"I pray that the Creator will bless you on your journey," Fraxinus said. "May He protect you always." Then the old druid's eyes locked on Melony. "And, Aralyn," he said. Melony's eyes widened in surprise. "You don't have to hide yourself from us. My people eagerly await your arrival at Alden." Melony bowed her head to him. A wave of confusion hit Jonathan. *Why did the druid call her Aralyn, not Melony?* he wondered. But no explanation came, and Jonathan was left with yet another question burning in the back of his mind.

Jonathan adjusted his pack as Melony said goodbye to Fraxinus and the other druids. And Micah spent a good deal of time saying his goodbyes to the druid children whom he'd played with the last two days.

"Wait," Micah said just before they set off. "Where's Belnor? He didn't say goodbye." Jonathan looked around, but the black-haired druid was nowhere to be seen.

"I don't know," Jonathan said. "But we have to go." So they strode into the woods, the sun just peeking over the horizon.

"What was that about?" Jonathan asked Melony after they were out of earshot of the camp.

"What?" replied Melony.

"Why did he call you Aralyn?" he asked.

"I don't know," Melony said. But Jonathan sensed that Melony wasn't telling the whole truth.

As the morning progressed, the shadows of the trees shortened and the forest air warmed. Squirrels scampered back and forth across the forest floor, and birds chirped high above the trio. The crunching of the leaves under their feet was rhythmic as they strode across the forest floor. But Jonathan's feet were growing soar from the seemingly endless hours of walking. And his stomach was begging for them to stop for some breakfast.

"Let's stop a moment," Jonathan said.

"Why?" Melony asked.

"I'm hungry," he said as he started to pull off his pack. But even once they had all stopped moving, the crunch of footsteps lingered a moment longer.

Something isn't right, Jonathan thought. He pulled his pack back on and signaled Melony and Micah to keep walking. They moved a few yards, and he again signaled them to stop. The crunching lingered once again. Melony looked pestered, and an expression of confusion was written on Micah's brow. A few more yards. More crunching. A few yards further. Again, more crunching. Melony looked greatly annoyed now. She opened her mouth to say something, but Jonathan held a finger to his lips to signal her to be quiet. He waved at Micah and Melony to go ahead. Then he moved towards the nearest tree and hid in its shadow.

When Melony and Micah were a good distance from his hiding spot, Jonathan saw something move in the shadows. He strained his eyes, but all he could see was a dark figure sneaking from tree to tree. Finally, a sliver of sunlight momentarily touched the mysterious figure. Jonathan immediately recognized the black hair, the ivory skin, and the green druid cloak of Belnor. He had followed them from the camp. But why? There was only one way to find out. Jonathan let Belnor get ahead of himself, then he pursued.

He observed Belnor as he followed the druid boy. He had traveling boots on his feet and a large pack on his back, not very different from his own. But Jonathan saw no sign of a sword or dagger. In fact, he saw no signs of a weapon of any kind. As Belnor crouched behind a thick tree trunk, Jonathan crept behind him and cleared his throat.

"Well, Belnor. You sure did get far before getting caught," Jonathan said. Belnor spun around to face him.

"Jonathan," Belnor exclaimed. "How did you–" Jonathan easily dragged Belnor up by his cloak and escorted him in the direction of Micah and Melony.

"Micah! Melony!" Jonathan shouted. "Look who I found tagging along!" There was no response. *They must be too far ahead to hear me*, thought Jonathan. He moved faster, dragging Belnor along.

"Ow! Let go!" Belnor cried. But Jonathan didn't let go. An uneasy feeling settled upon him.

"Melony! Micah! Wait up!" he said. Quickening his pace once more, Jonathan reached a small clearing. There, in the middle of the clearing, were two packs and a small, green cloak lying in a heap on the forest floor. Jonathan rushed into the clearing, finally letting go of Belnor's cloak. He picked up the cloak, instantly recognizing it as the one the druid boy had given Micah. Jonathan's heart began to race.

"What happened to them?" Jonathan asked Belnor, showing him Micah's cloak.

"I don't know," Belnor exclaimed.

"You don't know?" Jonathan asked sarcastically. "So the moment I caught you, they magically disappeared for no reason?"

"Jonathan–"

"I knew I shouldn't have trusted you or your people," Jonathan said.

"This isn't my doing," Belnor said defensively.

"Yeah?" Jonathan said. "Then who did it?"

"Look," Belnor said, pointing to a patch of leaves on the forest floor. "I think they were dragged away."

"What do you mean 'dragged away'?" Jonathan asked. Then he noticed the tracks to which Belnor was pointing. *How didn't I notice them right away?* Jonathan thought. Belnor moved over to the tracks, analyzing them carefully.

"They were dragged away by someone," Belnor repeated. "Or something." Jonathan picked up Micah's pack, shoved Micah's cloak into it, and slung it over his own shoulder.

"Come on," Jonathan said to Belnor. "I'm not losing my brother." Belnor nodded, picked up Melony's pack, and slung it over his shoulder. Then Jonathan nocked an arrow and two began following the trail deeper into the forest.

It wasn't long before the trail led to the edge of a gorge. The sloping sides were covered in dead leaves, and the roots of trees jetted out of the dirt like thick winding arms. A column of blue smoke rose from the bottom of the gorge, masking the floor below. *What's big enough in these parts of the woods to drag off two people?* Jonathan wondered. But he knew his question would be answered shortly. He barely hesitated before climbing down the side of the gorge. When he finally reached the bottom, the smoke was thick and determined to blind and suffocate him.

But Jonathan had barely reached the floor of the gorge when he heard a great grunt. Seeing a shadow in the smoke, Jonathan searched for something to hide behind. There were no trees. Instead, there were only a couple of small, wiry shrubs littering the floor of the gorge. Jonathan made for one of the shrubs, the crunch of dead leaves betraying him to whomever or whatever had made the grunt. Just as he lowered his body to the ground behind the shrub, a short creature stepped out from the smoke.

Through the thin branches of the shrub, Jonathan saw that it wasn't even four feet tall. The creature hunched over with a large lump on its back, like a hunchback. Course feathers clung to the creature's head and wing-like arms. The large patches of greyish-green skin that weren't covered in feathers were instead covered with nasty, giant warts and bruises. It snarled and grunted as it walked around on two bird legs, each with long, razor-sharp talons. It began sniffing the air with its beak-shaped face, like a predator sniffing for its prey.

But worst of all was the creature's scent. Jonathan gagged and held his breath to keep from vomiting. If he had describe it, it smelled like an egg had been left in the sun far too long. And then that egg had been thrown into a bog and left to rot. It was without question the worst thing Jonathan had ever smelled. It left him lightheaded and nauseous.

How did that thing steal my brother? Jonathan wondered. *It's tiny.* The creature, apparently unsatisfied with something, went back into the smoke, where he disappeared through the misty curtain. Belnor raced down the side of the gorge, and, reaching the bottom, lay low next to Jonathan.

"That was a tengu," Belnor said in a panicked whisper. Jonathan wasn't sure why Belnor sounded so panicked. He had never heard of a tengu. But Belnor seemed to have read his thought for he said, "It's a bird-goblin." Jonathan nodded his head slowly. He had heard of neither a tengu nor a bird-goblin. But it did explain why the creature had feathers.

At that moment, a scream pierced the silence of the gorge. Jonathan knew instantly that it was Melony's because it was the same scream she had let out when he had shot her.

"What are they doing to her?" Jonathan whispered to Belnor.

"I don't know," he replied. The next thing Jonathan heard was a loud grunt. Melony's screams suddenly stopped. Jonathan knew he had to save her and Micah, whatever was happening. He got up from his hiding place.

"Stop!" Belnor protested quietly. "You're going to get yourself killed."

"Then come with me and make sure I don't die," Jonathan whispered back. Belnor sighed and got to his feet, unwillingly following Jonathan further into danger. Jonathan, bow in hand, cautiously walked through the curtain of thick, grey smoke that separated him from this tengu.

Emerging from the smoke, Jonathan's eyes fell upon a horrendous sight. A blazing fire, from which the cloud of smoke had been conjured, was twenty paces away from Jonathan. He could see a dozen silhouettes of feathered bird-goblins gathered around the brilliant flames, a buzz of excitement emanating from them. Micah and Melony were tied with their backs to a towering ash tree on the other side of the great bonfire. Melony was unconscious and had a cut on her forehead. On the other hand, Micah was wide awake, his face white as a sheet.

In the corner of his eye, Jonathan spotted Belnor crouching behind a large rock. He was frantically waving for him to come closer. Jonathan ran and joined the druid behind the rock.

"What is it?" asked Jonathan.

"There's something you need to know about tengu," Belnor said with a hint of fear in his voice. Jonathan knew that whatever Belnor was about to say was going to be unpleasant. "They survive by eating human flesh." Jonathan felt a mixture of fear, anger, and adrenaline course through his body.

"We have to rescue them," said Jonathan.

"Alright," Belnor said. "I know a few spells that could–"

"No," Jonathan said firmly. "No magic."

"But, Jonathan–"

"I said no," Jonathan repeated.

"Then how would you suggest we rescue them?" Belnor asked aggressively. "There are at least a dozen tengu between us and your friends. And we'll suffer the same fate unless—"

"Unless we have a strategy," Jonathan interrupted. Both were silent, deep in thought, trying to come up with some sort of plan. The only sounds that could be heard were the crackle of the fire and the cries of the strange creatures. Finally, an idea dawned on Jonathan.

"I've got an idea. But I need to ask you something," Jonathan said. "Are you a fast runner?"

"I suppose," Belnor said. "But how does that help your friends?"

"You need to distract those bird-goblin things and lead them away into the forest," Jonathan explained. "While they're chasing you, I'll untie Melony and Micah. Then you'll run back, and we'll all get out of here as fast as we can."

"I don't like this plan," Belnor said.

"It's the only one we have right now," said Jonathan. "Please, I have to save my brother. And to do that, I need your help." Belnor hesitated, his nervous glance shifting between Jonathan and the tengu camp.

"Fine," he finally muttered. "I'll help you."

"Thank you," replied Jonathan. "Start distracting them on three. Ready?"

"I suppose I'm as ready as I will ever be," Belnor said.

"On three," Jonathan whispered. "One." He watched Belnor take a deep breathe. "Two." The druid anxiously bounced on the balls of his feet. "Three." Belnor jumped on top of the large rock that they were hiding behind, lifting the sides of his cloak like a set of bird wings to make himself easy to spot.

"Oy! Birdbrains! Over here!" shouted Belnor. All the tengu became silent and turned their heads towards Belnor. Apparently realizing Belnor was edible, they began creeping towards the large rock. Belnor shot into the cloud of smoke behind him, heading for the woods. After a moment's hesitation and a few exchanged glances, all twelve tengu followed in hot pursuit.

Once they were out of sight, Jonathan ran to the tree to which Melony and Micah were bound. He drew his sword and began to cut the ropes that held them captive.

"Jonathan! You found us!" Micah exclaimed.

"Of course I did," Jonathan said. "Now hold still. This sword is sharp." He cut through the first cord just as Micah's eyes suddenly widened.

"Jonathan! Behind you!" Micah cried. Jonathan heard a low growl behind him. He spun around to see what had made the noise when he felt a blow to his head. His sword flew from his hand, and Jonathan fell to one knee. Regaining his vision after the blow, he looked up. A very fat and feathery tengu stood in front of him, a jagged, twisted sword in his hand. The creature lifted his sword and swung it downwards towards Jonathan's head. Jonathan felt the blade graze his cheek as he tried to dodge the blow.

"Jonathan!" Micah cried. He nodded his head towards the base of the tree to which he was tied. There, sitting on the forest floor only three feet away from Micah, was Jonathan's own shortsword. Jonathan rushed to grab the sword. But the tengu leapt high into the air, using its wings to rise a few extra feet above Jonathan. It didn't take long for Jonathan to realize that the creature was aiming to land on him. Jonathan made a dash for his sword, grabbing it by its round pommel. With one swift motion, Jonathan spun around and slashed his sword at the landing tengu. The creature fell to the forest floor, thrashing in pain, a stream of dark purple blood flowing from the fresh gash on its stomach. Jonathan lifted his shortsword over the dying tengu and stabbed it through the heart. It let out one last raspy breath and then was still.

Jonathan fell to his knees in front of the dead creature. He could feel the adrenaline coursing through his veins. Remembering what he was doing, Jonathan turned around. Micah, still tied to the tree, was watching Jonathan with amazement.

"How in Iyuandil did you do that?" Micah asked.

"I got lucky," Jonathan said, wiping the purple blood from his sword before cutting Micah's remaining bonds. He handed his younger brother his pack. "Keep watch while I free Melony."

"Keep watch for what?" Micah asked.

"For more tengu," Jonathan said. "And also for Belnor."

"Belnor?" Micah exclaimed. "He's here?"

"I'll explain later," Jonathan said, starting to cut the ropes around Melony. But as he did, he discovered a small, gold medallion hanging around her neck by a thin, golden chain. When he looked closer, he saw that the image of a dragon with outstretched wings had been delicately etched in the gold surface. Jonathan recognized it instantly as the symbol of the house of Kathar, the royal family.

"Oy!" Jonathan heard Melony say. He quickly moved away from Melony as she got to her feet. "What do you think you're doing?" Melony shouted as she tucked her medallion into her dress and out of sight.

"I was just trying to untie you," Jonathan said defensively.

"Just keep your nose in your own business," Melony replied. "Now, what happened?" But before Jonathan could answer her, Belnor came running through the cloud of smoke.

"You better start running if you don't want to be bird food!" Belnor shouted. The druid grabbed a necklace with a purple crystal from around his neck and turned around to face the direction he had just run from. At that moment a tengu emerged from the trees.

"*Mortiac teldriin!*" Belnor shouted. A glowing purple orb shot from Belnor's fingertips and hit the tengu in the chest, knocking the creature backwards a good ten feet. Belnor didn't hesitate another moment before running past Jonathan and Micah, not stopping to see if they followed. Jonathan saw Micah begin searching the ground around him.

"What are you doing!" shouted Jonathan as Micah mischievously picked a stone from the ground.

"Watch this," Micah said, taking out his slingshot and aiming it at the smoke from which the tengu had emerged. At that moment, eleven more tengu emerged from the smoke. Probably fancying the four children as their next feast, the tengu ran towards the quartet as fast as their bird legs would carry them.

The rock flew from Micah's slingshot and hit a small and extremely ugly tengu square in the forehead, causing it to fall to the forest floor in a small, smelly heap. Jonathan rushed to Micah's side, pulling him away from the tengu.

"Did you see that!" shouted Micah. "I hit it!"

"Good for you," said Jonathan sarcastically. "Let's see how you do when they're three feet in front of you." Micah rolled his eyes. Jonathan grabbed his brother's arm and dragged him out of the gorge and away from the increasingly nearing bird-goblins.

Jonathan looked ahead, searching for Melony and Belnor ahead of them. But they were nowhere in sight. *Of course,* Jonathan thought. *They abandoned us. They probably thought they could escape by letting those goblins eat us first. They're probably–* Jonathan's thought was interrupted by the sudden sensation of being lifted into the air by the scruff of his cloak.

"Aahhhhh!" Jonathan heard Micah scream in terror next to him.

This is it, Jonathan thought. *Those wretched, feathered birdbrains have us. It's the end! It's—*

"Belnor!" Micah shouted. Belnor was sitting on a tree branch, his hands glowing purple with magic. Jonathan reached behind him, but felt nothing holding his cloak. He and Micah were set on the branch, their feet dangling high above the forest floor.

"You did that using magic?" Micah asked in amazement. Belnor nodded.

"Hush, all of you," Melony whispered from a tree branch above them. The cut on her head was still bright red, blood smeared across her forehead. Her sword was drawn and her hair was falling out of her braid. Her electric blue eyes searched the forest floor vigilantly. She glanced up at Jonathan. "What are you staring at?" she asked in an irritated manner.

Jonathan, not realizing he had been staring at her, replied with a short, "Nothing." A moment later, several tengu passed under the tree, taking no notice of their prey hiding in the treetops. After nearly fifteen minutes of crouching in the tops of the great tree, the four children slipped from the branches that had kept them hidden and safe from the tengu and continued their course south towards the mighty city of Alden.

Chapter 6
New Questions Arise

The medallion that hung around Melony's neck still haunted Jonathan's thoughts. How had she gotten it? Had she found it? Or had she stolen it? So many questions swam through Jonathan's mind.

"Melony," Jonathan said, "where did you get that medallion?"

"I told you it isn't your business," Melony whispered back.

"I was just curious," he said. Melony kept her eye locked on the path ahead.

"It was a gift," she finally said quietly.

"Who gave it to you?" Jonathan asked.

"I don't really want to talk about it." As soon as she had said this, she quickly marched to the front of their group, leaving Jonathan walking behind Belnor and Micah. The two boys stood side by side discussing odds and ends, such as monsters, the woods, and legendary battles.

Jonathan, ignoring Belnor and Micah's conversation, imagined what Silan was like right now. It had been nearly four days since he and Micah left home to escape King Alexander's men. Mum would be worried sick, hoping her sons were safe, and, more importantly, alive. But he knew that no matter how worried she became, Mum's head would remain high and her hair would still be in two braids, tied to the back of her head by the small strip of leather. He could almost smell her delicious corius-fruit pie sitting in the windowsill.

"We camp here," Melony said, interrupting Jonathan's thoughts. They had entered a small clearing, and Melony was already beginning to clear a space for a fire.

"Go gather some firewood," she ordered Belnor and Micah.

"Yes ma'am," Micah replied sarcastically, before he started walking in the direction of the woods with Belnor. Then Jonathan realized something.

"Wait a minute. You two get back here," Jonathan said. Micah and Belnor came back to where Jonathan stood. "You," Jonathan said, pointing to Belnor. "You need to go back to your clan."

"What? Why?" Micah asked.

"I didn't want a third person on this journey, but I definitely don't want a fourth," Jonathan said. "You need to go home, Belnor. Right now."

"I'm here to help," Belnor said.

"Help us what?" Jonathan said. "We can get to Alden on our own." Belnor stared at Jonathan for a moment. But then his gaze shifted to somewhere behind Jonathan. Jonathan turned around only to find Melony sitting on the forest floor behind him.

"Like I said," Belnor said to Melony, "I'm here to help." Melony stared back at Belnor. Jonathan didn't understand what exactly he meant. What did Melony need help with?

"He can stay," Melony said quietly. At that, Micah and Belnor ran into the woods to get firewood.

"What is it you need his help with?" Jonathan asked her after Belnor and Micah were out of sight. But Melony just ignored his question

"Why don't you go find us something to eat or something," Melony said. Her back was turned away from him, but Jonathan could tell that she was angry.

"Why are you angry at me?" Jonathan asked cautiously.

"I'm not angry at you," she said, but not convincingly.

"Look," Jonathan said, "I'm sorry about whatever you're mad at me about. In fact, I don't even know why you're angry at me." Melony turned to him. She stared at Jonathan with her piercing blue eyes.

"I'm not angry at you," she said. "It's just... my medallion." Jonathan was very confused now.

"Your medallion makes you angry?" Jonathan asked. "Is it magic or something?"

"No. It's not magic. I just–" she stopped herself. "Just forget you ever saw it, alright?" Then she went back to working on her clearing. Although hundreds of questions were swimming through his head, Jonathan could tell Melony wanted to be left alone. He took his bow off his back, and started to leave the clearing. He stopped at the edge of the woods and waited for something, though he didn't know what. Whatever it was, it did not come, so Jonathan slipped into the woods to hunt. He trekked through the woods until he was a good distance from the camp and then perched himself in an old, large tree.

Hunting always helped Jonathan think. The stillness of the trees and the quiet of the woods helped him to concentrate. Finally, he could analyze his and Micah's situation. First, they were on a long journey south to Alden, far from home and help. Second, they were traveling with a girl who tried attacking them and a druid boy who had followed them with no explanation. And finally they had almost gotten killed only hours ago. And for what? Why hadn't they just hidden in the woods until the soldiers had left?

Because Mum wanted us to be taken care of, said the little voice in the back of his mind. *But I'm sixteen years old,* Jonathan thought. He could take care of himself, as well as his brother and mother. He had for years now.

When he was seven, two years after his father had left, Jonathan started working as a farm hand on Old Man Bynum's farm. There, he had helped with every seeding and every harvest to get just enough money for his family to eat and purchase the bare necessities for winter.

At the farm of that grouchy old man, Jonathan had met Henry, the blacksmith's boy. Henry had always been the outgoing one, the one who made tedious day-to-day work fun. It wasn't long before Henry became Jonathan's best friend. Four years ago, to Mum's great surprise, Martin Smith, Henry's father and the town blacksmith, had taken on Jonathan as his apprentice. The blacksmith had also been so generous to provide food for their family. Jonathan knew Mum would never allow it in any other circumstance, but she pretended that she was alright with it, for her sons' sakes.

Jonathan's thoughts drifted to Melony. Why had she been so secretive about her medallion? He wondered why she needed to get to Alden if she feared the king's soldiers. He asked himself why *he* needed to go to Alden if he himself also feared King Alexander's men. Jonathan decided that whatever happened, that night he was going to ask Melony why she had to get to Alden. And he was determined to get an answer. As he was lost in thought, a squirrel scurried past. He tried to shoot it, but his arrow zipped several feet above it. So Jonathan forced himself to push his thoughts aside.

In fifteen minutes, Jonathan shot three squirrels: one larger one with dull, grey fur and two smaller ones with rusty, red fur. He was about to shoot another when Belnor and Micah came clambering through the woods, now discussing monsters of the mighty mountains. Both of them had their arms full of firewood so that they could hardly see over the tops of their loads.

"Oy! Jonathan," shouted Belnor. "Do you think you can give us a hand?" Jonathan grabbed his squirrels and put them in his bag. He leapt from the tree branch and grabbed some of the top pieces of wood the boys were carrying so they could at least see. The trio walked back together. When they arrived, they found Melony looking over the map Fraxinus had given her.

The squirrels were skinned, gutted, skewered, and devoured by the time the sun had sunk below the horizon. Melony found a corius-fruit tree nearby so the four children ate the ripened fruit as well. Each layer of the fruit Jonathan ate was sweeter than the last, while, at the very center, the rather large seed, about the size of a walnut, had a nutty flavor and was always Jonathan's favorite part. They didn't use any of the food the druids had given them, since there was no point in wasting it when they had enough already.

Stars began to appear in the sky, but there was only a thin sliver of moon to be seen. Melony, all this time, had not spoken to Jonathan. She again pulled out the map of Iyuandil. The three boys surrounded her, all trying to see the map. It had not been damaged by the tengu, which was good. They needed the map to get to Alden quickly.

"We're not far from Lenz," Melony said, pointing to a small dot next to a crooked blue line.

"I'd say it's only a two days journey from here," Belnor said.

"If we can get there," said Melony, "then we can take a boat on the Anafract River all the way to Alden." Jonathan had never thought of the possibility of taking a boat to Alden. The journey would be much less treacherous and much faster than walking.

"That could work," Jonathan said. "I say we do it."

"Great," Melony said, rolling up the map. "We'll leave for Lenz in the morning."

The four of them spread their bedrolls on all sides of the crackling fire. Soon after he had settled into his own bedroll, Jonathan could hear the soft snores of Micah beside him. But he could not sleep. He stared up at the unending field of stars, questions swimming through his head.

Later in the night, Jonathan could hear Melony tossing and turning in her sleep. She moaned, and her breathing quickened. Slowly, he turned onto his side, propped up on his elbow, and faced Melony.

"No. I won't go," she muttered. Her brow furrowed, but she remained asleep.

"Melony?" Jonathan said.

"Please, don't kill him!" Melony said, a little louder than the first time.

"Melony, are you alright?" Jonathan asked.

"No. Stop! Ethan!" Melony screamed. Her eyes opened and she quickly sat up. For a second she sat there staring into the distance, gasping for breath.

"Melony," Jonathan whispered. "Are you alright? You were shouting in your sleep." Melony turned and looked at Jonathan.

"Sorry," she said. She sounded almost embarrassed. Melony lay back on her side and turned to face Jonathan. He could see the stars reflecting in her blue eyes. "It was just a dream," she said.

"Sounded more like a nightmare," Jonathan said.

"It wasn't a nightmare," Melony said.

"Then close your eyes."

"Close my eyes?" Melony asked.

"Yeah," Jonathan said. Melony gave him a questioning look, but then closed her eyes. Immediately, a painful expression filled her face. Her eyes snapped back open.

"So I was right: it was a nightmare. And a bad one by the sound of it." Melony rolled her eyes at Jonathan. An owl hooted in a nearby tree. "I know when I have a nightmare, I like to talk to someone about it. Usually my brother." Melony didn't say a word. "Well, if you don't want to talk about your nightmare, maybe we should talk about something else to get it off your mind."

"Like what?" Melony asked

"Like why you need to get to Alden." There was a seemingly unending silence.

"Because," she finally said. She turned on her side, facing away from Jonathan. The answer he had dreaded had reached his ears. But he was determined to get a proper answer. He was about to ask again when he heard a long, yet quiet, sigh. "Because I need to find my uncle."

"Your uncle?" Jonathan asked. She was looking for her uncle in the same place *he* was looking for his uncle? Jonathan was intrigued. "Why?" Melony turned back to face him.

"He's the only family I have left," she said.

"Don't you have parents? A mother? A father?" Jonathan whispered.

"No. They're both dead."

"I'm sorry," Jonathan said. "How did they die? If you don't mind my asking."

"My mother died when I was three," she said. "She was captured during the Second Fae Raid. Soon after, she was killed. Or so my nanna said." Jonathan knew about the Second Fae Raid. He had only been four years old. Fae warriors from the east had pillaged and ravaged the kingdom and eventually raided the capital, Alden.

"My father…" Melony started. Jonathan couldn't hear exactly what Melony said next, but he didn't press the matter. "What about you?" Melony asked, surprising Jonathan.

"Me?" Jonathan said.

"Yes. Why are you going to Alden?"

"I'm looking for my uncle too."

"Are you joking?" Melony said.

"It's true!" Jonathan defended himself.

"Well, why do you need to find *your* uncle?"

"Because of King Alexander," Jonathan explained. "His men came to our village in search of young men and boys for his army. Our mother told us to find our Uncle Eli in Alden so he can take care of us while King Alexander searches for boys in the north."

"What about your father? Can't he protect you from Alexander's men?" Melony asked. Jonathan was silent and lowered his head. "Oh. I'm sorry. I didn't realize he's dead."

"He's not dead," Jonathan said. "I wish he was, though. Then he'd have an excuse for not being here."

"What happened to him?" Melony asked.

"He left," he said. "I was about five. Micah was only a year old. I don't even know his name."

"I'm terribly sorry," Melony said. Jonathan could almost see tears welling up in her eyes.

"I try not to think about him," said Jonathan. He fingered his bow lying beside him. "Besides, I don't need him. I have his bow. I can protect my family without him."

"It's your father's bow?" Melony asked.

"Yeah," Jonathan said. "Some stranger brought it to our home after my father left. The folks in Silan say my father was the best archer in miles. He could shoot an acorn dead center from a mile away."

"That sounds impossible," Melony said skeptically. "Was he a farmer?"

"No," he said. "My father was a soldier. He served King Alexander when he was still a prince. I don't think it honorable, though. The king is a tyrant."

"He might not be all that bad."

"But he's taken everything from everyone! I used to make two maltra a day when I was a farm hand, but with King Alexander's taxes, there was hardly enough to feed my family. And, you attacked us because you thought we were some of King Alexander's soldiers."

"For the last time, I didn't attack you," Melony said. "Anyways, it's the soldiers that are horrible, not necessarily him. Have you ever met the king? No. But have you met his soldiers?"

"Yes," Jonathan said. "They took my best friend and broke into our home."

"Yes, they're terrible," Melony said. "But that was the soldiers, not the king."

"I think it's both."

"I think he actually wants to help and defend his people," Melony said. "That's what I would do if I were the ruler."

"What would you know about being a ruler?" Jonathan said. Melony was quiet. She turned away from Jonathan. "Melony?" But she still didn't reply. So Jonathan turned around and went to sleep, wondering.

When Jonathan woke up, Melony had relit the fire and prepared breakfast from the food the druids had given them. There were a few slices of sizzling bacon, biscuits that had been baked the day before in the druid camp, and some more corius fruits from the nearby corius tree. Belnor brewed a tea with some dried herbs he'd brought. He said the tea had medicinal qualities, but Jonathan found it quite repulsive and threw it into the grass when Belnor wasn't looking.

Melony made no mention of their late-night conversation. *Did I dream the whole thing?* he wondered. There was no evidence that it had happened. But as the quartet was packing up their bedrolls, Melony came beside Jonathan.

"I'd rather you not tell the others what I told you last night," she whispered. Jonathan nodded in agreement. *So it had been real,* he thought. Then Melony got up and doused the fire with water from her waterskin. After the four children packed up their bedrolls, they each tried to stuff as many corius fruits as they could into their packs. When they were satisfied with their load, they said a short prayer to the Creator, Melony said, "Move out," and they were off to Lenz.

Chapter 7
The Dancing Fiddler Inn

The quartet pushed through the forest for two days. Finally, by mid-afternoon on the second day, Jonathan emerged from the last few trees of the woods. Before him lay a wide, green expanse. It was the Canian Plain. The winding Anafract River was a long, blue snake on a vast, green carpet, cutting through the plain with natural beauty and grace. A large, black smudge rested on a bend of the river, on the same side that they stood. It was the town of Lenz.

Never before had Jonathan been to a village outside of Silan, much less a bustling town on the banks of the mighty Anafract. Even there at the edge of the wood, he could hear the buzz of movement from the town, where, Jonathan imagined, life was never boring. As they neared the entrance of the town, Belnor pulled his hood over his face.

"What's wrong?" Micah asked Belnor.

"Lenz is a noisy, bustling fishing town full of rowdy, cowardly, bargemen and fishermen," Belnor explained. "But worst of all, the people there are not very friendly toward druids. So excuse me if I hide my face. I'd rather not get run out of town."

The closer they came to Lenz, the more pungent the smell of rotting fish became. When they entered the town, Jonathan was surprised to find that the streets were filled with people, some dancing, and others throwing flowers into the air. The four children weaved their way through the crowd, only to find that the whole town was like this.

"What is going on?" Micah asked Jonathan.

"I have no idea," he replied.

"It's the autumn equinox," Belnor said behind Jonathan.

"The autumn equinox? Already?" asked Melony. Jonathan was also surprised. There were so many people in the streets, one would think the holiday was more than just the changing of the seasons. In Silan, the villagers didn't really celebrate the autumn equinox. Mostly, they were busy preparing the village for the band of merchants that could arrive any day. Some of the men did go to the tavern in the evening to drink beer, ale, and mead, but that was a pretty regular practice anyway.

"You do know what that means about getting a boat to Alden, right, Melony?" Belnor said.

"No," Melony said.

"It means that no boats will be sailing on the river until tomorrow," Belnor said.

"Great," Jonathan said sarcastically.

"What do we do?" Micah asked.

"If we aren't able to sail out of here today," Melony began, "then we'll have to stay the night."

"Where?" asked Micah.

"Outside town?" Jonathan suggested.

"Please outside town," Belnor mumbled.

"We should stay somewhere in town, an inn probably," Melony said. Jonathan had never slept in another town besides Silan. He knew in his gut that he would rather sleep in the middle of the woods surrounded by bandits than sleep in an inn with a bunch of strangers in the same building.

"But how would we pay for a room in an inn?" Micah asked. "We don't have any money." Melony reached for the satchel at her side. She put her hand in the bag, and when she pulled it back out, she was holding a small drawstring bag. The three boys gathered around Melony as she opened the bag slightly. Jonathan looked inside and saw it was full of gold coins.

"Where did you get that?" Micah said loud enough that a few people stared at them. The other three all made shushing sounds at Micah.

"Where *did* you get that?" Jonathan whispered.

"I earned it," Melony said. "I used to fight giants in northern Nimberia." She closed the drawstring bag and put it back in her leather satchel.

"No really, where did you get it?" Jonathan asked again. Melony began walking away, ignoring Jonathan.

"Come on," she said. Jonathan and the others followed closely behind Melony, making sure to stick together and not get lost in the crowd of celebrating people.

For almost two and a half hours they wandered the streets of Lenz, and Jonathan became very hungry. They hadn't eaten since breakfast that morning and the sun was now beginning to set. Clouds were rolling in from the north, giving off low rumbles of thunder, announcing the coming storm. Jonathan heard someone's stomach growl, which only made his gradually increasing hunger worse.

Suddenly, Melony stopped in front of a small building. A sign hung above the door with a picture of a man dancing with a fiddle. However, since he had never learned how to read, Jonathan couldn't read the words that had been painted on the sign.

"The Dancing Fiddler Inn," Belnor read aloud.

"I think we found ourselves an inn," Melony said happily. The four had already found three other inns, but each time they had tried to get a bed for the night or even a meal, they were turned away because the inns were too full.

Melony straightened herself and stepped through the door of the Dancing Fiddler Inn. Jonathan followed right behind her. The inside of the building was full of laughter and the smell of ale, beer, and whiskey. The room was filled to the brim with people dancing, drinking, and singing songs. A man in a dirty apron stood behind a tall counter near the front of the room, pouring a beer for another man.

"Can I 'elp you?" said a voice to Jonathan's left. A young woman stepped forward, three beer steins in her left hand and two in her right. Her hair was chocolate brown, with soft curls, and her eyes were dark and sparkled like sapphires.

"Yes," Melony answered. "We're looking for a place to stay for the night and something to eat." The woman looked at Melony, then Jonathan, then Micah, then Belnor, and then Melony again.

"We 'aven't much room," she said. Melony fished out the bag of gold and shook it.

"We're prepared to pay," Melony said. The woman's eyes widened, and a faint smile appeared at the corners of her mouth.

"I believe I 'ave a room I can fit you four in," the woman finally said. "Follow me." She turned and set the beer steins on the bar counter. She weaved her way through the endless maze of crowded tables and people, Melony, Jonathan, Micah, and Belnor following closely.

After leaving behind the crowd of people, the young woman led the four weary children up a flight of stairs. At the top was a long hallway, both walls lined with doors every few feet. The woman walked past most of the doors, nine of them Jonathan counted, and eventually stopped in front of one near the end of the hall. She took out a ring of keys, which had been hidden between her apron and her dress, and unlocked the door.

When Jonathan saw what was inside, he suddenly felt his weariness catch up to him, for inside were four beds, each with a straw mattress, a wool blanket, cotton sheets, and a fluffy pillow. A wide window was on the other side of the room, while the four beds were pushed up against the wall right of the door.

"Will this do?" asked the woman.

"Yes," said Melony. "This will do nicely."

"I'm Felicity if you need somethin' later," said the woman.

"Thank you, Felicity," Melony replied. Then Felicity turned and left the four children to themselves. By the time Jonathan had taken his own pack off, Micah had already claimed the bed nearest to the window. Jonathan claimed the bed closest to Micah, and Belnor claimed the one after that. Melony was left with the bed nearest to the door.

As soon as the sun sank below the horizon, Jonathan's stomach roared with hunger.

"What was that?" Micah asked.

"My stomach," Jonathan said. "We haven't eaten since this morning."

"We should get something to eat then," Melony said. The four of them went back down the stairs and reentered the crowded tavern. It was difficult to find an empty table, but soon they sat themselves at a small table in the corner. It was beginning to rain very hard outside when Felicity came and brought them each a bowl of steaming hot potato'n'fish soup, a Lenz specialty.

When Jonathan had slurped up the final drops of his second bowl of soup, he felt so full he thought he would burst. And when Felicity brought out thirds, Jonathan groaned at the idea of eating another bite. But both Micah and Belnor accepted their third helpings gladly. Each gulped down the hot soup as if their lives depended on it.

Melony, too, had declined a third bowl of the soup. She seemed deep in thought, maybe about getting a barge to Alden, or maybe about her uncle, but Jonathan didn't know for sure. After a while, Micah let out a long yawn.

"You should go upstairs and get in bed," Jonathan said.

"But I'm not tired," replied Micah.

"It's late and we've been walking all day," Jonathan said. "Go to bed."

"But—"

"Come on, Micah," Belnor interrupted him. "I'll go up with you. I'm tired." So Micah and Belnor slipped up the backstairs into the upstairs hallway. As he watched the boys go upstairs, Jonathan noticed that three scruffy-looking men were laughing hard at the table next to theirs. They all smelled strongly of fish and looked like they hadn't bathed in a month. And by the looks of the dozen empty ale mugs sitting in front of them, they were all extremely drunk.

"Hey, little missie," shouted one of the scruffy men, trying to get Melony's attention. Melony looked up. "Ain't you a pretty little thing." Melony turned her head away from him in disgust.

"Don't be shy, little lady," one of the other men said. The three men got to their feet. Jonathan looked down to see Melony tightly gripping the handle of her sword. The men walked over to their table.

"We don't want any trouble," Jonathan said standing up, his hand on the shortsword at his side.

"We don't want no trouble neither," said the third man. "All I want is a kiss from your lady friend here." Melony stood up suddenly, her face red.

"How dare you," she said.

"Oh come now," said the first man. "Just one kiss." At this the man puckered up his lips and leaned towards Melony. Before Jonathan could even think of what he was going to do, Melony pulled back her arm and punched the drunken man in the jaw. The man quickly pulled back and yelped in pain. The largest of the three men stepped forward and reared his arm back to smack Melony. But before he could inflict the blow, Melony ducked under the table.

Jonathan drew his sword and brandished it in front of the tallest man. But before either of them could do anything, the man fell face forward onto the table. Melony was standing behind the tall man, having just pulled his legs out from under him. Seeing their friend groaning on the floor, the other two drunken men scurried out of the inn.

"What in Iyuandil?" Jonathan muttered. "How did you do that?"

"I told you I used to hunt giants," Melony said. "Now I'm going to bed." She marched towards the stairs that led to the upstairs hall.

"But I thought that was a joke," Jonathan said, following her up the stairs.

"Well, it wasn't," Melony replied. Melony and Jonathan walked into the room to find both Belnor and Micah fast asleep in their beds.

Jonathan sat on his bed, taking off his boots. He could hear Micah's soft snores nearby. Then, Jonathan pulled the blanket over himself and laid his head on the small pillow. The moment he put his head on that pillow, he felt his exhaustion catch up to him. A bolt of lightning flashed across the sky, and thunder rolled outside his window. Jonathan let his eyes close and sleep befall him.

Chapter 8
Gorlan the Bargeman

T he next morning, Jonathan was awoken by the sound of bustling streets, the shouts of fishermen, and that scent one smells after a good storm. At first he was confused about where he was and how he'd gotten there. But then he remembered he was in Lenz.

Micah was still asleep, his blanket covering his head, as he had always done in Silan. Belnor was muttering in his druid tongue in his sleep. But Melony was already awake. She looked like she had been up for a while and had freshly braided her hair. She was analyzing Fraxinus's map at the foot of her bed.

"Why do you look at that map so much?" Jonathan asked Melony.

"Good morning to you too," Melony said. "I'm trying to learn the kingdom's geography. Come here." Jonathan went over to see what Melony had to show him. She pointed to a name of a place on the map that was slightly smudged. "Can you make out what this says?" Jonathan looked at it. But he knew it would be in vain.

"I– I can't," Jonathan said.

"I think it says Borko or Bonla. What would you say it was?" Melony asked.

"I can't read," Jonathan replied.

"Oh," Melony said. "I didn't realize–"

"It's alright," Jonathan said.

"You know, if you wanted to learn," Melony started, "I'm sure I might be able to teach you."

"Really?" asked Jonathan.

"Sure."

"What are you two talking about?" Micah asked groggily, sitting up in bed.

"Nothing," replied Jonathan.

Once the four of them had gotten out of bed and gotten dressed, they gathered their belongings and headed down to the docks. It was when he smelled the stench of old fish and heard the sound of rushing water that Jonathan knew they had made it to their destination.

"All we have to do is find a bargeman that can take us to Alden as quickly as possible," Melony said. Several small river barges were in port. Some were laden with goods from Alden, located at the mouth of the river. Others were empty, awaiting their next voyage. Men, women, and children alike bustled around the docks. Several men were shouting to other men on the barges. Some were unloading crates, while others were putting crates on the barges. The four children passed several barges and fishing boats alike. Many were large and made for passengers, while others seemed hardly big enough to hold one man. Melony passed by every single one.

Soon, Jonathan saw a smaller barge that was slowly falling into disrepair. A large man stood on the gangplank, yelling at a boy who had dropped a fish on the man's boot. The man looked the type that was mean and got angry for no good reason. Jonathan stood back, hoping Melony would not try to gain passage to Alden on *this* man's barge. To his disappointment, she did.

"Excuse me, sir," Melony said. The man turned around. His face was covered with bristles. His teeth were black and a few had fallen out. But what really put Jonathan aback was the smell the man gave off. It smelled like the man had bathed in raw fish his entire life. Jonathan had to resist the urge to gag. In the corner of his eye, he saw that Micah, too, was gagging silently, his face now slightly greener.

"Is that your barge?" Melony asked, nodding to the barge that looked like it might fall apart at any second.

"Yes indeed, lass. The *Tiffany*," said the man proudly, in a gruff voice. "And I'm her captain. Gorlan's the name. Judas Gorlan."

"We need passage to Alden, immediately," said Melony. "May we gain passage on your barge?"

"I don't take passengers on my barge," he said gruffly. "Especially folks without a copper dil to their name."

"We're willing to pay ten bid for passage.," Melony said calmly. Jonathan's heart seemed to skip a beat. Ten bid was a good sum of money. A bid was equivalent to about five maltra, and one maltra was the equivalent of about thirty dil. When Jonathan had worked in Silan as a farm hand, he had earned about two maltra a day, nowhere near ten bid!

"Ten bid, you say?" said the bargeman, scratching his balding head.

"Yes, sir. Ten bid. Five before the voyage." She pulled a glimmering, gold bid coin from her pouch. "Five after the voyage." She pulled out a second bid. The bargeman looked like he was weighing the offer in his mind. After a few moments, Gorlan extended his hand out to Melony, who shook it.

"We have a deal," Gorlan said. "We cast off this afternoon."

"Perfect," Melony replied. The bargeman walked back onto his barge, taking his stench with him. Jonathan gasped for a breath of fresh air.

That afternoon, after paying what they owed at the inn, Jonathan, Micah, Melony, and Belnor all boarded the *Tiffany*. Melony handed Gorlan five gold bid coins, and the captain shoved off, whistling an unfamiliar tune. It was only a one-day trip down stream, but since Gorlan was leaving so late in the afternoon, they would be traveling through the night.

"You four can sleep on deck if you wish," the smelly bargeman said. "There ain't any other place for you to sleep otherwise."

"Thank you," Melony said.

"Well, I'll leave you to it," Gorlan said with a grin that brought Jonathan nothing but suspicion and discomfort. The bargeman retreated to his position at the stern of the boat, where he manned the rudder.

Soon the sun sank into the horizon, and darkness fell over the *Tiffany*. The quartet laid their bedrolls on the creaking wood floor of the deck. The moon floated above the horizon, surrounded by thousands of twinkling stars. Jonathan lay on his back staring up at the beautiful, sparkling heavens. But he didn't feel tired. Something in the back of his mind was keeping him awake; an instinct telling him that he shouldn't sleep. That danger was near.

Micah, Belnor, and Melony were settling into their bedrolls, none showing that they felt the same as Jonathan. So he put aside his troubled mind and settled into his bedroll. He watched the stars twinkle innocently above him, still not feeling the least bit tired.

Squeak.

Jonathan woke with a start. He must have dozed off. The others seemed to be sound asleep. He wondered what the sound that woke him was.

Squeak.

He heard it again. Someone was trying to walk across the very squeaky floor. The noise was coming from the stern of the barge. Jonathan rolled over and pretended to be asleep, but he kept his eyes open. He could see the silhouette of a large, plump man creeping slowly towards the place where he lay. He could clearly see that the man held a long blade that flashed in the moonlight. Jonathan was as still as a mouse.

The silhouette of Gorlan came closer and closer until he was so close that Jonathan could smell him from where he lay. He watched as Gorlan moved towards Melony, whose sleeping face was turned towards Jonathan. But to Jonathan's surprise, Melony opened her eyes and moved her hand slowly towards her lips, signaling him to be quiet. Finally, Gorlan reached Melony and tried to lift her satchel from the floor without disturbing her.

Suddenly, Melony sprang from her bedroll, her sword unsheathed, and had Gorlan at sword point. He lifted his hands, letting Melony's satchel fall to the floor.

"What do you think you were trying to do? Rob me?" Melony shouted. Micah and Belnor sat up, rubbing their eyes and yawning.

"I– I just wanted to– to– keep your money safe. That's it!" said Gorlan, his voice trembling. Melony stared at Gorlan, unblinkingly, as she had done to Jonathan when they had first met.

"You stay away from me and my company," Melony said. "And I don't ever want to catch you stealing from us again."

"Y– yes, ma'am," stammered the frightened bargeman as he scrambled back to his place at the stern of the barge.

Chapter 9
A Sea Serpent

The *Tiffany* was quiet after Gorlan's attempt to steal Melony's gold. Gorlan had long stopped eyeing Melony's satchel and was silently sitting at the rudder once again. The children one by one fell asleep, though Melony stayed awake as long as she could to assure Gorlan did not try to steal from them again. Jonathan couldn't sleep either. He watched the stars in the dark silence of the night.

But suddenly, out of the silence, Jonathan heard a bubbling sound. It was coming from the river. Jonathan crept to the side of the boat to see what had made the noise. The moment he looked over the side, a giant, serpent-like creature broke the surface of the water. It stared at Jonathan with its great, black eyes. Then, it jumped out of the water, over the boat, and into the water on the other side. It did this a second time, wrapping its huge, scaly body around the barge.

"Stop!" Jonathan wanted to yell. But the words wouldn't leave his mouth. The monster squeezed the boat with its serpentine body, the sound of splintering wood echoing all around. Jonathan wanted to scream and wake up the others, who were all still asleep. The tail of the great creature knocked the sleeping Micah into the roaring water below. Jonathan ran to save him and fell into the water after him. The black waters blinded

Jonathan. He tried to get a breath, but the waters filled his lungs. He was drowning! Help! He was drowning!

Jonathan woke up with a start, his heart racing. It had only been a dream. A nightmare. He assumed it was from listening to too many of Micah and Belnor's conversations about monsters. The others, including Melony, were still asleep. And there was no monster to be seen.

Jonathan got up from the deck. His head hurt terribly. He thought it might have something to do with the awful smell that emanated from Gorlan and the *Tiffany* alike. The bargeman was still sitting on his stool next to the rudder at the stern, his head nodding as he tried to stay awake. The sound of rushing water filled the air. But it was not the calm sound of the river flowing downstream. This was a wild roar of water. Jonathan noticed that the noise became louder and louder as they sailed downstream.

Suddenly, the boat jerked hard to the left. Jonathan almost fell to the floor, but he managed to keep his footing. He ran to the side of the barge and saw what had caused the jerk. Rocks as large as the barge were protruding from the water. The river was a frothing storm, pushing the barge unforgivingly back and forth.

"What's going on?" said Gorlan, with a snort. His words had been slurred, as he had just woken from a nap, so they reached Jonathan's ears as "wasging un?" The bargeman yawned and rose, unsteadily, to his feet. His face turned red with anger when he saw Jonathan. "Why in Iyuandil did you wake me, boy?"

"I didn't!" Jonathan said, pointing overboard. "Look!" The moment Gorlan looked overboard, his anger turned into pure terror.

"Wake your friends!" Gorlan shouted, no longer sleepy. Jonathan didn't have to be told twice. He rushed to Micah.

"Micah!" he shouted. "Melony! Belnor! All of you! Get up!" Micah groggily sat up, trying to rub the sleep from his eyes. Belnor awoke in a similar manner, though he quickly stood up after looking at the worried expression on Jonathan's face. Melony, however, was up and wide awake the moment her name was called, her sword at the ready in case Gorlan was trying to steal from them again. The boat jerked, almost knocking Jonathan to the deck of the barge, as it hit another large rock. The four raced to the side of the barge. The rapids, in their rage, had torn a great hole in the starboard side of the barge.

Jonathan's heart beat wildly in his chest. He raced to the stern, where Gorlan was trying, unsuccessfully, to steer the ship out of the rapids.

"Why are there rapids? Haven't you been to this part of the river?" Jonathan shouted over the roaring rapids at the bargeman.

"I have!" Gorlan shouted back. "The rains caused flooding and must'a made us drift over to them rocky banks." Then Gorlan spoke as if to some invisible person next to him, "Don't you worry, Tif. I'll get you out of this." Jonathan raced back to the edge of the boat where the others were watching in horror. Again, the barge jerked violently. This time, Jonathan was thrown off the deck of the barge. He heard the cries of Micah, Melony, and Belnor falling from the barge as well.

Jonathan had always been a good swimmer. He, Henry, and Micah would often go down to the water hole near the village in the summertime. But that was when it was hot and all were sticky with sweat from the workday, not in the middle of autumn when all water was freezing cold.

Dark, heart-stopping cold water surrounded and penetrated his skin. His lungs burned, begging for air. He swam upward with every ounce of strength he had left. It seemed to Jonathan that he would never reach the surface. Finally, his muscles aching and his lungs searing with pain, Jonathan felt his head break through the surface of the water.

Coming out of the water was almost worse than being in the water. The chilly autumn air felt ice cold against Jonathan's wet scalp. His teeth chattered, and his toes felt as though they would turn to ice at any moment. Huge, jagged rocks towered around Jonathan, each trying to impale him. The roaring, rushing rapids tossed Jonathan like he was a ragdoll, small and helpless.

Suddenly, Jonathan caught a glimpse of Micah's head. He was flailing and panicking in the water. Jonathan tried to get Micah's attention and get his younger brother to swim towards him. But it was no use. Jonathan would have to go to him. The rushing current couldn't stop Jonathan. He fought against the waves and the wind, trying to reach his little brother. Finally, Jonathan reached Micah and grabbed him by the arm. Micah, panicking in the water, did not realize what Jonathan was trying to do. He kicked at Jonathan and pushed him away.

"Micah!" Jonathan shouted over the roar of the river. "I'm trying to help you!" Micah, to Jonathan's relief, finally realized what Jonathan was trying to do and began swimming with him to the bank of the river.

After using more energy to fight the current than Jonathan thought possible, he and Micah reached the riverbank. Jonathan was climbing up the muddy bank when he saw a hand extending towards him. He looked up. Melony was standing there, dripping wet, holding out her arm to him. Jonathan took hold and, with Melony's help, hauled himself out of the water. Out of the corner of his eye, he watched as Belnor helped Micah out of the water nearby.

"Thank you," Jonathan said through his coughs. He was exhausted. His legs felt like they were about to give way beneath him. "Where's Gorlan?" he asked, just noticing the smelly bargeman's absence. Melony looked down at the ground. Then she pointed out at the river. A ways downstream, Jonathan could see the remnants of the *Tiffany*. It had been smashed and bashed until it was merely a pile of wood floating on the river. There was no sign of Gorlan.

"I saw him get thrown off the boat," Melony said. "But it was towards the rocks. I never saw him come back up." Jonathan shuddered. Even though he hadn't liked Gorlan, he still felt sorry for the barge captain.

The rain began falling again, like a thin mist. Jonathan stumbled to the nearest tree, the other three following closely behind him. He dropped to his knees under the tree as his legs finally gave way beneath him. He was cold. He was wet. He ached all over. But Jonathan was too tired to care. He sat with his back against the tree. Micah curled up next to him, shivering. The river continued to roar, but the sound grew muffled and distant. Finally, Jonathan felt his eyes drift shut.

Chapter 10
The Magnificent City of Alden

I n what seemed like moments later, Jonathan woke up suddenly, the sunlight almost blinding him. The sun had already passed its peak and the afternoon hours were settling over the land. Micah and Belnor were still asleep near him, both with dirt in their hair and on their faces. Their packs from the druids were gone. And so was Melony.

"Melony?" Jonathan called, getting to his feet. But there was no reply. "Melony?" he shouted again. *Where could she be?* he wondered.

Jonathan searched along the riverbank for Melony, but she was nowhere to be seen. He walked a good ways down the bank, until he got a rather sharp rock stuck in his boot. Jonathan sat down in the mud of the bank and began to take his boot off to take out the rock. After he'd gotten out the troublesome pebble, Jonathan looked around as he pulled his boot back on.

He scanned the river's edge until he finally spotted someone. A girl in a red dress, a green cloak, and long, blonde hair was sitting not far from him on a large rock. Jonathan walked over to Melony. Her tongue was sticking out slightly and she was staring into the river, not even noticing Jonathan standing near her.

"Good morning," Jonathan said. Melony didn't even move.

"I think you mean good afternoon," she said. She went back to her thinking.

"What are you thinking about?" Jonathan asked.

"What? Oh, nothing," Melony replied vaguely.

"Oh come on," he said, taking a seat on a rock across from her. Melony just looked at him, saying nothing. "Why can't you tell me?" Melony looked down at her feet.

"I just can't," she finally said. She absent-mindedly took out her medallion and began fiddling with it.

"Is this about your medallion?" Melony's stare shot straight at him. She slipped her medallion out of sight. Then she looked away again. "So it is about the medallion?"

"Sort of," Melony whispered.

"Where did you get something like that anyway?" Jonathan asked curiously.

"I can't say," replied Melony.

"You don't know?" he asked.

"No, it's just," she started, "I can't really tell you." Jonathan was getting sick of all her secrets.

"Fine. Don't tell me." Jonathan stood up and began walking back to where Micah and Belnor where sleeping.

"Jonathan," Melony called after him. He stopped in his tracks. "All your questions will be answered by the end of the day." Melony got to her feet and walked past him. And as she did, Jonathan thought he heard her say, "And hopefully so will mine."

The two walked in silence to where the two boys lay sleeping under the tree. Jonathan went and woke them. They sat up groggily, still phased from what had happened the night before.

"The only food I have is two corius fruits," Melony sighed.

"You got your pack?" Jonathan exclaimed.

"No," Melony said. "Just my satchel and my sword. I put them on after Gorlan tried to steal from me. Did any of you get your packs?"

"No," Belnor said, getting to his feet. "But I know some herbs we could make tea with."

"No thanks," Jonathan said. He knew that if he drank that disgusting tea again, he'd probably be sick for the rest of the day.

"So just corius fruit," Melony sighed. "Well, we better eat quickly. If we get walking soon, we should reach Alden by early evening. I think we came pretty far downstream before the wreck."

So, the four of them sat down in the damp grass and divided the two corius fruits. Jonathan didn't realize how hungry he was until he took his first bite. He quickly devoured his half a fruit, as did the others. And all too soon for Jonathan, the food was completely gone. His stomach silently begged for more, but he could do nothing. He would have to wait until they reached Alden. Jonathan watched as Melony peeked into her money pouch. He looked over her shoulder and saw three bronze dil sitting at the bottom of the pouch. This was barely enough to get food for the four of them.

"I thought you had five bid left," Jonathan exclaimed.

"I must have lost it in the river," Melony said, her brow furrowed. "But there's no point worrying about it now. There's no getting it back." Melony returned the pouch to her satchel.

The company set off southward, and it wasn't an hour before they climbed to the top of a tall hill and saw the great city in the near distance, the smell of the salty sea in the air. The quartet, filled with the excitement that their journey was coming to an end, quickened their pace towards the city.

But Jonathan was only slightly excited. Sure he was happy that he would be seeing his Uncle Eli soon and that he and Micah could get good rest. But he was also sad. He wondered, after he had found his uncle and Melony hers, would he ever see her again? But Jonathan didn't have much time to ponder this because at that moment the quartet reached the city's western gates.

The city's walls were thirty-five feet tall and made of massive stones. The ten-foot-tall gates stood wide open, revealing the crowded city within. Guards were posted at the gates, but they let the children go through without a second look. As soon as Jonathan walked through those gates, he was in awe.

The city of Alden was just as magnificent as the merchants of Silan described. The mouth of the Anafract River flowed into the harbor where grand ships were docked, waiting to be laden with cargo and to sail to new destinations. Beyond the harbor lay the vast Southern Sea. Jonathan had never seen the ocean. It was a brilliant blue-green. Reflections of the sun, the clouds, and the ships danced on the waves. He was amazed by its beauty and vastness.

"Whoa!" Micah breathed. His younger brother, too, was gawking at the magnificent ocean.

"Come on," Melony said, smiling at their reactions to the sea. The company continued down the street into the city.

Shops lined every street. Jonathan walked past the shops of blacksmiths, silversmiths, and goldsmiths. Shops of seamstresses and tailors were at every corner. Merchants at the docks sold spices and pearls from the Isles of Mirrum in the Southern Sea. Others sold fine fabrics and furs from Kacuskri, which was to the east, beyond the Kingdom of Terren.

Jonathan had almost completely forgotten he was hungry until he caught the scent of freshly baked bread wafting from the small bakeries. His stomach growled, begging for supper. The four hungry children didn't even have to say a word before they rushed over to the nearest bakery. A half door separated the children from the steaming buns and cooling loaves sitting on wooden tables inside. The baker, a tall man wearing an apron, was near the back of the bakery, putting a loaf of unbaked bread into a hot oven. Jonathan could both see and feel the glowing red heat of the oven from the door.

"Excuse me," Melony called to the baker, who came over to them as soon as his bread was in the oven.

"What can I do for you today?" the baker asked with a broad smile.

"We'd like four of those buns, please," Melony said. The baker walked over to the basket and gently picked up four of the small, warm buns. He brought them to the door.

"That'll be two dil," the baker said as he handed Melony the buns. She pulled out two of the three remaining dil and handed the copper coins to the baker.

"Thank you, sir," Melony said.

"You're very welcome," the baker replied. "Have a good evening." Melony handed out the buns, and Jonathan bit into his. It was delicious and warm, which made Jonathan feel less chilled by the autumn cold. While they all ate, they continued walking through the city streets.

Jonathan was amazed by how so many people could live in one place. And there were so many different people, each with their own jobs, families, and histories. That immediately reminded Jonathan why he was there. His uncle was one of these many people in the city.

As the quartet walked through Alden, Jonathan asked people on the street if they knew an Elijah Beckett of Silan. Many ignored him and walked by, while the few who answered him said that they'd never heard of him. Micah, too, asked people about their uncle, and finally, someone told them that he had heard of an Elijah Beckett in the merchants' part of the city.

So they walked to the merchants' division of the city. By then, not only Jonathan and Micah but also Melony and Belnor were inquiring about Uncle Eli. After almost an hour of wandering through the merchants' area of the city, Jonathan finally found someone who could tell him where his Uncle Eli was. It was a woman with brown hair and green eyes who looked a great deal less wealthy than the other women Jonathan had seen in the merchants' area of city.

"Elijah Beckett, you say," said the woman.

"Yes. Do you know where he lives?" Jonathan asked, impatient with his search.

"Well, he used to live as a boarder in my husband's and my home," she explained. "But I'm afraid he left about two or three years ago. He became a crew member of a merchant vessel, I believe." Jonathan couldn't believe it. All that searching had been in vain. Not knowing what else to do, he relayed to the others what the woman had told him.

"I'm sorry, Jonathan," Melony said.

"What are we going to do?" Micah asked Jonathan.

"I– I don't know," he stammered. They had nowhere to go and no one to turn to.

"I know what we're going to do," Melony said. "We are going to find *my* uncle. He can help all of us." Melony began walking in the opposite direction. Jonathan, Micah, and Belnor, realizing Melony wasn't going to wait for them, hurriedly raced after her.

Melony led the company through the streets of Alden in an endless journey of lefts and rights. Jonathan had no idea where they were heading. Finally, she stopped directly in front of Castle Galador. The palace's huge, stone walls rose above the quartet and all the surrounding buildings. Sitting along the walls were beggars, some calling for help, others seeming to be asleep. Jonathan tried to ignore them. He didn't know why but they deeply disturbed him.

Suddenly Jonathan heard a croaky voice call out, "Do you have any bread?" He saw Melony turn around, but Jonathan continued to ignore the beggar. But when he realized Melony had stopped, he stopped and turned around. A very old woman, dressed in rags and very weak, was sitting with her back to the wall of the palace.

"I don't have any, sorry," Melony said. "What happened to all these people?"

"King Alexander," said the beggar woman. "Some were servants in the palace whom he forced out into the street after the death of King Darius. Others, he took their homes to make housing for his army."

"King Alexander did this?" Melony asked, horrified.

"Yes," said the old woman. She was examining Melony. "Funny," she finally said, "you remind me of someone I knew when I worked in the castle, many, many years ago."

"Who?" Melony asked.

"King Darius's daughter, the princess. I was one of the maids in her nursery." The old woman had a look in her eyes, like she was thinking of another time, another life. "But you couldn't be her. She was killed by the same horrid man who killed the king." Melony looked down at her satchel. She carefully slipped her hand inside it and pulled out a small, bronze coin. Her last coin.

"This is all I have," Melony said, slipping the woman the coin.

"Bless you, child," the woman croaked. "What did you say your name was?"

"My friends call me Melony," Melony said. "But you may know me as Aralyn." Then she quickly walked away towards the palace gates without saying another word to the woman. Jonathan followed closely, Belnor and Micah behind him. He looked back briefly to see the old beggar woman with wide eyes speaking to a beggar sitting beside her, pointing at Melony. Melony plowed onward.

"Aralyn?" Jonathan whispered to Melony. "I thought that was just the name the druids called you."

"I told you earlier that all your questions will be answered soon," Melony replied in a whisper. Jonathan was confused as to why they were walking along the walls of the palace; he thought they were supposed to be searching for Melony's uncle.

The company reached the palace gates, and by this time, the sun was setting. A guard in full armor sat on a stool, his back leaning against the wall of the gate. His snores were thunderous, and his head rested on his chest. Besides this snoring guard, the gate was unguarded. Jonathan expected Melony to walk in the opposite direction from the gates and begin heading down the main road to search for her uncle. But to Jonathan's surprise and utter horror, she walked straight through the palace gates.

"Melony! What are you doing?" whispered Jonathan. Although the snoring guard seemed to be undisturbed, Jonathan was taking no chances on letting Melony get caught trespassing on royal property. Melony looked back at the three boys.

"Well, are you three coming or not?" Melony whispered to them. Jonathan, Micah, and Belnor exchanged pained glances. Then they walked past the sleeping guard just as Melony had. The company strode through the main courtyard. A few servants looked up, and a few gave them confused expressions, but no one stopped the company from entering into the throne room.

Melony threw open the large doors that led into the king's throne room, and Jonathan was hit by the magnificence of the palace. The ceiling seemed to go up forever. On either side of the room, twenty throne-like chairs, all gilded with silver and bronze, lined the walls in rows two chairs deep. At the opposite end of the room was a great throne, completely covered in gold, silver, and precious stones. On it sat a tall man.

The man had dark, curly hair and a small goatee that curled at the tip, both with streaks of grey throughout them. He wore a royal robe of regal red, made of silk and trimmed with gold embroidery. But what stood out to Jonathan the most were the man's eyes. To Jonathan, his dark brown eyes looked bloodthirsty. There was no doubt that this was King Alexander.

Standing in front of the throne was a knight dressed in black armor and and black tunic. It was the same knight that had come to Silan and taken everyone. The two were having a loud conversation when the four walked in.

"But sire, I can't take them all," the Black Knight said. "The harvest is suffering, and the peasants need their menfolk to support them. And a number of the younger men and boys have run away from their farms and villages."

"I don't care how many men you have to take," King Alexander shouted. "If my army is going to be large enough to invade Nimberia, I need you to put aside your petty feelings and take every man and boy that can lift a sword. And I want you to punish any runaways you find. If they will not obey their king's commands willingly, they will obey them by force."

Melony made a coughing sound in her throat, which echoed throughout the hall. King Alexander looked up. He was startled, but soon became full of rage.

"What peasant dares to come before me without invitation?" asked King Alexander as he rose to his feet. Jonathan saw Melony draw a deep breath. And then she shocked him with what she said next.

"I am no peasant," Melony announced, pulling out her medallion so the king could see it. "My name is Aralyn Melony Eleanor Kathar, daughter of King Darius, Princess of Contaria, and rightful heir to the throne." The king and the Black Knight stared at Melony in disbelief. "I have come home, Uncle." Death-like silence filled the room.

"Guards!" King Alexander finally shouted. "Seize them!"

Chapter 11
The Dungeons of Castle Galador

"What?" Melony cried. Guards, each wearing a chainmail shirt, a red tunic, and a sword at his side, entered the throne room from the many doors around the room. Two guards seized Melony as she tried to draw her sword in defense. But they knocked the sword from her grip, letting it skid across the floor of the throne room. Jonathan wanted to rush towards the guards and help Melony when he felt someone grab his arm and pull it behind his own back. A guard was towering above Jonathan. Out of the corner of his eye, he saw that Micah and Belnor, too, had been too slow for the king's men. The Black Knight stepped towards the new prisoners.

"You're making a mistake!" Melony cried. "I'm Princess Aralyn! Let us go!"

"Follow me," the Black Knight ordered the guards. The guards followed the Black Knight out of the throne room, dragging Melony, Jonathan, Micah, and Belnor with them. As they were almost out of the room, Jonathan turned to see the king picking up Melony's sword off the ground.

"No!" Melony shouted to the king. "That's my father's sword! Please!" But the doors of the throne room slammed shut, cutting off their view of the king. The Black Knight led them through a maze of doors, corridors, passages, and hallways.

After a few minutes of walking, the Black Knight stopped before a large, wooden door. He pulled a key off the ring at his side and put it into the keyhole. A click came from the door. Then it swung open. But Jonathan couldn't see anything inside. It was just a dark nothingness. The guards led the children into the darkness.

"Light a torch," the Black Knight shouted. A moment later, bright flames burst to life in the darkness. A guard handed the Black Knight the torch. In the torchlight, Jonathan found there was a staircase starting at the door that spiraled down ever deeper.

"Move," one of the guards ordered, forcing Jonathan to walk down the staircase.

At the bottom, Jonathan found himself in a large room. A pillar stood in the center of the room with a torch burning in a torch stand. Cells lined the outer edges of the room, thick iron bars standing like the black teeth of some frightening creature. More guards were sitting at a table next to the pillar, playing a game of chess. They stood as soon as they saw the Black Knight and gave a low bow to him. The knight signaled for them to rise.

"Take their weapons," the Black Knight said, nodding to the quartet.

"Be careful with that!" Jonathan shouted at the guards as they took his bow from him. Ignoring him, the guards carelessly threw Jonathan's bow onto the table. They took his sword, his quiver, and his hunting dagger. Then they took Melony's dagger and Micah's slingshot. And finally, they took all of Belnor's charm necklaces.

Then, after a last, yet vain, struggle to escape by Micah, who tried biting the guard holding him, the guards shoved the four of them into a small cell that had no windows of any kind and was as cold as death itself. Bars made of solid metal made up the front and side walls, while a thick, cold, stone wall was at their backs.

"Let us out!" Micah screamed. The guards only laughed at him. But Micah kept banging at the bars and yelling at the guards to let them go. Micah had never liked the dark and had always hated confined spaces. Now he looked terrified. Jonathan went to his brother and pulled him to the back of the cell and sat him down.

"It's going to be alright," Jonathan whispered calmly. However, he didn't feel calm. His heart was racing and he was unsure what would happen next. He took off his own cloak and wrapped it around Micah. Micah looked up to Belnor.

"Can't you use magic to do something?" Micah asked him.

"They took my charms," Belnor replied.

"So do magic without a charm," Micah said. Jonathan could tell that his brother's fear was driving him into anger.

"I won't," Belnor said.

"Why not?" Micah asked.

"Because it's dangerous," Belnor said. "Now drop it." Micah opened his mouth to say something else, but Belnor's glare made him close it again.

"We're going to get out of here," Jonathan assured them. "Right, Melony?" Melony had claimed a spot in one of the corners and was fiddling with her gold medallion, turning it over in her hand again and again.

"He'll let us out soon," Melony whispered confidently to Jonathan. "Alexander will realize his mistake and release us. And then everything will be alright."

"He'll never let you out," said a weak, dry voice. Jonathan looked around for the speaker. A man was cowering in the corner of the cell next to theirs. He was shrouded in darkness and shadows.

"Who are you?" Jonathan asked.

"Just a lonely prisoner," the man said from the shadows.

"What is your name?" Jonathan asked.

"I cannot say. It brings too many memories. Painful memories," said the man, sadness ringing in his voice. His sad, hazel eyes locked onto Melony. "King Alexander will never release you, of all people. In fact I wouldn't be surprised if he executes you in the morning."

"You don't even know who I am," Melony said.

"You're Princess Aralyn if I'm not mistaken," he replied.

"How do you—"

"How do I know who you are?" the man asked. "Because I saw the golden medallion in your hand. I've only seen it one other time, and that was eleven years ago. The night I helped the princess escape the city." He emerged from the shadows. His hair was a dirty blonde, and was so long it touched his shoulders. He had a bushy beard and looked as though he hadn't seen sunlight in years, for he was as pale as pale could be. And he smelled like he hadn't bathed in just as many years.

"You!" Melony exclaimed. "I remember you!" To Jonathan's own surprise, the man seemed familiar to him as well, as if Jonathan had once seen him in a dream long forgotten.

"I am so sorry for all that has happened to you, my lady," the man said.

"Thanks to you I'm not dead, so you have nothing to apologize for," Melony said. The man was silent. "But I still do not understand why you say my uncle will never let me out."

"You don't know?" the man asked, astonished.

"Don't know what?" Melony asked cautiously.

"The man who killed your father was merely a hired assassin," the man said. "An assassin hired by Alexander himself." Melony's eyes widen with horror.

"Alexander was the one who killed my father?" Melony said in shock. "That can't be true."

"I'm afraid it is, my lady," the man said.

"How did you find out about it?" asked Melony.

"I was one of Alexander's men," the prisoner explained. "But when I found out about Alexander's plot, I knew I had to do something. First I went to your father's chambers, but it was too late. He was dying. But with his dying breath, he begged me to go and help you escape. He gave me his royal sword to give to you. So I ran as quickly as I could to your nursery. I told your nursemaid that you had to go far away from the palace and never return. And I gave her your father's sword to keep for you. Then she took you and fled just in time."

"My own uncle," Melony said in disbelief. "He killed my father? He tried to kill me? How does no one know?"

"The man he hired was an infamous assassin," the man explained. "But when the deed was done, the prince had the assassin arrested to draw suspicion away from him. Now the assassin's a prisoner, like myself."

"Is he still here?"

"He is."

"Where?" Melony asked, raising her voice.

"Get some sleep, my lady," the man whispered.

"Where is he?" Melony shouted at the man.

"I will tell you," the man said, still whispering. "But not tonight." Melony stood up and sat herself in the farthest corner from the man.

Then from across the cell, Melony asked, "Can you at least tell me his name?"

"Yes," the man replied. "His name is Acillion." Melony nodded thankfully. But Jonathan could now see a glimmer of hate in her eyes.

Micah and Belnor had been sitting in another corner this entire time. Micah still looked frightened. Jonathan sat next to his little brother and leaned his head against the stone wall. Micah's eyes were wide with terror and his hands were as cold as ice.

"Are you going to be alright?" Jonathan asked. Micah merely nodded. "Just close your eyes and imagine someplace bright and happy."

"Like home?" asked Micah.

"Yeah," Jonathan replied. "Like home."

"I wanna go home," Micah whispered, curling closer to his brother. Jonathan looked down and saw a single tear trickling down Micah's cheek.

"We'll be home soon," Jonathan whispered back. His gaze shifted to the dark corner in which Melony was sitting. He could still see the glimmer of her eyes in the dim cell. She was staring off into space, deep in thought and absent-mindedly fiddling with her hair.

"You didn't tell us," Jonathan said coldly. "Why?"

"I don't know," she said. She didn't say any more.

"You could have trusted us, you know," Jonathan said.

"But I couldn't, could I?" Melony replied.

"What do you mean?"

"Well, you were just two boys I'd met out in the woods. Plus, you shot me."

"But then I saved your life. You couldn't even trust us then? You couldn't trust *me* then? You obviously thought the druids should know. What was that? About a hundred and fifty strangers?"

"I didn't mean to tell them, alright!" Melony finally cried. She covered her face with her hands. The dungeon was quiet.

"What do you mean?" Jonathan asked cautiously.

"I made a promise," Melony said.

"To who?" Jonathan asked. Melony sighed.

"When I was as little girl, I took pride in being the king's daughter," Melony explained. "But my nanna thought it would be safer to hide my true identity while in exile. So I hid. I hid myself for so long. So long that I lost who I truly was. I lost Aralyn. But then my nanna died. And on her deathbed, she reminded me who I was and made me promise not to tell anyone who I was until—"

"Until you returned," Jonathan said. Melony nodded.

"But I wasn't even going to come back until Ethan said…" Melony choked.

"Who's Ethan?" Jonathan asked, confused.

"Just someone I knew in Nimberia," Melony said quietly. "But he's gone now. And now I'm here because I was lost and had no one else to turn to. I thought my uncle might take me in."

"But how did the druids know your true identity," Jonathan asked.

"She talks in her sleep," said Belnor.

"I never meant to tell anyone," Melony said. There was an awkward moment of silence.

"So," Jonathan started. "Do you want me to start calling you Aralyn now?"

"No," Melony replied. "I've been called Melony so long that Aralyn seems like a stranger to me. And no 'Your Highness' or 'Your Majesty' either. Just Melony."

"Alright then, Just Melony," Jonathan said. Melony gave him a weak smile. But it soon faded. Jonathan could see the shadow of fear in her eyes. "Are you going to be alright?"

"Why do you ask?" Melony asked.

"You look afraid," said Jonathan. Melony sighed.

"I *am* afraid," Melony admitted. "I just found out that my uncle is the man my nanna tried to hide me from for the last eleven years. And now I'm his prisoner."

"What are you going to do?" Jonathan asked.

"I don't know yet," Melony said. "I should probably figure that out." She went quiet, and her brow furrowed as she thought. The questions that had been swimming in Jonathan's mind the past few days had been answered. And yet, he was left with more unanswered questions than before. And it felt strange to know that he had been travelling with a long-thought-dead member of the royal family for days. Jonathan wondered what would happen to them. What would King Alexander do to Melony? What would he do to them all?

Chapter 12
The Council of Contaria

I t was late in the evening when the guards returned to the cell. Jonathan was fiddling with a piece of straw on the floor when the click of a key came from the cell door. He looked up and saw the Black Knight and three other fully armed guards standing just outside the cell.

"Get up," yelled a guard as he walked into the cell. Two guards dragged Jonathan to his feet.

"Get off of me," Jonathan said, pulling away from the guards.

"What's going on?" Melony demanded.

"The king has summoned you four," said the Black Knight.

"Why?" asked Melony.

"You'll find out soon enough," the knight replied. The guards and the Black Knight led Jonathan, Micah, Belnor, and Melony back up the stairs and out of the dark dungeon. It was dark outside. The faintest streaks of pink and purple rested on the western horizon, the colors singing the sun's farewells for the night. The guards standing behind Jonathan shoved him out the door. They led them through the endless palace corridors, finally stopping in front of a large, solid, wooden door: the door to the throne room.

The Black Knight knocked four times. For a moment, nothing happened. Then the doors slowly swung open, revealing King Alexander sitting on his throne. His golden crown sat on his head, and a silver scepter inlaid with red jewels rested in his hand. Tied to his belt was an ornate sheath. It took a moment, but Jonathan finally recognized the hilt of the sword at the king's side as Melony's sword.

The twenty seats around the throne room, which had been empty earlier that day, each held a man. Each man was clad in garments trimmed with fur, gold, silver, or, in some cases, all three. Jonathan realized in an instant that these were the great lords of the Council of Contaria.

But why had they been summoned? Did the king believe Melony now? Was he accepting her as the princess, his long lost niece? Or was the man in the dungeon right and Alexander wanted Melony dead? Whatever the case, Jonathan couldn't tell exactly what was going on. The room was dead silent except for the sound of footsteps and the clanking of the guards' armor.

When they reached the center of the room, the Black Knight stopped the guards and the prisoners. King Alexander stood. The knight and guards bowed low to the king. And Micah, Belnor, and Jonathan all found themselves bowing to the king, though they knew not their fate.

After a second, Jonathan looked up slightly. All were standing and bowing to King Alexander. All but one person. Melony stood tall.

"How dare you not bow before your king, girl?" shouted the Black Knight. The knight stood, pulled his hand back, and struck Melony across the face, knocking her to the ground.

"You'll pay for that," Jonathan heard Melony mutter.

"Let the hearing commence," said one of the lords. *A hearing*, Jonathan thought. *So that's what this is about.*

"Bring forward the accused," another lord said. One of the guards pulled Melony to her feet and pushed her forward. An older lord stood with a roll of parchment in his hand. He looked like he could compete in age with Fraxinus, but his eyes did not hold the same kindness as the old druid.

"You have been charged with treason," croaked the elderly lord.

"This young girl? Charged with treason? How can this be?" asked another lord.

"She thinks, Lord Stephen, that she is the late Princess Aralyn," said King Alexander.

"I do not *think* I am Princess Aralyn," Melony interrupted. "I *am* Princess Aralyn." A murmur rippled through the lords.

"As you can see, lords of the Council, the girl has broken our laws," Alexander continued. "She has claimed to be a princess, and as such has claimed to be not only a member of the royal family, but the rightful queen. This is high treason!" Many of the lords nodded in agreement. "And, according to the laws established by King Atel II, the punishment for treason is death by hanging." Many of the lords shouted their agreements, while others were silent, not daring to show their opposition to the king's opinion.

Jonathan was frightened. They were going to hang Melony. What did that mean for him and Micah, or even Belnor? Would the king let them go? Or would they hang in the gallows as well? Suddenly, the room was silent. Lord Stephen was standing with an old, hole-riddled piece of parchment in his hands.

"If I may, Your Majesty," began Lord Stephen. "I have here the law of our land in which it says 'One who is found guilty of impersonating a member of the royal family shall be cast out from the city and the kingdom and banished on penalty of death, thus shall be the law of the land.' So hanging would not be the appropriate punishment for her crimes. Instead, banishment must be the sentence."

"We must obey the laws of our forefathers," said another lord. Alexander glared at Lord Stephen with disbelief, anger, and hatred.

"Then, according to the laws set by my forefathers," the king started, "I banish you from this city and this kingdom, beyond the western mountains, never to set foot in these borders again. Do you have anything to say for yourself?" Melony glared at the king.

"That's my father's sword," she said through her gritted teeth. "And someone like you doesn't deserve to have it."

"Take her away," shouted Alexander. Two of the guards that had brought them in escorted Melony out of the throne room.

"Bring forward the others," said a lord. Jonathan felt the guards standing behind them push the three of them forward to where Melony had been standing. He had no idea what was going to happen to him. He saw Micah out of the corner of his eye. He looked almost as scared as he had when he'd been tied up by those bird-goblins. Jonathan drew closer to him. Whatever happened, he had to protect his brother.

"You three are charged with trespassing on royal property," said one of the lords. "Normally you would be sentenced to a day in the stocks. But you were also found in the company of a traitor. Why were you with her?"

"We all had the same destination," Jonathan said. "We had no idea who she was or what she was doing."

"Not even the slightest hint?" asked Lord Stephan. Jonathan hesitated.

"No, my lord," he finally said. But he was lying. He had seen Melony's medallion. The moment the lie slipped from his lips, Jonathan first felt a pang of guilt. Not because he has lied to the

Council, but because his words had ensured Melony would be sent into exile alone.

"Then to the stocks with them," a lord called. King Alexander nodded silently. The guards started pushing them out of the throne room. Jonathan looked up to the enthroned king. His cold, blood-thirsty eyes rekindled Jonathan's anger towards the king. That man had taken his best friend. That man had driven Jonathan from his family. And now Jonathan knew that that man had murdered Melony's father.

Melony, Jonathan thought. *She's the rightful queen. What if she can make this right?*

She can't do that alone, replied the little voice in the back of his mind. Jonathan felt courage bubbling in his chest. He looked down and saw a dagger in the belt of the guard next to him. Then, without thinking, Jonathan pulled the dagger from the guard's belt and slipped out from the guards' grasps. He ran to the center of the throne room. All eyes shifted to him, and a gasp rose from the lords.

"No," Jonathan shouted.

"What?" the king said.

"I will not go to the stocks," Jonathan shouted. "I will not tolerate a king who has taken everything away from his people. And if that means following the rightful queen of this land to the ends of Iyuandil, then that's what I'll do."

"How dare you," King Alexander started, rising to his feet.

"Melo— I mean Aralyn is your niece and the princess, whether you like it or not," Jonathan said. "She is the rightful queen and now she knows what you've done." Jonathan paused and tried to think of something brave to say. Finally, he said, "Your reign will soon come to an end." Jonathan stared at the king, trying his best to look brave and intimidating. The king glared back, not even having to try to look the same. But

Jonathan caught a glimmer in King Alexander's eyes: a glimmer of fear.

"If those are your thoughts," the king started, and Jonathan prepared for the worst, "then you all shall be hanged." Jonathan's heart nearly stopped. That had not been the result he'd wanted. A murmur went through the room. The Black Knight approached the throne. "What is it, Sir Wallace?" the king asked in annoyance.

"My lord, all three of these boys would make fine soldiers for your army," the Black Knight said. "Send them to Borlo to the training camps." King Alexander pondered this for a moment.

"I suppose that would be a worse fate than the gallows for them," Alexander finally said. "They shall be banished to Borlo, along with the girl." Jonathan knew he should be scared, but he wasn't. He felt braver than ever. He had stood up to the king that had driven him from his home and tyrannized the kingdom. He even felt a smirk creep onto his face.

Besides, Jonathan thought, *it can't get much worse than banishment.*

Chapter 13
The Sins of the Father

The guards grabbed hold of Jonathan, pulling the knife from his hand, and led the three of them back down the long way to the dungeons. They threw Jonathan, followed by Micah and Belnor, into the same cell. Melony was already there, and she looked pale. Her head was held high, but she was clearly shaking. Micah and Belnor sat down on the cold, damp floor while Jonathan moved to Melony's side.

"Melony, are you alright?" he asked.

"What are you guys doing here?" she asked.

"We've been banished," Jonathan replied quietly.

"What? But why?"

"Jonathan stood up to the king," Belnor said. "And he banished us because of it."

"You did?" Melony asked Jonathan. He nodded.

"Would we be back in this cell if he hadn't?" Micah replied. "I'm glad Jonathan did it. I didn't like the king."

"You were right about him," Melony said to Jonathan. "That night after the tengu attack, when you said that King Alexander was a tyrant and evil. You were right."

"I'm sorry," Jonathan said.

"I think we should go to sleep," Belnor interrupted. "We may have a long day of travelling in the morning. Borlo is a long way from here." A few minutes later, Micah's head rested on his older brother's shoulder. His soft snores assured Jonathan that he was sound asleep. Jonathan heard Belnor whisper a prayer to the Creator, though he could not make out the druid's exact words. Then Belnor stopped and curled up on the dirt floor of the dungeon. He, too, fell asleep quickly. Finally, Melony's head nodded as she drifted off to sleep.

But Jonathan, however hard he tried, could not sleep. He was worried about Mum and what might happen to her now. He had acted in the throne room without thinking, something he almost never did. But now he was thinking of the consequences that his actions would have on not only himself, but also his brother and mother. Jonathan tossed and turned until—

"Can't sleep, boy?" Jonathan was startled. It seemed like the man who had spoken to them earlier was watching him. Jonathan had almost completely forgotten about the man until he had spoken again.

"I'm just… thinking," Jonathan said. Then he went back to his thoughts.

"Are you thinking about your home?" the man asked.

"Maybe," Jonathan said, beginning to be annoyed with this man's questions.

"And where might home be for you?" asked the man

"Silan," Jonathan replied. "It's a tiny village in the north."

"You're from Silan?"

"You sound like you know the town."

"I do. I used to live there." Jonathan was stunned. What were the odds that this man had lived in the very town he had been born and raised in? A town of which hardly anyone knew and in which fewer lived.

"Really?"

"Yes. Many years ago, I lived there with my family."

"I don't remember you."

"I wouldn't expect you to," the man said. "I was forced to leave by Alexander over a decade ago."

"Did you bring your family with you?"

"No. I had to leave them in Silan," said the man. Then he gave Jonathan a questioning look. "Perhaps you know my family." Jonathan began thinking of all the families he knew lived in Silan. "I had a wife and two sons. My sons were about four years apart in age. The elder would be about your age by now."

"What were your sons' names?" Jonathan asked.

"Jonathan and Micah Fletcher," the man said. "Do you know them?" Jonathan felt like the breath had been knocked out of him. This couldn't be happening. His father, whom he had hated for so many years for leaving him, was standing in front of him. His mouth went dry as he tried to speak.

"Well, do you know them, boy?" the man in asked desperation. "Are they still alive?"

"I know them," Jonathan said.

"Are they well?"

"I… I think Hannah is well," Jonathan said.

"What about the boys?" the man asked.

"They're… um…" Jonathan was at a loss for words. He didn't know what to say to the man.

"What's wrong, boy?" the man asked.

"I spent years wondering where my father was," Jonathan said, half to himself. "Years wondering why he'd left me and why he never came back."

"What are you talking about?" asked the man, extremely confused.

"I'm talking about you," Jonathan said. "My name is Jonathan Fletcher. My mother's name is Hannah and my brother, right over there, is Micah."

"It can't be."

"I—" Jonathan could hardly get out the words because a lump was forming in his throat. "I— I'm your son."

"Jonathan? My boy? Oh, my precious son!" the man cried, reaching through the bars for Jonathan. But he moved out of his father's reach.

"You're like a stranger to me," Jonathan said. "I don't even know your name."

"Well, then I suppose it's time you learned it." Jonathan's father leaned closer. "My name is Acillion Fletcher." Jonathan felt the blood drain from his face.

"Your name is Acillion?" Jonathan repeated. "I thought you said that was the name of the assassin who killed the king." His father's gaze shifted downwards. Acillion. The man that stood before him was his father and the man that had killed the king.

Jonathan stood up, his legs shaking, and slowly backed away from Acillion. He tried to put as much distance as he could between himself and the murderer that was his father. He soon could back no farther, for the wall of metal bars blocked his way.

"I know what you must be thinking, son," Acillion said. "But I did it to protect our family." Jonathan began moving towards the corner, forgetting that Melony lay asleep there. He tripped over the princess, who awoke with a jolt and a yelp.

"What's going on?" she asked, sleepily. Jonathan didn't answer her.

"You did it," Jonathan whispered.

"Did what? What did he do?" said Micah, who was now awake and sitting up.

"Tell him, Jonathan," Acillion said loud enough to wake Belnor. "Tell your brother who I am. Tell them *all* who I am."

"What is he talking about?" Melony asked, now standing next to Jonathan. He still couldn't speak. A lump had filled his throat and a single tear was slowly trickling down his cheek. But this was a tear of neither sadness nor joy; it was a tear of anger and hate.

"Tell them, Jonathan!" Acillion shouted.

"It's him," Jonathan cried. "He's Acillion, the assassin who killed the king." Jonathan paused. Melony looked like she was about to explode. "He's my father." He said this last part very quietly, as though if he said it quietly enough, it would no longer be true. Melony rushed towards Acillion. The metal bars kept Acillion just out of Melony's reach.

"You– you treacherous beast!" Melony screamed. "You coward! Traiter! Murderer! You– you–" Then Melony sank to the floor and burst into tears.

"Our father?" Micah said. He got up and walked cautiously towards Jonathan. "How could he be our father? I thought Father left us." Jonathan had no answer. Melony's sobs echoed through the dungeon. A guard walked over to their cell and banged against the bars.

"Stop yer bawlin'," the guard bellowed. Melony sniffed and muffled the sound of her cries in her arms.

"Jonathan, I–" Acillion started.

"No," Jonathan said. "I don't want to hear it. You've been gone for eleven years. I thought you abandoned us. Now I wish I'd been right."

"Jonathan–"

"I don't want you to come near us ever again," Jonathan said. Silence fell over the dungeon. Jonathan sat down and turned away from Acillion. He was drained from the shock of the day and soon found that he could keep his eyes open no longer. With Micah dozing off at his side, Jonathan closed his eyes and drifted to sleep.

Jonathan stood at the top of a rock ledge. The sounds of a raging battle roared all around him. He looked down from the rock ledge into a small gorge. Below him, Melony wore full plate battle armor, her sword gripped tightly in her hand. A crimson cloak flew behind her, standing out against the pure white snow. She was fighting a soldier with her sword and shield, all her focus directed towards getting past this enemy.

Then Jonathan saw a tall knight in black armor creeping up behind Melony. The knight drew his sword and prepared to run her through. But she hadn't noticed him.

Jonathan tried to scream her name, but the sounds of battle drowned out the noise. He reached for an arrow, but his quiver was empty. He looked down to see his father's bow broken in his hands. What was he supposed to do? How could he save her?

Jonathan looked to his other hand and saw a sword, the kind only knights carry. He gripped it tightly and knew what he had to do.

"No!" Jonathan screamed as he raced down the gorge. He slipped between Melony and the knight, lifting his sword as the knight began to strike. The next thing he felt was a sword being pushed through his chest.

Jonathan woke up suddenly, his heart pounding. He looked about to see he was still in the dungeon. The nightmare was unsettling, and it took him several minutes to fall back to sleep. But when he did, his slumber was not interrupted until the next morning.

Chapter 14
Fort Borlo

When dawn finally arrived, four palace guards came to the cell and unlocked the doors. The Black Knight stood just behind them. Jonathan got to his feet.

"It's time to go," said the Black Knight. One of the guards stepped into the cell, a pair of shackles in his hands. He grabbed Jonathan's hands and locked the shackles around his wrists.

"You won't be slipping away this time," the guard muttered as he finished tightening the shackles. The shackles were tight and cut into Jonathan's wrists. None of the others were forced to wear the wretched things. Only he had to wear them because of his incident in the throne room the day before.

The guards led Jonathan, Belnor, Micah, and Melony through the palace to the stables. Jonathan counted nearly fifty huge, majestic horses as he was led through the massive stables. Finally, he saw that he, his brother, and his friends were being led to a carriage with a rough, wooden floor surrounded by vertical bars, with a roof covering the top. Two black horses were being harnessed to the front of the carriage by three stable boys. The Black Knight unlocked a door on the side of the carriage. The four prisoners stopped.

"Well, come on," said the knight impatiently. None of them moved. Then, Melony stepped forward. She didn't say a word as she walked to the carriage and stepped through the door.

As she walked past him, the Black Knight made a low bow and said, mockingly, "Your Highness." Melony sat down in the straw that littered the carriage floor. Then Belnor stepped forward and joined her in the cage. Then Micah hurriedly joined them. Jonathan was the last standing outside the cage. One of the guards unlocked the shackles around Jonathan's wrists and pushed him forward.

"Get in there, lad," said the Black Knight. Jonathan slowly walked toward the carriage. He walked so slowly that it seemed he might never reach it. But, all too soon, he reached it and climbed in to join Micah, Melony, and Belnor. He was afraid. They were all afraid. The Black Knight, after locking them into the cage, commanded the stable boys to lead the horses and the carriage outside the city.

As the carriage was led to the courtyard, all eyes fell upon the four prisoners inside. Some of the servants snickered and sneered, while others remained silent and solemnly watched as the carriage and the prisoners were led out of the palace.

Suddenly, Jonathan heard a young boy yell out with a sneer, "Everybody, bow down to the princess!" Then another said, "Behold, the new queen," while another laughed saying, "Someone bring the queen a crown." It seemed as though Melony's claim had spread throughout the palace. It wasn't long before even the stable boys leading the carriage joined the mockery, yelling, "Make way for the Queen of Contaria."

When they reached the gates of the palace, many of the city dwellers stopped and watched the sad carriage. The old beggar woman that Melony had spoken with the day before stepped out in front of the carriage and scolded the stable boys, saying, "Why do you treat your queen this way?" Then she hobbled to the bars of the carriage and, as she walked along, whispered, "Why don't you fight back, Aralyn?" Melony only lowered her head and closed her eyes.

The children were led down the main road of Alden, city dwellers looking on them with pity, while the stable boys, still leading, continued to yell out, "Make way for the Queen of Contaria. Make way for the Queen of Contaria. Make way for the Queen of Contaria!" But none laughed. To all, they were just four children being treated unjustly by their tyrannical king.

When they reached the outer wall of the city, Jonathan saw a great caravan of colorful wagons laden with goods from Alden and her ports. The stable boys led the carriage to the back of the caravan, where they handed the reins of the horses to a large, gruff-looking guard.

A half hour later, the caravan gave the signal and they headed off, following the long line of dreary wagons. The guard sat in front of the children, his hands holding tight to the reins. Melony's head remained lowered, but Jonathan knew she wasn't asleep.

They rumbled along the dirt road, now wet and filled with muddy puddles. The wheels of the carriage were quickly covered in thick, black mud that made a loud squish with each rotation of the wheels. The grass glittered with dew drops, and the clouds were stained with shades of pink, red, and yellow in the morning light. They rode through the countryside, past farmers working hard in their fields, past shepherds guarding their sheep, and past a group of small children playing with a dog. Melony stared off into the distance, towards the city that had long since left their sight. Her fingers fiddled with the medallion on the chain around her neck.

"Melony?" Jonathan said. Melony didn't respond. "It's going to be alright." Melony continued to stare off, as if she hadn't heard Jonathan at all.

The hours passed slowly. Micah dozed off in the straw after noon passed. His snores broke the deafening silence of the empty land. Belnor settled himself into a corner, his cloak wrapped tightly around him. Jonathan also dozed off and when he woke up the sun was setting in the west. The caravan had stopped.

"What's going on?" Micah asked drowsily.

"We've stopping to make camp for the night," Belnor said.

The guard got up from his seat in front of the cage and opened the door for the children to go out and do their business before forcing them back inside. He didn't let them out of the cage again, though Belnor and Micah begged to be let out to stretch their legs. Then the guard began pitching a tent that had been stowed below his seat. Next, he pulled a small bag out of a chest that was kept underneath the carriage. The guard handed them the sack. Jonathan opened the cotton sack and inside was their supper: cold bacon and stale rolls. Then the guard handed Jonathan a small canteen with water for them to share. As the guard proceeded to build a roaring fire at such a distance that the carriage was just out of reach of its heat, the prisoners ate in silence; everyone except for Melony. She refused eat or drink.

Despite sitting around in the carriage all day, they all were tired. Micah scooched over next to Jonathan and laid his head on his older brother's shoulder. It was comforting to Jonathan to know that they were together in this frightful journey.

"Good night," Jonathan said softly to Melony, who didn't respond. Jonathan whispered a short prayer to the Creator, asking Him to protect Mum and to protect them, and then drifted off to sleep.

The next morning, the guard's banging on the metal bars awoke Jonathan. Then the guard passed them a small bag through the bars. Jonathan opened it to find four more rolls, a single corius fruit, and a canteen of water. Jonathan divided the food among the four of them. But, like the night before, Melony refused to eat.

"You need to eat something," Jonathan insisted. She merely pulled her knees up to her chest. "Melony, you'll be no use to anyone if you die of starvation. Now eat." He tossed a roll to her. Melony stared at it for a moment before half-heartedly picking it up, eating a few bites, and setting it down again. It wasn't much, but it was a start. The guard let them out again for a minute, but soon they were back in the cage and on the road.

Every day was the same. Wake up at dawn, eat, ride until sunset, eat, sleep. Wake up, eat, ride, sleep. Wake up, eat, ride, sleep. Jonathan became tired of the cycle. The days became long and dull. They hardly ever talked. And Melony spoke the least of them all. For six days it went on like this.

Then, on the seventh day, they finally reached it. A towering fortress lay before them, small farms surrounding the area. The stone walls were tall and menacing, and guards marched across the top of the walls. Large, iron gates were open and wide, but Jonathan knew that they would probably close before sunset.

The guard drove the carriage through the gates and along the narrow streets of the fort into a large courtyard with a cobblestone floor. Two horses were tied to a post near one wall, both whinnying and stomping their hooves impatiently. Six doors lined the walls of the courtyard.

Once the guard had stopped the carriage, a stable boy came running to tend to the horses. He looked no older than Micah. Jonathan heard the creak of a door opening. He turned around to see an older woman emerge from one of the doors on the other side of the courtyard, a scowl on her face.

"What have you got for me today?" she asked impatiently.

"Three lads and one girl. Banished here," replied the guard.

"Children banished?" exclaimed the old woman.

"That's what I thought. But orders are orders. The boys are to be trained. You can do whatever you want with the girl."

"We've been meaning to find another kitchen servant," the woman said. "And she looks healthy enough. Yes, she'll do nicely. Right then. Take them in there." She pointed to the door from which she had just come.

The guard fumbled with his keys before selecting one and slipping it into the lock of the cage door. When the door finally opened, the guard grabbed Micah by the arm.

"Let go of me," Micah shouted. He looked back to the carriage. "Jonathan!"

"Oh, be quiet, you," the guard grumbled. He shut the door to the cage once again and locked it. Micah struggled as the guard dragged him to the door to which the old woman had gestured. Micah looked back at Jonathan, pleading silently for help before going through the door. After about two minutes, the guard returned. Micah was nowhere to be seen.

"What did you do with my brother?" Jonathan cried. Paying Jonathan no heed, the guard reopened the door and grabbed Belnor. He walked Belnor to the door as he had Micah, and again the guard returned alone.

Next the guard came and grabbed Melony. She didn't struggle or try to escape. She just walked with her head down. Jonathan was scared for her. In just the few days he'd known her, he knew that she would not normally act like this. The guard led her through the door and they disappeared. But the guard had left the cage unlocked. Jonathan stared at the door that guard had had taken Micah and the others through. No one came from it. Was this his chance to escape? He knew that he could make it out of the fort. But what then? Where would he go? He could try to help the others escape, but without a plan he would likely fail. Then what would happen to his brother and friends? Micah had already grown up without a father. Jonathan knew he wouldn't be able to go on without an older brother, especially in this place.

The guard returned to the cage, where Jonathan still sat. He grabbed Jonathan by the shoulder and led him through the door. Just inside was a long hallway. The guard led him down the hall and past the many closed doors that lined it. Finally the guard opened a door and pushed Jonathan through it, slamming the door shut behind him. He heard a click and knew that the door had been locked.

"Jonathan!" Micah cried. He was standing near the door, his face white as a sheet. Belnor was in the room too. The druid was looking out the room's only window, tall, narrow, barred, and not even wide enough to fit one's shoulder through. The room was fairly large. About a dozen cots littered the floor, and large trunks lined the walls. Why there were so many cots, Jonathan didn't know.

"Where's Melony?" Jonathan asked.

"I don't know," Micah said. "Is she still in the carriage?"

"No, I was the last one," Jonathan replied. They weren't able to anything else before the old woman who had greeted the guard came in with a bundle of dark-colored clothes.

"You all will be needing to change into these," said the woman. She tossed the clothing at Jonathan. Then she marched out of the room, shutting the door behind her.

Jonathan passed out the clothes from the bundle. He himself got a black wool tunic, black trousers, a black leather belt, and a small black cloak. The image of a red dragon, the crest of King Alexander, had been embroidered on the shoulder of the shirt and the back of the cloak. After changing into these, Jonathan put his old clothes into the only empty trunk. Micah and Belnor had almost identical clothes, like some kind of uniform.

The door opened once more, but it was neither the guard nor the woman who walked through. Instead, a stream of young men and boys, ranging from ages thirteen to twenty-one by the looks of them, flowed in through the door. They all looked exhausted and glistened with sweat, and they all wore the same black uniforms. Most of the boys headed straight for their cots, completely ignoring the three newcomers. However, Jonathan caught a small gesture of sympathy from one or two of the boys.

The very last person in the group to walk in was a boy about Jonathan's age. He was about as tall as him too. His face was dirty and hair matted. If it weren't for the flaming, red hair, Jonathan might not have recognized him immediately.

"Henry?" Jonathan said. The boy turned around. There was no mistaking it. Even through the dirt and sweat that covered his face of freckles, that longing for adventure still shined in his eyes.

"Jonathan?" Henry said in disbelief. "You're here?"

"Yeah," Jonathan replied. "How are you?"

"Well I was taken from my family and have been training to be a soldier for the last three weeks," Henry said. "So how do *you* think I'm doing?"

"Henry, I'm sorry," Jonathan said. "I should have tried to stop them."

"If you'd have done that, you would've gotten caught too," Henry said.

"Well, I ended up here anyway," Jonathan said.

"How far did you get before they caught you?" Henry asked.

"We didn't get caught," Micah said. "Well, not exactly."

"Then why are you here?" Henry asked.

"That's a very long story," Jonathan said. At that moment, Jonathan heard the sounding of a horn.

"What was the horn for?" Micah asked.

"That means dinner," Henry said. All the other boys in the room were scrambling for the door. "Come on," Henry said and joined the crowd of boys heading out the door. Jonathan, Micah, and Belnor followed Henry and walked down the main hallway as several more boys from other dorms joined the crowd.

As Jonathan walked down the hall, he passed a door that was slightly ajar. He peeked inside and saw Melony sitting on a cot. Jonathan looked around him, making sure no one saw him. Then he slipped into the room.

He came in unnoticed by Melony, who was looking at an object in her hands. She had changed into a simple grey dress that looked like it was made of wool. Jonathan caught sight of a golden glimmer from Melony's hand and knew at once she was holding her medallion. She still hadn't noticed him.

"Ahem," he said. Melony jumped and looked up. Jonathan walked over and sat on the cot next to Melony. "Melony. How are you?" There was a long silence.

"I'm sorry I dragged you into this mess," Melony finally said after days of silence.

"Don't say that, Melony," Jonathan replied. "You didn't drag us into anything. I got myself here."

"But if I had never stepped out from behind that tree, then none of you would be here," said Melony.

"Melony, if you hadn't stepped out into the open, then *you* wouldn't be here. You'd be *dead*. The tengu would have killed you."

"And if I'd survived the tengu?"

"Gorlan would have stolen your money. Or you might have drowned when the river overflowed."

"And if I'd made it to Alden alone?"

"Then you would have been banished. And alone," Jonathan said. Melony turned away from him. "I did it on purpose, you know."

"What do you mean?" Melony asked.

"I stood up to Alexander so that he'd banish us."

"Why?" Melony asked. "You could be heading home!"

"I wanted to help you," Jonathan said. A faint smile spread onto Melony's face as she shook her head.

"Ethan, why'd you make me leave Nimberia," Jonathan heard her mutter, though he was pretty sure she hadn't meant to say it outloud.

"Why did you leave Nimberia?" Jonathan asked.

"It doesn't matter why I left now," Melony said. "What matters is if I can get out of here. And if I can avenge my father's death. I'll do whatever it takes."

"And if that means killing the king?" Jonathan asked.

"Then that's what it takes," Melony said. "But it all depends."

"Depends on what?"

"Whether I have a sword in my hand the next time I see him." Jonathan didn't know how to respond.

"We should probably go to the dinner hall," Jonathan finally said.

"Is that where they were going?" Melony asked.

"Yeah. Come on," Jonathan said. They stood up and stepped out into the hall. It was almost empty now with the last few boys running through the doors at the end of the hallway.

"Melony," Jonathan said as they walked to the end of the hall. "We're going to get out of here."

"How?" Melony asked. Then sarcastically she said, "We're going to escape?" Jonathan stopped and looked straight into Melony's piercing blue eyes.

"Yes," Jonathan replied.

Melony and Jonathan walked into the dining hall. Dozens of long wooden tables with long wooden benches filled the hall. The light of torch fire flickered across the walls. A long line of boys and young men snaked between the tables, all waiting to reach the cook, who was ladling greyish gloop into small wooden bowls.

The two of them stood in the line, received their own bowls of food, and went to find a seat. In the corner of his eye, Jonathan thought he saw someone waving at him. He turned and there at the very back of the hall was Micah, waving vigorously and sitting beside Belnor and Henry.

"Over there," Jonathan said to Melony, nodding in the direction of the others. The duo weaved their way through the maze of tables. Jonathan took a seat between Micah and Henry, while Melony sat next to Belnor on the other side of the table. No one spoke for a good four minutes. All of them scarfed down their food, which was surprisingly tastier than it looked and was far more satisfying than what the guard had given them during their journey. Finally, they all stopped, pushed their bowls back and sighed.

"Well, should I start the introductions?" Henry asked cheerfully. Jonathan wondered how Henry could be so positive in such a dark and foreboding place. Henry turned to Belnor, extending his hand. "I'm Henry Smith."

"My name's Belnor," Belnor said, shaking his hand.

"And what might your name be?" Henry asked Melony.

"Melony," she replied. "Melony Wilson."

"A pleasure to meet you, Melony," Henry said with a broad smile. "Now tell me how you four ended up here."

"I'll tell you later," Jonathan said.

"Oh, come now," Henry said. "We've got time."

"I said later."

"Fine," Henry said. "Maybe your friends could tell me about themselves in the meantime." He turned to Melony. "Where are you from?"

"Ravan," Melony said. "It's in Nimberia."

"Really?" Henry asked. "Have you ever seen a giant?"

"Maybe," said Melony.

"Oh come on," Henry begged. But Melony was silent. He sighed and turned to Belnor. "What about you?"

"I'm from the Tetwes druid clan," Belnor said.

"A druid?" Henry said. "You mean you do magic?" Belnor nodded. Henry shared a concerned glance with Jonathan.

"What?" Jonathan asked.

"I just thought—"

"I'll explain later." Just then, a horn sounded, ending the meal.

"Later is getting nearer and nearer," Henry said. "We've gotta return to our rooms. Curfew is in fifteen minutes." He got up from the bench and began walking toward the door they had entered from. Jonathan quickly got up to walk beside him.

The company walked down the hall to their rooms. When they reached Melony's, Henry turned to her, gave a dramatic bow, and said, "Until we meet again, my lady." Melony's eyes widened and she looked at Jonathan.

"You told him?" Melony asked.

"Told me what?" asked Henry.

"No, I didn't tell him," Jonathan said.

"What are you two talking about?" Henry asked in frustration.

"Just give us a second, Henry," Jonathan said. He grabbed Melony's arm and pulled her out of Henry's earshot.

"How did he know?" Melony asked in a whisper.

"He doesn't," Jonathan said. "He's just like that. But at some point I'm going to have to tell him that—"

"No."

"Hear me out," Jonathan said. "You know how I told you we were going to escape?"

"Don't tell me you've decided to stay," said Melony.

"No, of course not," Jonathan reassured her. "It's just that Henry's my best friend. And if we do leave this place, I'm bringing him with us."

"Alright," Melony said.

"But Henry won't do anything without a good reason," Jonathan said.

"I think escaping this place is a good enough reason," Melony commented.

"I know," Jonathan said. "But I'm a really bad liar. So he's going to find out you're a princess eventually."

"She's a princess!" Henry exclaimed. Apparently, they hadn't gotten far enough away from Henry to speak privately. "She's a princess and you didn't tell me?"

"Keep your voice down," Jonathan said urgently.

"Oh, sorry," Henry whispered. "But seriously, you couldn't even mention it? Given me a hint? A wink? Anything?"

"We've been here all but an hour," Jonathan said. "There wasn't much time to mention that."

"Fine, but when we get back to our room, you have to tell me everything," Henry said, walking towards the room they were sleeping in. Jonathan turned back to Melony.

"I'm sorry, I should have been more careful with my words," Jonathan said.

"It's fine," Melony sighed. "Like you said, he was bound to find out eventually." A horn sounded in the distance. "Goodnight, Jonathan," Melony whispered as she slipped into the girls' bedroom. Jonathan turned back around to see the hallway was empty. He walked quickly to his room and closed the door behind him.

"Now it's time to tell me what happened," Henry demanded as soon as Jonathan walked in the door. So as the four boys readied themselves for bed, Jonathan retold their journey and how they'd gotten to Borlo. He told everything except for meeting his father in the dungeon.

"And that's everything," Jonathan concluded.

"Unbelievable," Henry said. "You actually fought goblins?"

"Bird-goblins," Jonathan corrected him. "And yes."

"That's amazing," Henry said. "And what you said to the king! I wish I'd been there."

"Believe me, if you had, you'd have been in the dungeons with us too," Jonathan said. "And that was not a good time."

"Well, I'd love talk about this until the sun rises, but we should probably get some sleep," Henry said. "You three will have a lot of getting used to starting in the morning." They all lay down on their cots, each with a thin, cotton blanket. Jonathan listened to the shuffling of the other young men in the room as he stared at the ceiling, preparing for sleep.

Jonathan stood at the top of a rock ledge. The sounds of a raging battle roared all around him. He looked down from the rock ledge into a small gorge. Below him, Melony wore full plate battle armor, her sword gripped tightly in her hand. A crimson cloak flew behind her, standing out against the pure white snow. She was fighting a soldier with her sword and shield, all her focus directed towards getting past this enemy.

Then Jonathan saw a tall knight in black armor creeping up behind Melony. The knight drew his sword and prepared to run Melony through. But she hadn't noticed him.

Jonathan tried to scream her name, but the sounds of battle drowned out the noise. He reached for an arrow, but his quiver was empty. He looked down to see his father's bow broken in his hands. What was he supposed to do? How could he save her?

He looked to his other hand and saw a sword, the kind only knights carry. He gripped it tightly and knew what he had to do.

"No!" Jonathan screamed as he raced down the gorge. He slipped between Melony and the knight, lifting his sword as the knight began to strike. The next thing he felt was a sword being pushed through his chest.

Suddenly, Jonathan woke up. It was pitch black outside and the snores of a dozen boys and young men filled the room. He sat up and accidentally knocked Belnor with his foot.

"Jonathan?" Jonathan heard Belnor whisper in the dark.

"Sorry," Jonathan whispered back. "I didn't mean to wake you."

"Why are you awake?" Belnor asked.

"Nothing," Jonathan assured him. "I just had a nightmare."

"Are you alright?" Belnor asked suspiciously. "You sounded nervous when you woke up."

"It's just," Jonathan started, "I've had this dream before. In the castle dungeons."

"What was in the dream?" asked Belnor.

"I was standing at the edge of a gorge," Jonathan explained. "A battle was raging around me, and Melony was fighting a soldier below me. Then, a knight snuck up behind Melony and prepared to strike. Then I ran between the knight and Melony, and he…" Jonathan stopped.

"What?" Belnor asked.

"The knight stabbed me in the chest," Jonathan said.

"He stabbed you?" Belnor exclaimed.

"More like impaled," Jonathan corrected himself. "Then I woke up."

"Why would you dream that?" Belnor asked. "And why twice?"

"Who knows," Jonathan sighed. "But, it's over now. I'm going back to sleep. See you in the morning."

"Goodnight," Belnor replied slowly. He seemed like he was deep in thought and paying little attention to Jonathan's goodnight.

Chapter 15
The Cage

Jonathan awoke to the sounding of the same horn that he had heard at dinner the night before. He sat up groggily and looked out the thin, barred window. The sun hadn't even risen yet. Henry was already up and was quickly putting on a black tunic identical to the ones that they had been given yesterday.

"Get up and get dressed," Henry said quickly, throwing Jonathan's new black tunic at him. Jonathan pulled the thin blanket off his body, but regretted it the moment he did. Though there were almost two dozen boys in the room, it was freezing cold. Nevertheless, he got up, goosebumps crawling up every inch of his body.

He slipped the black tunic over his head and fastened the belt around his waist. The wool trousers and cloak easily kept the chilled air from freezing Jonathan to the bone, but the boots were uncomfortable and the belt was one belt notch too small. But he would have to deal with it.

Jonathan walked over to his brother's cot and ripped the blankets off Micah's and Belnor's sleeping bodies.

"Wake up, you two," Jonathan said, "and get dressed."

"Quin snadu ichnu te illac?[13]" Belnor groaned in his native tongue before rolling out of bed and slipping on his black tunic. Micah took a little more persuading.

"Why do we have to get up so early? It's so cold," Micah complained, pulling his blanket back over his head.

"Stay in bed if you'd like," Henry said. "But don't come crying to me when you're flogged or sent to the Cage for being late."

"What's the Cage?" Micah asked.

"It's a tiny cage in the cellars. It's cold and dark and wet," Henry explained. "I've heard of boys who were shut down there for days for being late. It wasn't pretty."

After Micah heard that, he shot out of bed and got dressed so fast that Jonathan wondered if anyone could ever dress faster. After the four of them had gotten dressed, they headed to the dining hall for breakfast. As he went down the long passageway to the dining hall, Jonathan stopped at Melony's door. He knocked lightly.

"Melony," Jonathan called. Only silence came from beyond the wooden door. "Melony? Are you there?" Again, Jonathan received no reply. Disappointed, Jonathan slowly walked away from the door and towards the dining hall.

When he finally reached the hall, it looked no different than the night before. It was still dark, dingy, and heavy with an ever-present stench. Like the night before, Jonathan went and got his breakfast, which consisted of a greyish porridge, a stale roll, and a piece of burnt bacon. Then the four boys sat at one of the tables.

"So, Henry," Micah said. "What do we do today?"

"Train," Henry said. He continued to eat his breakfast without the visible inclination to continue.

---

[13] Why would you do that?

"What do we do to train exactly?" Jonathan asked. "Do we just spend all day hitting each other with sticks?"

"Everyone is divided into different units based on age," Henry said as he swallowed his porridge. "Each unit trains in weaponry and tactical formation. And each unit has a commanding knight. We practice combat with each other and things like that."

"So basically we're going to spend all day hitting each other with sticks," Jonathan repeated.

"Yeah, basically," Henry said and took another large mouthful of porridge. "Oh, and there's one more thing you should probably know. Micah won't be in our unit. He's too young. He'll be in a unit with boys his age."

"What?" Micah said. "But– but–"

"What about Belnor?" Jonathan asked.

"I don't know," Henry said. He turned to Belnor. "How old are you?"

"Fourteen," Belnor said.

"Then he'll be in our unit," Henry said.

"But–" Micah said.

"I'm sorry, Micah, but there's nothing we can do to change it," Henry said. "But we'll still have meals at the same time and sleep in the same chambers."

"But–" Micah stammered. The sound of the horn rang through the dining hall. A hundred benches scraped across the stone floor simultaneously. A river of boys began to flow between Jonathan and Micah, ever widening as it separated the two brothers and swept them in different directions.

"It'll be alright, Micah," Jonathan half yelled to him. "I'll see you later." Then Micah was swept out of sight. Jonathan and the others were pushed down the long, narrow hallway. It was so crowded, Jonathan couldn't get a good look at the hall, but he just assumed it was just like the one they entered their room from. The large group of boys began to crowd around Jonathan, closing him in. He felt the air becoming thick, and his breathing quickened as he lost more and more space.

"Are you alright?" Henry asked.

"I'll be fine," Jonathan quickly assured him.

"That's where we're heading," Henry said. He pointed to an arch leading into a large courtyard. Belnor, Henry, and Jonathan pushed and shoved their way through the sea of boys until they reached the door. Beyond the doorway, Jonathan saw the clear blue skies and heard the faint chirping of a bluebird. He took a deep breath of the crisp, fall morning air. It reawakened his hope for freedom.

The trio walked through the archway and into the courtyard. But this courtyard was different from the one they had entered into when they arrived yesterday. This courtyard was slightly larger than the first, and there were no horses or posts for horses. Instead of cobblestone, the ground was covered with sand. Not a fine layer of sand, but a good five or six inches' worth. In the center of the courtyard was a large circle made of rope. About two paces from the edge of the circle was a large chest that was closed and padlocked.

In the courtyard stood about two dozen boys. Most of them were either Belnor's or Jonathan and Henry's ages. One or two of them Jonathan even recognized from Silan. But they merely acknowledged him with a slight nod of the head. Everyone else stared at the new recruits. Jonathan could feel the cold, pitiless stares from his new peers like one feels the chill in the air before the first frost of winter. Although he tried to make eye contact, none could bear to look him directly in the eyes.

Jonathan's attention was quickly averted by the entrance of a man into the courtyard. He was tall and dressed in a yellow tunic with a black bear embroidered on the front. His peppered hair was cut short, and his beard was carefully shaped. His eyes were cold and observant. He was the perfect image of a great knight.

"That's Sir Marcus," Henry whispered, nodding toward the man. "Steer clear of him if you can."

"Why?" Jonathan asked.

"Because he sent the last newcomer to the Cage for snickering during formation practice," Henry replied. At that moment, Sir Marcus seemed to stare directly at Jonathan, right into his eyes and into his soul. It was almost like Melony had done the first time they'd met, but more unnatural. And most bizarre of all, Jonathan had the strangest feeling that the knight knew him. A shiver ran down Jonathan's spine, and goosebumps began to form all over his arms. That stare was like ice. As the knight drew nearer to the group of boys, deadly silence fell over the courtyard.

"Line up," shouted Sir Marcus, almost making Jonathan jump as the complete silence was broken. The dozens of boys scrambled to make a single line, each shoulder to shoulder. Sir Marcus turned to the chest Jonathan had seen earlier and unlocked it. He pulled out an object Jonathan couldn't quite see, but from the momentary glimpse he did get, it looked like some sort of hand-held weapon.

"Today, we will begin learning how to use a flail," said Sir Marcus. He held up the weapon he'd pulled from the chest. It had a leather-bound handle about a foot long attached to a chain. At the end of the chain was a metal ball the size of an apple. The most frightening of all was that the ball was covered in spikes.

"This is a simple weapon," Sir Marcus explained. "You swing it and hit your enemy. The spikes penetrate the flesh and cause bleeding. The more blows, the more bleeding, the quicker your enemy dies. Any questions?" When Sir Marcus asked that, it was more like he was saying, "I dare you to say a word. And if you do, I'll use this flail on you." There was an awful lot of

139

uncomfortable shuffling from the boys, but none decided to take Sir Marcus's veiled challenge.

"Now that you know the basics, let's have two of you give us a demonstration," Sir Marcus continued. *A demonstration?* Jonathan thought. *He's going to make us fight each other with those things?* Sir Marcus pulled two more flails from the chest. These had no spikes as Sir Marcus's did. This made Jonathan feel a little better. At least they wouldn't be driving spikes into each other.

Sir Marcus slowly paced back and forth along the line of boys. A sense of tension seemed to squeeze the air out of Jonathan. Finally, the knight stopped in front of one of the younger boys. He looked about Belnor's age. But he was shorter and plump. Sir Marcus handed the boy one of the two flails. The boy turned pale and slowly accepted the weapon with a shaky hand. Then Sir Marcus began pacing again, staring at each boy with cruelty lurking behind his eyes. Again, Sir Marcus stopped, and this time directly in front of Jonathan.

Jonathan felt the pit of his stomach drop out. Sir Marcus extended the weapon to Jonathan, who carefully took it as if it would catch on fire at any second. The flail was heavier than he had anticipated. The leather handle squeaked in his hand; the chain swung and clanked with the slightest movement. Though the ball at the end of the chain had no spikes, it was still very heavy, and Jonathan could tell it would deliver a painful blow to any man foolish enough to come near the person holding the weapon.

"Step into the circle," Sir Marcus ordered. Jonathan took steps at a snail's pace towards the ring of rope resting on the sandy floor like a snake. He hesitated when he finally reached the circle's edge before stepping over into the arena. The other boy, who had dark brown hair and blue eyes, stepped in at the other side of the circle. His face had now changed from ghostly white to sickly green. The dozens of boys that had not been chosen to fight gathered around the edge of the arena, a buzz coming from them like the fight was some sort of long-anticipated performance.

"Begin," Sir Marcus shouted. Neither of them moved. The boy stood there with the handle of the flail in his left hand and the ball of it in his right. He stared at that flail as if he hadn't heard Sir Marcus's word to start. "I said begin!" Sir Marcus yelled. The other boy broke his stare and began to cautiously approach Jonathan.

The boy swung his flail, but Jonathan easily moved to his left to avoid the blow. A few cheers rose from the crowd of unchosen boys. Jonathan looked to Belnor and Henry. They were standing on the opposite end of the arena. Belnor wore a clear expression of horror at the situation. Henry, however, was earnestly trying to mouth a message to Jonathan. It was hard to decipher at first, but Jonathan finally understood: *Try not to hurt him too badly.*

Henry's message was interrupted by the other boy's flail hissing past Jonathan's right ear, narrowly missing his shoulder. But Jonathan didn't even try to swing his flail. He knew Henry was right. He knew his own strength and that he could seriously hurt the other boy with a single swing.

"Get in there," Sir Marcus yelled at Jonathan. He unwillingly took a few steps towards the boy. The boy took another swing at Jonathan, horribly missing. The two were close enough now that Jonathan could see terror in the other boy's eyes. Not mere fear, but terror. Jonathan didn't understand why the boy was terrified. This was just to prepare them for battle. This was just practice. Wasn't it?

Jonathan tried to go easy on the other boy, but the boy was so plump that going easy was too much. And if he tried to go any easier, Sir Marcus would surely notice. Jonathan swung his flail to the left, then to the right. But the other boy was too slow. The second blow caught him in the side, just under the armpit. The boy cried out in pain. Jonathan saw Sir Marcus in the corner of his eye, solemn and emotionless. Jonathan wasn't sure what to do next. He didn't want to hurt the boy any more.

"Throw the flails aside," Sir Marcus instructed. Hoping the fight was over, Jonathan did as the knight instructed. "Take his arm." Confused, Jonathan crossed the arena to where the boy, still dazed from his wound, was sitting on his knees. Slowly, Jonathan grabbed the boy's arm. "Good," Sir Marcus said. "Now, break his arm."

Jonathan's head shot up. Break this boy's arm? How could he? That boy had never done anything wrong to him. Jonathan didn't move. Now he understood the boy's terror. This wasn't just a practice fight. Sir Marcus was weeding out the boys who weren't strong enough to fight, by making them fight each other.

"Why are you hesitating?" Sir Marcus asked. "Finish it." This was too far. Breaking this boy's arm was too far.

"No," Jonathan mumbled. He let go of the boy's arm, and the boy scuttled away.

"What did you say?" Sir Marcus spitted.

"I said no," Jonathan stated firmly. "I won't do it." The boy scampered out of the circle, but Jonathan stood his ground, his heels digging into the sand.

"What's your name, boy," Sir Marcus asked.

"Jonathan. Jonathan Fletcher," Jonathan replied.

"Jonathan Fletcher?' Sir Marcus said. The knight was silent for a few moments, a far away look in his eyes like he was revisiting some sort of memory. Then he shook himself back to reality.

"Jonathan, you're one of the new boys here," the knight said. "You may not know the way we do thing here in Borlo, but everything revolves around discipline and taking orders." The knight began to walk around the inside of the circle, glaring at each of the boys. Some of them were trembling, and Jonathan didn't think it was from the cold.

"Discipline is the key to a good soldier," said Sir Marcus. "If you follow commands and do as you're instructed, you will be rewarded. Fail to follow my orders," he stopped directly in front of Jonathan, "then I'll have to break you." Suddenly, the knight punched Jonathan in the stomach, knocking the breath out of him and bringing him to his knees.

"Take him to the Cage," Sir Marcus ordered two of the bigger boys standing in line. Jonathan looked up at the cruel knight. From that angle, Sir Marcus seemed almost familiar. Like someone from a distant childhood memory or a fleeting dream. But that couldn't be possible. Jonathan had never seen this man before that day. As the two boys pulled Jonathan to his feet, the sense of familiarity faded away.

The boys dragged Jonathan out of the courtyard and to a door in the hallway. When they opened it, it was much like the door down into the dungeon of Castle Galador. They led him down into the cellar, into the darkness. When they reached the bottom, Jonathan saw a head with snow-white skin appear from the darkness like a phantom.

"Wha' are yeh doin' down 'ere?" wheezed the pale man.

"Sir Marcus sent this one to the Cage for the night, Wentworth," one of the boys said.

"Alrigh'," Wentworth said. "Throw 'im in there." It took a minute for Jonathan's eyes to adjust to the darkness. But soon he saw the large cage made of iron bars looming directly ahead of him. It was barely tall enough to stand in and had hardly enough room to hold more than three people. A small stool sat next to the Cage, an unlit candle sitting on it. The larger of the two boys threw Jonathan into the Cage and slammed the door. Jonathan heard the door click as it was locked.

"Yeh be'er ge' used to the dark," Wentworth said. "Yeh'll be down 'ere for a long while."

Jonathan sat in the darkness of the Cage for a seemingly endless amount of time. He knew that if this was what life in Borlo was like every day, they couldn't stay here. He refused to accept a life of serving the king who had driven him from home, banished them to this hellish place, and destroyed all of their lives. They had to escape. All five of them.

The next morning, Jonathan woke up lying on the cold floor of the Cage. He could hear the sounding of the horn faintly above him. Wentworth was nowhere to be seen. But the door of the Cage was now open wide. Jonathan got up, his body stiff and aching. He flew up the spiral staircase and into the morning light. The dim light of dawn seemed blinding after the darkness of the cellar. Jonathan raced to the dining hall, painfully hungry since he hadn't eaten since breakfast the day before. He burst through the entrance of the hall and got into the quickly growing line for breakfast.

Once he had finally gotten his bowl of grey porridge, Jonathan looked about the hall and spotted Henry, Belnor, and Micah sitting together in the back of the hall. Jonathan walked over to them.

"Can I sit there?" Jonathan asked.

"Jonathan!" Henry exclaimed, scooching over to make room for him. "You're back!"

"Yeah," Jonathan said, sitting down and beginning to shovel food into his mouth.

"What was it like?" Micah asked cautiously.

"The Cage? Jonathan asked. Micah nodded. "Cramped, dark, and cold. That was about it."

"Last time I was in there, a rat bit me," Henry said. "I still have the scar."

"I didn't see any rats," Jonathan said. "It was too dark."

"Well don't get on Sir Marcus's bad side again today," Henry said. "Or you'll be in there two nights instead of one."

"That's terrible," Belnor exclaimed.

"He's done it more than once," Henry assured Belnor. "Sir Marcus had Robert Evans in there for two nights and two days. When Robert got out, he was wide-eyed with terror. He told strange stories of demons and warlocks coming to him in the dark. Some of the other boys still believe the Cage is cursed. But we sensible people know Robert probably dreamed them up, figments of his nightmares."

"Well, I didn't hear anything," Jonathan said. At that moment, the horn sounded. Jonathan stuffed the rest of the porridge into his mouth as Micah said goodbye. Then the three of them walked out of the dining hall and into the courtyard where Sir Marcus stood, waiting.

Chapter 16
An Unlikely Ally

I t had been almost a month since they'd arrived in Borlo,
but every day had been the same as the first. Jonathan
woke up before sunrise at the sound of the horn and ate a
breakfast of tasteless, grey porridge in the dining hall with Belnor,
Henry, and Micah. After the sun rose, Sir Marcus led them
through formation exercises until the noon horn sounded. Then
they would eat a lunch of cold meat and a stale roll each.

After lunch, Sir Marcus taught them how to use different
types of weapons. One day they learned to use a mace, which had
a similar use as a flail only you had to stand closer together when
you fought. Another day they used crossbows. Jonathan hated
that lesson because as a demonstration Sir Marcus made them
shoot arrows at a target someone had to carry like a shield. And
despite his skill with a bow, Jonathan could never hit the center
and came close to being sent to the Cage for misfiring too close
to Sir Marcus's head. Another day they learned to use poleaxes,
and so on. Though the weapons had been blunted, he, Belnor,
Micah, and Henry always came back to their room black and blue
from demonstrations.

Jonathan hardly ever saw Melony. She didn't eat with the
boys in the dining room after the first night. He never saw her in
the halls either. The only time he did see her was in the evening

just after dinner when he was trudging to his room. Even then, she was at the other end of the courtyard drawing water from a well and there was no time to speak. Jonathan wondered what she did all day and if he would be able to talk to her any time soon.

One day, when the sun had finally come out after two weeks of grey gloom. Jonathan was heading down to the courtyard for the second half of the day. He had just finished lunch and had left almost ten minutes early because he wanted to think. He could never concentrate when the sounds of people bustling and talking surrounded him. He needed silence. And he needed a plan.

That's what he was thinking about. How they were going to escape. Every plan he came up with lacked one element: someone on the inside. That was what he needed for a foolproof plan. But none of the staff were kind enough or brave enough to show any sign of pity or assistance.

As he walked into the courtyard, Jonathan's thoughts were set aside when he noticed that several large targets had been lined up along one side of the courtyard. A rack of simple longbows sat at the other end, and a quiver of arrows was sitting ten feet ahead of him on the cobblestone floor. It had been ages since he'd laid his hands on a bow.

Jonathan scanned the surrounding area. No one was in sight. He quickly went to the rack of bows and chose one that suited him. Then, he took the quiver and chose a single arrow. The longbows were harder to draw back than his recurve bow, but Jonathan still managed to draw the string back to his chin. He took a deep breath and let the arrow fly.

Several things happened in an instant. First, Jonathan heard the *twang* of the bowstring, then the satisfying *thwump* of the arrow hitting the center of the target, and then, unexpectedly, a low whistle. Jonathan lowered the bow and turned in the direction of the whistle. There, at the entrance of the courtyard, stood Sir Marcus.

"Sir Marcus," Jonathan said, stunned. "I– I was just–"

"I know what you were doing," Sir Marcus interrupted him. "I should have you sent to the Cage for using the equipment without permission."

"Sir, I didn't mean any harm," Jonathan said. "I was just–" Sir Marcus held up his hand to stop Jonathan.

"I meant for you to come out here and do that," said Sir Marcus.

"Y– you did?" Jonathan stammered. "Why?"

"Because of your name. It sparked my interest," Sir Marcus said. "Fletcher you said it was, if I'm not mistaken."

"Why would *my* name spark *your* interest?" Jonathan asked.

"Because," Sir Marcus said, "I used to know a man who went by the name of Acillion Fletcher. He was a great archer and one of my closest friends." *How could Sir Marcus have possibly known my father?* Jonathan wondered. *Maybe this is a trick.*

"So why might I interest you?" Jonathan asked. "I'm sure there are a lot of people with the name Fletcher in the kingdom."

"I'm sure there are," Sir Marcus said. "But after seeing what you just did there, there isn't a doubt in my mind."

"About what?" Jonathan said.

"You're his son, aren't you? You're Acillion's boy?" Jonathan was speechless. "Well, aren't you?"

"Um… yes," Jonathan said softly.

"I knew it!" Marcus said excitedly. "You probably don't remember me from when you were a boy. You were only five or so when I last saw you. Such a tragic night that was." Then it clicked. Jonathan finally realized why Sir Marcus had seemed so familiar.

"You!" Jonathan cried. "You're the man who came that night eleven years ago. You told Mum that Father had left. You gave her my father's bow."

"Yes, that was me. After that I was sent here by King Alexander," explained Marcus. "I'm sorry if I've been too hard on you. I have to keep up appearances, or I'll lose what little respect I have in this god-forsaken place. I hope that you can forgive me."

"You wanted me to break a boy's arm on my first day," Jonathan said.

"I knew you wouldn't do something like that," Sir Marcus said. "I could see it in your eyes." *What if he is just saying this to put me off guard and give him an excuse to put me in the Cage again?* Jonathan thought. Despite this, Jonathan wondered if Sir Marcus might be willing to help him. This was his chance to gain the trust of someone on the inside, the last piece he needed for his plan. He couldn't pass it up. Besides, what did he have to lose?

"Sir Marcus, if you had a chance to overthrow King Alexander, would you take it?" Jonathan asked cautiously.

"What kind of question is that?" exclaimed Sir Marcus.

"Just hear me out," Jonathan pleaded. "If you had even the slightest chance, would you take it?"

"You do realize those are treasonous words, don't you?" Sir Marcus said quietly.

"Would you take the chance?" Jonathan repeated. Sir Marcus stared very hard at Jonathan, deep in thought. Then he looked around the courtyard, making sure that no one else could overhear.

"Yes," Sir Marcus finally said. "Most definitely."

"Alright," Jonathan said. "Then there is a great deal I need to tell you. First, it was King Alexander that hired my father to kill King Darius."

"You think that's news to me?" Sir Marcus said. "Alexander was speaking to your father when we found him after the king was killed. He accused Acillion very dramatically. Too dramatically for me to believe. But I never thought Acillion would actually kill the princess."

"Actually, that's the second thing you need to know," Jonathan said. "The princess isn't dead."

"What are you talking about?" Sir Marcus asked.

"My father let her escape with her nursemaid that night," Jonathan said. "Apparently she's been living in exile for the last eleven years. But a few weeks ago, she went to Alden."

"Why haven't I heard about this?" asked Marcus.

"The king didn't announce it," Jonathan said. "Instead he banished her, but we're determined to escape."

"We?" Marcus said.

"I meant *she*," Jonathan quickly corrected himself. "*She's* determined to escape. Not *we.*"

"Jonathan, are you saying Princess Aralyn is *here*? In Borlo?" Sir Marcus asked. "I'm sure the king would pay a fortune for her head."

"What!" Jonathan exclaimed. *I should never have trusted him,* Jonathan thought. But now he'd dug too deep a hole to get out. "You'll never find her."

"It's alright, Jonathan, that's not how I meant for it to come out," Marcus reassured him, seeing how defensive he was becoming. "I don't want to harm the princess. If what you're saying is true, the rightful heir to the throne is within these walls. And if it's your intention, I will help you and the princess escape."

"Really?" Jonathan asked in astonishment. Maybe he had placed his trust in the right place after all.

"Really," replied Sir Marcus. "I know a very simple way out that would be perfect for two young people to slip through undetected."

"Two people?" Jonathan said. "*Only* two people?"

"Yes," Marcus said slowly. "Yourself and the princess."

"I'm afraid that won't work," Jonathan said.

"What? Why not?" Marcus asked.

"Well, there aren't just two of us," Jonathan said.

"How many are you?" asked Sir Marcus.

"Five," replied Jonathan.

"Five? Why five?" the knight asked.

"Myself, the princess, my brother Micah, his friend Belnor, and my friend Henry."

"Hmmm. That makes it difficult. Much more difficult." Sir Marcus slipped into silence for a long while, thinking.

"Actually," Jonathan finally started, "I think I've already got a plan that might just work." Then he went on to explain his plan. By the time he finished, the other boys were filing into the courtyard.

"I do believe that could work!" Sir Marcus whispered. Then, he pulled a piece of parchment and a small charcoal pencil from one of the trunks. "Take this. You'll need it."

"Thank you," Jonathan whispered back.

"Now get over there before I whip you, boy," Sir Marcus said loud enough for the entire courtyard to hear. And Jonathan ran back to Henry and Belnor, who were waiting for him.

"What was that about?" asked Henry.

"I just found us a way out of here," Jonathan said with a grin.

"Everybody gather around," Sir Marcus shouted. Everyone immediately did as he said. "Today you'll be learning the basics of archery. And I don't care what you think you know; if any of you try and get ahead of my directions, you'll be in the Cage for the night. Now everyone grab a bow and three arrows. I said three, Peter!"

As Jonathan, Belnor, and Henry grabbed bows, Jonathan whispered to them, "Follow my lead." He grabbed the bow he'd used earlier and three arrows. His friends did the same.

"Now everyone step up to the rope so that everyone has a target," Marcus called. Everyone did just that. "Now pull back and aim at the target. Do not fire until I say so. Ready? Aim—" But Sir Marcus was interrupted by the twang of a single bowstring and the *thwump* of an arrow hitting the center of the target. These sounds were shortly followed by two other shots, neither hitting the exact center of their targets, but hitting the targets all the same.

Just as he'd planned, Jonathan, Belnor, and Henry had fired their shots early. Sir Marcus's face turned red as a radish.

"Fletcher! Smith! Yuovech!" Sir Marcus shouted. "You will report to my chambers after dinner. You're all staying in the Cage tonight." Jonathan turned to his friends. They looked shocked and confused and looked at Jonathan as if he were crazy. Jonathan slyly smiled back. After the incident, Jonathan, Belnor, and Henry followed the rest of Sir Marcus's commands to the letter. Jonathan knew his friends were dreading a night that would seem cold, cruel, and endless. But Jonathan just smiled to himself. All he had to do now was contact Melony.

After practice, the trio trudged into the dining hall where they found Micah. He was pale as snow.

"Micah, what's wrong?" Belnor asked.

"I– I got sent to the Cage for the night," Micah said. "I don't know why. Sir Marcus just came up to me before dinner and told me I have to go to his office and then the Cage."

"You know, that sounds very familiar," Henry said sarcastically, turning to face Jonathan. "How could you do that!

You got us all sent to the Cage for the night! Why in Iyuandil would you do that?"

"Henry, calm down," Jonathan said. "It's all part of the plan."

"Plan? What plan?" Belnor asked, also obviously unhappy with their fate.

"The plan to escape," Jonathan explained.

"Wait. We're escaping?" Henry asked. Jonathan merely nodded his head.

"When?" Micah asked.

"Tonight," Jonathan said.

"But what about Melony?" Belnor asked. "How are you going to tell her the plan? There's no time."

"I'm going to need your help there, Belnor," Jonathan said. "I need you to write a letter to Melony explaining the plan. I'll get it to her on the way to Sir Marcus's office. Can you do that?"

"Of course," Belnor said. "But I don't have anything to write on or with."

"Here," Jonathan said, pulling a piece of parchment and a charcoal pencil from his pocket.

"Where did you get that?" Henry asked in bewilderment.

"From Sir Marcus," Jonathan explained. "He's going to help us escape."

"*Sir Marcus* is *helping* us *escape*?" Henry said. "You've gone insane. If anything, Sir Marcus will be the one stopping us."

"You don't understand," Jonathan said. "He wants to help because he was a friend of my father."

"My father is friends with one of the merchants that comes to town, but that doesn't mean I trust him," Henry said. "Quite the contrary in fact."

"If you don't want to escape, then you don't have to," Jonathan said. "But we're taking this chance."

"Why?" asked Henry.

"Because so far it's the only chance we've got," Jonathan replied. "Besides, it'll be an adventure." Henry gave a long sigh.

"Fine," Henry finally said. "But when we're all walking to the gallows, I'll say I told you so."

"We still don't know what the escape plan *is*," Micah said.

"I'll explain while Belnor writes the letter," Jonathan said. "But we'll need to be quiet. We don't want the word spreading to the guards." Jonathan went on to dictate the letter to Melony and explained the plan to Henry, Micah, and Belnor. When the letter was done, dinner time was almost over.

"If I'm right, I should be able to get this to Melony before the end of dinner," Jonathan explained. Then he grabbed the letter and hid it in his pocket, left the dining hall, and headed for the courtyard where he knew Melony would be. But when he reached the courtyard, Melony wasn't there. Jonathan was confused. He couldn't wait long for her; dinner was almost over. He heard the footsteps of guards coming towards him. Jonathan quickly ran for the bushes near the well and hid among them just as three guards came into sight.

Just then, Melony walked around another corner in the courtyard, carrying two large buckets. He was surprised at how dirty and tangled her golden hair had become and how weary she looked. Melony tied the rope to the handle of one of the buckets and slowly lowered it down into the watery depths of the fort's well. When the guards disappeared around the corner, Jonathan inched closer to the edge of the bushes.

"Pssst!" Jonathan whispered. "Melony!" Melony's head shot up, looking around. It was a few seconds before she finally spotted Jonathan.

"Jonathan!" she softly exclaimed.

"I don't have long," Jonathan said. "I just need to tell you that I have a plan to get out of here." Melony's eyes seemed to light up.

"What's the plan? How can I help?" Melony asked.

"Here," Jonathan said, and he handed her the letter.

"What's this?" Melony asked.

"The plan," Jonathan said quickly. "Read it carefully. It'll explain everything." Jonathan heard the bell signaling the end of dinner. "I'm out of time." And he started to turn and leave when he remembered. "Oh, Melony, one more thing. Don't forget to get the key."

"The key to what?"

"The Cage."

Chapter 17
Escape!

J onathan scrambled up the narrow, spiral staircase to Sir Marcus's office as the sun sank lower in the sky. When he finally reached the wooden door of Sir Marcus's office, he almost ran into it headfirst. His legs aching, Jonathan knocked on the door.

"Enter," Jonathan heard Sir Marcus's voice call from the other side of the door. Jonathan pushed it open, revealing a room in the shape of a semicircle with stone walls. The flat wall, which faced the door, had a single door near the left corner of the two walls. Jonathan assumed this led to Sir Marcus's bedroom.

Against the curved wall near the door was a simple wooden desk. On the desk was a pot of ink, a few pieces of blank parchment, and one piece of parchment covered in small scribbles of writing. On the center of the flat wall above a roaring hearth hung a huge shield with a black bear on a yellow background. On the floor near the hearth was a large, brown, bear-skin rug, its teeth still bared. The fire crackled merrily, illuminating the two chairs sitting in front of it. In one chair sat Micah, and in the other sat Belnor. Henry stood behind Micah's chair staring into the flickering flames. Sir Marcus stood with his back to the flames, facing the boys and holding an envelope. When Jonathan walked in, all heads turned to him.

"We're all here then?" Jonathan asked.

"Yes," Henry said.

"So, we're really doing this?" Belnor asked.

"Yes," Jonathan said. "We have to for Melony's sake." He looked to Sir Marcus. "Do you have what I asked for?" Sir Marcus nodded and handed the envelope to Jonathan.

"Remind me why this plan has to be so dangerous?" Belnor asked.

"It's the only plan that could possibly get all five of you past the guards," Sir Marcus said.

"Plus it's the most exciting," Henry said with a grin.

"Wait," Micah interrupted. "You said possibly. Are you telling us that we might still get caught?"

"Of course," Sir Marcus replied. "And here's some inspiration so that that doesn't happen: don't get caught or you'll be swinging tomorrow."

"Swinging?" Micah said.

"Hanged," Henry said as he held an invisible noose around his own neck. Micah gulped.

"Every plan has its risks," Jonathan said. "But I know we can pull this off."

"Then if you're ready," Sir Marcus said, "I will escort you to the Cage." Sir Marcus walked over to the door, opened it, and began the long descent back to the bottom of the keep. It took a few seconds for any of the boys to begin following. But Jonathan gathered all his courage and followed after the knight. Micah closely followed his older brother. Behind him came Henry, with Belnor bringing up the rear.

The journey down was much longer than the journey up because this time they were going all the way down to the cellars. All the while, Sir Marcus whispered last minute information and advice to Jonathan.

157

"I've arranged clothes and fresh supplies for your journey," Sir Marcus said. "You'll find them with the village cobbler, Mr. Dribbles. Once you've gotten out, go southwest and through the Black Mountains. That'll be your best bet to get to Alden quickly. Travel by day and whenever you come to a stream, or a pond, or even a puddle, go *through* the water. It'll cover your scent from tracking hounds."

Now they were nearing the bottom of the staircase. The only sources of light were the torches that sat in torch-holders along the walls of the spiral staircase. Finally, the five of them reached the very bottom of the staircase, which was blocked by a simple, wooden door. Sir Marcus suddenly turned to Jonathan, firmly grabbed both his shoulders, and looked at him directly in the eyes.

"No matter what happens, you must keep the princess safe," Sir Marcus whispered. The knight took a long look at Jonathan. "You look just like your father," he muttered.

He turned back around and banged on the door three times. It slowly creaked open, nothing but darkness on the other side. Then, Wentworth's snow-white head emerged from the darkness.

"Yeh, Sir Marcus?" wheezed Wentworth.

"I have four for you tonight, Wentworth," Sir Marcus said. Wentworth's eyes shifted to Jonathan.

"So yer back?" Wentworth said with a toothy grin. "I knew yeh would beh. You had that look in yer eye. A troublemaker."

"They're to be under constant supervision," Sir Marcus said, ignoring Wentworth's comment. "I want you to personally see to that."

"I'll guard 'em myself, sir," Wentworth said, a yellow grin spreading across his face.

"Perfect," Sir Marcus said. "They should be let out in the morning, but after breakfast ends."

"O' course, sir," said Wentworth.

"Then I leave them in your hands, Wentworth," Sir Marcus said, immediately turning and heading back upstairs. They were on their own now.

Wentworth escorted them through the dark with only a single candle in his hand to light the way. It took a minute for Jonathan's eyes to adjust to the darkness, but he soon saw the faint outline of the Cage. Wentworth set down his candle on a chair that leaned against the Cage.

"Alrigh', oo's goin' first?" Wentworth said. After a minute of hesitation, Henry stepped forward. Wentworth searched Henry for anything that might help them escape. But they had planned for this, so Wentworth found nothing on Henry and opened the door to the Cage with a long squeak. He pointed to it, and Henry stepped in. Jonathan went next. The only thing Jonathan was carrying was a small envelope of powder. Wentworth opened the envelope and smelled it.

"Wha' yeh got smelling salts for?" he asked as he handed the envelope back. Jonathan ignored him and entered the Cage. Next was Belnor. Wentworth eyed Belnor's druid charms and merely laughed.

"What?" Belnor asked, confused.

"Yer one o' those magic-lovers, ain't yeh," Wentworth asked. Belnor didn't answer. "Bah. Magic's no'in' more than a thing fer babies."

"You don't believe in magic?" Belnor asked quietly.

"Ain't ever seen it, so I ain't believin' in it," Wentworth said. Belnor rolled his eyes and entered the Cage. Micah went last with nothing on him.

Once they had all gotten into the Cage, Wentworth snickered and said, "Make yerselves comferble." Then he slammed the door closed. Wentworth lifted the candle off the chair, sat down, and began whistling a very sad tune.

159

Now was their chance to carry out the rest of phase one. Jonathan signaled Belnor with a nod. The druid nodded back. Belnor hurriedly took off one of his charm necklaces: a shiny black stone that had been roughly carved in the likeness of a crescent moon. Jonathan watched as the druid gripped the charm so hard in his left hand that his knuckles were beginning to turn white. Belnor crept like a cat behind the chair where Wentworth was sitting. He leaned in close to Wentworth until he was next to the man's ear.

"*Dorminu,*" Belnor muttered. The charm in Belnor's hand glowed blue for a moment, and at the same time Belnor's eyes faintly glowed green. A second later, Wentworth's candle fell to the floor and went out, plunging them into utter darkness. Jonathan heard the man slump over and begin to snore so loudly that Jonathan was afraid everyone in the fort would hear.

"Now what?" Henry asked.

"We wait," Jonathan replied, taking a seat on the cold floor, his back against the bars. Silence reigned through the dungeon-like place, with the exception of Wentworth's snoring. So they waited. And waited. And waited. It was hours before Jonathan heard the sound of footsteps from the stairwell.

"Someone's coming," Micah whispered. But they couldn't do anything but sit and wait to see who it was. The doorknob rattled. The click of the door unlocking rang through the dark room. A crack of light appeared out of the darkness where the door had been. Melony slipped through the doorway.

"Jonathan?" Melony whispered.

"Over here," Jonathan whispered back. Melony slowly walked towards the cage, her arms stretched in front of her.

"Where are you guys?" Melony whispered.

"We're ten feet in front of you," Micah said.

"Did you get the key?" Jonathan asked.

"Of course I did," Melony said irritably just as she reached the cage. "Where's the door?"

"On this side," Belnor said. Melony moved over to the far side of the cage, keeping her hands on the bars and avoiding the sleeping Wentworth. Jonathan could hear Melony insert the key into the keyhole. A click came from the lock and Jonathan heard the squeaking sound of the door swinging open.

"I got it!" Melony whispered.

"Good going, Melony," Henry said quietly. In single file, the four boys silently filed out of the Cage.

"Let's go," Jonathan said.

"Wait," Micah said. "Shouldn't we bind Wentworth? You know, so he doesn't set off any alarms."

"You're right, Micah," Henry said. "I thought I saw some rope in the corner over there. We can use that." Henry crept into the darkness of the corner. When he emerged, he was carrying a few coils of rope, just enough to bind and gag Wentworth. Jonathan and Henry set about tying the rope tight so the man could not escape. Surprisingly, his slumber didn't seem disturbed by this.

"Now we can go," Jonathan said. Taking the lead, Jonathan ran quietly through the door and out of the Cage room. When the five of them had gotten out, Melony locked the door and tucked the key in her apron. They didn't have to talk much after that since they all knew the plan. They all climbed the stairs until they had reached the ground floor, which only took a minute. They had just completed phase one of the plan. Next was phase two, which was going to be much harder.

The company snuck through the winding corridors and hallways of the fort, trying their best to stay in the shadows and out of sight of the ever-present guards patrolling from the fort's walls. It was a good fifteen minutes before they finally reached the courtyard that Jonathan, Henry, and Belnor had trained in with Sir Marcus.

In the far corner of the courtyard, hidden in the shadows, was the faint outline of a box. As they came closer, Jonathan saw that it was Sir Marcus's chest. The five of them gathered in the shadows around the chest just as a guard came into view on top of the wall. Jonathan's heart pounded. He kneeled in front of the old chest and reached out his sweating hands to open it. Thankfully, it opened easily and noiselessly.

There, lying at the very top of the chest, was a longbow. Jonathan couldn't help but grin. He pulled the bow from the chest and began stringing the bow and testing it for any flaws. He found none. Underneath the bow, Jonathan discovered two quivers. One was filled with eighteen black arrows, the long, iron-tipped kind the military archers used. The other was shorter and filled with two dozen crossbow bolts. Jonathan took the first quiver and put it on his back. The other he placed on the ground. Under that was a crossbow made from the wood of a corius tree.

"I'll take that," Henry said.

"Alright," Jonathan said, handing Henry the crossbow and the other quiver. The next weapon in the chest was a shortsword.

"Melony, you're the best with a sword. You should take this," Jonathan said, handing her the sword and continuing to look through the chest. He could see Melony in the corner of his eyes swinging the sword around, testing its weight and balance. Finally, Jonathan found the flail with spikes that Sir Marcus had shown them their first day of training.

"Micah should take the flail," Belnor said. "I've got magic on my side."

"Is that alright with you, Micah?" Jonathan asked his brother.

"Yes," Micah said smiling. "Besides, I'm better with the flail than Belnor."

"I never said that," Belnor retorted.

"Oy," Henry whispered. "This is no time for messing around." Micah's smile faded and he would have glowed a bright enough shade of red for all to see if his face had not been hidden by the shadows.

"We better get moving," Jonathan said. They all crept along the shadowy edges of the courtyard, trying their best not to make a sound. They weaved through more halls and passages until they came to the door outside the main dining hall.

"Alright, now we split up," Jonathan said. They had all known this was coming. It was necessary for the plan. But now that it was time to do so, they were hesitant to part ways. Any number of things could go wrong once they were separated, and no one would have any idea if the others got caught or injured. All these thoughts were running through Jonathan's head. However, he had to push these thoughts aside.

"Come on, guys," Jonathan said. "Henry and I will head to the gatehouse while you three head to the stables. Just like we planned." No one moved.

"I have a bad feeling that something is going to go wrong," Micah said.

"Come off it," Jonathan said bravely. "Nothing bad is going to happen." But in reality, Jonathan had the same feeling. It had been growing in him ever since they had left the courtyard.

"All the same," Belnor said, "I think we should say proper goodbyes to each other. Just in case."

"I agree," Melony said.

"Oh come on," Henry said. "I'm not saying goodbye because I know we can do this and that we're not going to fail."

"Just say goodbye, Henry," Jonathan said in frustration.

"I will not," Henry said.

"We don't have time for this," Jonathan sighed. "We'll see you three soon." Melony nodded. Then Jonathan watched

Belnor, Melony, and Micah turn and disappear into the night, headed for the stables on the east side of the main courtyard. Jonathan and Henry raced to the other side of the courtyard and pushed the door open.

"You should have said goodbye," Jonathan muttered as they began to climb the staircase into the gatehouse.

"Saying goodbye would have only made me doubt," Henry replied.

"Doubt what?" asked Jonathan, though he already knew the answer.

"That we can do this," said Henry.

"We *can* do this," Jonathan said, reaching the top of the flight. The light of a candle made flickering shadows across the walls. A man, who was in fact the gatekeeper, was nodding off in the far corner. Jonathan grabbed the envelope of powder. He tore it open and spat into it. Then he took from his quiver a very small arrow, about the length of his hand, which had a very thin point. Jonathan dipped the tip of this small arrow into the wet powder and handed it to Henry. Henry nodded and placed the arrow in his crossbow.

Twang.

The gatekeeper slumped over, asleep, much like Wentworth had done. The tiny arrow stuck out of the man's thigh. Jonathan and Henry emerged from the dark staircase and into the gatehouse.

The gatehouse was a small room. There were two small windows facing the outer wall and two facing the inner wall. Each window had wooden boards used to close the windows when the fort was under attack. Now they had been propped up by sticks to allow the gatekeeper to look out at coming wagons. There were two doors that led out onto the walls, one on either end of the room. In the center of the room was a large wheel that looked like a giant bobbin with thick chains wrapped around it

164

instead of thread. Pegs stuck out at intervals around the top of the wheel, which helped guards and gatekeepers turn the wheel to open the gate.

"Bolt the doors," Henry said. Jonathan ran to one side of the room and bolted the door as Henry did the same on the other side. Jonathan went to the gatekeeper and pulled the arrow from his thigh.

"He's going to have a headache in the morning," Jonathan muttered. Just then, he noticed something on the floor: a small bolt and two hinges. Curious, Jonathan approached them. He unbolted the latch and pulled upwards. A door came swinging open leaving a dark, square hole in its stead.

"Henry, come look at this," Jonathan whispered. Henry hurried over and knelt beside his friend.

"It's a trapdoor!" Henry said excitedly. "And it's right above the gate."

"That'll be helpful," Jonathan said. He looked around and found a large coil of rope sitting half hidden in the shadows of the corner. Jonathan took this and threw one end down through the trapdoor and tied the other to the bottom of the large wheel.

Then, in the distance, Jonathan heard the clopping of horses' hooves on cobblestone. Henry and Jonathan raced to the windows that faced the inside of the fort. Just outside in the dark courtyard, Jonathan could see horses approaching with figures on their backs. But these were not guards; the riders were too small to be guards. It was Melony, Belnor, and Micah returning from the stables.

"Excellent," Henry said. He walked away from the window leaving Jonathan to watch their friends draw closer. "Well, are you gonna to help?" Henry said. Jonathan turned around and saw Henry beginning to turn the large wheel. He came over and took hold of a peg on the other side and began pushing. The wheel turned, the chains clanked, and the grey light of dawn began to peek over the distant horizon.

"Jonathan," Micah whispered from below. Jonathan stopped pushing and rushed to the trapdoor. Micah looked up at him from a beautiful white horse with a black tail and mane. Belnor was riding a bay steed with a long, brown mane. And Melony sat on a grey horse with white spots. But those were the only horses he saw.

"Why are there only three?" Jonathan exclaimed. "There are five of us! We need two more horses!"

"We only had time to get three out," Melony said.

"What do you mean?" Jonathan asked, sweating from panic.

"There was a stable boy," Micah explained, "and we accidentally woke him up."

"You what?" said Henry. Just then, a horn sounded three times, echoing across the castle. Fires flared up in the towers that made up the outer wall. Jonathan heard the shouts of guards coming from all sides.

"Jonathan!" Melony cried from below. Jonathan looked through the trapdoor. He saw Melony draw her shortsword.

"We need to hurry," Jonathan called to Henry. He again grasped the other side of the wheel and pushed with all his might. The shouts were getting closer and now the light of a dozen torches was flickering nearby. Then came a banging at the door.

"Open this door!" shouted a guard. Jonathan kept pushing.

"Go find an axe," another guard cried. It wasn't long before Jonathan heard the splintering of wood as the guards began hacking away at the door. Jonathan's arms and legs burned. His back ached. Sweat trickled down his brow and his heart raced. Jonathan's eyes shifted for an instant towards the trapdoor. If they ran now, they might get away.

Suddenly, the soldiers made a hole in the door about the size of a man's lower arm. Jonathan and Henry kept pushing. One guard poked an arrow through the hole and drew. Jonathan and Henry kept pushing.

"Stop or I'll shoot," the guard with the bow called. Jonathan and Henry kept pushing. The twang of the bow rang through the air, but neither of the boys had been shot. Instead, Jonathan saw that the guard had broken the peg which was supposed to hold the wheel in place once they had stopped turning. Jonathan and Henry kept pushing.

"It's high enough for us to get through," Melony shouted from below. Jonathan and Henry made a dash for the trapdoor. But the moment they let go of the wheel, it began to unwind. Henry rushed back and held the wheel in place once more.

"Stupid guards," Henry muttered. "They broke the mechanism."

"We need someone to hold it open," Jonathan said.

"You go," Henry said. "I'll hold it open as long as I can."

"What? No!" Jonathan said. "I'm staying right here with you."

"This is your only chance," Henry said. "Go!"

"But you'll be left here," Jonathan said. "They'll hang you for trying to escape."

"That's a risk I'm willing to take," Henry said. "Now get down there and go!"

"I am *not* leaving you behind!" Jonathan said.

"You *have* to," Henry replied. Jonathan didn't want to leave his friend. His best friend. But there was no other choice. Henry was giving them a chance.

"I promise I'll come back for you," Jonathan said.

"Not until the princess is back where she deserves to be," Henry said. "She must reclaim her throne."

"But–"

"Go!" Henry shouted. The guards were again hacking at the door and had almost made a hole big enough for them to get through. With a final glance at his friend, Jonathan ran to the trapdoor and slid down the rope.

"About time you got down here," Melony shouted as she knocked the hilt of her sword against the helmet of a soldier. The man fell to the ground. A few feet away, Micah was trying to use the flail, but he wasn't making much progress against the soldier facing him. Jonathan pulled an arrow out of the quiver and fired it straight through the soldier's knee. The soldier screamed in pain. Micah ran over to his brother.

"Thanks," Micah said, winded. Jonathan looked around for Belnor. He finally saw him standing in the center of the courtyard, fighting another guard. Jonathan could see that the druid was tightly gripping one of his charms. But as Belnor knocked the guard away with a burst of purple light, Jonathan saw the guard grab Belnor's charm and yank it out of his hand. The guard crashed into the wall, unconscious.

"Belnor, let's go!" Melony shouted. But at that moment, nine more guards entered the courtyard through the door in front of Belnor. Belnor looked back. Then he took a step towards the guards.

"What is he doing?" Jonathan asked.

"He's going to get himself killed," Melony gasped. Belnor slowly lifted his arms, and his hands began to glow red. That's when Jonathan noticed Belnor wasn't holding any charm.

"I thought he could only do magic when he's holding a charm," Jonathan whispered to Micah.

"Belnor!" Micah shouted. Belnor's head whipped around suddenly. To Jonathan's horror, the druid's eyes were glowing bright red.

"What in Iyuandil," Jonathan gasped. Belnor turned back around and faced the guards. As they began to charge, Jonathan heard Belnor shout an incantation.

"*Ventoc draegonachn fortimu mie*," Belnor shouted. A wave of red energy shot through the air from Belnor's hands. The blast knocked the guards backwards and threw them against the courtyard walls. Belnor lowered his hands and turned back to them, his eyes still glowing red. When the light faded, Belnor's normal brown eyes rolled back into his head, and he fell to the ground. Melony rushed to Belnor's side and shook him.

"Wake up, Belnor," she shouted. Belnor stirred slightly, then his eyes slowly opened.

"What happened?" Belnor asked in a moan.

"Help me, Jonathan," Melony said. "We need to go before more come." Jonathan ran to Belnor and Melony. She was right. Already Jonathan could hear the rushing footsteps of more soldiers coming their way.

"Can you ride?" Jonathan asked Belnor, helping him to his feet.

"I think so," Belnor replied. They ran to the horses. Jonathan climbed onto the back of the same horse as Micah, sitting just behind his little brother.

"What about Henry?" Micah asked.

"He's not coming," said Jonathan. "He's keeping the gate open long enough for us to get away."

"We can't leave him," cried Micah.

"Come on," Jonathan shouted.

"He'll die if we leave him," Micah screamed. But Jonathan didn't listen. Henry had made his choice, and Jonathan wasn't going to let his best friend sacrifice himself in vain.

"Ya," yelled Jonathan.

"No!" Micah cried. Away the white horse galloped, its black tail and mane billowing behind it. They rode through the gate, across the drawbridge, and into sweet freedom. Just as the three steeds passed through the gate, it came crashing down. Jonathan looked up at the gatehouse and saw Henry in the window, four guards approaching him. Jonathan forced himself to look away. There was nothing he could do now.

Ahead of them was flat, open country. And in the distance were the dark shapes of a small village. They galloped across the fields and the frosted-over plains towards the town as fast as their horses could run. But as they rode, Jonathan felt the occasional drop of water splash into his face or his arms, almost like rain but falling horizontally towards him. However, when he tasted the drops, he knew they were the salty tears of Micah sitting in front of him.

Closer and closer the dark shapes came until finally they reached the village. Jonathan pulled back on the reins and the horse slowed to a trot. The village was deathly silent and uncomfortably still. The main street was lined with shops and stands. But no one was out. The sign of a large mug above the tavern was visible in the dim light of dawn. It was completely silent, as if everyone was holding their breath.

"Pssst!" Jonathan heard ahead of them. Jonathan looked around to see where the sound had come from. Just ahead of them on the right side of the street, Jonathan saw a man holding a lantern.

"Are you the runaways Sir Marcus told me about?" the man with the lantern whispered.

"Yes sir," Jonathan replied.

"Then come in," the man said. "We haven't got much time." The four children rode to the building and dismounted. They hurried inside the shop and the man shut the door behind them.

"I thought there was gonna be five of you," the man said. None answered him.

"You must be Mr. Dribbles," Jonathan said.

"Yes, I am," Mr. Dribbles said. Mr. Dribbles was a very thin man. He was balding on top and wore a leather apron with several pockets for putting his cobbler tools in. "Your packs are in the corner over there," said Mr. Dribbles, pointing to the pile of packs. "The missus has packed some bread, potatoes, and bacon along with the supplies Sir Marcus requested."

"Thank you," Melony said quietly. Jonathan went to the corner, opened a pack, pulled out a cloak, and put it on over his black training uniform. When he looked up, he saw Belnor lowering himself onto a stool.

"Are you alright?" Jonathan asked.

"Just a little dizzy," Belnor muttered. "What exactly happened?"

"You don't remember?" asked Melony.

"I remember riding into the courtyard," Belnor said. "Then everything went... red. And then I was lying on the ground. And my hands..." Belnor stopped.

"What about your hands?" Melony asked with concern.

"It's nothing," said Belnor, slipping his hands under his cloak. Melony walked over to Belnor and held her hand out, silently demanding to see his. Belnor sighed, pulled his hand out, and placed it in Melony's.

"Belnor!" Melony gasped.

"What?" Jonathan asked, rushing over to see. Belnor's hands were completely red, his palms charred black.

"If one of you could tell me what happened instead of staring at the result, that would be very helpful," Belnor said with a hint of sarcasm.

"You stopped nine guards with a blast of magic," Micah said. "You didn't use any charms, and your eyes glowed red."

"Red?" Belnor said in surprise.

"We have to dress your hands before we leave," Melony insisted.

"We don't have time," Belnor said, pulling back his hands and getting to his feet. He grabbed his pack, trying to hide his pain when his hand made contact with the fabric. This left one pack. None of them wanted to touch it. It was Henry's and Henry's alone. Jonathan opened the thin curtains just a crack and peeked out the window. The sun was about to burst over the horizon and bathe Iyuandil in its colorful morning light.

"Time to go," Jonathan said. Melony opened the door and peeked her head out.

"It's all clear," she whispered.

"May the Creator bless you all," Mr. Dribbles said.

"Thank you," Melony replied. They all snuck out the door one by one, Melony leading and Jonathan taking the back, bow in hand. Belnor mounted his horse and Melony hers. Micah mounted the white horse and sat there. He offered no help to his brother when Jonathan almost slipped off the horse trying to mount. Jonathan could still sense how upset Micah was. But they would have to deal with it later. They turned their horses west.

The Black Mountains stood tall and intimidating ahead of the company. Their snow-capped peaks glowed pink as the morning sun peeked over the eastern horizon. The trees dotted the distant mountainside and looked like they were the size of ants from so far away. Streams and waterfalls shimmered like golden rivers in the morning light. Jonathan realized that, as he had tried to take in the mountains' beauty for the last few seconds, he had been holding his breath. He let out a long breath and saw it like a tiny cloud before him.

Jonathan thought of Henry and how he would have loved to go on the adventure on which they were embarking. All at once Jonathan felt as though his very soul had been torn in half. He had just lost his best friend in the entire world. He had abandoned him, not just once but twice. Jonathan knew he had left Henry to his death. Jonathan felt his eyes begin to sting as salty tears began to trickle down his cheeks.

Chapter 18
Aamar

The company rode hard most of the day. By the time the sun had begun to set they were well into the foothills of the mountains. Melony spotted a small group of rocks that formed a cave-like space. They decided to stop there and make camp. Jonathan slipped off the horse and helped Micah down. Then he dropped the reins in the grass and began taking off the horse's saddle.

"Shouldn't we tie up the horses?" Belnor asked as he set his pack down on the earthy floor of the cave.

"No," Melony said. "We don't have enough supplies to take care of all three of them. Plus, there won't be many places to graze since the mountains are snowy this time of year. And the two bigger horses won't do very well on the narrow mountain roads." So they left the horses untied in the small clearing outside the outcrop, expecting them to go back to their stables in Borlo as soon as they had finished grazing.

"I'll go gather firewood," Belnor said.

"No you won't," Melony said. "Your hands are still burnt." Belnor looked down at his cloak and grabbed the end of it. Then, with a long rip, Belnor tore off part of the hem of his cloak and began wrapping the cloth around his injured hands.

"If I can't help you guys, then I'm just a burden," Belnor said.

"I still don't understand how that happened," Melony said. "You've done magic before, and you were fine then."

"I used focuses then," Belnor said.

"What's a focus?" asked Micah.

"Focuses are like my charms," Belnor said. "They act as gateways for magical energy and bear the strain that comes with that. But if there is no focus, then the human body has to bear the strain." He held out his charred hands. "A magic burn like this is the result." When he finished bandaging his hands, Belnor got to his feet.

"I'm coming too," Melony said. They left the cave-like shelter and disappeared into the woods.

Micah still wasn't speaking to Jonathan. He had taken a seat with his back resting against the stone wall of the cave. Jonathan knew Micah blamed him for what had happened to Henry. Micah thought of Henry like a second brother and was almost as close to Henry as Jonathan. So Henry's sacrifice was as much a blow to Micah as it was to Jonathan. Jonathan went over to his brother and sat next to him.

"You left him to die," Micah whispered.

"No, I didn't," Jonathan replied. But he was trying to convince himself more than his brother. "He sacrificed himself so that we could get away." A lump was beginning to form in Jonathan's throat. "It's the noblest thing anyone could ever do." Micah hugged his brother tight and buried his head into Jonathan cloak. "It's alright, Micah," Jonathan whispered as he held his younger brother. "Everything's going to be alright."

"I hope the Creator will keep him safe," Micah whispered.

"Me too, Micah," Jonathan whispered back. "Me too."

Ten minutes later, Belnor and Melony returned to the cave, both their arms loaded with sticks and dry branches. They laid these down on the floor of the cave near the entrance. Without speaking, Melony grabbed the flint and steel that Mr. Dribbles had put in her bag while Belnor set up a small pile of kindling and dry leaves from the corners of the cave. Melony knocked the steel against the flint, sending sparks flying into the air. Suddenly, the leaves began to burn at the edges and then they burst into flames.

After an hour, the fire was more coal than flame and Jonathan's stomach was growling. Micah pulled the small, cast-iron skillet from his pack and set it on a pile of hot coals that Melony had set aside with a large stick. Melony pulled some bacon from her pack and put it on the skillet. Immediately, the bacon began to sizzle and pop, and the delicious smell of cooking meat filled the cave. They set some potatoes to cook in the coals. Jonathan pulled four biscuits out from his pack and passed them out. His mouth began to water as he put the biscuit to his lips.

By the time the bacon was done cooking, they had all scarfed down their biscuits. They each got two thin slices of bacon, and those were soon gone as well. For the grief-stricken and travel-worn children, the food was heavenly. They drank long drinks from their leather canteens and took large bites from their hot potatoes, too hungry to care if they burned their tongues. But, as always, the food was gone all too soon. Though they had all been tired before the meal, the food had renewed their energy.

"What do we do now?" Melony asked.

"No idea," Jonathan replied.

"How about a song?" Belnor suggested.

"I've got one," Micah said quietly. Then he cleared his throat and began to sing. The moment Micah began to sing, Jonathan recognized the song. It was a song that his mother had sung to him and Micah many times in the dark of long winter evenings.

Oh Sir Miles, what is seen on yon' battlefield?

For I cannot see from my realm
I heard the cries of men from that field
Now I ask, what's seen on yon' battlefield?

Blood stains red on the battlefield
And the moon shines bright from above
Weapons lay scattered and helms are bent
That's what is seen on yon' battlefield

Oh Sir Miles what do you feel on yon' battlefield
When the battle is over and done?
What goes through your mind, what gnaws at your heart
When you stand on yon' battlefield?

I feel death all around, filling the air
And my heart throbs from grief
For my son has died on yon' battlefield
And forever there he'll lie

There was silence after the song ended.

"That was a very sad song," Belnor finally said as he fiddled with the coarse bandages wrapped around his hands.

"Yes, but also beautiful," Melony said.

"I'm still not tired," Micah said.

"How about another song?" Belnor suggested. "Maybe something less sad." Jonathan, however, was tired. He laid himself down on his sleeping roll and closed his eyes. Then Jonathan heard Melony begin to sing into the night with a voice like he'd never heard.

A long time ago, in the time of Atel
Jack, Rebecca, and Faith
Wandered the lands to the west, north and east

And as they traveled they saith:

Be warned oh evil that lurks in the dark
Take heed all en'mies of light
Take heart all men, all women, and child
For we will bring justice tonight

In the lands beyond mountains and ice and snow
The warriors did behold
The darkest of sorcerers dwelling inside
The darkest of dark strongholds

A mighty black dragon did surround
The sorcerer's dark stronghold
One thousand arrows to bring the beast down
At the hand of Rebecca the Bold

To the top of the tower, the heroes did climb
While the sorcerer waited with dread
Jack, Rebecca, and Faith fought with all f their strength
Until finally the sorcerer was dead

After the battle the trio did return
To the palace they called their home
King Atel did rejoice and the kingdom made noise
And sang praise to the great heroes

Seven years passed and the kingdom did thrive
In peace and prosperity
The heroes did face every foe that did race
To destroy their kingdom's beauty

One morning in Castle Galador

King Atel found Prince Jack alone
Nowhere around could the gils be found
Not a trace, not a hair, not a bone

Ten days of searching and fin'lly they found
Faith the Fearless's shield
Lying gently beneath a great oak tree
Which stood in the middle of the field

And so they say if you lift Faith's shield
In the highest of oaken boughs
Faith the Fearless and 'Becca the Bold
Will return to these lands of ours

"That was a nice song," Micah said.

"It was beautiful," said Jonathan. Melony smiled and blushed in the firelight.

"Why is it you three only know sad songs?" Belnor said in exasperation.

"How about you sing something then?" Micah suggested.

"Maybe some other time," Belnor replied. Just then a huge yawn escaped his mouth.

"I think it's about time we went to sleep," Melony suggested.

"But I'm not tired," said Micah, yawning as well.

"Come on, Micah," Jonathan said. "Get in bed." Micah did as he was told.

As Micah lay under his blankets, Jonathan heard him whisper, "I'm still not tired," followed by his soft snores. Jonathan smiled and rolled his eyes. He got up and stoked the fire. Belnor had already settled into his bedroll and was drifting off to sleep. But Melony stood at the mouth of the cave.

"I'll take first watch," Melony said.

"Watch? For what?" asked Jonathan and instantly regretted it. How could he be so stupid? They were refugees now and there would be people hunting them down. Of course they would need to keep watch. "How about I take first watch instead," Jonathan said, trying to make up for his ignorant statement.

"No, you need rest," Melony said.

"Then I'll take second watch," said Jonathan.

"Belnor already called second shift," Melony explained. "You'll be last."

"Are you sure you don't want the last shift?" Jonathan asked.

"I'm sure," Melony replied. "Besides, I can't sleep right now. I have too much on my mind."

"Like what?" Jonathan asked.

"Just some things," was Melony's only reply. "Belnor will wake you up when it's your turn."

Though he was still curious, Jonathan was too tired to question her any further or argue about the watch shifts. He went to his bedroll and got under the blankets. The warmth of the fire was at his back, his face towards the cold of the night. He closed his eyes and drifted off to sleep.

The next thing Jonathan knew, Belnor was shaking him awake for his shift. He still felt groggy but he forced himself to get up and walk to the entrance of the cave. He sat with his back against the stone wall outside of the cave. He could hear the rustling of blankets as Belnor got into his bedroll. He heard Micah's soft snores and the crickets chirping all around. The leaves rustled in the gentle breeze, and the bright moon was beginning to fall into the western horizon, making way for her sister, the sun.

Jonathan sat there for hours with no sign of danger. But just as he thought they'd make it safely through the night, he heard a sound in the distance. It sounded like the barking of hounds. Then a bone-chilling howl rose from the woods. It was the hounds from Borlo. They had tracked the four of them down. Jonathan got up and ran into the cave.

"Wake up, everybody," Jonathan whispered frantically. His three sleeping friends groggily shuffled under their blankets. "We need to go now."

"What's wrong?" Belnor asked.

"Hounds," whispered Jonathan in reply. At that, three of them shot out of bed and began to pack all of their supplies. Jonathan stomped out the remaining glowing coals of the previous night's fire and then kicked dirt over it. The cave was now only lit by the grey light of dawn struggling to penetrate the darkness of the night. After only a minute, they all stood at the entrance of the cave, ready to make a run for the mountains.

Jonathan peered into the dark woods to make sure the coast was clear. Not far off he could see the flickering flames of torches. The barking hounds were very close now, their keepers at their heels. Jonathan grabbed Micah's hand.

"Run," Jonathan whispered to the others. Then he ran off into the woods, still holding onto Micah. He could hear Belnor's and Melony's footsteps just behind them. They didn't speak, they didn't shout, they just ran. Jonathan could hear the hounds chasing after them, but he kept running. Among the shouting of the guards and the barking of the dogs, Jonathan thought he heard the sound of horses' hooves chasing after them. *If they're chasing us on horseback,* Jonathan thought, *then we have no chance on foot.* Just then, Jonathan saw a creek just ahead of them. The advice from Sir Marcus came flooding back to him. He felt a new wave of adrenaline course through him as he ran through the black water of the creek. The freezing water quickly soaked through his trousers as the water rose to his knees. But Jonathan was too focused to care.

The four of them kept running. Jonathan's lungs burned, his legs throbbed, his heart pounded. But after a little while, the sound of the hounds began to fade. The dogs were losing their scent. After another ten minutes, the dogs were too far away to hear. Though strangely, Jonathan could still hear the sound of a horse trotting behind them. Jonathan slowed to a walk and looked back. About thirty feet behind them was the white horse with black hair that he and Micah had ridden the day before. It was wet up to its knees.

"What in Iyuandil?" Jonathan muttered.

"What?" Micah said and then looked behind them. "It followed us?"

"Why?" asked Belnor. Jonathan stopped dead in his tracks and turned to face to horse.

"Shoo!" Jonathan ordered the horse. "Go home!" The horse made a snort-like sound and stopped. Jonathan and Micah turned back around and kept hiking. As soon as they started walking, Jonathan heard the sound of the horse's hooves walking. For a minute, he thought the horse was going back down the mountain. But the sound of clopping hooves continued to follow, not fade away.

"We don't need you here," Jonathan said over his shoulder. "Go home." But the horse ignored him and kept following. Jonathan heard Micah snickering next to him. Jonathan turned to his younger brother.

"Maybe it likes us," Micah suggested, trying to hide his laughter. No matter what Jonathan did, the horse kept following them. It wasn't long before Jonathan gave up and just let the horse follow them. *When it wants to go home, it will*, Jonathan thought.

Finally, the grey light of dawn began to seep over the horizon. It wasn't long before the clouds turned pink, and the sun rose from the east in its golden glory.

Jonathan remembered Mum had always said that sunrise was her favorite time of day. He suddenly felt the great distance between himself and home. He knew Mum would be worrying about them and what had happened to them. She probably thought they were with their Uncle Eli. *If only it were so*, Jonathan thought. He whispered a prayer to the Creator asking for courage. Who knew what could happen as they crossed the mountains?

They hiked all morning, the horse always behind them. No one spoke. They didn't stop for breakfast for fear the guards and their hounds would catch up to them so by the time noon arrived, they were so hungry that every few minutes someone's stomach growled loudly. When they stopped to eat and rest, the horse stopped too and began to eat a small patch of grass nearby. They drank from their leather canteens and rested under the shade of the towering wall of rock.

"I don't think that horse is going to stop following us," Belnor said after he'd eaten his second cake.

"I don't think it is either," Melony said.

"Well, we can't take care of it. You said that last night," said Jonathan.

"I know, but as long as it can find its own food from the mountain grass then I say we keep it," Melony said. "We can send it back home when we get to the higher, snowier part of the mountain."

"Great!" Micah exclaimed. "Belnor, what's the druid word for stowaway?"

"Aamarasekin," Belnor said. "Why?"

"Because that's what I'm gonna call him," said Micah decisively. "Aam... Aamaras... Aamar... Oh well, maybe I'll just call him Aamar for short."

"Call who Aamar?" Jonathan asked.

"The horse, of course," Micah said matter-of-factly. No one disagreed with the name so it was decided. The horse's name was

Aamar. Micah got up, went over to Aamar, and began stroking the horse's muzzle.

"You're a good boy, aren't you, Aamar?" said Micah gently. Jonathan rolled his eyes but couldn't help but smile. After they had finished their lunch, the four of them, five including Aamar, hiked onwards. Jonathan let Micah place a makeshift bridle on Aamar and they placed their packs on his back. Onwards they trudged into the mountains, the steady clopping of hooves never ceasing. Jonathan still didn't like having Aamar around. It was like having a fifth member of their company. But Henry was supposed to be their fifth companion, not a stowaway horse.

Chapter 19
An Underground World

I t had been three days since they had escaped from Fort
Borlo. Though it was only the beginning of the eleventh
month, winter had already fallen over the mountain range.
Snow shot down from the dark clouds hanging over them,
stinging Jonathan's face. He pulled his wet, ragged traveling cloak
closer around himself. He was glad he had put his second pair of
clothes on under his black uniform from Borlo. But the cold of
the mountain sank deep into Jonathan's bones, and the biting
wind found its way through every layer of clothing, wet or dry.

Micah, trudging just behind Jonathan, was no better off. His
black cloak was wet, though not as soaked as Jonathan's. In his
hand was the lead rope for Aamar, who had lowered his head
against the bitter winds. Belnor stood behind them, his lips blue
and his dark hair whipping in the unrelenting wind. Melony had
taken the lead once again. She had braided her long blonde hair
to keep it from whipping in the howling wind, and her hand
rested on the hilt of her sword.

Jonathan rubbed his hands together, trying to bring some
feeling back to them. He saw Melony reach into her satchel, pull
out Fraxinus's map, and stare intently at it. She looked to the
north, then the south. She looked again at the map. Again she
looked up, this time to the west and the east.

"What's wrong?" Jonathan asked Melony. He had to shout these words a second time before Melony heard him over the wind.

"I just can't figure out…" Melony trailed off.

"F– f– figure out w– what?' said Micah, his teeth chattering loudly together.

"Come on, I think it's this way," Melony said. She headed westward, into the wind.

"Think what is this way?" Micah asked Jonathan.

"Don't ask me," Jonathan replied. The four of them marched onward, Aamar trudging behind them. They climbed through the mountains all day, Jonathan's nose, toes, and fingers becoming numb and ever colder. He had never thought it was possible to be so cold.

The sun began to set, or at least the sky became slowly darker than it had been with the dark clouds. They had little food left, no fresh water, and nothing to warm themselves with. But they continued through the snow, the ice-cold winds stinging their faces. Jonathan was tired. He wanted to rest, but they couldn't. There was no place to rest. The last signs of grey in the sky faded into the black and white of the dark, snowy night. There was no sun to guide them and no moonlight to light the way. They were lost in the night.

Finally, Melony stopped. She yelled to them over the cries of the wind. But all Jonathan heard her say was, "I… oun… ca… we cou… warm." He had no idea what she meant. And he couldn't say anything for his teeth were chattering together too quickly.

Melony turned and began to walk into the side of the mountain. Then she disappeared. When Jonathan reached the spot where she had disappeared, he found a small cave entrance just big enough for someone to duck into. So that's exactly what he did. He ducked his head and slipped into the cave. All of a sudden, the wind stopped whipping around him, the snow stopped stinging his face, and the sounds of the storm became distant and muffled.

"What is this place?" Jonathan asked. Melony only shrugged. Belnor entered behind him and quickly began to inspect the cave.

"I think it's an abandoned dwarvish mining shaft," Belnor concluded. Jonathan looked back towards the entrance of the cave. Outside, Micah was stroking Aamar's nose. He was talking to the horse, but Jonathan couldn't hear what he was saying over the howling winds outside. Finally, Micah tumbled into the cave. A single tear rolled down his cheek.

"Aamar's heading home," Micah said. "He couldn't fit." Then he saw where they were. "Whoa." Belnor was walking to the back of the cave now, Jonathan just behind him. Suddenly, Belnor disappeared. He had fallen through the floor.

"Belnor!" Jonathan shouted. He came to the spot Belnor had fallen. But it was not just a hole. It was a cliff, and Belnor was hanging for his life on the edge.

"Grab my hand," Jonathan said as he extended his hand to the druid boy. Belnor let go of the cliff with one hand and reached for Jonathan's arm. Jonathan felt Belnor's bandaged hand in his own and pulled Belnor up, back on top of the cliff.

"Thanks," Belnor said.

"We should stay near the front of the cave." said Melony. "Just to be safe."

"Good idea," Jonathan said. Then he turned to see Micah crouched at the edge of the cliff looking down into it. "Don't get too close to the edge, Micah!"

"I won't," replied Micah. Jonathan walked away and searched every corner of the cave for any spare twigs that might be used to build a fire. But there was nothing. They would have to go without a fire tonight.

Suddenly, Jonathan heard Micah scream, his cries quickly growing farther away. He turned to see that Micah was nowhere in sight

"Micah!" Jonathan cried out. After a second, he heard a splash below them. Jonathan, Melony, and Belnor raced to the edge of the darkness.

"Micah!" Jonathan called. "Micah, where are you?" His own echoing voice answered back, saying, "Are you? Are you? Are you? Are you?"

"I'm alright!" Micah finally yelled from below them. "There's water at the bottom. It broke my fall."

"I told you not to go too close to the edge," Jonathan shouted.

"I wasn't that close," shouted Micah back. "Something pushed me."

"How are we going to get him up here?" Melony asked. But no one had any idea.

Suddenly, as he looked over the edge into the darkness below, Jonathan felt someone push him from behind. He fell down into the darkness.

Splash.

Jonathan was completely immersed in dark, cold water. He instinctively swam upwards towards the surface. His head broke the surface, and Jonathan gasped for air.

"What just happened?" Jonathan asked through chattering teeth as he tread water. He heard two more splashes nearby. Belnor and Melony came up soaking wet.

"Something pushed me," Belnor cried.

"Me too!" Melony said.

"Are you all alright?" Jonathan asked them.

"I'm alright," Melony said.

"I'm cold," Micah said through chattering teeth.

"Nothing broken?" asked Jonathan.

"No," Micah said.

"Who pushed us?" Belnor asked.

"Who knows," replied Jonathan.

"It's pitch black down here!" Melony said.

"Does anyone have a match?" Micah asked. "A candle stub? Anything?"

"They wouldn't do us any good; we're soaked," replied Jonathan.

"*Quendel achnevenal,*" Belnor whispered. Suddenly, Jonathan saw Belnor's eyes faintly flash green. A moment later, a white light began to emanate from Belnor's hand. A small, white ball of magical light rested in the palm of his hand.

"Thanks, Belnor," Melony said.

"Whoa!" Micah said. "Can I try?"

"Sure," Belnor replied. "But I'll warn you, it won't work. Only a few people can perform magic and even then it takes months or years of practice to master the simplest of spells."

"Let me try already," Micah said.

"Alright!" Belnor said pulling off a necklace with a white crystal. "Hold this charm in your left hand. Your other left. There you are. Now say the words 'quendel achnevenal.'"

"I don't think this is a good idea," Jonathan objected.

"*Quendel achnevenal,*" Micah said. At first, nothing happened. But after a few seconds, Jonathan saw Micah's eyes flash gold. A small ball of white light flickered into existence in Micah's right hand.

"You– you did it," Belnor stammered. "You actually did it!"

"Yeah, I did, didn't I?" Micah said grinning.

"But you've never practiced magic," Belnor exclaimed. "How could you have…"

"That's amazing," Micah murmured. Suddenly, Belnor's light went out and the sound of a splash echoed through the cavern. Micah's light also went out, plunging them back into darkness.

"Belnor?" Melony called.

"Let go of me!" Jonathan heard Belnor shout. A second later, a torch was set ablaze outside the pool of water and the cavern filled with its fiery light. Belnor was on his knees at the edge of the water. He was soaking wet from head to toe and his lips were blue. A very muscular, very hairy, and heavily scarred arm was at Belnor's neck holding him close to his captor. After his eyes adjusted to the new light, Jonathan saw it was a dwarf that held Belnor. Melony drew her shortsword and began to swim towards the edge of the pool and the dwarf, and Jonathan followed after her.

"Don't come any closer," the dwarf said in a gruff voice, "or I'll slit his throat." Jonathan saw the flash of a blade in the torchlight. But he had reached a part of the pool where he could stand with the upper half of his body above the water. He pulled his bow off his back and grabbed an arrow. He nocked it and drew back, aiming at the dwarf's arm.

"I wouldn't do that if I were you, boy," the dwarf said as he brought the knife to Belnor's neck. Jonathan saw Belnor's lips move and then his eyes quickly flash green. Suddenly, a blast of light came from Belnor's hand. The dwarf let go of the druid to cover his eyes. Belnor had just enough time to run into the water and to safety when the dwarf got to his feet, though he was still dazed. He picked up his knife and pulled a battle axe from beneath his coat. Jonathan pulled his arrow back and aimed again.

But before he could let his arrow fly, the dwarf gave out a long, high-pitched whistle. Confused, Jonathan hesitated. Only seconds later, a dozen more dwarves lit torches all around them and emerged from the darkness. They were surrounded by dwarves. Some had bows drawn while others brandished large clubs. But most held double-sided axes engraved with intricate dwarvish glyphs.

"I would lower your weapons if I were you," said a rather tall dwarf who was obviously the leader. Reluctantly, Jonathan lowered his bow and returned the arrow back to his quiver. He heard the sound of metal on leather as Melony placed her sword in her sheath.

"Now, who are you and why have you trespassed in our territory?" said the head dwarf.

"Trespassing?" Micah said very loudly. "We didn't know! We were just–" Jonathan stopped Micah by stomping on his foot rather hard. "Ow!" Micah exclaimed. Melony quickly stepped forward.

"We are merely travelers passing through the mountains," Melony said calmly.

"And where might you be travelin' from?' asked another dwarf.

"I'm doing the talking," scolded the head dwarf. "Where might you be traveling from?"

"From the eastern side of the mountain," was all Melony said.

"The eastern side, eh?" the head dwarf repeated. "You wouldn't happen to be coming from Borlo, would you?"

"Yes, we are. In fact–" Micah began, but he was again interrupted, this time by Jonathan covering his mouth with his hand.

"We have no quarrel with you," Melony said. "Let us go, and we'll be on our way."

"I'm afraid we can't do that," the head dwarf said. "You see, we kill any who trespass in our lands. I won't have any spies going back to Janus, telling him about our plans."

"We're not spies," Melony said frantically. "There has to be some way you'd let us go."

"There is none," said the head dwarf. He nodded to a group of dwarves holding bows. They drew back and aimed at the four children.

"Wait, Horgath!" said the dwarf who had taken Belnor hostage. The head dwarf held his hand up and the archers stayed their bows.

"Why do you speak out of place, Cremthol?" Horgath asked.

"I believe these children may be of use to us," said Cremthol. "The one with dark hair has magic. Perhaps he can solve our problem." Horgath silently contemplated this statement. Jonathan's heart was racing, fear and adrenaline coursing through him. He was scared to move and yet scared to stay still.

"Come out of the water," Horgath commanded.

"What do we do?" Jonathan whispered to the others. He met Melony's eyes.

"Do what he says," Melony said, wading towards the shore. Reluctantly, Jonathan followed suit. The dwarves backed away from the shore to make room for them. When they were finally out of the water, their clothes soaked and sticking to them, Horgath gestured to the children. Jonathan had just noticed that he was nearly a foot taller than Horgath when the dwarves standing behind them knocked the back of their legs, forcing them to their knees.

"Oy," Micah cried.

"Quiet," Jonathan hissed.

"Take their packs," Horgath said. Jonathan felt his pack get ripped off his back. The dwarves threw the four packs into a piled at Horgath's feet. Then the dwarf leader spoke to Belnor.

"Is it true, boy?" Horgath asked. "Are you a magic wielder?"

"I'm a druid," Belnor said.

"Good," said Horgath. "I've had enough of sorcerers. Tell me, have you ever used a spellbook?"

"A few times," Belnor said. "What of it?" Horgath nodded to the archers again. This time they all lowered their bows. Jonathan let out a long breath, realizing he had been holding it.

"Have you ever broken a curse, boy?" Horgath asked.

"If you want something of me, just tell me what it is already," Belnor said in frustration. A murmur rippled through the crowd of dwarves.

"There is a sorcerer inside the walls of the king's palace, named Janus," Horgath explained. "He's put a spell on the king and now rules through him, like a puppet master pulling a puppet's strings. We few are those still loyal to the true king and have been looking for a way to break the enchantment holding our king captive."

"But you need someone with magic to break the spell," Belnor finished for Horgath.

"Indeed," Horgath replied. "I will make a deal with you. If you can sneak into the sorcerer's chambers and break the enchantment, you and your friends may go free."

"And if I fail?" Belnor asked.

"If you fail, none of you will see the light of day again," said Horgath, glaring at Belnor.

"I will do it," Belnor said. "Just don't hurt my friends."

"I'm going with Belnor," Micah announced.

"Fine," Horgath said.

"No," Jonathan shouted.

"He has already volunteered. He is now a part of the deal," Horgath said decisively.

"Then I'm going too," Jonathan said forcefully.

"Fine," said Horgath. "But the girl stays. If you fail, I promise you, she'll never again see the light of day." Jonathan gulped. "Show them to the entrance," Horgath shouted. The dwarves began to scuffle about. Rough hands dragged the four of them to their feet and down a long, dark passageway. Jonathan had to bend over to keep his head from hitting the ceiling.

It felt like hours before they finally reached a dead end. Jonathan was very confused. Wasn't there supposed to be an entrance of some sort? One of the shorter dwarves stepped past Jonathan, his grey beard dragging along the ground. From his pocket he pulled a large key. He moved his hand across the rock. When he stopped, he inserted the key into a small hole in the tunnel's wall.

Slowly, the rocky dead end swung inwards and open. Beyond the door was the passageway of a luxurious palace.

"There you are," Horgath said.

"How are we supposed to find the sorcerer's room?" Belnor asked.

"I almost forgot," Horgath said and began digging through his pockets. When he pulled out his hand, in his palm was a pinkish crystal the size of a pumpkin seed.

"What is that?" Micah asked.

"This, my boy, is an enchanted crystal," Horgath stated. "It will become brighter as you near the sorcerer's spellbook." Then he handed the crystal to Belnor and pushed the boys into the passageway. "If you come back, and I say *if*, just knock on this wall seven times." The door to the tunnel began to close slowly, beginning to cut them off from the caves.

"Good luck," Melony murmured as the door was inches from shutting. Then it shut. It looked as if there had never been a door there in the first place. Jonathan looked at Belnor. His face was pale, but stoic. Jonathan watched as the crystal in Belnor's hand began to glow ever so faintly.

"I think we should try that way," Micah said in a whisper, pointing down the corridor to their left. Jonathan nodded in reply and took the lead. They went down one hall and up another, three rights, two lefts, up some stairs and found themselves in an enormous hall.

Tapestries lined the stone walls that rose so high that the ceiling was barely visible. Torches filled the hall with red flickering light as the howling wind from the storm tried in vain to squeeze its way through the thick stone walls.

Despite the hall's beauty, there was one danger: everything echoed. Jonathan was used to moving silently through the woods when he hunted, but sneaking around in the dwarf palace was much different. Every sound echoed for at least a minute, even the slightest drop of a pin. Jonathan began to walk on his tiptoes in order to keep the entire palace from echoing their presence. Belnor and Micah were behind Jonathan, trying to keep quiet, but it seemed quite impossible for them to do so.

"This way," Belnor whispered. He slipped through a small doorway that was almost completely covered by a tapestry. When Jonathan slipped into the passage, he found himself facing a spiral staircase. Micah and Belnor were already climbing upwards. All the while the crystal glowed brighter and brighter.

Jonathan's legs burned by the time they finally reached a door at the very top of the staircase. The crystal glowed so bright that Jonathan had to squint to see the strange runes gracefully engraved in the door. Micah got on his knees and peered through the tiny keyhole.

"Nobody's in there," Micah whispered. He tried the handle. "It's locked."

"I can unlock it," Belnor said.

"Well," Jonathan sighed, "let's get this over with." Micah pulled himself up from the floor and made room for Belnor. The druid grabbed the black, moon-shaped onyx charm from around his neck in his hand.

"*Teltalima*," Belnor whispered. His eyes flashed green. Then the lock in the door clicked. Belnor took hold of the handle and pushed the door open.

The room behind the door was rather large and circular. A four-poster bed sat in the left side of the room, its purple curtains tied neatly to each post with golden tassels. Directly across from them was a fireplace. There was nothing left but hot coals in the fireplace, but Jonathan could still see the heat rising off them. On the right side of the room was a desk. And on that desk was a large book decorated with gold leaf and precious gems, and a beautiful purple gem stone the size of an apple rested in the center.

"Is that it?" Jonathan whispered as he pointed out the ornate book.

"I suppose," replied Belnor. Belnor approached the book slowly. Jonathan watched him open it cautiously and flip through the pages slowly and carefully. Jonathan looked over Belnor's shoulder to catch a glimpse of the book. The book was the most magnificent book Jonathan had ever seen. Each page was covered in beautiful images and illuminated manuscripts. The pictures were so realistic that they seemed to come to life and dance on the page.

"This is it," Belnor whispered, pointing to a highly decorated page. "This incantation should break the enchantment." Belnor cleared his throat and began to read.

Auditule, obscuritoc incantatioc,
Teachn tempac venetu
Perdoc yip finioc

Solvatac catenac
Quip ligo illis animacinac
As illis nakteg anciatoc humoc

Jonathan heard the door creak behind him, but he was so fascinated by the book that he paid the sound little notice.

Tollu incantatiac
Quip caecitiac illac oculec
At sel corporic opique

Tenebrac—

Suddenly, Jonathan felt someone knock the wind out of him, throwing him to the ground. Belnor's incantation stopped.

When Jonathan finally caught his breath and came to his senses, he saw a man in flowing purple robes with a silver mustache had tackled Belnor to the ground, knife in hand.

"Where is the book?" the man screamed at Belnor.

"Who are you?" Jonathan asked throw gasping breaths.

"I am Janus," the man said. "And you will tell me where the book is."

Jonathan could see Micah hiding behind the open door of the closet. He was clutching the book tightly against his chest. Then, to Jonathan's bewilderment, Micah opened the book, found the page Belnor had been on, and began reading the incantation. What baffled Jonathan the most was that Micah had never learned to read.

Tenebrac nakteg, fuge en terseg
Illac li atpropiec tentic
E praecipic te solvac rivinic teachn

Jonathan watched the sorcerer hit Belnor over the head with the butt of his knife. Belnor's struggling body went limp. Janus got up and turned to where Micah was hiding. A rush of anger surged through Jonathan.

Portoc libertac, pos illac mortalic
Qua factic
Perptac divac aciesac

Jonathan grabbed an arrow from his quiver and quickly fired it at Janus. But instead of being struck in the back, Janus moved at an inhuman speed and turned to face the arrow. The arrow stopped three inches from the sorcerer's nose, hung in the air a moment, and then clattered to the floor. Jonathan charged at the sorcerer, his face red with fury. But Janus didn't even look dazed. He held out his hand and whispered a few words. Suddenly, Jonathan was flung to the opposite side of the room and pinned to the wall by some invisible force. All the while, Micah continued to read from the spellbook.

Succidu yip vinculu bondajac
Nit illis obsec
En wistiloc yip corpec

Jonathan couldn't move his arms. He couldn't move anything. Janus crept towards Micah, preparing to take the book. The sorcerer stepped over Belnor's seemingly unconscious body. Suddenly, Belnor grabbed Janus's ankles and pulled him to the ground.

Yip requisnac xaxi

"Let go of me, boy," Janus shouted. But Belnor wouldn't let go. The sorcerer squirmed until he got his legs loose enough to

197

kick the druid boy in the face. Belnor's nose began to ooze with blood.

Zinba carcerec tenebrac

Janus was only a few steps away from Micah. He pulled out his dagger and lifted it over his head.

"No!" Jonathan screamed.

Quip hostielac hominis, illac te syrenu

Jonathan saw Micah's eyes brightly flash gold as they had in the cave. The stone on the front of the book glowed brightly. Janus froze in his tracks. His entire body began to shake.

"What have you done?" Janus screamed in anger. Micah's eyes widened. In an instant, the sorcerer turned into black sand and fell as a heap of dust on the floor. Micah sank to his knees, trembling. Jonathan fell from the wall, his face smacking the floor as he landed on the ground. After that, everything was still.

"Did it work?" Micah asked in a whisper, still clutching the spellbook.

"I think it did," Belnor replied. Jonathan lifted himself from the floor and brushed the dust off his trousers. Belnor wiped off the blood from his nose with his sleeve. Micah got to his feet and set the sorcerer's book on the desk, his hands trembling.

"How did you do that?" Belnor asked. Micah only shrugged, his eyes with wide with disbelief.

Suddenly, Jonathan heard a rumble begin to grow steadily louder. Or was it coming nearer? Jonathan picked up his bow, which had been knocked to the ground. The rumbling now sounded distinctly like footsteps. A lot of footsteps. Whoever it was, they were coming up the stairwell. Jonathan's fingers longed to grab an arrow from his quiver, but he denied them. Then the rumbling stopped. There was utter silence for a moment. Nothing moved. Jonathan didn't dare to breathe. Someone knocked lightly on the door.

"Janus?" shouted a gruff voice. "Are you in there?" Jonathan, Micah, and Belnor looked at each other. Then there was a loud bang on the door. It sounded like they were trying to break down the door. Finally, with one final bang, the door broke from its hinges and fell to the floor with a loud crash. A dozen dwarves clad in armor and brandishing spears stormed into the room, surrounding the three boys. The leader of the group was dressed in black furs and wore a golden crown. His long grey beard went down to his knees and was adorned with gold, silver, and precious gems.

"You're not Janus," the lead dwarf exclaimed when he saw the boys on the other side. "Where is he?"

"He's been destroyed," Belnor said.

"He has?" the dwarf said in disbelief. "Who destroyed him?" the dwarf asked, his face turning red in anger.

"It was me," Belnor said

"No, it was me," Micah said in opposition.

"It was all of us," said Jonathan. "So if you're going to kill one of us, you'll have to get through me first." Jonathan realized just how stupid this sounded after he said it. They were outnumbered at least three to one and their height advantage wasn't going to help much.

"You have destroyed a man I trusted with my life," the dwarf said. Jonathan braced himself for the worst. "And now I must thank you! Janus made me trust him so he could put me under his spell. And now you have saved not only me, but my entire kingdom. Thank you, sirs, thank you!" Jonathan was utterly baffled and surprised that they hadn't already been impaled by the guards' spears.

"You're the king?" Micah exclaimed.

"Yes," said the dwarf. "I am King Nublae of Terren. And who might you three be?"

"I am Belnor Yuovech, a druid of the Tetwes clan," Belnor replied. "And my friends are Jonathan and Micah Fletcher."

"It's an honor to meet you, Your Highness," Jonathan said. "But we need your help, sire. Our friend is being held hostage by a group of dwarves hiding in the old mines. They were the ones who sent us to kill Janus. If we don't go back for her, they will kill her."

"Dwarves hiding in the old mines?" the king repeated. "Did you catch the name of any of these dwarves?"

"Their leader was named Horgath," Belnor said.

"Horgath?" King Nublae exclaimed. "My nephew?"

"Your nephew?" Micah repeated.

"Please, sire," Jonathan said. "There is an entrance in your palace where we are to meet them. We need to get there as soon as we can."

"Come. I know the entrance of which you speak," the king said. Then he turned and hurried out of the room and down the spiral stairs. King Nublae and his guards escorted them down the long hall of tapestries. Then, after several lefts and rights, they finally reached the location of the hidden door. Jonathan stepped up to the door and knocked seven times.

"Melony!" Jonathan shouted at the wall. "It's Jonathan. We did it! We stopped Janus!"

"Jonathan?" said Melony's muffled voice from the other side of the secret door. Almost instantly, the wall began to swing into itself, revealing Melony and the other dwarves. Melony ran out of the tunnel and right into Jonathan's arms before any of the dwarves could stop her.

"Sorry," Melony said, stepping away from Jonathan and blushing.

"Horgath!" King Nublae exclaimed.

"Uncle!" Horgath cried. The two dwarves ran to each other and then ran into each other, bashing their heads. Both were smiling broadly after the collision, so Jonathan assumed it had been on purpose.

"Evitor be praised!" King Nublae shouted, throwing his hands in the air. Then he turned to Jonathan, Micah, and Belnor. "Whatever you desire is yours. You have saved me and my kingdom."

"Well, I don't know about the rest of you, but I'm starving!" Micah said.

Chapter 20
A Deal with the Dwarf King

I f Jonathan had ever believed the rumors that dwarves ate worms, or moles, or rocks, he found himself terribly mistaken that evening. King Nublae sent one of his guards straight to the kitchens as soon as Micah had made his request for food. After the dwarves closed the door to the caves, the rebel dwarves, the guards, the king, and the four humans began walking cheerfully to the banquet hall. It was only a matter of minutes before the delicious scents of a feast reached Jonathan's nose. By the time the party had reached the great banquet hall and had found seats near the front of the room, cooks and kitchen servants were laying glorious dishes on the long wooden tables: roasted mutton and fish, freshly baked breads and fruits, hot soups, steaming stews, and sweet-smelling ciders. Jonathan's eyes widened in wonder. He had never seen so much food in his life.

The great fire pit that sat in the middle of the hall was set ablaze, casting giant, flickering shadows of feasting dwarves on the tapestries that lined the room. Jonathan took a sip of his cider. The warmth from the drink spread through his whole body, but he couldn't decide what sort of fruit the cider was made from. It tasted like plums and apples and corius fruits and other flavors Jonathan couldn't name. It was delicious nonetheless. After a while of feasting, Melony began to speak with King Nublae.

"How did Janus trap you in his spell?" Melony asked the king.

"That is a long story," Horgath said, sitting next to his uncle.

"I have all night," replied Melony. Horgath smiled.

"About nine years ago," Horgath began, "a sorcerer named Janus came to the royal court saying he brought counsel for the king. King Nublae happily welcomed Janus to the court. I was suspicious of the man and wasn't keen on his joining the court. But I kept my thoughts to myself.

"It wasn't a year later that the king began acting rather odd. He didn't talk very much and what he did say, he said only to Janus. Even to me, his nephew and heir, he never uttered a word.

"So one day, while he was away on his daily morning ride, I decided to search the old sorcerer's chambers and see what was really going on. So I went to his chambers and looked about. And sitting on the bed was a large book. I took the book and brought it to the castle alchemist, Vendar. And the moment Vendar saw it, he said it was a book of enchantment.

"I took the book back to Janus's bedchamber, hoping he wouldn't notice I had moved it. But before I could leave the room, Janus came in the door and was so shocked that he was at a loss for words. I ran past the sorcerer and back to my chambers.

"The next day, the king declared I was banished from Eris, our capital city, on pain of death. And by that point I had realized my uncle was now merely a puppet of the sorcerer. I and those loyal to Terren left the city and fled into the dark, uncharted mines and caves of the mountains. And there we stayed until you four came along."

"That treacherous snake," King Nublae cursed. "He got less than he deserved."

"King Nublae," Melony started, "I actually I have very important business to discuss with you."

"Oh? And what would this business be?" King Nublae asked.

"It's about Contaria," began Melony. "You see, King Alexander is a tyrant. He's destroying the people of Contaria bit by bit."

"And what do you suppose I do?" replied King Nublae. "King Alexander is nothing like his father. Or his brother for that matter. He even destroyed the trade relations between my kingdom and his. But he is the rightful heir to the throne, so I have no grounds to do anything about him."

"But King Alexander isn't the rightful heir," Jonathan said. "Princess Aralyn is."

"Princess Aralyn has been dead eleven years, just like her father," Nublae said, taking a hearty drink of his ale.

"That's not true," Jonathan said. "She's sitting right next to you." The king choked on his ale. Then he began to laugh, his large stomach shaking like pudding.

"That's a good one, boy," King Nublae said. "I almost believed you."

"It's true, Your Majesty," Melony assured him. She pulled out her medallion and placed it on the table next to the king. Slowly, the king picked up the medallion and eyed it carefully. Then he smiled.

"So its true," the king said. "You really are the princess."

"Uncle, you can't really believe she's the princess from a medallion," Horgath said. "She could have stolen it."

"On the contrary, nephew," King Nublae said, leaning over so Horgath could see the medallion. "It's dwarvish gold."

"I see," Horgath said in surprise.

"I don't," Micah said.

"Dwarvish goldsmithery is very special," said King Nublae. "It's enchanted so that only the person who was given the piece of jewelry can keep it in pristine condition. If it is stolen or lost, then it will tarnish. And only returning it to the owner will restore the piece to its original glory."

"It helps keep track of stolen heirlooms," Horgath added.

"But this medallion is in perfect condition," the king said. "And I know for a fact it belongs to Princess Aralyn."

"How do you know?" Horgath asked.

"Because I made it myself," the king said, handing it back to Melony. Melony fastened the chain around her neck and tucked the medallion into the front of her dress again. "So what is it you want, Your Highness?"

"I want to save my kingdom from Alexander's tyranny," she said, "and take my place as rightful Queen of Contaria."

"That's big talk from someone so small," Horgath said.

"How do you plan to do that?" King Nublae asked Melony.

"I…" Melony said. "I suppose… I guess… Maybe…"

"You have no plan? No strategy?" Horgath scoffed. "Why are you asking for aid without any idea of what you're talking about doing?"

"I just thought–"

"The only way that you could possibly retake your throne is taking it by force," Horgath said. "By war." Jonathan choked violently on his cider.

"War?" Jonathan said. "You can't be serious."

"My nephew is right," King Nublae said.

"But Alexander's forces are enormous," replied Melony. "He has thousands of men, horses, and weapons at his disposal. Not to mention that I have no army of my own."

"That's definitely a problem for you," Horgath said. "I will enjoy watching you try to solve it."

"Silence, Horgath," the king said. "You will not be rude to our guest."

"Yes, Uncle," Horgath muttered. The king turned to Melony.

"I think I can help," King Nublae said. "You see, the dwarves of Terren are always ready for battle. Our armories are always full, and our soldiers at the ready. If we help you battle King Alexander and get back your crown, then all I ask for is that when you are queen, you will reforge the alliance between dwarves and men and open trade between our kingdoms once again. I sense dark times are ahead and I think it would be wise for us all to create strong alliances while we can." Melony opened her mouth to speak, but Jonathan stopped her and leaned close to her ear.

"Think about what you're doing," Jonathan whispered. "Wars and battles aren't something to be taken lightly."

"I *am* thinking, Jonathan," Melony replied, also whispering. "Besides, what would you know about battles, anyway?" She turned her attention back to King Nublae. "I am willing to accept your offer."

"Excellent," King Nublae said. "I will have a scribe draft a treaty in the morning. In the meantime, you four need rest. I will have some bedrooms aired out for your use. Did you bring anything with you?"

"We *had* packs," Micah said. "But Horgath took them."

"Right. Sorry about that," Horgath said. "I'll have them brought to your rooms."

"Thank you," Melony said, smiling with gratitude. Jonathan, however, was not smiling. They finished supper with a magnificent winterberry pudding, which Jonathan would have greatly enjoyed had he not been deeply concerned about what Melony had just done. She had just agreed to go to war with her uncle. And Jonathan had a sickening feeling that it would not end well.

After everyone had finished eating, King Nublae ordered two of the servants to lead them to their rooms. A she-dwarf named Valina showed Melony to her room, on the side of the castle where the women's chambers were. As they parted, Melony smiled at Jonathan, but he didn't smile back. He still had that sick feeling in his stomach.

Jonathan, Micah, and Belnor were escorted to the other side of the palace where the men's chambers were. Leonard, the second servant, led them down dark but richly decorated hallways to a large wooden door. When he opened it, it revealed a large, royally decorated bedchamber. There was a grand fireplace with a roaring fire on one side of the room with two armchairs sitting in front of it. On the other side were three large four-poster beds, each with sheets made of fine silk and covered with furs and wool blankets. At the foot of each bed was a trunk one could use to put linens or spare clothing in. Sitting on top of the trunks were their packs. A broad but rather short wardrobe sat against the wall as well. It was full of traveling cloaks, thick fur coats, boots, and wool garments perfect for the freezing cold of the mountains.

Of the three beds, Belnor and Micah chose the ones on either side of the center bed. So Jonathan took the bed between the other two. Micah was the first to jump into bed. He hadn't even bothered to take off more than his cloak and boots before scrambling under the sheets and falling into a deep sleep. Jonathan took off his traveling cloak and peeled off each layer of clothing. Even with the roaring fire in the hearth, his skin began to tingle in the chilled air of the bedroom. Jonathan pulled a wool nightshirt out of the trunk at the foot of his bed and slipped it over his head. As soon as he had done this, he scrambled to get under the blankets of his bed. Belnor sat in one of the armchairs near the fire and merely gazed at the flames, obviously deep in thought. Not wanting to disturb him, Jonathan let Belnor be and soon fell asleep.

Jonathan stood at the top of a rock ledge. The sounds of a raging battle roared all around him. He looked down from the rock ledge into a small gorge. Below him, Melony wore full plate battle armor, her sword gripped tightly in her hand. A crimson cloak flew behind her, standing out against the pure white snow. She was fighting a soldier with her sword and shield, all her focus directed towards getting past this enemy.

Then Jonathan saw a tall knight in black armor creeping up behind Melony. The knight drew his sword and prepared to run Melony through. But she hadn't noticed him.

Jonathan tried to scream her name, but the sounds of battle drowned out the noise. Jonathan reached for an arrow, but his quiver was empty. He looked down to see his father's bow broken in his hands. What was he supposed to do? How could he save her?

He looked to his other hand and saw a sword, the kind only knights carry. He gripped it tightly and knew what he had to do.

"No!" Jonathan screamed as he raced down the gorge. He slipped between Melony and the knight, lifting his sword as the knight began to strike. The next thing he felt was a sword being pushed through his chest.

Jonathan woke up suddenly, covered in cold sweat. Micah was still sound asleep in the bed next to him. But Belnor's bed was still empty, neatly made and untouched. Then Jonathan looked to the chair near the fire where Belnor had been. But he wasn't there either. Instead, Belnor was pacing back and forth across the room, his brow furrowed.

"Belnor?" Jonathan said groggily. "What are you doing up?"

"I couldn't sleep," Belnor replied as he continued to pace.

"What are you pacing for?" Jonathan asked after a minute or two.

"I'm thinking," Belnor said. "Pacing helps me think."

"About what?" Jonathan asked. Belnor kept pacing for a few minutes without answering the question before he sat on his own bed across from Jonathan.

"Did you know about Micah?" Belnor asked Jonathan. "Did you know he had magic?" Jonathan hesitated a moment. "Jonathan?"

A memory flashed briefly before Jonathan's eyes: a baby resting in gold and white flames and sparks burning his own eyes. Then, as that memory faded, another came to light. A six-year-old Jonathan trudged through the snow from the wood pile carrying three smaller logs in his arms. Suddenly, Micah, who had just turned three, came running around the house to Jonathan.

"Jontan," Micah called to his brother. "Look! Flowers!" Micah held up three small purple wildflowers for his brother to see. Jonathan set down his small load of wood and gently took the flowers, baffled. These flowers grew abundantly around their house in the summer. But now it was the middle of winter. *So where*, young Jonathan wondered, *could these flowers have come from?*

"Where did you get these?" Jonathan asked. Micah smiled and crouched in the snow. He held out one hand and touched the snow. Jonathan saw Micah's eyes flash gold. Then, slowly at first, a small, perfect circle of snow melted where Micah's hand had been. Green grass began to spring up in the circle and two small purple flowers bloomed.

"Mum!" Jonathan called. "Micah's doing something." Mum ran out of the house, ladle still in hand, and saw Micah melting the snow.

"Micah!" Mum said sternly. She threw her ladle to the side and ran to her son scooping him up in her arms.

"Mum, how did Micah do that?" asked Jonathan in bewilderment.

"It's magic, Jonathan," Mum whispered as though she didn't want anyone to overhear them, even though they were at least a quarter mile from any other home.

"Magic?" Jonathan exclaimed.

"Magic?" Micah repeated.

"Yes," Mum said. "And it's very dangerous."

"Are you scared of magic, Mum?" Jonathan asked curiously.

"I'm scared for Micah," answered Mum.

"Why?" Jonathan asked.

"You'll understand when you're older," said Mum. "But until then, I need you to make sure Micah never does *any* magic ever again. Do you understand?"

"Yes, Mum, but–" Jonathan tried to say.

"No buts," interrupted Mum. "You have to promise me."

"I promise, Mum," Jonathan said.

"Thank you," Mum said. "Now let's go inside before we all catch cold."

"Jonathan?" Belnor repeated, snapping Jonathan back to reality. "Did you know?"

"Yes," Jonathan replied in a whisper.

"Why didn't you say anything?" Belnor asked rather loudly. Jonathan made a shushing sound.

"Because Micah didn't know," said Jonathan. "My mum made me promise to never tell him. He hasn't done any magic since he was little and he can't remember it. But thanks to you, he's at it again."

"I don't see why you're afraid of magic," Belnor said.

"Because magic is a curse," Jonathan said.

"Magic is a gift!"

"Not for Micah," Jonathan mumbled under his breath.

"What are you not telling me?" Belnor asked, standing as he did. Jonathan remained silent. "Fine. Don't tell me. But Micah knows he has magic now, and right now he's dangerous to others and himself. Without proper training he might never learn to control it."

"If you're suggesting he join the Druid Order, the answer is no," Jonathan replied, getting to his feet. He towered over Belnor by at least a head.

"You can say no all you want, but ultimately it's not your decision," said Belnor.

"You breathe a word of this to Micah, I swear I'll–"

"You'll what?" Belnor said. "Whatever you do, I'll remind you I have magic as well. Powerful magic."

"Jonathan? Belnor?" Micah said groggily. "What's going on?"

"Nothing. Go back to sleep," Jonathan said, still glaring at Belnor. Micah pulled the blankets back over his head. Jonathan and Belnor stood another minute before they finally got back into their beds. Jonathan got under his blankets and closed his eyes. However, he couldn't fall asleep. He had broken the first promise he had ever made. His promise to keep Micah away from magic. And now he wondered if he would be able to uphold the others.

Chapter 21
Confusion

"Jonathan. Jonathan. Jonathan. Jonathan," Micah repeatedly whispered at Jonathan's bedside.

"What, Micah?" asked Jonathan, still half asleep.

"It's time to wake up," Micah replied with a grin. Then he walked away and began digging through the wardrobe on the other side of the room. Jonathan looked at the bed to his left and saw Belnor was still asleep.

"You didn't wake up Belnor?" Jonathan asked Micah.

"Oh, I tried to wake him up first," Micah replied. "But he's still sound asleep." He continued to dig through the wardrobe, now occasionally throwing an article of clothing behind him.

"What in Iyuandil are you doing?" asked Jonathan.

"I'm looking for something to wear," Micah replied from inside the wardrobe. "Come on, there are plenty of warm things in here. I even think I saw some stuff that would fit you."

Jonathan pulled the blankets off himself, but the moment he did, he regretted it. The fire had died down, and the room was now chillier than it had been the night before. Micah, however, seemed to be unhindered by the cold. He hardly took notice when his bare feet pattered across the ice-cold floor.

By the time Jonathan had inched his way to the wardrobe over the cold floor, Micah was beginning to get dressed. He pulled on a reddish wool tunic and a pair of wool trousers. Around his waist he fastened a belt with a small pouch. He pulled on a leather vest and a pair of knitted, fingerless gloves. And finally he donned a dark blue cloak that went down to just past his knees.

Jonathan dug through the wardrobe and quickly found some socks for himself. After pulling them on, he searched through the dwarf-sized clothing for something that might be suitable for him to wear. It took him a few minutes, but he finally found a tunic and a cloak that would fit him, though he couldn't find any trousers. Instead he decided to use the black pair he had gotten from Borlo. While Jonathan was getting dressed, Micah ran to Belnor's bedside.

"Come on, Belnor," Micah said, throwing a wool shirt at Belnor's head.

"I'm up," Belnor's muffled voice said groggily through the shirt. Jonathan was pulling on his boots when Belnor blundered out of bed and pulled the wool shirt on. Belnor hardly made eye contact with Jonathan all morning. And when he did, there was a look in his eye that made Jonathan wonder if it was anger or concern or both. After they had all gotten dressed, they heard a knock on the door.

"Are you three ready to go?" Melony asked from the other side of the door. Jonathan opened the door and Melony stood in a red wool dress with a fur vest, thick mittens, and a wool cloak with her green cloak on top of it. She had a wool cap on top of her hastily braided hair, her pack on her back, and her sword swinging at her side.

"I thought you were going to sign a treaty before we left," Jonathan said. Perhaps he could still change her mind about the war.

"I woke up early to sign it," replied Melony. "Come on. We're heading to the stables." She turned around and headed down the hall and then took a left, disappearing from view. Belnor grabbed his pack, squeezed past Jonathan, and started heading down the hall like Melony.

"Are you two coming?" Belnor said without turning around. Micah rushed out the door as he scrambled to put his other arm into his pack's arm hole and followed Belnor around the corner. But Jonathan stood still in the doorway, watching the empty hallway, his face turning pale. There was going to be a war. And there was nothing he could do to stop it.

Lost in thoughts of the horrors ahead of them, Jonathan had to shake himself back to reality before he too slung his pack on his back and followed the others towards the stables. He walked slowly down the hall and took a left. From there, he could only follow the sound of footsteps ahead of him. It was a long while and several flights of stairs before Jonathan heard the braying of horses and the stomping of hooves.

Jonathan descended another flight of stairs and took a right to find himself at the doors of the royal stables. The concentrated scent of hay and horse manure choked him when he walked through the door. The dwarf stables were not the largest stables one could find in Iyuandil. But for a people who lived under the mountains and snow and hardly ever left their underground homes, the stables were more than sufficient. Several rows of stalls held ponies and a few traveling horses. The walls were lined with stacks of hay and barrels of water. And at the end of the stables was a wide, double door that led out to the mountainside.

"Aamar!" Micah shouted just as Jonathan walked into the stables.

"This one belongs to you?" asked the stable boy holding Aamar's reins. The young dwarf looked even smaller next to the large horses around him.

"Yes. His name is Aamar," Micah replied. Then to Aamar he said, "I thought you'd gone back to Borlo like I told you."

"We found him wandering around the mountainside," the head stable boy said, walking over to Micah. "If he's yours, you might as well take him with you."

"Thank you," Micah said. He gingerly took Aamar's reins and began stroking Aamar's nose. Jonathan watched from the doorway as the stable dwarves bustled about to find appropriately sized horses for the rest of them.

"I don't understand," Jonathan finally said loud enough for everyone to hear. "We just got here. Why are we leaving? And I thought you signed that treaty to get an army. I'm surprised you want to leave after you were so eager to start a war with your uncle." All eyes turned on Jonathan. At any other time, Jonathan would have felt embarrassed to have become the center of attention. But right now he didn't care. He was angry that Melony had signed the treaty.

"We're leaving to ask for aid from the Nimberians," Melony replied as she continued to saddle the horse she had chosen. She didn't even glance at Jonathan. Jonathan stomped over to Melony.

"This isn't going to help get revenge on your uncle, you know," Jonathan said.

"Do you want to try and talk to him then? Because that worked perfectly the last time." Melony asked sarcastically. "If you have a better plan, I'm open to suggestions."

"Listen to me," Jonathan said as calmly as he could. "You're just going to make this bloodier than it needs to be."

"What are you talking about?" Melony replied.

"The war. It's just going to get more innocent people killed," said Jonathan. "There are other ways to reclaim your throne."

"Jonathan," Melony said, now looking intently into Jonathan's eyes. "I'm not planning on starting a war. The plan is for us to go north to Nimberia to the court of King Richard. I have a letter from King Nublae explaining who I am and our treaty. If he joins the cause, our army will be larger than Alexander's. I'm going to intimidate my uncle, not fight him directly."

"Oh," Jonathan said quietly. He didn't know what else to say. If everything went as planned, there would be no war after all. But he was still angry at Melony for not telling him anything until that moment. All of a sudden, someone made a loud coughing noise behind Jonathan. When he turned around, he found one of the stable dwarves impatiently holding the reins of a large grey horse. It was so big, Jonathan was almost afraid to take the reins from the stable dwarf. Jonathan took hold of the reins and slung his pack onto the saddle, just behind the spot he was to sit.

Once all four of them had saddled their horses, fastened their packs and extra supplies to the saddles, and packed enough coal for fires to last them the mountainous journey, they climbed upon their horses. Jonathan mounted Ganathor, the grey horse, with a bit more difficulty than the others since the steed was so much taller than the other horses. Then the doors of the stables were flung open, revealing the snowy mountains. The storm from last night had passed and now the sun was rising behind the mountain. The western horizon they faced was still grey with the dawn, and the air was crisp and fresh. Jonathan looked down the side of the mountain to see the faint green earth below.

Melony was the first to head out into the cold of the mountains. She led her brown mare onto the snowy outcrop and turned to head down the narrow path. Jonathan followed closely after, with Micah and Belnor at his tail. Jonathan wasn't sure which way they were going, but Melony kept Fraxinus's map out, a new circle drawn in red ink north of the tiny illustration of mountain ranges.

Around sunset, they made camp on the cliffside of the mountain. They used the coal they had been given by the dwarves to quickly start a roaring fire. Then they roasted some slabs of lamb the dwarves had sent with them. When Jonathan had had his fill, he lay down on his sleeping mat. He wrapped himself in his blankets and cloaks to fight against the cutting wind and biting cold of the night and watched as the stars peeked out of the darkness one by one.

By that time, a bluish fog was beginning to form around the camp. But Jonathan was so tired from the journey down the mountain that he hardly felt the unearthly chill that the fog brought with it.

Four days had passed since the company had left Terren, but the fog that had formed the first night still hadn't dissipated. Jonathan thought this was curious, but he dismissed it since there was usually a good amount of fog around that time of year. Dark clouds had covered the sun, and the trees that towered around them looked dim and fuzzy in the mist as they travelled onward. With the rhythmic, monotonous clopping of horses hooves mixed with the silence of the forest, Jonathan caught himself dozing off while sitting up on Ganathor's back. That's when he heard one of the horses behind him stop.

"What's wrong?" Micah asked.

"Shhh," Belnor shushed hurriedly. Jonathan turned his horse to face the boys. Belnor sat on his horse's back, keeping completely still as he listened for something. "Do you hear that?" Jonathan strained his ear, but he didn't hear a sound.

"I hear it," Micah said.

"I don't hear anything," Melony whispered to Jonathan.

"Neither do I," he replied.

Belnor quickly dismounted from his bay mare. He slowly crept towards the fog and stretched out his hand into the mist, briefly letting his hand bathe in the fog. Then, he jerked his hand back.

"This is no fog," Belnor muttered just loud enough for Jonathan to hear.

"What is it then?" Jonathan asked, his brow furrowed in confusion.

"They're rachin," Belnor said. "A whole pack of them." He hastily backed away from the fog. "We need to get out of here." Suddenly, the fog thickened even more around the company, as though it had formed a grey wall around them. That's when Jonathan noticed figures moving in the fog. He grabbed his bow, nocked an arrow, and drew to fire.

"Don't waste your arrows, Jonathan," Belnor whispered. "They will have no effect on the rachin right now." Belnor got down on one knee and started digging through his pack. Jonathan kept his bow pointed at the mist-like spirits. Even if it was pointless, having a weapon in hand made Jonathan feel safer.

"What do they want?" Melony asked Belnor.

"They are spirits of confusion," Belnor replied as he continued to dig through his pack. "Their sole desire is to confuse travelers on their path. Make them go in the wrong direction until eventually they walk off a cliff or something. Where is that charm?" This last thing Belnor said half to himself out of frustration. But a second later, Belnor's face lit up as he pulled a small object from his pack and held it up at the fog. It was a small crystal. Then Belnor began to yell, "*Iyuan apol quitel nadu!*"

A wave of light emanated from the charm when Belnor finished the spell. The figures Jonathan had seen in the fog solidified so that he could see every feature of their faces and bodies. The spirits all looked like women, beautiful women at that, all clad in long, flowing robes of thick blue mist.

"Shoot them, Jonathan!" Belnor shouted. Jonathan let his arrow fly at the rachin directly in front of him, shooting it through the forehead. The spirit dissipated in a cloud of mist. An unbearably loud screech came from every direction, forcing them all to quickly cover their ears. Another rachin advanced on Jonathan. He quickly pulled out another arrow, and the spirit hissed at him as it rushed towards him. Jonathan shot this one too, this time right through the heart, and watched as it also dissipated in a cloud of fog.

"Jonathan, watch out!" Melony cried. When Jonathan turned, another rachin was directly behind him. Its solid form loosened and turned into a mist. The cloud charged at Jonathan, but he had no time to stop it. It forced itself up Jonathan's nose. He could feel the mist filling his lungs. He tried to cough it out, but nothing came out. He couldn't breathe. Jonathan fell to his knees, gasping for air, but it was in vain. His lungs burned, and his body began to shake. His vision became blurry.

Suddenly, Belnor raced to Jonathan's side and rested his hand on Jonathan's chest. Jonathan could barely make out a small charm in the druid's hand.

"*Arapel lilecot*," Belnor cried. Jonathan's lungs burned as the mist forced its way out of him. Then, before his eyes, the rachin glowed orange and then dissipated. Jonathan gasped for breath.

"Thank you," Jonathan whispered. Belnor nodded in reply. Jonathan grabbed his bow from the ground and looked up. But before he could draw another arrow, he saw the other rachin hesitate, glance at each other, and then fly away from the company.

"They're leaving," Melony exclaimed. Then, suddenly, the entire fog lifted.

"Whoa," Micah whispered. Jonathan looked around them and the entire forest had disappeared with the fog. Instead, a vast desert lay before them with rolling, golden sand dunes that spread endlessly in every direction. The clouds too had dissipated, and now the hot desert sun beat down on them with its piercing rays.

"Where in Iyuandil are we?" Jonathan screamed at the desert. He didn't understand. Where had the forest gone?

"This must be the desert of Sembal," Belnor said.

"We've gone south?" Melony exclaimed.

"We must have fallen too deeply under the rachin's spell to realize where we were really going," said Belnor. "And I was too slow to detect the spirits in time. I am so sorry."

"It's alright, Belnor. It's not your fault," Melony said. "We just need to go back the way we came and get out of here. We can start by heading north again."

Chapter 22
The Woman with the Golden Tooth

The desert sun slowly peeked over the eastern horizon. The chill of the night still blanketed the dunes. Meanwhile, the flames of the campfire glowed red on the sand. All four of them had already been up for hours, too cold to sleep. The horses, whose reins had been secured to metal stakes that they had hammered into the ground, were shuffling nervously in the cool morning, keeping near each other for warmth.

"We've been stuck in this desert for three days now," Micah said in exasperation as he stirred the last of the coals with one of Jonathan's arrows. They had finally used the last of their coal and hadn't found wood of any kind in all the miles of desert they had crossed.

"Are we even heading north?" Jonathan asked. "We should have gotten to the Black Mountains by now."

"Honestly, I don't really know where in Iyuandil we are," Melony admitted. The coals gave one last bright glow before they died out. Belnor gave a long sigh. Then Jonathan stood up.

"Right," he said. "It's my turn to lead. And I say we go that way." Jonathan pointed towards the western horizon.

"West? Why?" Melony said.

"In the few tales I've heard, the sea is always to the west of Sembal," Jonathan said. "If we find the sea, we can get our bearings and then… and then… well, at least we'll know where we are. Sort of."

"Wait a second," Belnor said.

"Don't tell me that you hear more rachin," Melony said.

"No. I smell smoke." Everyone watched each other for a moment, then all at once they scrambled to their feet. Jonathan grabbed his pack and the arrow they had used to stir the coals. There was no need to stomp them out now. As soon as he gathered his things, Jonathan climbed onto Ganathor and galloped up the highest dune nearby. From there, he looked out in every direction. The dim light of dawn made it hard to see his surroundings, but Jonathan, with the eyes of a hunter, still caught the wispy trails of smoke in the corner of his eye.

"This way!" Jonathan shouted in excitement. With Jonathan on his back, Ganathor trotted down the other side of the dune and across the loose sand towards the thin column of smoke. When he got to the top of the last dune, Jonathan saw a small hut in the middle of the desert. A small well stood next to the hut, and a goat, tied to the side of the house, lay sleeping. When the others had caught up to Jonathan on their steeds, they all descended the dune and approached the hut.

"Hello?" Melony shouted, slipping off her mare and cautiously nearing the house. Jonathan handed Ganathor's reins to Belnor and then loudly knocked on the front door. Only silence answered them.

"I don't think anyone's home," Micah said after a minute.

"Wait! I'm here," a voice said from inside the house. The door swung open and out came an old woman with dark skin and very curly grey hair streaked with silver. Her brown eyes gave a merry twinkle like starlight. But what caught Jonathan's eye was her front tooth, which had been replaced by a small nugget of gold.

"You are right on time," the woman said.

"You must be mistaking us for someone else," Melony said. "We just stumbled upon this place. We're lost."

"No, it was you I was waiting for," the woman replied. "I saw you coming last night."

"You saw our camp?" asked Jonathan.

"No, no, dear," she replied. "I *saw* this happening last night."

"You're a seer?" exclaimed Belnor. The woman didn't reply but gave him a warm smile.

"I should probably introduce myself," the woman said. "I am Calypso, a humble seer. Now come inside. The morning tea's getting cold."

"But our horses—" Micah said.

"They won't go anywhere," Calypso said with a wave. Then she turned around and walked back into the hut. They stood there for a second before Jonathan shrugged his shoulders and stepped into the hut. Belnor, Micah, and Melony let go of the horses' reins and followed him inside.

It was a small place, made of dried mud walls. There was an assortment of brightly colored stones and pieces of glass hanging from the ceiling. A small cot had been shoved to the edge of the room, and a wooden shelf was nailed to the wall. A table had been set with five clay cups, each filled to the brim with hot, golden tea.

"Please, take a seat," Calypso said. Jonathan sat in the seat nearest to the door, Micah and Melony on either side of him, Belnor on the other side of Micah, and Calypso sitting between Melony and Belnor. They sat in silence for a long while, Calypso sipping her tea. Jonathan lifted the teacup in front of him and breathed in the herby aroma. It smelled a lot like the tea Belnor had made for them once. Jonathan moved his lips to the cup and

223

cautiously took a sip of the steaming tea. The moment the tea entered Jonathan's mouth, he had to keep himself from gagging. It was much worse than Belnor's tea. When he looked at the others, Melony and Micah were also trying to hide their disgust. Belnor, on the other hand, was gulping down the tea like it was cold apple cider. A minute later, he was on his third cup of tea.

"Now, we haven't much time, and there are many things I must tell you," Calypso said. She took another sip of tea. "First, one of you is going to die."

"How dare you," Melony said, her stool clattering to the ground as she stood and gripped the handle of her sword.

"There is no need for you to go for your weapons," Calypso said. "I am not going to harm you."

"What did you mean then?" Jonathan asked defensively, fingering his bow under the table.

"I have foreseen it," Calypso said. She turned to Melony. "I'm afraid that your quest to Nimberia is doomed to fail."

"What?" Melony exclaimed. "But I must go to Nimberia."

"You will not find what you seek there," Calypso said solemnly. "And if you do go, one of you will die."

"Is that a threat?" Melony asked.

"No," said Calypso. "It is a warning." She stared directly at Jonathan. Everyone was silent. Then her gaze shifted to Belnor. They stared at one another for a minute until finally Belnor broke his gaze away from her, his eyes wide and his face pale. Then Calypso continued to speak to them.

"But do not lose hope," Calypso finally said. "The Creator has found favor in you four. He will guide you on your journeys."

"What about the war?" Micah said.

"Yes, the battle is coming fast," said Calypso. "If I were you, I would start preparing yourselves."

"Prepare how?" Jonathan asked.

"However you see fit," replied Calypso gravely. Jonathan gave Melony a fearful glance, but she returned it with one of confidence and determination.

"Then where do we go now?" Jonathan asked.

"I would suggest your travel directly west for two days or so," replied Calypso. "You'll soon reach the port of Talar. I expect you will find an old friend there." Then, before Jonathan could ask any more questions, Calypso changed the subject. "And now I have something for each of you." She stood up and took a small, wooden box off the highest shelf. Then she sat back down and carefully opened the box.

"Melony," Calypso said. Melony looked surprised. None of them had told Calypso their names and yet she said it as though they had known each other for years. "I give you this amulet. A tree to remind you that you will never be alone. True family is never dead." Melony took the amulet carefully and slipped it into her satchel.

"Belnor, I give you this amulet of a sacred eye. No matter where you go, you can have courage, for the Creator will always be watching you." Belnor took the amulet with shaking hands and slipped it on an extra leather cord and added it to the other charms in his collection.

"Micah, you fear monsters," Calypso said. "I give you this amulet of a dragon. You may fear monsters now, but soon monsters will fear you." Micah grabbed the amulet nervously and held it in his fist.

"And finally, Jonathan," Calypso said. She hobbled over to the corner and put her hand underneath the small cot in the corner. From under it, she pulled out a sheathed shortsword and set it on the table in front of Jonathan. "This is the second time you have been gifted a sword," Calypso said. "Only once more shall you be given a sword before the coming day."

"What day?" Jonathan asked. Calypso was silent. But a moment later, Jonathan heard her voice ringing in his head, though the seer's lips were not moving.

"You have a gift, Jonathan Fletcher," her voice said in his mind. "A gift that is both a blessing and a curse. And I will tell you this. Your vision will come true." Jonathan thought his heart stopped for a moment. Just a moment.

"My– my vision. My dream?" Jonathan said in his mind. "Is that the day you were talking about? The day that's in my dream?" Calypso nodded gravely. They all sat in silence for another minute before Calypso stood up suddenly.

"I think it's time you four get going," Calypso said. "You have a long journey ahead of you and there isn't any time to waste."

"But we need supplies. Water. Something," Jonathan said, grabbing the sword as Calypso rushed them from their seats and out the door.

"Oh you don't need supplies from me," Calypso said with a warm smile and a chuckle. "You keep going west and you'll come to an oasis by nightfall. And there was one more thing I was going to say. It's on the tip of my tongue," Calypso said, tapping her chin. She stood there for a moment trying to remember what she was going to say. "Oh well, it probably doesn't matter," she finally said. "Come back soon!"

Jonathan looked out to the south for a brief second and then looked back to the hut. But when he turned back around, the hut, the well, and Calypso had all disappeared without a trace.

"I don't believe it," Melony said, staring unblinking at the spot that Calypso's hut had been.

"Where do we go now?" Micah asked, the dragon amulet still clenched in his fist.

"I'm not sure," Melony said. "Belnor, what do you think? You've dealt with this kind of stuff before, right?"

"I– I don't know," Belnor said.

"I say we go west, then," said Melony. Aamar whinnied loudly to get their attention. None of the horses had left, but they all still looked confused to find that the house had suddenly disappeared. The four children climbed onto the horses and continued to watch the spot where Calypso's hut had just been, half expecting it to reappear any second.

Jonathan, however, stared blankly into space. *Your vision will come true*, Calypso's words rang in his head. *I'm going to sacrifice myself to save Melony*, Jonathan thought. Fear ran rampant through his veins, making his hands tremble slightly.

"Let's go," Melony said. She snapped her horse's reins and headed west. Jonathan hesitated another moment before following.

About an hour later, they all dismounted to give the horses a break and walked with their horses' reins in their hands. Jonathan was still dwelling on Calypso's words. But now, he was thinking of the second piece of advice she had given them. *The battle's coming fast. I would start preparing yourselves if I were you.* If Jonathan was to fight in a battle like his vision predicted, he would have to practice. Jonathan pulled the shortsword Calypso had given him out of its sheath.

"What are you doing?" Melony asked.

"Calypso said we needed to prepare for the battle," said Jonathan, throwing Ganathor's reins to Micah to hold. "Let's practice."

"But, we need to walk. We need to reach the oasis Calypso was talking about before nightfall, or we're not going to have enough supplies to last us the night."

"Then practice while we walk," Jonathan said. Melony sighed and kept walking. Jonathan kept his sword out. He was about to insist again when, suddenly, Melony turned around quick as a flash, threw her mare's reins to Belnor, drew her sword, and slashed her blade two inches from his face. Jonathan raised his sword just as Melony came for another swing, the clang of the clashing steel ringing across the dunes. His brief training at Borlo had not prepared him for that.

"What was that?" Jonathan shouted.

"You wanted to practice," Melony said as she moved her sword to strike Jonathan on the left. "This is how I practice." She lifted her blade again and tried to stab Jonathan through the liver. But Jonathan used his sword to push hers away. As he did this, Melony used the pommel of her shortsword to push Jonathan in the back, nearly knocking him flat on his face.

"You're not fighting back," Melony said.

"It's hard when I can barely stay on my feet," Jonathan said as he regained his balance from Melony's last blow. He lifted his sword and turned to face Melony. He raised his sword and brought it down near her ear. But Melony quickly lifted her blade to block it. Then, Melony twisted her blade around Jonathan's, and Jonathan's sword flew from his hand.

"Where did you learn to use a sword like that?" Jonathan asked as he grabbed his sword out of the sand.

"When I was nine, a giant-hunter named Ethan Blackhill came to my village," Melony said. "I was fascinated by his sword and scars, but I wasn't able to speak with him. That was until I was robbed by a couple of older boys in town. Thankfully, Ethan came to my rescue. The next day, I saw Ethan practicing with his sword. Despite the little I knew about swordplay, I could tell he was an expert. I asked him if he would teach me. And after I proved myself, he said yes."

"Is that how you became a giant-hunter?" Jonathan asked.

"Yes," Melony said. "When I was eleven, Ethan decided to go back home to his band of hunters. And I decided to go with him. So I ran away from home. Ethan's band treated me like one of their own. And I learned to fight with them." Then Melony rolled up her sleeve. On her upper arm was a brand in the shape of an eagle. "I became a giant-hunter and took on their mark," she said, pointing to the eagle brand.

"Why did you leave?" Jonathan asked. Melony rolled down her sleeve as her face fell.

"The village where my old nursemaid lived, Ravan, was attacked by giants," Melony said. "My nursemaid died in that attack. And Ethan found out who I really was. He was the one who convinced me to go home. And he came with me to ensure I got there safely."

"Wait," Micah said. "Then where was he when you stumbled on our camp?"

"We were attacked by some of Alexander's men just a few hours before I stumbled on your camp," Melony said. Jonathan could see tears welling up in her eyes. "Ethan held them off and told me to make a run for it. But as I ran, I heard the soldiers run him through."

"I'm sorry, Melony," Jonathan said. "I didn't know."

"It's alright," Melony said, giving a smile to try and hide her tears. "But now I guess you see why I thought you were soldiers in the woods that night. And why I attacked you."

"Wait a second, I thought you said I attacked you?" Jonathan said with a smirk. Melony rolled her eyes and smiled.

"Your attacks are sloppy," Melony said. "Use the flat of the blade instead of the edge. And try to keep your power in your core, not your arms. It'll give you more control." Melony took her mare's reins back from Belnor and mounted. Jonathan did the same, and Belnor and Micah followed. They continued trudging through the deadly heat for hours, but to Jonathan it felt like days. They would walk for about an hour and then ride for an hour, on and off throughout the day so the horses didn't wear out. But Jonathan thought Aamar would have carried Micah on his back all day and night, non-stop, if Micah had asked it of him.

They tried to sing songs and start up conversations to pass the time, but the heat left everyone drained and too tired to speak. And with every passing hour their throats became drier, and soon they completely ran out of water.

"Look!" Micah said in a dry voice near sunset. He pointed to the west across the sand to a greenish area. Palm trees were silhouetted against the disk of the sun as it crept slowly towards the horizon. It was the oasis.

Chapter 23

Paradise

T he oasis was a beautiful place. The trees provided long-awaited shade and shielded them from the setting sun. A small lake sat in the middle of the oasis with water so cool and sweet that one might have thought a wagonload of sugar had been dumped into the lake. And there were flowers. Oh so many flowers. Red, pink, blue, yellow, and violet, all kinds Jonathan had never seen in his life. It was wonderful. The children tied the horses to a log with some spare rope and made a camp a ways away so that the horses had space to graze and roll around. They made camp near the lakeshore and found plenty of dry firewood among the trees and lush brush to build a roaring fire.

Belnor was able to find several wild herbs and greens that were edible, but strangely they couldn't find any small animals or birds for them to hunt, nor any fish in the small lake. Not a single one. The silence was almost disturbing without the chirping of birds harmonizing with the rustling songs of the wind in the trees. So instead of hunting, they foraged for more greens and stuffed as many as they could in their packs, eating what they couldn't fit, which was quite a lot.

They wouldn't have dealt with a fire that night since they didn't need it for cooking, but they had been so cold the night before so they took the time to get a fire going. Once the sun had set and the cold of night washed over the desert, Jonathan was very glad they'd started the fire. None of them spoke much that night. They all quenched their thirst at the lake and filled their water skins to the brim. After that, they were too exhausted to move. One by one, Micah, Melony, and Belnor laid down on their bedrolls and fell into long-awaited sleep.

Jonathan decided to take first watch and sat alone in the dark, cold night. The warmth of the dying fire made him drowsier and drowsier by the minute. He tried to rub his eyes open and shake himself awake, but no matter how hard he tried, there was no getting rid of that draw towards a long, delightful, dreamless sleep.

Jonathan jerked himself awake. He must have dozed off for a second. The four horses whinnied nearby. Then, he heard a loud crunch, and the sound of a thousand mouths gnawing filled the camp. Then, only three of the horses were whinnying. One had gone dreadfully silent. Jonathan silently got to his feet and grabbed his bow and quiver. He crept away from the lakeshore and towards the horses. He weaved his way through the darkness-cloaked trees and finally saw the horses nervously stomping their hooves in the distance. But before Jonathan stepped out of the line of trees, he stopped dead in his tracks.

"What in Iyuandil are those?" he whispered, his eyes wide with terror. Surrounding the remaining three horses were hundreds of terrifying creatures. They were about a foot tall and looked like flowers, though these were not the kind of flowers one would like to go and smell in a garden. No, these flowers had two arms made of leafy stems with three thorny claws on the end of each hand. Their ten legs looked like those of a spider, long and spindly and red. Worst of all were their heads. The heads looked like large tulip buds. But each bud split in half, revealing a mouth with three rows of razor-sharp teeth. Only three horses stood tied to the log now. But where the fourth horse had once been, there was now a pile of bones and four bloody hooves.

After he had gotten over the shock of seeing such awful creatures, Jonathan slipped back to the camp. He silently ran to the closest sleeping mat, which belonged to Belnor, and vigorously shook the druid awake.

"Jonathan?" Belnor said groggily. "What's going–" but he was interrupted by Jonathan's frantic signals to be quiet. He signaled Belnor to wake Melony. Belnor nodded in reply and then headed over to Melony while Jonathan went over to Micah and shook him awake.

"Five more–" Micah began to groan rather loudly. But Jonathan quickly put his hand over his little brother's mouth and put his finger to his own lips. Belnor had already awakened Melony, and she was tying her sword to her belt.

"What's going on?" she whispered.

"Get your things," he whispered to them all. "We can't stay here any longer." Without hesitation, they all quickly stuffed their few belongings into their packs and slung them on their backs. When they were done, Jonathan gestured for them to follow him silently.

Jonathan again crept through the trees in the direction of the horses, Melony, Belnor, and Micah at his heels. Soon, he could see the clearing with the horses up ahead. He knelt behind a large tree at the edge of the woods and signaled for the others to follow his example.

The terrifying tulip-like creatures were beginning to climb up the legs of Melony's mare as they watched. The horse whinnied frantically as the gnawing sound began again, getting louder with every passing second. Jonathan held his hand over Micah's eyes and closed his own tightly. The panicked whinnies grew louder as the gnawing increased; then, suddenly, it all stopped. Jonathan cautiously opened his eyes to find that there was now a pile of horse bones where the horse had been standing. Jonathan exchanged glances with Melony, who was now green in the face and looked like she was about to be sick.

When Jonathan looked back, the creatures were beginning to surround Aamar. Jonathan looked to Micah. His little brother was beginning to tear up as he looked back up at his brother. Suddenly, Micah sprang to his feet and ran back in the direction of the camp. Jonathan dared not call after him and instead drew his shortsword from its sheath. He sensed they couldn't remain hidden for long. He heard Belnor mutter a spell under his breath. He looked to Melony as she drew her sword. She nodded to Jonathan.

Then, all at once, the three sprang out from their concealment and charged at the terrifying tulips. Jonathan began to swing at all the creatures in his reach, sending them flying behind him. But as the trio went farther, the creatures grew closer together. Jonathan felt tiny teeth sink into his ankles every few seconds, making it increasingly difficult for him to run. But he kept hacking at the terror tulips until he reached Aamar's side. The horse whinnied in slight relief, but they all knew the battle wasn't over yet.

Jonathan stayed at Aamar's side, chopping and hacking at the creatures, but he was beginning to be overwhelmed. It was as if the tiny army never ended. A minute later, Jonathan looked down and was horrified to find the tulips climbing up his shins. He kicked frantically at them with little result. Jonathan looked around to see Melony and Belnor were also being overwhelmed. Jonathan heard Belnor cry out as a tulip tried to take a large bite out of his thigh. *This is the end; we're going to die*, Jonathan thought.

Then among the trees, Jonathan noticed a faint, flickering light drawing steadily nearer. He squinted into the darkness, but he could not see where the light came from. A few seconds later,

Micah burst from the tree line. His hands were engulfed in gold and white flames, and his eyes glowed the same color.

"Get away from my brother," Micah screamed at the army of tiny terrors. Then, without hesitation, Micah extended his arms and the gold flames lashed out at the terrifying flowers. But the gold flames didn't move like ordinary flames. They snaked in between the creatures, roasting each into a crisp in less than a second and then moving onto the next. Soon, the four of them were surrounded by a wide circle of ash. The flames dissipated. For just a moment everything was still.

"Micah?" Melony said. Micah didn't answer. A moment later, he collapsed to the floor. Jonathan raced to Micah's side and gathered his little limp body in his arms.

"Micah, wake up," Jonathan shouted anxiously.

"We need to get out of here," Belnor said quickly. Jonathan looked up and saw that, just beyond the tree line, another hundred or so terror tulips were quickly drawing nearer. Jonathan quickly lifted Micah from the ground and rushed to the horses. He set Micah so he was sitting on Aamar's saddle and then climbed on behind him. Belnor and Melony climbed onto Ganathor, the only other surviving horse. Then, just as the first few tulips emerged from the treeline, Jonathan snapped the reins and Aamar bolted.

Chapter 24
The Desert Ball

The wind rushed past Jonathan's face, clouds of sand and dust rising like a storm from the trail Aamar had just blazed. Micah's limp head bobbed up and down with the movement of the horse while Jonathan tried to keep him from falling off. The oasis was now far from sight, but the quartet hurried onward. The farther they got from those terror tulips, the better. They ran until Aamar and Ganathor could run no longer. When that happened, they slipped off the two horses. Jonathan slipped the still-unconscious Micah off Aamar's back and laid him in the sand. As soon as he had dismounted, Belnor stormed over to Jonathan.

"You can't run from this anymore, Jonathan," Belnor said. He knelt by Micah and grabbed his hand. He lifted it gently for Jonathan to see. Micah's hands were burnt as badly as Belnor's had been at Borlo. His peeling skin was red, and the edges were charred black. "Do you see this? This happened because Micah hasn't learned to control his magic. And if he doesn't learn, it will only grow worse."

"No," Jonathan said. "He's not going to study magic. That's final."

"You may not have a say in the matter," Belnor replied. "You need to stay out of Micah's way."

"Is that supposed to be a threat?" Jonathan asked.

"If you want it to be," replied Belnor.

"I should never have let you come with us," Jonathan said, anger bubbling in his chest.

"You shouldn't have," Belnor replied. "Then I wouldn't have to listen to a self-centered, overbearing troll."

"That's a lot coming from a magic-worshipping twerp," Jonathan quipped back.

"You know, you're exactly like you father," Belnor shouted. "A bucket full of excuses to cover up whatever you want to do."

"I am nothing like my father," Jonathan hissed. "I'm no coward."

"Prove it!" Belnor said. Jonathan pushed Belnor in the chest. Belnor stumbled backwards as he tried to regain his balance. Then he rushed at Jonathan and pushed him back. Jonathan underestimated the force behind Belnor's push and was knocked off balance. He fell backwards into the sand. Belnor straightened himself and began to turn away. But Jonathan hurried to his feet and pushed Belnor face first into the sand. Belnor turned onto his back and kicked Jonathan in the shins. As the druid got to his feet, Jonathan kicked a shower of sand into Belnor's eyes. Enraged, Belnor came at Jonathan, teeth bared and fists raised.

"What is wrong with you two?" Micah shouted. They both stared at Micah. He was still sitting in the sand, Melony kneeling next to him. Micah glared at Jonathan with disgust and disappointment.

"Micah, I–" Jonathan started.

"Why are you two fighting?" Micah asked firmly.

"We–" Belnor started.

"We just had a disagreement," Jonathan interrupted him.

"Well, stop it," Micah scolded. Jonathan gave Belnor a cold, threatening look. Belnor returned it.

✧ ✧ ✧

Jonathan built a small fire with a few bits of firewood that they had stuffed in their packs. Then, they quietly spread their bedrolls on the sand. Belnor stayed further from the fire than the others. Jonathan did not oppose this.

"I forgot my sleeping mat," Melony said in surprise.

"You can have mine," offered Jonathan, holding out his mat to her.

"No, I can't," Melony replied. "It's not mine to take."

"I insist," Jonathan said. Melony sighed. Then she carefully took the mat out of Jonathan's hands.

"Thank you," Melony said. One by one, they all lay down on their mats and began to fall asleep. All except Jonathan. He stared up at the blanket of stars above him and tried to get himself to go to sleep. But no matter how hard he tried, he could not fall asleep. Jonathan watched the stars twinkle and shine, wide awake, the adrenaline still pumping through his veins. He listened to Micah's soft snores and Belnor's soft breaths as they drifted off into peaceful sleep. He listened to the wind howl over the dunes. Then he heard Melony sigh.

"Melony?" Jonathan whispered. "Are you still awake?"

"Yeah," Melony whispered back. "I can't sleep."

"Why not?" said Jonathan.

"I just remembered that today was my birthday," Melony said, half to herself.

"Happy birthday," Jonathan said. "How old are you?"

"Sixteen," Melony replied, a hint of disappointment in her voice.

"What's wrong? You've come of age! Shouldn't you be celebrating?"

"I guess," Melony said. "It's just that when I was little, I always dreamed I would be living in Castle Galador with my family, as a princess."

Jonathan was puzzled. "Why does being *there* on your sixteenth birthday make a difference?"

Melony sighed and began to explain, in a dreamy manner. "In the royal court of Contaria, a great ball is held in honor of a royal child on the eve of her sixteenth birthday. The greatest chefs are summoned from across the kingdom. And the most talented tailor in the land is commissioned to sew a brilliant ball gown for the princess. Then, at the ball at exactly midnight, the princess is asked by a suitor to have her first dance."

"That sounds..." Jonathan trailed off. He didn't know what to say. It sounded fancy and elegant, too much so for him. "Interesting," he finally said.

"But I suppose I'll have to wait a long time for my first dance." She looked out towards the horizon as though she was trying to imagine what her life might have been like.

"I'm sorry," Jonathan said. They were quiet for a long while, staring up at the endless, starry sky. Suddenly, an idea dawned on him.

"You know, just because you're not in a palace with fancy dresses or feasts doesn't mean you can't have your first dance," Jonathan said.

"What do you mean?" Melony asked. Jonathan stood up, rubbed the sand off his trousers, and straightened himself. He couldn't believe he was about to do this. He extended his hand out to Melony.

"May I have this dance?" he asked. A huge smile bloomed on Melony's face. She was speechless. She grabbed Jonathan's hand, and he pulled her up from her bedroll.

That night, the Princess of Contaria had her first dance with the poor boy from Silan. They danced in the desert sand for what felt like hours. Unheard music filled Jonathan's heart and made him feel like he could fly all the way to the moon and back. He just wanted time to stand still so he and Melony could remain forever in each other's arms, dancing under a star-filled sky.

"Look," Melony whispered. Jonathan looked out to the eastern horizon. The first grey light of dawn was beginning to emerge from the edge of the world. "It's going to be dawn soon. We should probably get a little sleep. What do you think?" Jonathan could only nod. He was filled with such a feeling deep inside him that he could hardly speak. But they hadn't slept enough that night, and Jonathan knew that they had a long day's journey ahead of them. They needed their rest.

"Thank you, Jonathan," Melony whispered.

"You're welcome, Your Majesty," he replied, giving her a low bow, smiling all the while. Then, Melony pecked a kiss on Jonathan's cheek. He felt himself blush. The two went to their separate bedrolls. Jonathan lay on his back looking at the stars. *I just danced with a princess*, he thought. *I just danced with Melony.*

Jonathan slept well after the dance and was undisturbed until Micah shook him awake after the sun had been in the sky for at least an hour or two. The fire had died and all that was left were the smoldering coals. There were no signs of the monsters from the oasis, which brought comfort to Jonathan. They weren't being hunted for now.

Jonathan and Melony made eye contact only a few times that morning, and every time they did, Melony blushed slightly. And every time, Jonathan's heart fluttered with happiness. He rolled up his blankets and tied them to his pack. They were going to walk most of the day. Aamar and Ganathor were still exhausted from their midnight ride so the fewer supplies and people they had to carry on their backs, the quicker their recovery. When they were ready, they all headed out. The port of Talar couldn't be that far now.

Chapter 25
The Port of Talar

I t was just after sunrise the next day when they saw it. A dark spot at the edge of the shimmering sea. A blemish in the sand. The port of Talar. Jonathan had expected that the port city would be something like Alden, but he was soon proven wrong. The only similarities between the two were that there were ships and the whole place was bustling with activity. The market was filled with fruits, spices, goods, and colors that Jonathan had never seen before. Beautiful men and women with caramel-colored skin and silky black hair filled the streets. All spoke with one another very quickly and in a language Jonathan didn't understand.

As Jonathan walked through the market, the shopkeepers yelled after him with broad smiles on their faces, holding up whatever they were selling, be it fine jewelry or fresh fish.

"So what's the plan?" Micah asked amidst all this.

"I think we should find a ship that can take us to Contaria," replied Melony.

"Oh, right! Because that worked out great the last time we used that plan," Micah said sarcastically.

"We're going to be fine," Melony replied.

"To the docks then," Jonathan said. They couldn't ask anyone for directions. But it didn't take long for Jonathan to catch the smell of the salty sea in the air and follow the breeze that blew the scent their way. "This way," Jonathan said. It only took them a few more minutes to find the road that led to the docks and, once they had found it, it was a rather short walk to the docks.

A crowd was already at the docks, some unloading ships of their cargo, others preparing a few ships to set sail. Jonathan was the first to dive into the crowd. He waded through it like a river, avoiding men with large crates and sailors with bundles of rope. But on the other side of the crowd, Jonathan saw two Contarian sailors talking to each other, paying little attention to the bustling crowd behind them. Then, as if by some miracle, Jonathan realized he actually *knew* one of the two sailors. It was Elijah Beckett. It was his uncle.

"Uncle Eli?" Jonathan exclaimed. The man looked up and combed the crowd with his eyes. Jonathan lifted his hand and waved to his uncle. However, Uncle Eli only gave him a look of confusion. Jonathan pushed his way through the crowd, Micah trying to keep up behind him. Finally, Jonathan stumbled out of the crowd and onto the dock.

"Uncle, it's me, Jonathan. Jonathan Fletcher," Jonathan explained. Upon realizing who Jonathan was, a broad smile spread across Uncle Eli's face.

"Jonathan?" Uncle Eli exclaimed. "Is that really you?"

"Yes," Jonathan said excitedly. Uncle Eli grabbed Jonathan by the shoulders, his face glowing with joy.

"How in Iyuandil did you get here?" said Uncle Eli. "And where's your mother?"

"Mum isn't here," Jonathan replied. "And how we got here is a long story."

"A very long story," said Micah.

"You've grown so much," Uncle Eli said to Jonathan. Then he turned to Micah. "But this can't be? Little Baby Micah?"

Micah nodded. "I hardly even recognize you. Why, you're almost a man!" Just then, Belnor, holding onto the reins of Ganathor and Aamar, and Melony pushed their way through the crowds and were now running towards Jonathan and Micah.

"Who's this?" Melony asked, gesturing to Uncle Eli.

"Melony, Belnor, this is my uncle, Elijah Beckett," replied Jonathan.

"You mean the one you were looking for in Alden?" Belnor asked. Micah nodded enthusiastically.

"It's an honor to meet you, Mr. Beckett," Melony said, extending her hand to shake his.

"It's Captain Beckett, actually," Uncle Eli replied, shaking Melony's hand heartily.

"Captain?" exclaimed Jonathan.

"Why, yes," Uncle Eli said. "I started out as just a sailor on the merchant vessel *Regina* about five years ago. That's her, right over there. Anyway, I became close friends with all the crew and especially the captain. About two years ago, he decided he was going to come ashore and live the rest of his days in Alden with his wife. And he made me the new captain."

"Mum always said you left to find adventure in your life," Micah said. "Did you find it?"

"A life at sea is the best adventure anyone could ever ask for," Uncle Eli said with a wink at Micah.

"Captain Beckett," Melony started, "you wouldn't happen to be sailing for Contaria anytime soon, would you?"

"Actually, I'm casting off for the Isles of Mirrum very soon. And then from there I sail to Contaria."

"Could you take us with you?" Jonathan asked earnestly.

"Of course," Uncle Eli replied.

"Ahem," said the second sailor.

"Ah yes, I almost forgot," said Uncle Eli. "This is John Carroll, my first mate. John, these are my nephews, Jonathan and Micah Fletcher."

"A pleasure to meet you," said John Carroll in a very formal manner.

"John," Uncle Eli said, "inform the crew to prepare the ship. She needs to be ready to cast off in the next half hour."

"Aye, sir," replied Mr. Carroll.

"Now, follow me, and you four can tell me how in Iyuandil you got here," Uncle Eli said.

"What should we do with our horses?" Micah asked.

"What horses?" their uncle asked.

"Wait," said Melony. "Where's Belnor?" Jonathan turned and looked around wildly for Belnor. But the druid and the two horses were nowhere in sight.

"Belnor!" Micah called.

"Where could he have gone?" Melony asked frantically.

"I don't know," Jonathan said, trying to stay calm. "But he couldn't have gotten far." He turned to his uncle. "Uncle Eli, take Melony and Micah aboard your ship. I'll look for Belnor."

"But–" Micah said.

"Go," Jonathan said. "It won't take long."

"Come on, you two," Uncle Eli said. Melony and Micah both hesitated before following Uncle Eli up the gangplank of the *Regina*. Jonathan took another sweeping look of the docks. Suddenly, Jonathan spotted a trailing green cloak in the corner of his eye.

"Belnor," Jonathan called and ran after him into the crowd of Sembalese men and women. He didn't know exactly where he was going, but Jonathan kept pushing through the crowd, saying "excuse me" every time he ran into someone even though he knew they didn't understand him.

Jonathan was just passing a small pier when he saw him. Belnor was at the end of the pier, standing with Aamar and Ganathor, his back to Jonathan.

"Belnor?" Jonathan said running down the pier. Belnor turned when Jonathan spoke. "What are you doing here?"

"Nothing," Belnor said quietly.

"Well, the ship is going to cast off soon," Jonathan said. "We need to go aboard." He turned around and began to walk back to the *Regina*, expecting Belnor to follow. But he didn't.

"Jonathan," Belnor started, "I'm not coming."

"What do you mean you're not coming?" Jonathan said, turning back around and standing next to Belnor.

"I mean I'm not coming," Belnor repeated.

"Why not?" asked Jonathan. Belnor lowered his eyes to his feet. "Is this about our fight?"

"No," Belnor said after a moment's hesitation. "I can't go because I have something I must find."

"What is it?" Jonathan asked.

"A key," Belnor replied quietly. "Calypso spoke to me in my mind when we were in her home."

"She spoke to you in your mind?" Jonathan said. "She did the same thing to me. What did she say?"

"She gave me a quest," Belnor said. "She told me that I must find a certain key or…" Belnor stopped.

"Or what?" asked Jonathan.

"I– I can't tell you," Belnor said. At that, Jonathan noticed Belnor was trembling.

"Are you alright?" Jonathan asked. They sat in silence for a minute.

"You better get back to the ship, Jonathan," Belnor said quietly. Jonathan hesitated.

"Right," he finally said. "I suppose this is goodbye." Belnor nodded in silence, but he didn't move. He continued to stare longingly into the west. Jonathan turned and walked slowly away. When he reached the place where the pier attached to the mainland, Jonathan looked back. Belnor hadn't moved an inch. Jonathan sighed. They may have had their disagreements, but leaving Belnor behind seemed wrong. But it was Belnor's choice. So reluctantly, Jonathan turned his back to the druid and headed in the direction of the *Regina*. But before he'd gotten far, he heard Belnor call out to him again.

"Jonathan," Belnor said.

"Yes?" replied Jonathan.

"Don't tell the others about the key," Belnor said. "It could put them in danger." Jonathan was confused about this.

"What danger could a key cause?" Jonathan asked. But Belnor ignored him. Jonathan watched as the druid began checking Aamar's saddle. Without another word, Jonathan left.

"Did you find him?" Micah asked earnestly as Jonathan walked up the gangplank of the *Regina*.

"Yes," Jonathan replied hesitantly.

"Well, where is he?" asked Melony.

"He's not coming," Jonathan said.

"Not coming?" Micah repeated. "But he can't just stay here."

"He said he has to find something," Jonathan said.

"What?" asked Melony. Jonathan hesitated.

"I'm not sure," he lied. "But it's his own decision to leave."

"Are we ready to cast off?" Uncle Eli asked.

"No," Micah shouted.

"Yes," Jonathan said.

"What about your druid friend?" Uncle Eli asked with concern.

"He's not coming," Jonathan said. A moment of silence washed over the four of them.

"Right, then," Uncle Eli said gravely, breaking the silence. "We'll cast off." Uncle Eli turned and nodded to Mr. Carroll.

"Lower the sails," Jonathan heard Mr. Carroll shout to the crew. But it sounded distant and far away. "Raise anchor. Pull in the gangplank." All these commands were carried out quickly by the crew and, before Jonathan could even think, two sailors removed the gangplank. The ship began to drift slowly from the dock, first a foot, then two feet, then a yard. Jonathan could see Belnor standing on the other dock, staring at the Regina, the reigns of Ganathor and Aamar in his hands. Then, Belnor turned and walked into the bustling crowd without looking back.

During the first couple of days of their voyage on the *Regina*, it felt strange not having Belnor around. His absence weighed on the remaining trio, Micah the most. Micah was quiet and downcast, sad at the loss of his friend. But Jonathan was not able to easily comfort him. On the second day of the voyage, Jonathan became violently seasick. The constant rocking of the ship back and forth and back and forth made Jonathan endlessly dizzy and his stomach churn.

But after Jonathan got over his sickness, he was able to better enjoy his time on the *Regina*. The first things Uncle Eli taught Jonathan were how to untie the sails, what the crow's nest was, and how to stay on his feet when the seas became rough. Micah liked the crow's nest so much that, at almost any time of the day, one would only have to look up to find him in the nest with Uncle Eli's telescope looking out across the waves. Melony spent most of her time reading the few books in Uncle Eli's quarters or analyzing the sea charts and trade route maps.

Jonathan preferred the bow of the ship, especially the figurehead. The figurehead of the *Regina* was a large fish holding a great trident. It had been hollowed out and one could get inside of it by going below deck and taking a set of ladder-like stairs into the back of the figurehead. There, Jonathan could sit alone and think as he looked at the vast, crystal-clear, blue sea.

The first night that he was well again, Jonathan joined Melony, Micah, Uncle Eli, and most of the crew in the galley to eat supper. Jonathan enjoyed the stew that Mr. Cliff had prepared, though he had no idea what was actually in it. But along with the stew there were stale biscuits to eat that the crew called hard tack and Jonathan called disgusting.

"There's something moving in my biscuit!" Micah shrieked.

"Those are just little bugs," said one of the crew members, who was called Billy by the crew, though his real name was William Jefferson. "They give you extra protein." At that point Micah gagged quite loudly. After that, meals were excellent as long as the three of them remembered not to eat the hard tack.

The weather at sea was unpredictable and uncontrollable. About a week into their journey, dark clouds blotted out the sun and the rainstorm made the boat rock so violently that Jonathan thought he might be seasick again. He had just retired to his cabin and was lying in bed when he heard a soft tapping on his door.

"Come in," Jonathan said, sitting up in bed. It was Micah who entered.

"Jonathan," he said, "can I talk to you?"

"What's wrong?" asked Jonathan. Micah closed the door and sat on the bed next to Jonathan. "Are you alright?"

"I'm not sure," Micah replied. He was rubbing his hands together nervously. Jonathan glimpsed his brother's palms and saw that they were black.

"What happened to your hands?" Jonathan asked.

"Nothing," Micah said as he tried to hide his hands behind his back.

"Let me see them," Jonathan demanded.

"Please don't be mad," Micah said.

"What did you do?" Jonathan asked.

"I– I–" Micah stammered. "I was trying to make a ball of light, like I did in the caves with Belnor. I remembered the words so– so I tried it. And it worked. But…" Micah pulled his hands out from behind his back and presented them to Jonathan. Micah's hands had just been starting to heal since the incident with the terror tulips. But now they were newly blistered and blackened. Jonathan gently took his little brother's hands in his own.

"Why did you do magic?" Jonathan asked Micah. But it came out harsher than he had meant it to. Micah lowered his head.

"I'm sorry, Jonathan," Micah said. "It's just, every time I've done magic in the past few weeks, it feels… right somehow. I don't know how to explain it."

"You know how dangerous it is," Jonathan said.

"Just because *you're* afraid of magic doesn't mean it's always dangerous," said Micah. "If I learn to use it, to control it, maybe this won't happen anymore."

"What are you saying?" asked Jonathan.

"Well, Belnor and I were talking a while ago," Micah said. "He said that I could learn to control my magic if I join the Druid Order. And then I could use it to help people. And I could–"

"No," Jonathan interrupted him.

"No?" Micah repeated. "But, Jonathan–"

"I said no," Jonathan said.

"Why not?" Micah asked. "If I did magic, I could–"

"No means *no*, Micah," said Jonathan. "I won't allow you to join the Order."

"I'm old enough to make my own decisions, Jonathan," Micah said.

"You're twelve," Jonathan said.

"Thirteen as of two days ago," Micah said. "But with everything that's been going on you forgot about it. You forgot about me."

"That's not true," Jonathan shouted. Micah jumped off the bed and stomped towards the door. "Magic will ruin your life, Micah. That's why I'm saying no. To protect you." With his back to Jonathan, Micah straightened himself.

"I'll keep that in mind when I make *my* decision," Micah said. Then he stomped down the ship's narrow hall to his own cabin.

Jonathan felt the fury building in his chest. Belnor had talked to Micah behind his back. Now that druid had infected his little brother with a dangerous desire. How could he have done this?

Chapter 26
The Twins of Mirrum

J onathan sat in the open mouth of the ship's figurehead and watched the shore move ever closer to the ship. They were heading directly towards Gush Harbor on the island called Tak. Three weeks had passed since they had set off from Talar, and Jonathan longed for the firmness of the earth beneath his feet.

"Jonathan," Melony called from the bottom of the ladder. Jonathan pulled his gaze away from the green shores and looked down the ladder hole. Melony stood at the bottom, looking back up.

"Yeah?" Jonathan responded.

"We're about to dock," Melony called up.

"I'll be up in a minute," Jonathan called back. He watched Melony disappear from the ladder passage. Then he shuffled out of his nook and shimmied down the ladder. He made his way down the narrow hall, up the stairs, and out onto the bright deck. The salty air, though it penetrated everything on the *Regina*, smelled especially strong on the deck. A dozen seagulls circled high above the ship, their cries piercing the monotonous sound of the waves crashing against the hull.

Gush Harbor was a crowded, noisy place. Jonathan had become familiar with the sight of ports and harbors, having been to two in the same number of months. But he was still fascinated by the bustling crowds and colorful goods. Gush was more like Alden's harbor than Talar's. Even the people looked more familiar. Crates of chickens, goats, and other livestock lined the docks, prepared to be loaded onto ships. Many ships looked much like the ones Jonathan had seen in Talar with thin sails and small hulls, all full of Sembalese sailors shouting in their foreign tongue. Others were large with many masts and white sails like the *Regina*, sailed by men shouting in Contarian. When finally the *Regina* had been secured to the docks, the crew lowered the gangplank.

"We should go ashore," Melony suggested enthusiastically.

"What about Micah?" Jonathan asked, looking up to the crow's nest. Micah was grinning, calling down to the sailors below. But he showed no signs of coming down anytime soon.

"He'll be fine," Melony said. "Besides, we won't be gone long."

"Alright," Jonathan agreed. "Let's go." Melony led the way down the gangplank. When he finally felt solid earth beneath his feet, Jonathan realized that they were the first ones off the *Regina*. Almost the second Jonathan's foot touched the shore, he heard a fanfare sound not far from the dock.

"What's that?" Melony asked.

"I don't know," replied Jonathan.

"Come on," Melony said, dragging Jonathan along in the direction of the fanfare. Once they got close, Jonathan saw that a great procession was coming nearer. Dancers and acrobats in bright colored clothes led the grand parade, flying through the air like strange birds. Behind them were half a dozen guards dressed in full armor, spears in hand and banners flying. Behind these guards was a large litter, covered in brightly dyed silks and gold and silver tassels.

Jonathan watched the litter draw nearer, longing to see what great lord or noble sat in it. But what he saw was not what he expected. When the open side of the litter passed Jonathan's view, he saw two young boys inside. They were both about nine years old, decked head to toe in identical fine clothing and jewels. After a moment, Jonathan realized that the boys were identical twins, almost indistinguishable from each other. They were playing with small toy soldiers; in fact the litter was full of them, all with miniature weapons and matching, handmade uniforms. As the litter passed, one of the twins made eye contact with Jonathan. He nudged his brother and pointed in Jonathan's direction. The second twin grinned and nodded.

"Stop!" the two shouted in unison. The entire procession stopped in its tracks, waiting for its next command.

"Bring those two forward," said one of the twins, pointing directly at Jonathan and Melony. The guards automatically began pushing through the crowd, heading straight for Jonathan and Melony. Melony tugged at Jonathan's hand, and they tried to move away from the litter. But before they could get out of the way, the guards reached the two and surrounded them.

"You heard Prince Adrian," one of the guards said, directing Jonathan to the litter. Jonathan slowly began to walk towards the litter, Melony following him. The twin princes' grins grew broader the closer the two got to the litter. When they did reach it, Jonathan stared at the twins.

"Well, are you going to bow?" said the first twin.

"Oh, um…" Jonathan stammered out and then gave a quick bow.

"Who might you be?" the second prince asked.

"I'm Jonathan," Jonathan said. "And this is Melony."

"And you two are warriors?" the first twin asked.

"Warriors?" Melony exclaimed.

"Yes, you two are warriors," said the second. "And now you shall be our champions."

"Champions for what?" Jonathan asked.

"Would you like the boy or the girl for your champion?" said the second prince, ignoring Jonathan.

"I'll have the boy," said the other. "The girl can be your champion. Shall we take them back to the palace?"

"I don't think we can do that," Jonathan said. "You see, we need to get back to our ship so we can—"

"Silence!" shouted one of the princes.

"We order you to come to the palace with us," said the first twin.

"And if you don't, we'll have you beheaded," chimed in the second.

"You can't be serious," Melony said.

"Onward!" the princes commanded the procession. The guards that surrounded them poked their spears at Jonathan's back, urging him to follow. Reluctantly, Jonathan followed behind the gilded litter.

Jonathan and Melony had to walk on foot the entire way to the palace, which was completely uphill and on the other side of the city. By the time they reached the palace, it was mid-afternoon and Jonathan was out of breath after climbing dozens of staircases. The palace was a beautiful building of white limestone. Dozens of flights of stairs lined with statues of kings and queens in royal robes led up to the front gates. The litter stopped directly in front of the palace, and the twin princes jumped out, still grinning broadly.

"Welcome, champions," said the first prince, "I am Prince Adrian."

"And I am Prince Aurelius. But of course you already knew that. And your names are Jefferson and Melody?"

"Jonathan and Melony," Melony corrected him in frustration.

"Whatever," Aurelius said.

"Follow us to our bedroom," Prince Adrian said. "There, we can begin playing." The two boys raced through the great doors that served as the main entrance of the palace. Melony rolled her eyes and followed after them, Jonathan following at her heels. They followed the princes down grand halls, around countless twists and turns, and up three flights of stairs. Jonathan finally caught up to them when they stopped in front of a door that was as tall as his house and as wide as five men standing shoulder to shoulder.

"Welcome to our bedroom, great warriors," said Prince Adrian. Or was it Aurelius? Jonathan couldn't tell the difference between the two boys. The twin that had spoken clapped his hands twice. Slowly, the grand doors swung inwards, revealing the brilliant scene inside.

The room was enormous, almost as large as the grand dining hall in Terren. Two huge beds, one for each boy, stood at the end of the room, both large enough to sleep ten people comfortably. A large bookshelf stood between the two beds, reaching into the rafters. The only way to get to the higher shelves was to use the gold ladder that stood next to it. The books were all written, illustrated, and bound by hand and most of them, Jonathan would soon find out, contained stories of quests and adventures, or facts about magical monsters and creatures of Iyuandil. And there were strange books that no one really knew what was inside because Aurelius and Adrian never let anyone open them.

Expensive toys with intricate mechanisms and delicate decorations had been strewn carelessly across the floor, some broken and others extremely disfigured. Two scale-sized stone castles stood on either side of the room, one for each boy. They used these forts to play war, a game in which they used scale-sized ballistas and guards from the hall to attack each other's fort.

"Now, we should play war in the forts," said Prince Aurelius. Or was it Adrian?

"Maybe we shouldn't," Melony suggested.

"What do you mean?" Adrian asked. "We want to play war."

"Since we're great warriors, we don't need to play games of war," Jonathan muttered.

"Of course!" Prince Adrian said. "You go on real adventures!"

"What a wonderful idea," said Prince Aurelius.

"What idea?" Jonathan said. But the twins had already whispered together and raced to the great bookshelf. "What idea?" Jonathan shouted again.

"We're going to embark on an adventure," Prince Aurelius shouted back. Aurelius jumped up onto the gold ladder, climbed about two thirds of the way up, and pulled a thick book from the shelf. He flipped through it momentarily before stopping on a page in the middle of the book.

"How about we go find some gold?" suggested Aurelius.

"No," Adrian replied. "We need something more precious than mere gold or jewels." Aurelius nodded in agreement. He threw the book to the floor and took another book from the shelf above the first. Like the first book, Aurelius flipped through this one and stopped near the middle.

"A quest to find the Fountain of Youth?" Aurelius suggested.

"We're nine, Aurelius," said Adrian. "I don't think we need to get any younger."

"True, true," said Aurelius, throwing this book down as well. "Move me to the left a little." Adrian took hold of the bottom of the ladder and pushed it to the left. Aurelius grabbed the book that had been just out of his reach before and began flipping through its pages.

"Aha!" Aurelius shouted. "I found the perfect adventure." The prince climbed down the ladder and showed to his brother what he had found in the book. Adrian grinned broadly.

"Perfect! We'll leave immediately," Adrian said.

"Leave for where?" asked Jonathan. Aurelius turned the book so Melony and Jonathan could see. It was an illustration of a horn.

"What's that?" Melony asked, confused.

"That, great warrior, is the hycreni's horn," said Aurelius.

"Sorry, but what's a hycreni?" Jonathan asked.

"A hycreni is an enormous monster that lives in the caves not far from here," Adrian explained. "Legend says that if someone saws off the hycreni's horn and hangs it above his door, he will have anything he desires for the rest of his days."

"We want it, and you two are going to help us get it," Aurelius said.

"This can't be happening," Melony muttered in frustration. "Look, we aren't going to go anywhere with you two. We have to get back to our ship, and we don't have time to go on some childish adventure." The two boys looked crestfallen.

"Well if that's how you feel," said Adrian, disappointment ringing in his voice, "we'll just have you beheaded. Guards!"

"Wait, wait, wait!" Jonathan said. "We'll go with you. But as soon as we get the horn, you have to let us be on our way, alright?"

"Alright," the boys said in unison. Aurelius ran over to his bed and pulled a long velvet rope that hung next to it. A loud bell sounded through the entire room and, Jonathan guessed, the entire palace. A moment later, a servant boy entered through the large doors.

"You called, Your Highnesses?" asked the servant solemnly.

"Yes. Please have the *Beauregard* prepared for sea. We're going on an adventure," said Prince Adrian.

"Of course, Your Highness," said the servant boy. The servant turned and left the room, the great door swinging shut behind him.

"This is going to be lots of fun," Aurelius exclaimed joyously. Jonathan exchanged a concerned look with Melony.

"We shouldn't have left the ship," she said solemnly.

Chapter 27
The Quest for the Hycreni's Horn

The vessel that the princes had sent for was a magnificent boat. Like the twins' litter, it was covered in a thin layer of gold. The prow of the ship was tall and carved in the likeness of a swan's head. It had a small covered area in the center for the princes to lounge under in the cool shade. A crew of eight men was already aboard when the four arrived.

The princes had allowed Melony and Jonathan to choose weapons from the palace armory before they left. Melony chose a two-handed longsword that had good balance and fine craftsmanship. Jonathan chose a longbow and a quiver of arrows that were fletched with peacock feathers. The princes themselves were clad in handcrafted armor of the highest quality. It shimmered in the sunlight as the princes clambered on board their boat, their armor clanging with every step they took.

"Onward!" the princes demanded in unison. All the sailors scrambled to their rowing stations and began rowing vigorously out to sea. Jonathan looked back to Gush Harbor as they pulled out to sea. There, floating gently on the water, was the *Regina*. But it was so far away that no one would be able to hear him should he try to call for help. Jonathan turned back to face the open ocean. He had no idea where they were going exactly, but, wherever it was, he wondered if there truly was some fearsome monster lurking there.

"What are we going to do?" Jonathan asked.

"I guess we're going to fight a hycreni, whatever that is," replied Melony.

"I know, but what if hycrenies don't exist?" Jonathan asked.

"What do you mean?" Melony asked

"If there's no hycreni and no hycreni horn, will the twins let us leave?" Jonathan asked. "Or will we be stuck being these spoiled princes' champions for the rest of our lives?"

"We're not going to be stuck with these boys," Melony said. "I'll make sure of that." They stood in silence for a moment, watching Gush disappear into the horizon. "I wonder what Micah and your uncle are doing right now."

"They're probably looking for us," Jonathan said.

"Honestly, they're probably worried sick," Melony said. "We shouldn't have left without telling them. I'm sorry I dragged you along."

"Don't blame yourself," Jonathan said. "I agreed to come."

"What will we tell them when we get back?" Melony asked.

"I don't know," Jonathan said. "I guess it depends on if the hycreni exists." Countless hours later, a rocky island emerged on the horizon.

"There it is!" Prince Adrian exclaimed in excitement. The two boys ran to the prow of the ship and hung off the swan's head to get a better look at the island. Not a single green thing grew on the island. The dark, gaping mouth of a large cave was directly before them, sinisterly daring the four young adventurers to enter into its endless night.

"Captain," said Prince Aurelius, "take the four of us ashore. You and the crew will remain here while we get the horn."

"Of course, Your Majesty," the captain said. The boat's crew rowed up to the mouth of the cave and no further.

"Let's go, champions," said Prince Adrian, hopping off the boat and onto the shore next to the cave. Melony and Jonathan climbed out of the boat and followed the princes, who were already entering the cave.

"Wait up," Jonathan yelled after them. If there really was a monster in that cave, he wasn't going to let the boys get eaten by it in their carelessness. Jonathan pushed into the darkness until he couldn't see his own hand in front of his face. All he could do was keep walking and listen to the twins' footsteps in front of him and Melony's footsteps behind him. He could smell an awful scent that seemed to get stronger as they moved further into the cave. After a while, Jonathan heard something crunch beneath his step. He didn't know what it was. He wasn't sure if he even wanted to know.

After a few minutes of walking, the whole cave began to slowly brighten. Before long, it was just bright enough to see it was an enormous cavern that was several stories high and filled with stalactites and stalagmites. The roof of the cave was riddled with small holes that made it seem like stars were shining down from inside the damp, dark cavern.

But the light revealed something else as well. Scattered across the floor of the cave were bones of rats, bats, small creatures, and the occasional human. Weapons and armor were among the bones, many bent in strange shapes and postures. Shields lay split clean in half and helmets had deep dents in them. Most of the bones seemed to be concentrated at the mouth of a dark corridor. That's when Jonathan heard a deafening roar, like a goat and a terrifying dragon crying out in unison.

Instinctively, Jonathan grabbed Melony's hand and the shoulder of Prince Adrian, who was standing directly in front of him. Adrian grabbed his brother and they all ran to an enormous stalagmite that the four of them could all hide behind. Jonathan, his heart racing, peeked around the stalagmite.

He watched in horror as a huge creature slowly emerged from the darkness of the corridor. The beast was like nothing Jonathan had ever seen. The monster was almost twenty feet tall and had the torso of a man, muscular and bulging with inhuman strength. Instead of legs, the creature had a long, winding, snake-like tail almost thirty feet long. But the beast's head was neither that of a man nor a snake. Instead, it was the head of a billy goat. It's unblinking eyes with rectangular pupils were fiery red. A forked tongue peeked out every few seconds, green poison dripping from the corners of its mouth. Two goat horns the size of trumpets grew on its head, each stained with blood. Just looking at the monster made Jonathan's stomach turn so violently that he thought he would be sick right then and there on the floor of the cave.

"It's real," Melony whispered in astonishment.

"Who goesssss there?" the hycreni said.

"Don't make a sound," Jonathan mouthed to Melony and the twins, all of whom nodded in reply.

"I know you're there," said the hycreni. "I can sssssmell you." Jonathan stood perfectly still. His heart raced. The sound of his own breathing rang in his ears. So he held it.

"You sssssmell of man flesssssh," the hycreni hissed. Jonathan could hear its tongue dart out of its mouth and then quickly back in like that of a snake's. "You're young though. Very young. Children really. Why would children come to fassssse me? Do they really think me that weak? Come out, children, and I will make sssssertain your deathsssss are sssssswift."

Jonathan looked at Melony. If he didn't act fast, neither of them would make it out alive. He tightened his grip on his bow. He gave one last look of reassurance to Melony, and then he walked out into the light.

"I'm here," said Jonathan. The hycreni's head snapped in his direction.

"Ah… Not asssss young asssss I thought," the hycreni said. "You are either very brave to fassssse me, or very foolisssssh."

"I'm not afraid of you," Jonathan said, trying to sound bold and brave. But he didn't feel that way.

"Not afraid?" repeated the hycreni. "Well, I sssssupossssse that will change very sssssoon." The beast lunged at Jonathan, teeth bared. Jonathan rolled out of the way just in time to avoid the blow.

"Run!" Jonathan cried to Melony and the twins. He ran up an incline that got him level with the hycreni's head and pulled an arrow from his quiver. He needed to give the other three time to get away. He began shooting the hycreni in the head, first in its ear, then on the side of its nose. But before Jonathan could draw back a third time, the hycreni grabbed Jonathan around the waist. It squeezed him tighter and tighter, making it increasingly difficult for him to breathe. He gasped for breath, but it was no use.

"Hey!" Melony shouted. She held one of the twin's small daggers in her hand, lifting it over her head. As the hycreni turned to see who had shouted, Melony threw the dagger, striking the hycreni's eye. The hycreni writhed in pain and in so doing, lost his grip on Jonathan. Jonathan fell through the hycreni's clutches towards the stone floor of the cave twenty feet below him. Instinctively, Jonathan stretched out his hand and caught a stone ledge. He held tight, not daring to look down, and then struggled to drag himself onto the ledge.

The hycreni, enraged by Melony's dagger, began to chase her to the other end of the cavern. As it turned its body, Jonathan noticed a small exposed area of flesh on the hycreni's neck. An arrow shot there could stop the hycreni once and for all. Jonathan pulled an arrow out of his quiver to fire at the beast. But then he realized something: his bow was gone. *I must have dropped it when the hycreni grabbed me*, Jonathan thought. He didn't know what to do.

The hycreni was gaining on Melony. Jonathan could see she was heading straight for a dead end. She would be trapped. Jonathan knew he had to do something. He looked down from the ledge and saw another, much thinner ledge. The Creator must have been favoring Jonathan that day, for on the ledge, to Jonathan's great surprise and relief, was his bow. Jonathan looked back up to see Melony reach the end of the cavern, the hycreni at her heels. When she reached the stone wall of the cabin, she didn't stop. Melony began climbing the rock wall of the cave, reaching a thin ledge that was eye-level with the beast. She drew her sword and brandished it at the creature.

"There isssss nowhere for you to hide now," the hycreni hissed. Just then, Jonathan saw Adrian and Aurelius sneak out of the shadows and creep up behind the monster. Jonathan dared not cry out because then the beast would turn and attack them. The boys pulled out their swords and moved to the hycreni's tail. Just as the creature was about to strike Melony, the princes thrust their swords into the monster's tail. Again, the hycreni cried out in rage and pain. It whipped around and began to chase after the boys. As it turned, Melony leapt from the ledge and onto the hycreni's back.

Jonathan couldn't take it anymore. He lay down on his stomach, one arm holding onto the ledge, the other reaching down for his bow. His fingertips barely brushed against the string of the bow. He heard the hycreni cry out with a hiss-like scream, but Jonathan didn't look up to see what had happened. He let go of the ledge with his other arm and lowered himself just a little more, trying to hold on with his legs. Finally, Jonathan barely got a finger around the bowstring. He pulled it up slowly, balancing it carefully on one finger.

"I will feasssssst on all your flesssssh," Jonathan heard the hycreni cry. Jonathan pulled up his bow in one final effort and dragged himself back onto the ledge. The hycreni and the twins were racing towards him. Melony was still riding on its back, gasping its bloody horns as she tried to stab and slash at the creature's back.

"The hide is too thick!" Melony shouted. She looked towards Jonathan. "Shoot it, Jonathan! Shoot it!" Jonathan pulled an arrow from his quiver and shot at the hycreni. But the arrows glanced harmlessly off the creature's hide.

"It's not working," Jonathan shouted to her.

"The eyes!" she cried. "Shoot it in the–" Before she could finish, the hycreni reached to his back and grabbed Melony around the waist.

"Melony!" Jonathan screamed. The twins continued to run in Jonathan's direction, the hycreni chasing behind them, tightly gripping Melony. In a split second, an idea dawned on Jonathan.

"Turn around! Go the other way!" Jonathan shouted to the twins as he frantically waved his hands, trying to signal to the boys what he was trying to say. They must have gotten the message because they suddenly stopped and turned around so that they were now running towards the beast. The hycreni reached out to grab the boys, but they were too small and too quick for it. The boys ran around the monster in opposite directions. The hycreni began to turn around. As it did, Jonathan again saw the weak spot. He pulled back, aimed at the tiny spot, and let loose the arrow. The arrow flew through the air and struck the weak spot dead center. The hycreni thrashed about, screaming his terrible goat cry. Its grip on Melony loosened, and she fell to the ground. The creature choked horrifically on its own blood and with one last terrifying cry of rage, fell to the ground and went still.

"Is it dead?" Melony called, running back from the end of the cave.

"I don't know," Jonathan said from the ledge. "Does anyone have any rope?" Adrian ran back to the boat and, a few minutes later, he returned with a bundle of thick rope. They threw it up to Jonathan, who quickly climbed down.

"It's definitely dead," Melony said, poking the monster's head with the tip of her sword.

"That was a good shot," Adrian exclaimed. "You're going to teach me how to do that."

"No, I'm not," Jonathan said firmly. Jonathan walked over to the corpse of the hycreni, grabbed its horn, and broke it off. Then he did the same to the second horn. "We got you your horn and now you are going to let us be on our way." He handed one horn to Prince Adrian.

"What about the one for me?" Prince Aurelius said, reaching for the second horn in Jonathan's hand.

"You only need one," Jonathan said. "Besides, you don't always get what you want."

"What do you mean?" asked Prince Aurelius.

"I mean, you two need to learn how to share," Jonathan said. They stared at him, confused. "Do you know what *sharing* means?" Both princes looked at him with uncertain faces. "It means you take turns using things." They were both silent. Jonathan and Melony began to walk back to the entrance of the cavern while the two boys were still staring into space, baffled. The four returned to the *Beauregard* and were silent the entire boat ride to Gush. When they reached the docks, Jonathan and Melony left the weapons they had borrowed on the ship and began walking away, heading in the direction of the *Regina*.

"Where are you two going?" Prince Aurelius asked. "You must stay and play with us."

"We got you the horn," Jonathan said. "Now we get to leave."

"But–" Prince Adrian started.

"But nothing," Melony said sternly. "You two made a deal. And if you ever want to be anything more than spoiled princes, you will keep to your word and let us go free."

"You have no authority to speak to us like that," Prince Adrian shouted. Melony marched to the boys and stopped right in front of them. Then, quiet enough for the guards not to overhear, Melony whispered to them.

"I am the Princess of Contaria," Melony said firmly. "My kingdom holds ultimate authority in these lands. And I will not remain here any longer at the demands of two spoiled children." Then she turned and marched away. The princes stared wide-eyed as Melony walked away. Jonathan followed after her. And neither prince followed after them.

"That was a good shot," Melony said as they walked back to the docks. "When you shot the hycreni, I mean."

"Thanks," Jonathan said. "You jumping on its back was amazing. Where did you learn to do that?"

"A friend taught me," Melony said.

"Another giant-hunter?" Jonathan guessed. Melony smiled as she nodded. Finally, the *Regina* came in sight.

"Jonathan! Melony! Where have you been?" Uncle Eli cried when the two of them walked up the gangplank and onto the *Regina*. "I've been worried sick."

"You sound like my mum," Jonathan said.

"What happened? You just disappeared," Uncle Eli said.

"The princes of the island passed by in a procession and made us come to the palace," Melony said.

"We also fought a hycreni," Jonathan said nonchalantly, holding up the blood-stained horn.

"Is that what I think it is?" said Mr. Carroll, coming on deck just in time to see Jonathan hold up the horn.

"It's a hycreni horn," Jonathan said. "The princes took one and we took the other."

"You know," Mr. Carroll said, "they say that hycreni horns can grant you your greatest desire."

"I'm fairly certain that's just a legend," Uncle Eli said. "But it would make a lovely hunting horn. Loud too. You would be able to hear it for miles."

"Well, I didn't just come up here to talk about old legends and wives tales," said Mr. Carroll. "I came up to say we're ready to cast off, Captain."

"Excellent," Uncle Eli said. "Weigh anchor, men!" Suddenly, Micah emerged from below deck. His face was ash white.

"Where were you?" Micah asked.

"We were taken by the island's princes," Jonathan said.

"You didn't tell me you were leaving the ship," said Micah.

"I'm sorry, Micah," Jonathan said. "I didn't think I'd be gone that long."

"But you *were* gone," Micah said, glaring at Jonathan. He opened his mouth to say something else, but nothing came out. He closed it and began to climb the ladder to crow's nest. But as he did, Jonathan noticed that bright red burns now covered Micah's lower arms.

"Micah," Jonathan called after him. But Micah ignored him and reached the crow's nest. Jonathan turned to Melony.

"Go after him," Melony said firmly. He nodded and climbed the ladder after Micah. When he finally reached the top, he stood next to Micah, who silently looked towards the horizon.

"What did you do while I was gone?" Jonathan asked.

"It doesn't matter," Micah muttered. Jonathan eyed the bright red burns along Micah's arms. They weren't as bad as the last time, but the skin was still peeling off and Micah quietly hissed in pain when the skin made contact with anything.

"You can't keep doing magic, Micah," Jonathan said. "You're hurting yourself."

"Please go," Micah muttered.

"Micah—"

"Just go," Micah said. Jonathan reluctantly turned and climbed back down the ladder. When he reached the deck, Melony was standing with her arms crossed and a stern look on her face.

"What's going on with you two?" she asked.

"It's nothing," Jonathan lied. Melony's face clearly showed she didn't buy his excuse. But Jonathan didn't elaborate. He walked past Melony and below deck.

Chapter 28

A Red Flag on the Horizon

I t was a beautiful, clear morning, perfect weather for sailing. The sails of the *Regina* were filled with wind. The sea spray was cold against Jonathan's skin as he sat on the deck in the bright sunlight, the hycreni's horn in his hand and his knife in the other. He had spent every day since they'd left the Isles of Mirrum, six in total, working on turning the blood-stained hycreni horn into a fine hunting horn. A merchant had taught him how to make a horn the autumn before. However, he had never made one of his own. Now he was determined to make it the most splendid horn west of the Anafract.

But that day, Jonathan felt that something was watching him, watching the ship. He thought this was silly. He shook the feeling and completely forgot about it for the rest of the morning. It wasn't until that afternoon when Jonathan heard a shout from above him that the feeling returned.

"Ship ho!" shouted Micah. He was sitting in the crow's nest pointing towards the northern horizon. Jonathan looked out over the open seas, not seeing anything at first. Then, he saw it. Two white sails were peeking over the horizon. Uncle Eli came from below deck, Melony right behind him.

"What do you see, Micah?" shouted the captain.

"A ship, Uncle," Micah shouted down.

"A ship?" said Uncle Eli. Jonathan ran to the cargo-net ladder and climbed halfway to the top. The ship was just coming over the horizon so that Jonathan could see the whole ship. A small, red flag began to climb up the mast of the other ship. Jonathan turned to Uncle Eli, who had a look of horror in his eyes.

"What is it, Captain?" asked one of the sailors.

"Only one ship in these seas flies that red flag," said Uncle Eli. "And that is Captain Matthews, captain of the most feared pirate ship that sails the Southern Sea." Uncle Eli ran to the helm and shouted to his men. "Open the armory! Fly the colors! Prepare to defend our ship, men!" Then to Melony he said, "You and my nephews should hide in my quarters."

"Captain Beckett," Melony started, "we will not cower below deck while a battle rages above." Melony pulled a sword from the armory. "We will fight to protect this ship. Right, Jonathan?"

"Of course," Jonathan replied.

The pirate ship sailed closer and closer towards the *Regina*. Jonathan raced to his own quarters and grabbed his longbow and arrows he'd gotten from Borlo as well as the sword Calypso had given him. As he brought them back to the deck, Jonathan passed the armory. A few swords and harpoons were left, but there was not a single bow. Jonathan sat on the deck and instinctively began checking the arrows, making sure the shafts were straight and unbroken. In the corner of his eye, Jonathan saw someone wrestling with something. He turned to see if he could help, only to find Micah struggling to lift a large, steel sword. *How is Micah supposed to fight with such a weapon?* Jonathan wondered.

Jonathan looked at the bow in his hand and then looked back up at Micah. Then he walked over to his younger brother. Micah picked up the sword as Jonathan reached his brother. But

Jonathan grabbed the hilt of the sword and gently pulled it from Micah's hands, handing it to another sailor.

"What are you doing?" Micah asked. "I want to fight!"

"Fine. You will," Jonathan said. "But I promised Mum that I wouldn't let you get hurt." Jonathan handed the bow and quiver to his younger brother. "Take these."

"But–" Micah started to protest.

"Go up to the crow's nest."

"Jonathan–"

"Don't come down for any reason."

"Jonathan! This is the last bow," Micah said. Jonathan nodded his head. He held it out for Micah to grab. "No, I can't. I'm not as good a shot as you. You need to take it."

"Micah, take the bow and get up there," Jonathan said forcefully. Micah hesitated. Then reached out slowly and took the bow and the quiver from Jonathan's hands. Jonathan grabbed his brother and hugged him tight. Micah walked to the cargo-net ladder, put the bow and quiver on his back, and climbed all the way up into the crow's nest without looking back down.

The pirate ship was getting very close. Jonathan gripped the sword that Calypso had given him and tried to build his courage. He would fight until the last breath to protect his brother. He looked up at the crow's nest and saw the silhouette of Micah against the bright blue sky. Jonathan longed to have a bow in hand and a quiver on his back rather than a heavy sword. But he was glad Micah was safe. Well, safer. Soon, the pirate ship came near enough that Jonathan could see each pirate's dirty, ugly face.

"Are you ready?" Melony asked him, swinging her sword in anticipation.

"I don't think it matters if I'm ready or not," Jonathan replied. "We have to fight either way." Melony smiled. Jonathan looked up to Uncle Eli, who stood at the helm, sword in hand, looking fierce and ready for battle.

"No matter what happens, boys," Uncle Eli said to his crew, "each and every one of you has served this ship well."

Jonathan saw one of the pirates throw something towards their ship. Suddenly, a single grappling hook grappled onto the edge of the boat with a loud *thunk*. There was complete silence on the *Regina*. A pirate swung over to the *Regina*, planting his feet firmly on the side of the boat. He did not begin to attack.

"I am Odol," said the pirate. He was tall and muscular and his entire body was covered in tattoos. "My captain offers you the chance to surrender. Give us all your goods and you may leave unharmed. Resist, and we will take it from you and burn your boat to ashes."

"We will never surrender to a bunch of thieving pirates," shouted Uncle Eli. The entire crew of the *Regina* cheered.

Odol, the pirate, made a shrill whistle. Suddenly, a rain of grappling hooks flew over the gap between the two ships. Jonathan gulped and took a deep breath. He prepared for the inevitable. He could feel adrenaline coursing through his veins as he tightened his grip around the handle of his sword. Dozens of filthy pirates swung over to the *Regina*, swords in hand. Seconds later, the clanging and clashing of steel on steel filled the air.

One pirate finally came to Jonathan and their swords locked in battle. Jonathan did his best to block every attack, trying to remember what he had learned at Borlo and from Melony. But this pirate obviously had much more experience with a sword than Jonathan. If someone didn't come to his aid soon, he would surely be overpowered.

Thwump.

The pirate screamed as an arrow shot through his leg. Jonathan spun around to see Micah in the crow's nest, waving at him.

"Did you see that?" Micah shouted to him.

"Nice shot!" Jonathan called back. But before he could say anything else, Jonathan saw two pirates were working together to carry a large barrel and were pouring lantern oil across the deck, on the banisters, and on the masts. A third pirate was going around with a torch and lighting the oil. Jonathan raced to stop them. He swung his sword at the pirate holding the torch, knocking it out of his hand. When the pirate pulled out his sword, Jonathan quickly twisted his blade around the pirate's sword. The sword flew out of the man's hand, and Jonathan hit the pirate with the hilt of his sword, knocking him to the ground.

The second pirate rushed to attack Jonathan with a sword, swinging it above his head and bringing it down with all his strength. Jonathan dodged the blow and elbowed the pirate in the ribs, knocking him to the ground. The third pirate, frightened by Jonathan's lucky victories, turned and ran.

Jonathan turned around to continue defending the ship only to see Melony hanging onto the cargo-net ladder with one hand and standing on the *Regina*'s banister. She was fighting a pirate twice her size. No surprise to Jonathan, Melony easily disarmed the pirate with a flick of her sword. But Melony hadn't noticed a second pirate sneaking up behind her, a massive club in hand.

"Melony, turn around!" Jonathan shouted, but the sound of clashing swords drowned him out. The pirate behind Melony hit her in the back of the head with the club. Jonathan saw Melony go limp. Her grip on the ladder loosened and she fell backwards into the churning sea below.

Jonathan ran to the edge of the boat. If he didn't do something soon, Melony would surely drown. He threw his sword to the ground and, without even taking off his boots, jumped off the *Regina*'s edge, diving into the water. The moment he hit the water, he felt the chill of the sea rush through him. He looked around the surface of the water for Melony. Finally, he saw her only a few yards away. She was still just above the water. But she was quickly slipping under the waves.

When Jonathan reached her, Melony had sunk under the water. Jonathan ducked into the chilly, unending waters and stretched his arms out in search of Melony. But all he felt was the emptiness of the ocean. Finally, something brushed against Jonathan's hand. He grabbed hold of it and pulled it close. It was Melony. Jonathan wrapped his arm tightly around her. With his free arm, he pulled at the water, propelling himself towards the surface. He felt Melony, limp and heavy, in his arms. He kicked as hard as he could, but his boots didn't help. Jonathan's heart was pounding, his lungs were burning, his muscles were aching and beginning to give out.

Finally, Jonathan's head broke through the water's surface. He gasped for air, filling his burning lungs with the salty sea air, which now had the strong scent of burning wood in the mix. He held tightly to Melony, still limp and lifeless.

"Melony," Jonathan cried. "Wake up, Melony." But she didn't stir. He looked up to the bright bright blue sky. "Please, Creator. Help her."

Jonathan looked directly behind himself and saw the hull of the ship. How in Iyuandil they would get to the deck Jonathan didn't know. But something in his heart seemed to lighten at the sight of the ship. Suddenly, two ropes splashed into the water only a foot from Jonathan. He quickly grabbed the ropes before they drifted too far out of reach. He took one and tied it around Melony's waist. Then he held onto the second one for dear life. Someone on deck heaved the rope, and Jonathan felt himself being pulled skywards.

Jonathan looked up, expecting to see members of the crew of the *Regina* pulling the ropes that were raising him and Melony out of the water and towards the deck of the ship. But instead, he saw dirty, ragged men he'd never seen before pulling the rope.

They were pirates, and they were pulling him aboard *their* ship. Jonathan frantically turned to look for his uncle's ship. When he found it, his stomach gave a lurch and his heart skipped a beat. Where the *Regina* should have been there was now a great, red ball of fire bobbing on the waves and slowly becoming smaller as it disappeared in the vast black sea. Jonathan averted his eyes, hoping, praying that Micah and Uncle Eli were alive.

Finally, Jonathan was heaved aboard the pirate ship. He grabbed the lifeless Melony, quickly untied her, and laid her onto the deck of the ship. He placed his ear near her chest, but he could hear no heartbeat. He quickly moved his hand just below Melony's nostrils. But he couldn't feel her breath against his fingers.

"She's not breathing," he shouted. "She's not breathing!"

Chapter 29
Captain Matthews

I *t can't be true*, Jonathan thought in panic. *She can't be—* Suddenly, Jonathan was dragged to his feet and away from Melony by a pair of rough, strong hands. His arms were jerked backwards, and his hands were tied tightly behind his back by thick, coarse cords. A pirate had taken Jonathan's place at Melony's side. Then the pirate began repeatedly pushing on Melony's chest.

"Stop!" Jonathan screamed. He tried to pull free of the large pirate's grip, but the pirate only held him back with greater strength.

"Jonathan," Micah screamed from behind him. As Jonathan struggled against the pirate's hold, he was relieved to turn and see his brother alive. Uncle Eli stood at Micah's side, his hands also tied behind his back.

The pirate pushed against Melony's chest, just where her heart was. It was a moment before Jonathan realized what the pirate was doing. He was trying to get Melony's lifeless body to start breathing again. Jonathan's anger towards the pirate was replaced by fear for Melony's life. Silence filled the ship, only broken by the waves crashing against the hull. Jonathan held his breath and tried to hold back tears. Finally, Melony began coughing up seawater.

"Melony!" Micah exclaimed. Melony coughed up more water and took in raspy breaths. Then she opened her eyes.

"You're alive!" Jonathan exclaimed.

"What happened?" she asked. She sat up slowly, using her elbows for support. Jonathan looked at the young pirate who had just saved Melony's life. He looked about twenty or so years old. He was tall and handsome, his strawberry blonde hair cut short. His clothes were ragged, though far less so than many of the other crew members.

"You just brought her back from the dead," Jonathan said.

"She just needed a little encouragement, that's all," the pirate said with a grin.

"You saved my life?" Melony asked the pirate.

"Not really. It was that young man there," he said, gesturing to Jonathan. "You'd be at the bottom of the sea by now if it weren't for him."

"Thank you, Jonathan," Melony said smiling softly at him. Jonathan smiled back at her.

"This is an outrage," yelled Uncle Eli from behind Jonathan. Jonathan turned to see his uncle red in the face and baring his teeth. "I demand to speak with the captain of this vessel immediately."

"I presume you are the captain of that ship?" said a very tall and muscular pirate, pointing to the *Regina*. The beautiful ship was just slipping under the waves and out of sight.

"Yes," Uncle Eli replied. "And you must be Captain Matthews."

"I am not the captain, sir, only first mate," the pirate said.

"Then let me speak to the captain." A murmur rippled across the boat. The young pirate who had saved Melony got to his feet and crossed the deck to Uncle Eli.

"I am the captain," said the young man. "Captain Drinian Matthews."

"This must be a joke," protested Uncle Eli. "You're only a boy."

"And captain all the same," Captain Drinian said.

"How does someone your age become captain of a pirate ship?" asked Melony.

"Time for that later," Captain Drinian said. "If you'd like, you and the captain are welcome to join me in my quarters. There, we can discuss ransom prices in private."

"Ransom? Why would *we* be worth anything?" Melony asked.

"Ladies are never aboard merchant vessels without being of some value," Captain Drinian said. "I also have some blankets and drinks in there that might help warm you up."

"We won't go without my nephews," said Uncle Eli.

"Very well," said the captain. "Which ones are they?"

"The one you just pulled from the water and this one," Uncle Eli said as he gestured to Micah with his shoulder.

"Untie them, mates," Captain Drinian called to his crew lightheartedly. He began heading for the stern of the ship. The pirates let go of Uncle Eli, who followed Captain Drinian. As soon as their bonds had been cut, Micah and Jonathan also followed. Jonathan helped Melony to her feet. She was still weak, dripping wet, and shaking with cold. Jonathan shuddered to think what might have happened had he not seen her fall overboard. Suddenly, Melony's face turned ash white.

"What's wrong," Jonathan asked.

"It's gone," she whispered, her hand feeling around her neck. "My medallion's gone."

"What?" Jonathan whispered in shock.

"I must have lost it when I fell overboard," she said. Tears glistened in the corner of her eyes. "That was the last thing I had from my old life."

"I'm sorry, Melony," Jonathan said. "But there's nothing we can do."

"I know," she said, trying to hide the single tear gliding down her cheek. Then she let Jonathan lead her to Captain Drinian's quarters.

The captain's quarters were not at all what Jonathan expected. He expected a large cabin with treasure chests filling every corner, and a large bed with silk sheets and wool blankets with lace like he had heard from the tales of travelers. But instead, it was a rather small room. The bed was a cramped bunk built into the wall of the ship. A small desk sat in the corner, and maps covered the walls. With five people in the room, it was hard to move around. Jonathan helped Melony to the bed, bumping into both Micah and Uncle Eli on the way.

"Now, to business," Captain Drinian said with a grin. "Now you, Captain– what did you say your name was?"

"Beckett. Elijah Beckett," Uncle Eli said.

"Beckett, you say," repeated Drinian. "I don't think I've heard your name before. But by the looks of you and your ship, I'd say you're worth something. How about two hundred maltra?"

"No one's going to pay that," Uncle Eli said in disbelief.

"Well then," Captain Drinian said. "We'll figure something else out, won't we?" Then he turned to Melony. "As for you, young lady, what might your title be?"

"I don't have a title," Melony said.

"I find that hard to believe," Drinian said.

"Well, if I did have a title, I wouldn't announce it to a pirate holding me hostage."

"You have a lot of spirit for someone who almost died ten minutes ago," the captain said with a smirk.

"It wasn't the first time I've faced death," Melony muttered.

"I'm sure it wasn't," Drinian said. "Now, what's your name?" Jonathan watched as Melony's electric blue eyes watched the captain closely. He recognized that look. It was as if she was trying to look into the pirate's soul.

"How did you become a pirate?" Melony asked.

"Why should I tell you that?" Drinian asked slyly.

"Tell me how you became a pirate," Melony said, "then I will tell you my name and title. What do think of that?"

"Alright," agreed Captain Drinian. Then he began to tell his tale. "I've been a pirate for ten years now, ever since I was about ten. My father was the first Captain Matthews and the most feared pirate of the Southern Sea. I became a pirate because of him, and when he died, I became his successor."

"Why did your father become a pirate?" Micah asked.

"He was the admiral of the entire Contarian fleet before the death of King Darius," Drinian said. "He was a close friend to the king and had saved the king's life many times."

"Your father was a friend of the king?" Melony interrupted.

"Yes. Not only that but he knew who killed King Darius ten years ago. You see, after King Darius was murdered, my father soon realized that Prince Alexander had been the killer. He knew Alexander had always been secretly jealous of Darius. When my father tried to confront Alexander, the prince had him banished.

"My father's fleets had always been loyal to him, and many wanted to follow him to the open ocean. My father sent them back, telling them to watch Alexander and to wait for the princess, Darius's daughter, to return."

"Your father believed that the princess was still alive?" Melony interrupted.

"He didn't believe that the princess was alive. He *knew* that she was alive. You see, my father knew of Alexander's plot to kill the king. And he knew who the assassin was."

"And who was it?" Jonathan mumbled, half sarcastically.

"His name was Acillion Fletcher," Captain Drinian said. Jonathan had a sinking feeling in his stomach. He had almost hoped he had been wrong and that the nightmare of his father being an assassin was all a dream. But this only confirmed it.

"My father had hoped that he'd be able warn the king in time," Drinian continued. "But he couldn't. Fletcher got to the king before my father could."

"But surely the assassin killed the princess too?" Melony asked, pretending she didn't know what he was talking about.

"No. My father saw her that night. He saw the young princess and her nursemaid crossing the palace grounds in the dead of night. He followed them to the court physician's chambers. They never came back out. Just a few minutes later, he got word that the assassin had been arrested."

"But people can't just disappear into thin air," Jonathan commented.

"No. But later, my father went back and searched the physician's chambers. He discovered a secret trapdoor that concealed a secret passageway. It let out on the other side of the castle walls."

"Interesting," Melony said, still playing along.

"That's not all," Captain Drinian continued. "Rumors have begun to spread like wildfire through the kingdom."

"Rumors?" Jonathan asked. "What sort of rumors?" Drinian looked around the room cautiously as though he didn't want anyone to overhear even though there was no one else but the five of them in that crowded room.

"They say the princess is still alive and is trying to return to Alden to take back the throne," whispered Drinian. "You four wouldn't happen to know anything about it, would you?" he added suspiciously. Everyone stood perfectly still, not daring to look one another in the eye.

"Maybe we do," Jonathan finally said. "Maybe we don't. Either way, it's none of your business."

"Oh really?" said Drinian slyly. Then he turned to Melony. "Did you really think I wouldn't notice the royal seal on your medallion?" Melony's eyes widened as Captain Drinian pulled her golden medallion out of his pocket. The once shining dwarvish gold had tarnished, but the mighty dragon etched in the metal was still clear as day.

"You took it?" Melony asked, her face stained with disgust.

"Old habits," Drinian said, gently tossing the medallion back to Melony. The moment Melony caught the necklace, the medallion's tarnished face returned to its shining glory. "I had to be sure you were truly the princess." Melony glared at the pirate as she put her medallion back around her neck.

"What are you going to do with me?" Melony asked, an edge in her voice that seemed to dare Drinian to some unnamed challenge.

"I know exactly what I'm going to do with you, Aralyn Kathar," the captain said with a smirk. "I'm going to help you."

"What?" Jonathan said. "You're helping us? But you're a pirate."

"I may be a pirate, but I'm not a bad person," Captain Drinian remarked with a laugh. "Where are you going?"

"Why should we trust you?" Jonathan asked.

"Because you don't have much of a choice," the captain said. "So I'll ask again. Where are you going?"

"Erith," Melony said. "East of Alden."

"Really?" Drinian said. "So close to Alden? Are you sure you want to go there?"

"Yes," Melony said. "We must go there."

"Alright," Captain Drinian said. "I will take you all to Erith. I only ask for one thing in return."

"What would that be?" asked Melony. "My medallion? It will be of no worth to you."

"I know dwarvish gold when I see it, princess," the captain assured her. "No. When you see that tyrant of a king, I want you to give him a beating for my father's sake." Melony smiled slightly.

"Gladly," she replied quietly.

After everything had been settled and what was left of the *Regina's* crew had been untied, Uncle Eli and Captain Drinian looked at charts and planned a route back to Contaria. Thankfully for Jonathan and the others, it would only be a two-day journey since the pirate ship had only left Alden a few days earlier.

Later that night, Jonathan lay in his hammock, staring at the planks that divided the lower deck from the vast starry skies. The members of Captain Drinian's crew slept swinging in hammocks all around him. Jonathan found out the hard way, though he was not surprised, that Odol snored so loudly it was nearly impossible for Jonathan to fall asleep. All he could do was stare at the ceiling, his head aching, longing for rest. Eventually, exhaustion overcame him, and his eyes drifted shut.

Seconds later, Jonathan stood at the top of a rock ledge. The sounds of a raging battle roared all around him. He looked down from the rock ledge into a small gorge. Below him, Melony wore full plate battle armor, her sword gripped tightly in her hand. A crimson cloak flew behind her, standing out against the pure white snow. She was fighting a soldier with her sword and shield, all her focus directed towards getting past this enemy.

Then Jonathan saw a tall knight in black armor creeping up behind Melony. The knight drew his sword and prepared to run Melony through. But she hadn't noticed him.

Jonathan tried to scream her name, but the sounds of battle drowned out the noise. He reached for an arrow, but his quiver was empty. He looked down to see his father's bow broken in his hands. What was he supposed to do? How could he save her?

He looked to his other hand and saw a sword, the kind only knights carry. He gripped it tightly and knew what he had to do.

"No!" Jonathan screamed as he raced down the gorge. He slipped between Melony and the knight, lifting his sword as the knight began to strike. The next thing he felt was a sword being pushed through his chest.

Jonathan woke up sweating and gasping for breath. His head throbbed and his eyes wouldn't focus. The nightmare. It had come again. Jonathan heard Calypso's words as they flooded into his mind. *Your vision will come true. Your vision will come true. Your vision will come true.*

Chapter 30
The Beginning of the End

Two days passed and finally Jonathan saw the distant shore of Contaria on the horizon.

"Those are the cliffs of Erith," Captain Drinian said to Jonathan later that day. "We'll send you ashore around noon." Jonathan only nodded. The weight of the coming battle grew heavier as the shores of Contaria came closer. What's worse, Jonathan couldn't get Calypso's words out of his head. They continuously whispered in his ear like a constant breeze passing through the trees. *Your vision will come true. Your vision will come true. Your vision will come true.*

"Look!" Micah cried, pointing to the shore. At the top of the high cliffs facing the sea were hundreds of tents. Smoke drifted towards the sea, carrying the scent of roasting meat to Jonathan's nose. White and green banners blew in the breeze, all bearing the symbol of a green emerald: the royal symbol of the Kingdom of Terren.

"We will lend you a longboat to get to shore with your supplies," Drinian told Jonathan. "Once you three are off my ship, we'll head out to sea."

"Three?" Jonathan asked, looking to Uncle Eli. "You're not coming, are you?"

"No, Jonathan, I'm not," Uncle Eli said. "Captain Drinian and I have worked it all out. He's going to take my crew and me back to Gush so we can get a new ship."

"I see," Jonathan said, crestfallen.

"You could come with me, you know," Uncle Eli said. "You and your brother. You two could sail with me across the seas, see new places." Jonathan shook his head gravely.

"I can't, Uncle Eli. I…" Jonathan said. His eyes shifted to Melony. "I have to help her."

"I see," replied Uncle Eli. "Well, give my love to your mother. I'll try and visit." However, Jonathan doubted this. If his uncle hadn't come to visit them for the past twelve years, how could he expect him to visit in the next twelve? Despite this, Jonathan reached out and embraced his uncle for what might be that last time for a long time.

"Prepare the longboat," Drinian ordered his crew. Like a swarm of bees, the crew quickly got to work pulling ropes, adjusting pulleys, and positioning a longboat over the edge of the ship. Jonathan climbed into the boat, Micah and Melony piling in after him. Then the crew began to slowly lower the boat into the water.

Jonathan looked up to his uncle, who was looking over the banister, waving to his nephews. Jonathan waved back before the boat splashed into the water. He and Melony each took an oar and began rowing to shore as the pirate ship sailed into the distance, its red flag fluttering in the breeze. It wasn't long before the bottom of the longboat scraped against the sandy floor of the bay. Jonathan pulled in his oar and grabbed the anchor before jumping out into the water. Ice cold water soaked into his boots, numbing his toes. Melony followed and grabbed hold of the rope that was attached to the anchor. Together, the two of them pulled the boat onto the sandy shore of Contaria.

Jonathan had just shoved the anchor into the sand when he saw a party of six dwarves approaching them. Each dwarf was clad in full battle armor and carried battle axes that could chop a fully armored knight in half with a single blow. Horgath, the dwarf prince from the caves of Terren, was leading the party, his family crest of a green jewel worn proudly on his tunic.

"Princess Aralyn," Horgath said. "We thought you might not make it. And we didn't expect you to come by sea. Where are the Nimberian forces?"

"We never reached Nimberia," Melony explained. "We ran into some rachins that drove us south through Sembal. A seer told us that it would be better for us to head further south instead of backtracking north. So we came here by sea."

"No Nimberians then?" Horgath asked, a hint of excitement in his voice.

"No," Melony replied.

"That's disappointing," Horgath said, though by the sound of his voice he seemed to think the opposite. "I suppose we should settle you four– wait a moment. Where's the druid boy?" Jonathan and Melony exchanged uncertain glances.

"He left," Micah said quietly.

"Well then," Horgath said, "I suppose I'll escort you into camp. Then we will discuss a new battle strategy. Follow me." The trio and the six dwarves walked silently across the sandy beach. The great rocky cliffs towered next to them, and Jonathan saw no clear way up to the camp.

Suddenly, the dwarves turned into a small crevice in the wall, wide enough for three men to stand shoulder to shoulder. A wooden platform was hanging from ropes that reached all the way to the top of the cliffs. Horgath gestured for the three of them to step onto the platform. Hesitant at first, Jonathan stepped onto the platform. Horgath stepped on with them and once the four of them had settled on the platform, one of Horgath's companions blew through a large ram's horn.

The platform jerked upwards, making Jonathan lose his balance. He didn't regain it until he grabbed one of the ropes that lifted the platform. Horgath rolled his eyes as Jonathan straightened himself. Though he was a good foot taller than the dwarf, Jonathan didn't feel like he had gained any more of Horgath's respect.

When finally the platform reached the top of the cliff, Jonathan saw the contraption that had lifted them from the beach. It looked like a contraption used on wells to pull a bucket out of the water, but much larger. Five particularly muscular dwarves stood turning the crank that lifted the platform. As soon as the platform stopped moving, Jonathan stepped onto solid land. Only after he stepped off did he look down at where they had been standing a minute before. The place where the other five dwarves were standing was hundreds of feet below them and the height made Jonathan dizzy. The dwarves were just beginning to lower the platform back down when Horgath headed in the direction of the camp.

The camp was bustling with endless activity. Dwarves were everywhere, all with large bushy beards and eyebrows that hid the numerous battle scars on these fierce warriors' faces. Some were sharpening weapons, sparks flying from the stone sharpening wheels. Others were polishing helmets and breastplates until they could see their reflections perfectly in the metalwork. Horgath finally stopped in front of a pair of tents not far from the great pavilion.

"These tents are for you," Horgath said. "Settle in quickly. Princess Aralyn, if you would come straight to the pavilion when you're done, we can begin formulating our battle plans." Horgath turned and walked quickly in the other direction without saying another word. Once the dwarf had left, Jonathan and Micah chose one of the tents, and Melony entered the other.

Jonathan stepped inside and was surprised to find that the inside of the tent was much larger than he could have ever expected. There were three beds, one for Micah, one for himself, and a third empty bed. Jonathan assumed had been meant for Belnor. Light filtered through the fabric of the tent, giving the space a warm glow. A large trunk had been shoved into one corner of the tent. Jonathan threw his pack onto one of the beds. Micah did not, as he might have usually done, run to one of the beds and jump onto it, arms spread with a broad smile on his face. Instead, he slowly walked to the bed that Jonathan's pack wasn't on and silently sat on it.

Jonathan moved to the trunk and opened the lid. Inside, he found a helmet, a chainmail shirt, a pair of steel shinguards, a newly polished breastplate, a tunic to wear over the mail, a set of gauntlets, and a shield. Jonathan's stomach lurched at the sight of the armor. He didn't want to be reminded of his dreams or Calypso's words so he quietly closed the trunk. When he turned around, Micah was still sitting on the bed, staring into space.

"Micah?" Jonathan asked. Micah shook himself back to reality.

"Yes?" replied Micah.

"I don't think you need to come to the meeting for the battle plan," Jonathan said slowly. He expected Micah to demand to be allowed to go to the council, but, to Jonathan's surprise, he didn't.

"Alright," Micah said softly.

"Alright?" Jonathan exclaimed. "You're not going to fight with me or beg me to let you go?"

"No," replied Micah. "I just don't feel like it." Micah didn't say anything else so Jonathan decided he should head to the council.

"I guess I'll head to the pavilion," he said to Micah. "Keep out of trouble while I'm gone." Micah only nodded. Jonathan gave him a reassuring smile before he turned, pulled on his cloak, and left the tent. He could see his breath like smoke as he walked quickly to the grand pavilion. When Jonathan got to the pavilion, Melony was already there with Horgath, King Nublae, and a few of the dwarf generals, beginning the discussion as to what would be done in the coming days.

"Because you failed to contact the Nimberians, our initial plan to intimidate King Alexander's troops into surrender is no longer an option," King Nublae said. "Our forces are now facing a long and bloody war. There is no way Alexander will give up his power when he is only facing the armies of the dwarves."

"There must be another way," Melony said. "I can't risk the lives of thousands of innocent men and dwarves in a civil war."

"What about single combat?" suggested one of the generals.

"According to the laws of war, the leaders of each army must be the ones to fight in single combat," King Nublae said. "But in this case, Melony would be the one to face Alexander."

"But you can't face Alexander, Melony," Jonathan said seconds after he walked in. "He's twice your size and better with a sword, no doubt."

"Well, then what do you suggest?" Melony asked.

"You know what I suggest?" Horgath said in frustration. "War. It's the only option."

"Your warmongering will lead to your fall, nephew," King Nublae scolded Horgath.

"What if we just had one battle?" Jonathan suggested. The entire pavilion went quiet.

"What are you talking about?" one of the dwarf generals asked.

"A single battle to settle it all," Jonathan said. "Melony can't face Alexander in single combat, but we can't have all-out war. I say we challenge Alexander and his forces to a single battle. His troops are most likely scattered across the land and not as prepared as we are. Therefore, we're at the advantage."

"How'd you come up with that?" Melony asked in surprise.

"I don't know," Jonathan replied. "Maybe I picked it up in Borlo."

"That's not a bad idea," Horgath grumbled in agreement. "But what if he doesn't agree?"

"Then we go to war," Jonathan said. "But if we give King Alexander the challenge, we'll at least have a chance to avoid a war. We might as well try."

"Well, if that's the plan, then we need someone to deliver the message," Melony said. No one spoke for a long moment.

"I'll go," said Jonathan.

"Jonathan, you can't," Melony said.

"Please," said Jonathan. "I can do this."

"Why do you want to go?" Melony said. "We can send a messenger."

"I want to help," Jonathan said.

"Are you sure?" asked Melony.

"I'm sure," Jonathan said. Melony looked at him with concern in her eyes.

"Fine," she finally sighed.

"I'll go get ready then," Jonathan said.

"I'll draft a challenge," Horgath grumbled. "You should leave in the morning."

"Right," replied Jonathan. He took a deep breath and marched out of the tent. He had to admit to himself that he was afraid to go into Alexander's camp. But if it meant helping Melony, he was willing to do whatever it took.

Chapter 31
A Visit to the King

Jonathan slowly approached the intimidating camp of King Alexander's army. Hundreds of quickly pitched tents were scattered across the valley with one enormous, elaborate pavilion in the very center of the camp. Jonathan instinctively headed for the largest pavilion, squeezing the scroll of parchment for some sort of comfort that it did not offer. As soon as he came within thirty feet of the camp, two armed guards came to meet him.

"What is your business here?" one of the guards inquired.

"I'm here to deliver a message from Princess Aralyn to King Alexander," Jonathan said, holding up the scroll of parchment. The guards looked uncertainly at each other. "As soon as possible, please," Jonathan urged. One of the guards headed into the camp.

"Stay here a moment," the remaining guard said. Jonathan stood in silence for nearly ten minutes. Finally, the other guard returned.

"This way," the guard commanded. The two guards turned around and began marching in the direction of King Alexander's pavilion. When Jonathan and the guards finally reached it, one of the guards opened the tent flap. Jonathan's stomach felt like it had twisted into a knot and then turned inside out. Would

Alexander remember him from the hearing months earlier? Would he punish him for escaping Borlo and helping Melony? Jonathan hesitated before entering. He took a deep breath and quickly ducked his head into the tent.

Alexander and three of his commanding officers were standing around a table covered in maps and scale models of armies and cavalries and enemy forces. Alexander was more terrifying than he had been at Alden. Instead of royal robes and jewels, he was wearing battle armor. His breastplate and gauntlets were both gilded with gold. His helmet, tucked under his arm, was polished like a mirror and a red plume hung from the top of it.

Jonathan cleared his throat loudly to announce his presence. The four men looked up in unison. King Alexander's brow furrowed in annoyance.

"What are you doing here, boy? Get back to your duties," King Alexander commanded.

"I'm here to deliver a message," Jonathan announced. All eyes were on him.

"A message from whom?" one of the officers asked. "The dwarf scum?"

"No," Jonathan replied, holding up the parchment. "Princess Aralyn."

"That's imposs—" started one of the officers.

"What does it say, boy?" Alexander interrupted him. Jonathan took a deep breath. He didn't know how to read but Melony had helped him memorize the message word for word before he had left. He opened the parchment and, pretending to read it, recited the message.

To King Alexander Henry Joseph Kathar of the Kingdom of Contaria, second son of King Peter Kathar II, Lord of Castle Galador.

From Princess Aralyn Melony Eleanor Kathar of Contaria, firstborn daughter of King Darius Kathar I and rightful heir to the throne of Contaria.

Greetings,

On this the third day of the twelfth month of the year one thousand two after the establishment of the kingdoms, I, Princess Aralyn, offer King Alexander the challenge of a single battle. This battle shall be fought tomorrow, the fourth day of the twelfth month, on the Fields of Erith and shall be the battle to settle the matter of the throne of Contaria. If King Alexander and his allies are able to defeat the armies of my allies, then the throne shall be rightfully and undisputedly his. If my allies and I are able to defeat King Alexander and his allies, then I shall be crowned the true ruler of Contaria. The leader of the defeated force, if not killed during the course of the battle, shall be banished from Contaria and will never return on pain of death.

May your decision be made in good counsel.

Aralyn Melony Eleanor Kathar

Jonathan lowered the parchment to see Alexander's face, deep in thought.

"My lord—" one of the officers started, but Alexander held up his hand. The officer went silent.

"I remember you," King Alexander said. Jonathan's heart began to pound. "You were the boy that stood up for my niece during her hearing. You defied my power." Jonathan didn't know what to say. Still staring at Jonathan, Alexander said to one of the officers, "Have a letter of acceptance to the challenge be drawn up. And have this young man flogged." The two guards that had stayed standing at the door quickly grabbed hold of Jonathan so he could not run away.

"But I have to deliver your acceptance letter," Jonathan said, trying to find a way to get out of the trouble he'd gotten himself in.

"I have plenty of messengers of my own," Alexander said. "If your princess truly wants you back, she'll have to pay for it. Take him away." The guards pulled Jonathan out of the tent, leading him against his will further into the camp. They finally stopped in front of a wooden post that had been driven into the ground and had shackles bolted to it. The guards pulled Jonathan's cloak and jerkin off so that only his thin, cotton shirt shielded him from the cold winter air.

Jonathan knew he had to get away. As soon as one of the guards' grips loosened, he pulled his arm free and punched the other guard in the cheek. But before Jonathan could do anything else, the guard tightened his hold on him. And the other hit Jonathan so hard in the face that he saw stars. Then they forced Jonathan to his knees next to the post and shackled his wrists to it. His face to the post, Jonathan strained his neck to see what the guards were doing.

Crack.

Jonathan felt a sharp pain across his back. It came so suddenly that he bit down on his tongue. The taste of blood filled his mouth. Another crack of the whip, another slash across his back. Jonathan hissed in pain. By the time the whipping ended, his back was riddled fresh wounds criss-crossing each other and dripping with dark red blood. The whip had torn his his shirt, and now it was nothing but bloody rags hanging from his arms.

"If he doesn't die by tomorrow, I'll pay you ten bid," one guard said.

"I'll hold you to that," replied the other as they walked away, leaving Jonathan bloody and bruised. He leaned his forehead against the flogging post and tried to hide his face from passing soldiers as hot tears rolled down his cheeks. All he could do was pray to the Creator for some sort of miracle.

About an hour later, snow began to fall. Jonathan shivered violently as the freezing snowflakes stung his exposed back.

Jonathan could hear the footsteps of the soldiers all around him. A pair of boots stopped next to him. *Oh no,* Jonathan thought. *Now the mocking from the soldiers will start for sure.* But to Jonathan's surprise, he felt a thin blanket being draped over his back. It wasn't much but it was better than the pure biting cold of the snow.

"Well, well, well," said the owner of the black boots. His voice seemed oddly familiar to Jonathan. "Are you supposed to be a royal messenger? Last I knew, you were a refugee from Borlo, Jonathan Fletcher." At that moment, Jonathan knew exactly who was speaking and smiled.

"Henry?" Jonathan said as he lifted his head to look at his friend.

"You didn't get rid of me that easily," Henry said as he crouched next to Jonathan, a grin spreading across his face. His hair had gotten longer since the last time Jonathan had seen him. He seemed stronger too. "You look terrible."

"I didn't look nearly as bad when I arrived at this camp," Jonathan said. "How are you alive? We thought you'd been–"

"Hanged?" Henry finished for him. "Funny story that."

"Well, do tell," Jonathan said. Then gesturing to his shackles, he said, "I've got plenty of time."

"Right," Henry said with a grin. "Well, when those guards burst in, I pretended that I had been trying to stop you but you'd gotten away. They half believed me, but they took me to Sir Marcus anyway. Sir Marcus vouched for me and I went on my way, unscathed."

"You're joking!" Jonathan exclaimed. "Not even a lashing for letting us get away or anything?"

"Nope. Like I said, Sir Marcus vouched for me. In fact, the next day I was promoted."

"Promoted? Promoted to what?" Jonathan asked intently.

"Junior lieutenant," Henry said, a grin on his face.

"That's great, I guess," Jonathan said. He wasn't certain if Henry's happiness about being in promoted was a good thing or a bad thing. "Then what happened?"

"Nothing much, really," Henry said. "We trained as usual. I got to sit with the older and higher-ranked boys at meals. It was good fun. Then about two weeks ago, Sir Marcus received a message from the king ordering him to send everyone at Borlo to Erith for war. So we packed up and moved out. And we marched all the way here by foot. We've been here for about two days now, preparing for war." A soldier passed by and nodded to Henry. Henry nodded back gravely, trying not to act like he knew the prisoner. As soon as he was out of sight, Henry turned back to Jonathan "Now that I've told my end of it, what's happened to you?"

"I can't say right now," Jonathan said. "There's too much to tell. Right now I need to get out of here before the king rethinks his decision and decides to behead me."

"Alright," Henry agreed, disappointed that he would have to wait a while longer to hear his best friend's adventures. "I probably can't get you out until after dark, even with Sir Marcus's help."

"Good. More time to come up with an escape plan," Jonathan said.

"And a battle plan," added Henry.

"Battle plan?" Jonathan repeated.

"Yes," Henry said. "You think I'm going to fight for that tyrant against my best friend? No way. Sir Marcus and I are both going to fight with you and Melony."

"Alright, then what's the plan?" Jonathan said.

"Well, I was thinking about that," said Henry. "You see, Sir Marcus controls all the troops from Borlo. That makes up almost a fifth of Alexander's army. And I'll bet you anything he knows many other commanders who have the same feelings about

Alexander that he has. Say our forces come into battle and suddenly fight *against* Alexander's army. Wouldn't that be a shock for Alexander?"

"You're right, it would," Jonathan said, almost believing the plan could work. "But how would our armies tell the difference between your men and Alexander's men? You all wear the same uniforms."

"We can rub soot and black ink on our faces like the wild people of the east and Wanderers," Henry suggested. "So anyone with a sooty face is on your side."

"I think that might work!" Jonathan exclaimed excitedly.

"Lieutenant Henry," shouted another soldier.

"Coming, sir," Henry shouted back. Then to Jonathan, "I gotta go. I'll be back after dark to get you out of here."

"Take your time," Jonathan said sarcastically. Henry smiled and then ran off in the direction of the calling soldier.

Chapter 32
Sir Jonathan

T he snow finally stopped falling after a few hours. But the bitter cold left Jonathan's toes numb and his teeth chattering. And the blanket Henry had placed on his back wasn't helping much. Soon after Henry had left, King Alexander posted a guard beside Jonathan that changed every three hours. It was near the end of the fourth shift, around eleven o'clock, when Henry finally returned and approached the guard stationed there.

"Your shift's over," Henry said. "I'm here to relieve you."

"Aren't you a little young to be guarding the prisoner?" the guard asked.

"I don't ask questions, I just take orders. And I was ordered by Sir Marcus to relieve you," Henry barked. The guard shrugged, yawned, and then walked back to his tent without asking any more questions. As soon as the guard was gone, Henry pulled a set of keys from his pocket.

"Where'd you get those?" Jonathan asked quietly.

"I know people," was all Henry said. He quickly began unlocking the shackles around Jonathan's wrists. As soon as he was free, Jonathan looked down at his wrists. They were bruised and rubbed raw, and when he touched them, they stung unbearably.

"We need to get out of here," Henry said. "The next shift actually starts in ten minutes so we need to get as far away from here as possible before the next guard arrives." He grabbed Jonathan and helped him to his feet. As Jonathan stood up, his body ached from the whip lashes and the hours of kneeling against the post. Henry took off his own cloak and wrapped it around his friend. Then Henry didn't hesitate another moment. He grabbed Jonathan's arm and dragged him away.

"Where are we going?" Jonathan asked.

"To the edge of camp," Henry replied. "Sir Marcus is waiting there with a steed for you." The two boys ran silently through the camp, darting in and out of the shadows and avoiding any soldiers who happened to cross their path. The stars twinkled above them in patches as dark clouds began to roll over the sky. It was ten minutes before Henry and Jonathan reached the edge of the camp. There, holding the reins of a black stallion, was Sir Marcus.

"Sir Marcus," Jonathan whispered.

"It's good to see you again," replied Sir Marcus, shaking Jonathan's hand firmly. He handed Jonathan the horse's reins. "His name is Theseus, one of my prized warhorses. He won't fail to get back to your camp."

"Thank you," Jonathan whispered. "Has Henry told you of the battle plan?"

"He has," Sir Marcus said, digging a scroll of parchment from his satchel and handing it to Jonathan. "This is a copy of our plan and King Alexander's."

"Won't Alexander discover they're missing?" Jonathan asked.

"No, I ensured he won't find out," said Sir Marcus. Then he pulled something from Theseus's saddle. "I believe this is yours." Sir Marcus handed Jonathan a long, thin package. When Jonathan unwrapped it, he saw that it was his black, recurve bow: his father's bow. The one they had taken from him at Castle Galador so many months ago.

"Thank you," Jonathan whispered.

"The next shift has started by now," Henry said. "You need to get out of here fast."

"I'll see you on the battlefield," Jonathan said, taking Henry's hand and firmly shaking it.

"Not if I see you first," Henry said.

Jonathan climbed onto Theseus and put the bow in front of him across the saddle. Then he snapped the reins. The jet black horse ran like the wind across the valley, away from the enemy camp, and into the night. The cold wind stung Jonathan's cheeks as he tried to keep the cloak as close to his body as he could. He never heard anyone come after him, nor the howls of hounds coming behind him. After a half hour of hard riding, the lights of the dwarf camp came into view. A few minutes after that, they arrived in the camp, both exhausted. Melony and Micah ran out of their tents to him. Melony's face was pale with worry and Micah was green.

"Jonathan, what happened?" she cried.

"Alexander accepts the terms of the battle," Jonathan said quickly.

"We know," she exclaimed. "Alexander sent us a messenger. But you should have gotten back hours ago." Then she saw his bruised wrists. "Jonathan, your wrists!"

"It's not that bad," Jonathan lied.

"Your shirt is nothing but rags!" she exclaimed. "And why is it stained with blood? What happened?"

"Alexander wasn't exactly happy to see me again," Jonathan said. "But I had help getting away."

"Help? From who?" Micah asked.

"Sir Marcus," Jonathan said. "And Henry."

"Henry's alive?" exclaimed Micah.

"Yeah, and, even better, he has a plan that might win us the battle," Jonathan explained.

"I'm sorry I sent you into that, Jonathan," Melony said. "I should have known…"

"It's alright," Jonathan insisted. "I was the one who wanted to go. Now let's get to Horgath's tent. We have a lot to discuss."

"Wait," Melony said quietly. She fingered her sword for a moment before slowly pulling it from its sheath. "Jonathan, kneel." Confused, Jonathan got down on one knee. Melony lifted her sword and set it on Jonathan's right shoulder. Then she moved it to his left. "Rise, *Sir* Jonathan Fletcher, Knight of Contaria."

"You can't knight me," Jonathan said. "I'm a peasant."

"I can knight whomever I want," Melony said. "Besides, you deserve it." Then she turned the sword so the handle faced Jonathan. "Take it."

"This sword is made for a knight," Jonathan said in bewilderment.

"Well, you *are* a knight," Melony said. Jonathan reached out timidly and took hold of the sword's handle. It was a beautiful sword, simple yet elegant. The steely grey handle was wrapped in black leather, making it easy to grip. "What will you name it?"

"What?" Jonathan asked in confusion. "Why would I name it?"

"All the greatest swords have names," replied Melony with a smile. "Any ideas?"

"I'll have to think about it," said Jonathan. He didn't know exactly how to feel. He was happy and nervous and proud and unprepared, all in a single moment. But mostly he felt frightened. Everything was falling into place. He had been given a sword for the third time, just as Calypso had said. And in his dream, he had carried a sword like those only knights carried. Now, he held that very sword in his hands, and he would carry it into battle in only a few hours. But Calypso couldn't be right. His vision couldn't come true. Or could it?

Jonathan stood at the top of a rock ledge. The sounds of a raging battle roared all around him. He looked down from the rock ledge into a small gorge. Below him, Melony wore full plate battle armor, her sword gripped tightly in her hand. A crimson cloak flew behind her, standing out against the pure white snow. She was fighting a soldier with her sword and shield, all her focus directed towards getting past this enemy.

Then Jonathan saw a tall knight in black armor creeping up behind Melony. The knight drew his sword and prepared to run Melony through. But she hadn't noticed him.

Jonathan tried to scream her name, but the sounds of battle drowned out the noise. He reached for an arrow, but his quiver was empty. He looked down to see his father's bow broken in his hands. What was he supposed to do? How could he save her?

He looked to his other hand and saw a sword, the kind only knights carry. He gripped it tightly and knew what he had to do.

"No!" Jonathan screamed as he raced down the gorge. He slipped between Melony and the knight, lifting his sword as the knight began to strike. The next thing he felt was a sword being pushed through his chest.

Jonathan woke up, sweating and gasping for air. His heart was racing, and his head was pounding. He sat up in his cot and looked around. Micah was still sleeping soundly, a moonbeam lighting his face. Jonathan got up and quietly stepped out into the cool night air. The full moon bathed the surrounding landscape in the soft, silver glow of its unearthly beauty.

"Jonathan?" said Micah, standing at the tent's entrance. "What's wrong?"

"Nothing," Jonathan said half-heartedly.

"You're nervous about the battle, aren't you?" Micah said.

"Yeah," Jonathan replied. "What about you?"

"Honestly," Micah began, "I'm really scared."

"Why?" Jonathan wondered out loud.

"Well, it's a battle," Micah said. "I'm just scared that something will happen to you. That I'll be left alone."

"Micah, you will never be alone, I promise you," Jonathan said. "But if anything bad happens, I want you to know that you shouldn't be afraid."

"I'll try," Micah said. Jonathan sat there staring at the stars, not knowing exactly what to do or say. Sunrise might mark the last day of his life, and he didn't know what to say to his little brother. He mindlessly put his hand in his satchel and began fiddling with the red leather strap of the hycreni horn. *I'm going to die tomorrow*, Jonathan thought. *He needs to know that I'm not trying to abandon him. I'm not like our father.* He carefully pulled out the horn. *Am I?* He set it in Micah's lap.

"What's this for?" Micah asked.

"I want you to have it," said Jonathan.

"Really?" Micah said wide-eyed. "But, it's yours. You got it from the hycreni, and you made it into a horn. I couldn't–"

"Yes, you can," Jonathan said. "But you have to promise me something."

"What?" asked Micah.

"That you will stay here in the camp during the battle," Jonathan said. "No fighting."

"But I want to help," Micah pleaded.

"And I want you to stay safe," replied Jonathan. "So if something goes wrong, if I don't make it, I want you to go home. Go back to Silan and take care of Mum."

"But–" Micah tried to say.

"Promise me," Jonathan said.

"Fine," Micah sighed. "I promise." As they spoke, snow began to fall once more.

"Let's get inside," Jonathan said. "Tomorrow's a big day."

Chapter 33
The Battle at Erith

J onathan shifted nervously in the chainmail shirt he wore under his red and white tunic. The plates of armor on his shoulders and shins felt tight and heavy and held in his body heat like an oven. On the other hand, his face was freezing, his breath creating little clouds before his own eyes. Two quivers of arrows swung from the horn of the saddle, and Jonathan's black recurve bow sat in his lap. The longsword Melony had given him the night before swung at his side, the steel blade hidden by the leather sheath.

Melony sat on a proud warhorse next to him, her own armor shining in the late-morning sun. Her right hand gripped the handle of her sword while her left carried a wide shield, decorated with her coat of arms: a golden dragon on a white background with a diagonal red stripe crossing it. Her brow was furrowed as she prepared for the battle ahead.

On the other side of Melony sat King Nublae on the back of a mole the size of a horse. He and the mole both wore heavy plated armor covered in dwarf glyphs and scenes of ancient battles. The dwarf king had his sword unsheathed, and the mole bore its sharp buckteeth. Horgath sat on a similar mole, a battle axe in his hands and his helmet shining in the sunlight. Jonathan looked back and saw thousands of dwarves, all dressed in armor head to toe, ready to fight.

Suddenly, the earth began to shake. Jonathan thought it might be an earthquake, but he was mistaken. He heard a horn being sounded from *under* the ground. Then, a huge creature sprang up out of the earth. It looked like a giant earthworm. But its body was thick as a man's arm span, and its mouth was a beak the size of a man. The part that was sticking out of the ground was as long as a cedar tree is tall, and even more was still hidden deep below the surface of the earth. *So that's a whurm*, Jonathan thought. He had often heard of the giant war whurms of the dwarves in stories and songs, but he'd never thought he'd see one in all his life.

On the whurm's back sat a smaller figure with a large helmet that shimmered in the dazzling sunlight. From the helm flowed a long, greyish beard, the kind only dwarves have. Two more giant whurms sprang up from the ground, each with a small dwarf rider on its back. Soon after the whurms emerged, a tune began to rise from the army. It was quiet at first, but quickly became louder and louder. And soon, Jonathan could hear the words of the song.

Sound the drums of battle
Sound the horns of war
Come gather 'round the battlefield
Brothers wear' and worn
Brothers of the mountains
Sisters of the hills
Come gather 'round the battlefield
Brothers wear' and worn

Take up your sword, O brother
Take up your shield, O kin

Come meet us at our battle camp
Brothers wear' and worn
We fight for our mountain
We fight for our king
Come meet us at our battle camp
Brothers wear' and worn

Our en'mies shall surrender
We'll fly our vict'ry flag
Come shout our glorious battle cry
Brothers wear' and worn
Though blood doth stain our armor
And all around mourn kin
Come shout our glorious battle cry
Brothers wear' and worn

By the end of the song, every dwarf in the army was booming the song in unison. And when it ended, a great war cry rose from the army. The song stirred up something inside Jonathan: a desire to fight, to defend his friends and his family. He tightened his grip on his bow. Then he heard the faint sounding of a horn from the other side of the plain. Jonathan looked out across the soon-to-be battlefield and saw a great mass of soldiers holding spears, shields, swords, and other weapons that looked far more than deadly.

Jonathan said a silent prayer to the Creator. He prayed for safety for himself and the others. He prayed that his and Henry's plan would work and that this was the right thing to do. Finally, in one last desperate attempt, Jonathan prayed his vision would not come true. King Nublae raised his sword. The whole army fell deadly silent in anticipation. He turned to face his army.

"Brothers!" Nublae shouted. "Today we ride out to face a tyrant and a murderer of kin. If his reign persists, he will not stop until his empire covers Nimberia and the free kingdoms of the dwarves. So let this day long be remembered in songs and legends as one of valor, honor, and bravery. Let it be remembered as the day the kingdoms of dwarves and men were united under one cause. Let it be remembered as a day of victory!" An even louder cheer arose from the dwarf army. Nublae turned his mole steed back around to face Alexander's army.

"For Victory!" King Nublae cried.

"For Victory!" the dwarves cried.

"For Contaria!" Melony cried.

"For Contaria," Jonathan said quietly. His stomach twisted into a knot, endlessly and painfully untying and retying itself. A great roar came from the army of dwarves. Then, like one massive being, the army charged forward, pushing Jonathan and Theseus along with them like a great wave of the ocean. The warm blood pumped through Jonathan's veins, adrenaline rushing through him. His heart beat faster and faster as he neared the opposing army, which had also begun to charge.

Jonathan grasped the hilt of his sword, preparing to draw it when the time came. But, when an enemy soldier dressed in black and chainmail was merely thirty feet in front of him, Jonathan let go of the hilt of his sword, grabbed his bow, and quickly nocked an arrow. He let it fire, piercing the man in the shoulder.

And then, all at once, chaos reigned. Men and dwarves were knocked from their horses. Blood sprayed from every direction like rain, soaking Jonathan's hair and face. Dwarves and men stood locked in combat. Blood stained the clothes of almost everyone; whether it was the blood of the individual or the blood of a foe, Jonathan couldn't tell. Bloodied shields and broken spearheads were already strewn haphazardly across the ground alongside the bleeding corpses of fallen warriors. Jonathan's stomach lurched. But he continued fighting with all his strength, shooting enemies from atop Theseus.

Jonathan suddenly felt the blow of a shield against his body. The blow knocked Jonathan off Theseus's back, throwing him onto the ground. He felt something warm trickle down his brow. Jonathan touched his brow and when he brought his hand down, his gloved fingertips were tipped with blood. By the time he got back to his feet, Theseus had disappeared into the fray of the battle. But in front of Jonathan, sitting on a proud, black warhorse, was the Black Knight. He brandished his shield, which was now streaked with Jonathan's blood.

Jonathan looked around for his bow, which he'd lost his grip on during his fall. He saw it, just ten feet away. But the Black Knight spotted Jonathan and charged his horse. Jonathan rushed towards the bow, but he was stopped by a horse galloping across his path, trampling the bow into nothing but splinters. Jonathan felt a lump form in his throat. He shook himself violently. *There isn't time for being sentimental*, Jonathan thought.

The Black Knight was only twenty feet away, racing towards him. Jonathan drew his sword and stood ready to fight. The knight pulled out his sword and prepared to attack Jonathan from the saddle. He extended his arm downwards, blade out and ready to swing at Jonathan's head. Jonathan lifted his blade and barely blocked the blow, the clashing of the blades ringing out across the battlefield. The knight flew past Jonathan, and then turned to try another pass. Jonathan lifted his sword to ready for the second blow. The knight charged, sword extended, and hit Jonathan's sword. This time, the Black Knight struck with such force that it knocked the blade out of Jonathan's hand and out of reach. Then the knight turned around for one final blow.

Defenseless, Jonathan tried to run, but his legs wouldn't move. He was paralyzed with fear. The Black Knight galloped nearer and swung to behead Jonathan. But when the knight swung, Jonathan ducked the blow and grabbed the knight's arm. As the horse kept running, Jonathan managed to pull the Black Knight off the horse's back, throwing him and his sword to the ground. By the time Jonathan had pulled the sword out of the snow, the Black Knight was back on his feet.

Then, to Jonathan's surprise, the weaponless knight rushed at Jonathan headfirst. Jonathan raised the knight's sword and slashed at the Black Knight. But the blade merely clanged against his armor, doing nothing to the man inside. *This isn't going to work,* Jonathan thought. Suddenly, he had an idea. He turned the sword and grabbed the blade with his two gloved hands. The Black Knight again tried to tackle him, but Jonathan swung the sword's hilt at the knight's head as hard as he could. The force knocked the knight backwards and to the ground. Jonathan leapt onto the fallen knight and lifted his visor. The man inside was bleeding from the nose and trying desperately to get up. Jonathan lifted the blade over the Black Knight's face.

"Kill me already," the Black Knight cried in anticipation. But Jonathan didn't move. Instead, he lowered his blade.

"No," Jonathan said. "I'll let the queen decide your punishment." Then he hit the Black Knight over the helm with the hilt of his sword. The knight and his suit of armor went limp. He threw the sword down at the Black Knight's side. Suddenly, Jonathan heard another sounding of a horn: Alexander's reinforcements. Jonathan felt a surge of hope. Alexander was in for a nasty surprise.

Jonathan watched as another wave of men and boy soldiers approached the battlefield. He saw that, unlike the soldiers from the first wave, all these soldiers had painted their faces black. As the army entered the fray, the men didn't begin to fight the dwarves, to the surprise of the first wave. Instead, the soldiers with black faces began to fight the soldiers of the first wave.

Jonathan quickly grabbed the pile of broken wood that had once been his father's bow and shoved the splinters into his satchel. But as he placed the pieces into his bag, he paid little heed to the battle around him and did not notice the soldier rushing towards him. Only as the soldier was about to land his blow did Jonathan see him. Jonathan didn't have his sword; it had been knocked from his hands by the Black Knight. But miraculously he saw a blade flash before his eyes and come between the soldier's sword and his face. Jonathan looked to his right to see who had blocked the blow. It was Henry, his face covered in soot. Henry pushed the soldier backwards with his sword and stabbed him in the chest.

"Where in Iyuandil is your weapon?" Henry shouted.

"I dropped it," Jonathan replied.

"Then go pick it up!" said Henry. Jonathan rushed to his sword, lying a few feet away in the blood-soaked snow. When he turned around, Henry was fighting another soldier, and more were charging just behind him. Jonathan rushed to his friend's side. They slashed and stabbed at the oncoming soldiers, wary to block every blow. This wasn't training, where you had a second chance if you made a mistake. But no matter how hard they fought or how many foes they bested, the number of soldiers became overwhelming. Jonathan looked around and saw many dwarves being overwhelmed as well. It looked as if they were going to fail. Suddenly, Jonathan heard a voice on the wind.

"*Tunsonico yip crakisoua, mien naami en oppugido, ipche venetalu as mien axinak,*[14]" the voice cried. Dark clouds began to creep in from the north, and deep rolls of thunder bellowed across the battlefield. Suddenly, a bolt of lightning cut across the sky. Jonathan looked to the north. Belnor sat on the back of Aamar the horse, his right hand glowing with power and raised high in

---

[14] Thunder and lightning, my friends in battle, immediately come to my aid.

the air, his black hair whipping in the wind. Dozens more druids on horseback stood behind Belnor, swords glinting in the flashing lightning. All at once, they rushed into the valley, Belnor leading the charge, his green cloak billowing behind him.

Belnor rode directly into the fray and found Jonathan and Henry in the middle of the battlefield. As he approached them, he lifted his hand towards the sky. Bolts of lightning knocked many soldiers away from Jonathan and Henry. Then he rode up alongside them. Jonathan saw that the druid wore five rings, one on each finger. And each ring had a different color gemstone: one a blue sapphire, another a purple amethyst, the third a bright ruby, the fourth a white crystal, and the final an emerald.

"You're back!" Jonathan exclaimed.

"I thought you might want some help," Belnor said with a grin.

"You're amazing, Belnor," Henry exclaimed. "Absolutely amazing."

"What are those rings?" Jonathan asked.

"Their proeli rings," Belnor said. "Druid battle rings. They act as charms, but they're easier to use." Belnor looked around the battlefield. "Where's Melony?"

Jonathan looked around. Melony wasn't anywhere in sight. Then, he saw a gorge not ten feet away from them. Suddenly, six more of Alexander's men came charging at the three of them. Jonathan raced in the other direction, towards the edge of the gorge.

He skidded to a stop at the ledge and stood at the top, the sounds of the raging battle roaring all around him. He looked down from the rock ledge into the gorge. Below him he saw Melony, her sword gripped tightly in her right hand, her shield in her left. Her crimson cloak flew behind her, standing out against the pure white snow. She was fighting one of Alexander's soldiers, all her focus directed towards getting past this enemy.

But Jonathan soon saw a new enemy creeping towards Melony. It was not the knight that Jonathan had always dreamed about; it was King Alexander himself. The king drew his sword and prepared to run Melony through. But she hadn't noticed him.

"Melony!" Jonathan cried, but the sounds of battle drowned him out. Jonathan instinctively reached for an arrow, but the quiver was empty. He looked down at the splintered remains of his father's bow in his satchel. He felt the weight of the sword in his hand. He knew what he had to do. He looked up and tightened his grip on his sword.

"No!" Jonathan screamed. He raced down the gorge and slipped between Melony and the king, lifting his sword as Alexander began to strike, just in time to save Melony. Jonathan cried out in pain as the sword drove through his chest, just missing his heart. Jonathan saw Melony spin around, a look of horror on her face. Then, he saw it change. The horror in Melony's eyes turned into pure, white-hot fury.

King Alexander pulled his sword from Jonathan just in time to block a strike from Melony's blade. Jonathan staggered back and leaned against the rock's face and watched as Alexander and Melony circled each other like lions prepared to attack, their glares as sharp and deadly as their swords.

"Well, well, well," King Alexander said, "if it isn't my long-lost niece. I honestly didn't think you'd take things this far. I thought you might try the passive approach again." Melony tried to jab at him with the tip of her sword, but Alexander blocked it with his shield. "Though I have to admit, you are persistent, Aralyn."

"You don't even know," Melony said. Fury glowed in her eyes, making every stroke and blow a thing to be feared. But the king was an equal match for his young niece. They soon had their blades locked together, neither daring to move their blade first, their faces two inches from each other.

"You fight well," said Alexander. "But you're weak, like your father. The kingdom will never accept you as the queen."

"Maybe not," Melony said, "but at least I'm doing Contaria a favor."

"And what would that be?" Alexander asked her, a smile of triumph on his face.

"I'm getting rid of you," Melony said. She released her blade from the lock and ducked as the king's sword just missed her head. But Melony didn't run quite fast enough. Just as she moved from between her uncle and the wall, Alexander kicked her legs out from under her. Melony fell to the ground. She flipped over, Alexander standing over her. First, he stabbed her left arm, then her right leg. Melony screamed in pain. Alexander raised his sword, preparing to plunge the blade through her heart.

"Melony," Jonathan cried out. Alexander turned his head to Jonathan. A wicked smile crept onto the king's face.

"Yes. Yes, that's much better," Alexander said maliciously. He moved his sword away from Melony. "Aralyn, you've been a thorn in my side for too long now," he said. "Now I am going to make you suffer. First, You're going to watch me kill your friend. Then, it's your turn."

Jonathan watched the king turn and slowly walk towards him. He tried to shuffle away, but the pain in his chest was unbearable so he could only move a few inches before falling to his knees. He clutched at his chest, and his gloved hands came away soaked in blood. Alexander was so close now that Jonathan could see both the bloodlust and insanity in the king's eyes.

Jonathan looked past Alexander to Melony. He saw the white-hot fury in her eyes becoming hotter than before. Despite her wounds, Melony unsteadily got to her feet. Jonathan knew he had to buy her time.

"I bet you're disappointed," Jonathan said. Melony was picking her sword out of the snow.

"About what?" Alexander asked. Jonathan saw Melony take a step forward, but she hissed in pain as she stepped with her bad leg.

"Losing the battle," Jonathan continued. "Losing your crown. Maybe even your head."

"Oh I'm not going to lose," Alexander said, a devilish grin on his face. Melony raised her sword above her head. "I'm going to kill you, boy. Then I'm going to kill my niece. Then all your little friends. That's all the victory I need." Alexander was still focused on how much pain he was about to inflict upon both Jonathan and Melony, so he did not notice Melony charging towards him with bull-like anger.

But just in time, he saw Melony in the corner of his eye, her sword held high above her head. He lifted his sword in the nick of time and blocked his niece's blow. But he was unprepared for the newfound force in his niece's strokes. She thrashed, lunged, and swung as Jonathan had never seen. Alexander was barely able to block Melony's powerful blows.

Melony lunged at Alexander, aiming for his chest. But Alexander blocked with his shield and hit Melony's bad leg with the hilt of his sword. Melony hissed in pain, grabbing her leg. Alexander swung his sword at Melony's head, his face red with rage. Melony ducked the blow and rolled out of the way. Then Alexander lifted his sword over his head and swung it down directly towards Melony's face. Melony, in a last desperate effort, kicked Alexander's legs out from under him. His sword flew out of his hand. Melony scrambled to her feet and grabbed Alexander's sword from the ground. When she held it up, Jonathan saw it was her father's sword that Alexander had taken in Alden when they first saw him. As Alexander tried to get to his feet, Melony put one sword behind Alexander's neck and rested the tip of the other on his heart.

"Congratulations, Aralyn," the defeated king said maliciously. "Now what are you going to do? Hmmm? Kill me? Do you have the stomach for it? Or are you just a weak, cowardly, wannabe royal, just like your father?"

"Don't speak about my father that way," Melony hissed. She raised her father's blade, preparing to strike.

"Melony!" said a voice. Henry was just coming around the corner. Melony looked up. "Melony, don't do something you'll regret," Henry said. "Are you doing this for your people or revenge?" Melony glared back at him, fire in her electric blue eyes.

"What's the difference?" Melony muttered. She pushed her sword through her uncle's chest, straight through his heart. A surprised look was left on the dead king's face as he slumped onto the stony ground. Melony pulled the sword out of Alexander's chest, the blade dripping with dark red blood.

Jonathan thought he might be sick as he saw the deadly-fury in Melony's eyes. But he didn't dwell on it long. He was drowning in pain as blood oozed from his chest and formed small, dark red puddles staining the snow. His breathing was fast and shallow, his vision becoming dim and fuzzy. He was practically lying in the snow now, too dazed by the pain to move. Melony ran towards Jonathan and knelt beside him.

"Jonathan!" she exclaimed.

"Melony," Jonathan said, the pain searing in his chest.

"Don't speak," Melony commanded. "Save your strength." She sounded like she was trying to keep herself from crying.

"What have you done?" Jonathan asked her. "He was your uncle."

"He was a monster," she replied. "Monsters deserve to die." Suddenly, a burst of pain, pain like fire, shot through his chest. It was too great for Jonathan to contain. He gave an ear-splitting cry. Henry raced to Jonathan's side.

"Jonathan, it's going to be alright," Henry tried to comfort his friend. But it was no use. Jonathan knew what was happening. He was dying. "The plan worked perfectly," Henry continued. "Alexander never saw what was coming till it was too late." Jonathan gave a slight smile, crooked from the immense pain.

"We got that adventure you wanted," Jonathan said.

"It didn't turn out the way I thought it would, though," Henry said, tears glistening in his eyes.

"Henry," Jonathan said. It was becoming increasingly painful for Jonathan to breath. "When I'm gone–"

"Don't talk like that," Henry interrupted.

"Let me speak. When I'm gone, will you promise to look after my Mum and Micah? Can you do that for me?"

"Jonathan, I–" Henry tried to say.

"Promise me. Please." Henry merely nodded. "And can you tell Micah something for me?"

"What?" Henry asked, his voice breaking.

"Tell him to be strong," Jonathan said. "Tell him that he's got to be the man of the house. Tell him he can't forget what I told him last night. Will you tell him that?"

"Yeah," Henry said. "Yeah, I will." Jonathan heard soft sobbing coming from his right. A drop of water splashed onto his arm. Jonathan turned his head. Tears were streaming down Melony's cheeks.

"This is all my fault," Melony whispered.

"No, it's not," Jonathan said. "I was the one who ran between you and Alexander. If this is anyone's fault, it's mine."

"I can't do this, Jonathan," she said. "I can't be queen. I'm not ready."

"Of course you're ready," Jonathan said. "You've been ready since the day I met you." Jonathan could feel the life being drained from him. Everything was growing dark. Everything was fading.

"Hold on, Jonathan!" Melony said. But her voice sounded distant, almost like a dream. "Please hold on."

Chapter 34
The Creator

E verything was dark. But through the darkness, Jonathan saw images flash before him. He saw Belnor looking over him, herbs and bandages in hand. He saw Micah watching him from a corner, his cheeks pale and his eyes puffy and red from crying.

He heard Belnor say, "I'll do my best, but he really needs a miracle." But soon, the flashes stopped, and Jonathan felt himself being dragged down into the darkness again.

Jonathan didn't know what was happening to him, but he felt the pain in his chest increasing with every minute that passed. At least, he thought the minutes were passing. And yet, hours seemed like minutes and minutes seemed like hours. Jonathan felt as though the darkness was swallowing him.

Suddenly, Jonathan awoke. Bright white and gold light surrounded him and darkness no longer held him. His chest no longer seared with pain. In fact, he realized he was in no pain whatsoever. He touched his face and arms, searching for the scars and cuts from the past few months. But there was nothing. Not a single bruise or blemish. He looked down at the floor he was lying on. A reflection looked up at him from the polished, gold floor. He looked perfect and healthy. *Where am I?* Jonathan wondered. He was dressed in pure white garments and had nothing to cover his feet. The pure gold floor felt warm against his bare feet and his hands.

Jonathan looked around the magnificent hall he found himself in. He gawked at the enormous columns that lined the great hall. He could not see the roof above him, nor where the columns ended. The whole room was filled with light, but there were no windows, lamps, hearths, or torches of any kind to provide the light in the hall. Jonathan could only wonder where he might be.

"Jonathan, son of Acillion," said a booming voice. Jonathan trembled as he looked around wildly for the source of the voice.

"Y– y– yes?" Jonathan stuttered. "Who are you?"

"I am the Creator. The Lord of the Seven Realms and King in High Heaven."

"The Creator," Jonathan repeated in near disbelief. He fell to his knees in fear, his face touching the floor. "So it's true. I'm dead."

"No. You are not dead, Jonathan," replied the Creator.

"I'm not?" Jonathan asked. "But I did die! I was stabbed."

"You are not dead because your story is not complete," the Creator said. "My plans for you are not yet fulfilled." Jonathan didn't know whether he was relieved or not.

"What do you want of me?" Jonathan asked.

"The girl, Aralyn.," the Creator said.

"What about her?" Jonathan asked.

"She is to be a great leader. A beacon of hope in the dark times coming."

"What dark times?" Jonathan asked. But the Creator did not answer him.

"Jonathan," said the Creator, "I am going to send you back to Iyuandil. And I have a task for you: a task that will determine the fate of Iyuandil."

"What is it?" Jonathan asked nervously.

"Protect the young queen."

"Protect Melony? Is she in danger?" Jonathan asked.

"All of Iyuandil is in danger, Jonathan," the Creator replied. "A dark power has begun to rise. And if the girl is not protected, then the darkness will devour the realm." At that, a huge weight seemed to fall on Jonathan, weighing down his whole body and soul.

"Why me?" Jonathan asked. "I'm just a peasant boy from Silan."

"Because I chose you," the Creator said. "I chose you at the beginning of time, before the seven realms had even been created."

"But what if I fail?" asked Jonathan. "What if I—"

"Do not worry about what could happen," said the Creator. "I know my plans for all seven realms, just as I know my plans for you. Now return. They are waiting." Jonathan heard a horn resound in the distance, one of the most beautiful horns he had ever heard. Suddenly, he began to feel as though he was being pulled from a dream. But he still had so many questions.

"Wait! What is the darkness? Who is waiting? I need answers!" Jonathan's vision of the great hall began to grow dim.

"Do not tell Melony what I have told you," the Creator said. "I will be with you always." Jonathan's chest began to hurt and he felt an achiness creep upon him and spread throughout his body. His vision faded into black. The horn got louder and louder. Then it suddenly stopped.

Jonathan forced his eyes to open. They stung as they were greeted by the bright candlelight. As soon as his eyes adjusted to the light, Jonathan realized he was in the tent he and Micah had shared before the battle. He heard a fire crackling joyously outside. Many candles lit the tent, and it appeared to be twilight. Suddenly, Belnor walked into the tent through the front opening. His green cloak was torn and dirty. He had several fresh cuts, and his hair was singed at the edges. But Belnor also had an older scar that had not been there when they had parted ways in Talar. The scar ran down the left side of his face across his eye.

"You're awake," Belnor exclaimed when he saw Jonathan stirring.

"Yeah," Jonathan said. "What happened?"

"What do you remember?" Belnor asked.

"I remember fighting in the battle," Jonathan started. "Alexander stabbed me and then Melony…" It was too awful to say it outloud. So he decided to change the subject. "Did we win the battle? Is it still going on?"

"It's over," Belnor said. "It ended shortly after you blacked out. Melony and Henry brought you back to the camp."

"How long have I been out?" Jonathan asked.

"Six hours at least," replied Belnor. "Your wounds were severe. I'm surprised you're awake so soon."

"I should be dead," Jonathan said. "Alexander stabbed me. So how did I survive?"

"He barely missed your heart," Belnor said. "But thankfully he did miss. I would have been unable to heal you at all if he hadn't."

"You healed me?" Jonathan asked.

"I did what I could," Belnor said.

"Thank you," said Jonathan. Belnor nodded in reply. The druid was turning to leave when Jonathan asked, "Did you find what you were looking for?" Belnor stopped halfway through the door. Jonathan thought he heard him sigh.

"No," Belnor replied. He turned to face Jonathan again. "I traveled east to the place Calypso had told me to go. But when I arrived, the place was guarded by… creatures. I dare not say any more about them here. Only that I could not overpower them. I'm lucky to have escaped with my life." He gestured to the long scar that now streaked down his face. "They left me with this."

Just then, Melony limped into the tent. Her cheeks were tear stained and her eyes were red from crying, but when she saw Jonathan sitting up in bed, her eyes widened.

"Jonathan!" Melony shouted. "You're alive!"

"Was I dead?" Jonathan asked lightheartedly.

"No," Melony replied with a light smile. Then it faded. "We were all so worried. I don't know what I would have done if you'd—"

"I'm fine now, Melony," Jonathan assured her. "How's Micah?"

"He's alright," Melony said. "He's been blowing that horn of yours non-stop though. I should probably go and find him. He wanted to be told the moment you woke up. I'll be right back." Then she turned to leave the tent. As she left, Jonathan noticed the bandages tied around her leg where Alexander had stabbed her. Once she was outside, Jonathan heard her call for Micah and Henry.

"Jonathan," Belnor started, "the others don't know the real reason why I left. I'd prefer it to stay that way."

"Why?" Jonathan asked. But Belnor didn't have time to reply for just then, Micah dashed into the tent and crouched next to Jonathan's bed. Melony walked in after him.

"Jonathan!" Micah cried. He looked tired, and his eyes were red and puffy from crying. "It's a miracle."

"Actually, it was Belnor's healing," Jonathan said.

"But Belnor said you wouldn't survive without a miracle," Micah said.

"It's true," said Belnor. "I did what I could, but I didn't think you'd last the night."

"Then how—" Jonathan started. That's when he remembered his dream with the Creator. He had to have sent him back.

"The hycreni horn," Micah whispered.

"What?" said Belnor.

"Jonathan got a hycreni horn while you were gone," Micah explained. "Legend says it gives you what you want most. And I was blowing it a few minutes ago."

"You don't think—" Melony started. But just then, Henry walked into the tent.

"Jonathan Fletcher," Henry said. "Don't ever do that again. You had us all holding our breath and crying our eyes out."

"It's good to see you too," Jonathan said with a smile. He tried to sit up to see his friends better. But pain suddenly shot from his chest to his entire body. It was like he was on fire on the inside. It was almost unbearable.

"I wouldn't do that if I were you, Jonathan," said Belnor. "You're still recovering from your wounds. You need rest." Then to the others he said, "We should let him get it." Melony nodded. Belnor turned and left the room. Micah followed him closely and Henry went after them. Melony waited a few more moments before smiling at Jonathan and leaving. Then Jonathan was alone.

The silence was calming. Jonathan closed his eyes. Suddenly, an image flashed before his shut eyes: an enormous stone gate emerging from a cloud of smoke and flames. It made Jonathan sick to look at it. The doors of the gate were half open, and some dark energy was pulsating from it. Jonathan snapped his eyes open. *No*, he thought. *Not again.*

Chapter 35
A New Queen

Two weeks later, Jonathan stood in the throne room of Castle Galador. Sunlight shone through the large windows, giving the entire room a golden glow. The nobles of the Council of Contaria, all richly clothed in silks and gemstones, sat in their chairs lining the room.

Jonathan stood high above the entire scene in a balcony. He wore a silver cape, grey trousers, a cotton shirt, and a sky-blue tunic with a silver coat of arms embroidered onto the front. His family had never had a coat of arms. So Jonathan had chosen for himself a griffin on a blue plain with a silver chevron. His sword, which he had named Oathkeeper, hung at his side. Micah stood next to him, wearing a very similar outfit and looking like a royal page. On the other side of Micah stood Belnor. He wore a clean, green cloak and a single charm necklace around his neck: the eye-shaped charm Calypso had given him.

Suddenly, a fanfare of trumpets sounded. Jonathan heard the doors below him open. The entire room fell silent. All the nobles stood as a figure emerged from below the balcony, finally giving Jonathan his first glimpse of the new queen. A long, crimson cape trailed behind her, and her blonde hair was twisted into an intricate bun. She walked all the way down the golden carpet to the grand throne at the end of the room, the throne of her forefathers. She turned around to face her people.

Melony wore a beautiful, long, white dress with a crimson sash, crimson shoes, and a single ring on her finger. She was beautiful. She was nervous; Jonathan could tell even from way up in the balcony.

The lord of ceremonies walked to the throne. A young page followed him closely holding a crimson pillow with golden tassels. Sitting on the pillow was a gold crown with five glittering rubies set into it. The lord lifted the crown from the cushion and held it just above Melony's head.

"Do you swear to rule justly and fairly to the best of your ability for the rest of your days?" he said. Melony muttered something, but a few seconds later she seemed to realize her mistake.

"I swear," she said much louder.

"Do you swear to use your power for the good, the protection, and the preservation of the kingdom and her people?"

"I swear."

"Do you swear to serve the Creator and his will, not your own?"

"I swear."

"Then by the power vested in me, I crown you Queen Aralyn Melony Eleanor Kathar of Contaria."

The lord placed the crown on Melony's head. Then she turned and sat in the great throne. All at once, the entire hall erupted in a chorus of "Long live the queen! Long live the queen! Long live the queen!"

That evening, the great ball was the most overwhelming experience Jonathan had ever had. The noblewomen and great ladies were adorned with jewels and clothed in layers upon layers of silks and satins, making their ball gowns so wide that it was hard to walk between them. The noblemen, knights, and lords wore silk suits with feathery hats that, if he didn't watch where he was walking, Jonathan would run into and get a mouthful of feathers.

There were delicacies from every kingdom on the tables that lined the room, everything from chocolate-covered corius fruit to roasted peacock. And the dancing was so intricate and confusing that Jonathan was afraid he'd be trampled under the feet of the other dancers if he tried to join in.

Jonathan felt like a trapped animal among the noble guests of the ball. He pushed his way between the ladies' regal gowns and the lords' fancy feather hats. He didn't know exactly where he was going, but he needed to get out of there. Jonathan almost fell face-forward when he reached the edge of the crowd. Directly in front of him was an open double-doorway that led out onto a balcony. Jonathan slipped out onto the balcony and for the first time in hours, he could breathe once again.

"Jonathan?" Melony said. Jonathan turned around and saw her silhouetted against the bright lights of the ballroom, her white gown glittering in the candlelight. "Are you alright?"

"Yeah," Jonathan said, giving her a weak smile. "Why do you ask?"

"I saw you leaving," Melony said. "You looked flustered."

"I'm just not used to all this fancy royalty stuff," Jonathan said bluntly.

"Neither am I," Melony replied. She stepped out into the night and leaned against the banister next to Jonathan and looked to the city to the north side of the castle, the glowing lights of the houses and shops like stars in the darkness. Jonathan felt better having Melony next to him. He didn't feel so alone. A slow waltz began to play inside. It was a sad tune, but not too sad. It was the kind of tune that made you want to dance all night. Jonathan extended his hand to the new queen.

"May I have this dance?" he asked just as he had in the desert. Melony smiled and took his extended hand. The music played for what felt like hours as the moon rose steadily over the palace. Jonathan almost forgot about all the guests inside. It was just he and Melony.

"What are you going to do?" Melony asked after they had been dancing for who knows how long. "After the ball and everything, where are you going to go?"

"Home," Jonathan said. "Micah and I will leave tomorrow."

"So soon?" Melony said in surprise.

"I have to go home to my mum," Jonathan said. "We could be dead for all she knows." Melony nodded in understanding.

"You'll come and visit though?" Melony asked.

"All the time," Jonathan said. They danced a little while longer.

"You know, you are a knight now," Melony said.

"Yeah," Jonathan replied.

"Well I was just thinking," Melony started, "there's lots of room in the castle, and I never really repaid you for helping me."

"You don't owe me anything," Jonathan said.

"Yes I do," said Melony. "You saved my life. Many times. And you and Micah earned this as much as I have."

"Earned what?" Jonathan asked.

"A home in the castle, of course," Melony replied. "You're invited and so is Micah and your mum of course. Henry can come too."

"I don't know what to say," stuttered Jonathan.

"Just think about it," Melony said. "I guess you'll be headed out first thing in the morning?"

"Probably," Jonathan said.

"What are you two doing out here?" Henry asked playfully as he walked out onto the balcony. Melony pulled away from Jonathan.

"We were just talking," Melony said.

"Uh huh," Henry said.

"I should probably go back in," Melony announced. Then she quickly walked back into the bustle of the ballroom. Jonathan's heart was still fluttering as he watched her walk away. When she was out of sight, he looked to Henry, who was grinning broadly.

"What?" Jonathan asked.

"Nothing," Henry replied, unconvincingly.

"Why are you smiling like that?" asked Jonathan. Henry chuckled.

"It's just," Henry started, "she's very beautiful."

"Yeah, I guess so," Jonathan said. "You know you don't always need to say the first thing that pops in your head."

"I wasn't," Henry said. As he walked over to Jonathan, he patted him on the back. "I was saying what *you* were thinking."

"Wait, wait, wait," Jonathan said. "What are you talking about?"

"I've seen the way you look at her," Henry said, a grin on his face. "You, my friend, are in love."

"What? No!" Jonathan objected.

"Yes you are," Henry said. "I saw how you were looking at her. And how you danced with her."

"We're just friends," said Jonathan. "Besides, you can't know that someone is in love just by looking at them."

"Yes, you can," Henry replied. "And I think Melony's figured it out too."

"Great," Jonathan said sarcastically. Henry sat down on the thick balcony rail.

"Even if I did love her, and I'm not saying I do," Jonathan said, "I wouldn't be able to do anything about it. She's the queen! And if you didn't notice, I'm a poor, blacksmith's apprentice."

"Actually, you're a knight now," Henry corrected him.

"It doesn't matter," Jonathan said. "There are still... other issues."

"What do you mean?" Henry asked, still grinning broadly.

"There's some... family history between us," Jonathan said.

"What are you talking about?" Henry asked.

"I didn't tell you about something that happened before we were banished to Borlo," Jonathan said somberly. "While we were in the dungeons, we met my father." Henry's face fell.

"Your father?" Henry asked, gravely. "The one that left?"

"Yeah," Jonathan said.

"But what does that have to do with you and Melony?" Henry asked. Jonathan looked at his best friend and took a deep breath. Then he said the dreaded words.

"My father killed King Darius," Jonathan said. Henry stared dumbfounded at Jonathan.

"That's a good one, Jonathan," Henry said, clearly unsure whether he should be smiling or not.

"I'm not joking," Jonathan said.

"Come on, Jonathan. You can't expect me to believe that," Henry said carefully.

"Why would I make up something like that?" Jonathan replied.

"But why did he do it?" Henry asked.

"Because he was an assassin," Jonathan explained, "and Alexander had hired him to do the job."

"So by family history, you mean–" Henry whispered.

"*My* father killed *her* father," Jonathan said. "If Melony feels anything for me, it should be hate."

"Jonathan, you said it yourself," Henry said. "Your *father* killed the king. Not you. Why should she hate *you* for that?"

"I don't know," Jonathan sighed. He looked out over the harbor to the south of the castle, the moon's reflection on the water.

"So what are you going to do now?" Henry finally asked.

"We've got to leave in the morning," Jonathan said. "But I need to do something before we go." He turned back to Henry. "I just hope I have the courage to do it."

Chapter 36

Forgive or Forget

It was the early hours of the morning, just before sunrise. Jonathan and Melony walked solemnly down a long hall in the palace that led to the dungeons. Melony took the key in her hand and unlocked the door to her left. It swung open with a low creak, revealing the ominous stairwell that spiraled down into the darkness below. Jonathan grabbed a torch from the wall outside the dungeons. Then the two silently descended the stairs, deeper and deeper down. When they finally reached the bottom, two guards greeted them with a low bow. They moved silently past the guards and walked straight towards the cells.

It wasn't long before they came to the cell that they were looking for. Inside sat a pitiful figure with matted hair and a long beard, both dirty blonde. He looked up suddenly with his wild eyes.

"Jonathan?" Acillion exclaimed. Jonathan solemnly walked to the bars of the cage. "You've returned? Why?"

"I had unfinished business down here," Jonathan replied solemnly. "And because I have a question that needs to be answered."

"What?" Acillion asked.

"Why did you do it?" Jonathan asked. "Why did you murder the king?" Acillion gave out a deep sigh of regret.

"Alexander threatened to destroy everything I held dear," Acillion replied. "My family, my friends, and my village."

"And you chose to murder Darius instead?" Jonathan said.

"Yes," Acillion answered, guilt ringing in his voice. "It may not have been the right thing to do, but it was my only option. And not a day goes by that I don't regret killing Darius."

"Acillion," Jonathan began. "Every day since I was a boy I have thought about you. I've hated you and cursed you a thousand times."

"I'm sure you have," Acillion said. "And I don't blame you."

"Your crimes against me, Micah, and Mum are enormous and the scars from them will never fade," Jonathan said. "But, you are my father. And everything you did was because you loved us; you wanted to protect us. I see that now. And I think, after all these years, I am finally ready to forgive you." Though it was hard to tell in the torchlight, Jonathan thought he saw tears welling up in Acillion's eyes and trickling down his cheeks. The anger and hatred that Jonathan had felt burning inside him for so long was finally fading from his heart.

"Thank you," Acillion whispered, "my son." Jonathan felt some invisible weight leave his shoulders. But before Jonathan could say anything else, Melony quietly stepped forward. Her eyes flashed with hatred the same way they had when she first discovered her uncle's true nature.

"You killed my father," Melony said. "According to the laws of this kingdom, I should have you hanged. In fact I would feel that my father's death was truly avenged if I had you executed." Melony stared at Acillion with those electric blue eyes. Jonathan shuddered at the hatred emanating from her. "However, despite your crimes against my father and my kingdom, you spared my life when you could have taken it. And for that I am indebted to you. So to repay that debt, I shall let you live."

"Thank you, Your Majesty," Acillion said.

"But I promise you this, Acillion Fletcher," Melony said. "You shall remain in this dungeon for the rest of your days."

"Your Majesty, please," begged Acillion. "I had no choice!" But Melony ignored him as she turned around and began walking away from the cell.

"I'm sorry," Jonathan whispered. Then he too began walking away reluctantly, a pit forming in his stomach.

"No! You can't leave me here!" Acillion shouted after them. Jonathan's eyes were beginning to sting as his tried to hold back tears. He hurriedly climbed up the spiral staircase and out the door into the early dawn air. "Don't leave—" But Acillion's shouts were cut off by the slamming door of the dungeon.

"Melony, please," Jonathan said as soon as the door closed.

"I don't want to hear it, Jonathan," said Melony.

"He's my father," Jonathan said.

"He *killed* my father," Melony said, raising her voice. "I wish I could forgive him, for yours and Micah's sakes. But I just can't, Jonathan. I must know that those who killed my father have been brought to justice."

"And killing your uncle wasn't enough?" Jonathan shouted back. Melony averted her eyes.

"He deserved it," Melony muttered. Then she lifted her head. "We need to go to the stables. The others will be waiting for us." She marched away without waiting for Jonathan to follow. He lingered there a minute longer, not knowing exactly what to feel or what to say to Micah when he went back to their room.

If anything, at least my father's alive, Jonathan thought. *But I swear that one day my father will be given his freedom.*

Chapter 37
Home

Theseus's hooves sank into the snow as they trotted along the road. About two dozen boys and young men followed behind. Jonathan, Micah, Henry, Melony, and all the fellow villagers with them had traveled for five days now. Belnor had left their party the morning of the third day and headed in the direction of his camp.

"I'll visit soon," Belnor had said with a smile. By midday on the fifth day, Jonathan, Micah, and Henry began to recognize different landmarks. They were almost home.

The sun was beginning to set when Jonathan, who had taken the lead, rode over the final hill. Below him he saw the tiny buildings of Silan, thin ribbons of smoke rising from the chimneys. He could hear the clanging of metal on metal from the blacksmith. A roar of laughter from the tavern reached Jonathan's ears.

"I never thought I'd see it again," Henry said as he sat on his horse next to Jonathan. Jonathan nodded. He was too happy to say anything.

The four of them rode slowly down the steep hill, down the main road, and past the tavern. Five aged men came out to see who the travelers were. Micah waved to them from Aamar's back and a few waved back, eyes wide in disbelief.

As the parade continued through the town, boys and men broke away from the group and one by one to return to their homes. The village was filled with joyous noises. Men were reunited with their wives and children. Boys were reunited with their fathers and mothers. It wasn't long before Henry and Jonathan stopped at the blacksmith's shop. Mr. Smith was hammering away at the bent head of a hoe he was repairing, his back to the door. Henry stepped forward and knocked on the side of the door. Mr. Smith stopped what he was doing.

"I'm afraid we're closed," Mr. Smith said.

"That's alright," Henry said. "I'm not here to buy anything." Mr. Smith immediately turned around. Henry grinned at his father.

"Henry?" Mr. Smith said, tears of joy glittering in his eyes. Henry ran to his father and Mr. Smith hugged him so tight it seemed he would never let go. While Henry remained inside, Jonathan snuck back out onto his horse and rejoined the others.

All the other men and boys had gone their separate ways, so Jonathan rode straight to his home. He rode past the homes of the village, past all the fields of the farmers that he had long worked for, all the way to the edge of town near the woods.

His cottage home sat on the little hill, a thin pillar of smoke rising from the snow-capped chimney. The door, which the soldiers had broken into splinters all that time ago, had been replaced with brand new maple. The garden was completely dead and blanketed with snow, and only the dry stalks of old tomato plants were left sticking out. Jonathan looked at Micah, and Micah looked back at him, grinning ear to ear. The brothers dismounted as quickly as they could and scrambled to the door. When they were right in front of it, they stopped. Jonathan reached out and knocked softly on the new door.

"Just a moment," Mum's voice called from inside. A few seconds later, Mum, wrapped in her favorite and warmest shawl, opened the door. Her hair was tied in two braids and pulled together in the back with a piece of leather. She wore no smile on her face, and the sadness that had always lurked in her eyes seemed to have grown and seeped out of her. She looked like she had aged five years in just a few months. When she looked up and saw her sons standing before her, she covered her mouth with both her hands, and tears welled up in her eyes.

"Hello, Mum," Jonathan said softly. He stretched out his arms and Mum almost fell into them. Jonathan felt tears fall on his shoulder. Tears of joy. Then she let go to embrace Micah and held him close. Then she hugged both her sons at the same time, tears streaming down her face, overwhelmed with joy.

"My boys," Mum said, both of them in her arms. "My beautiful boys." But after a moment, Jonathan felt her embrace loosen. "Who is this?" Mum asked curiously. Jonathan turned around and saw Melony dismount and walk up to them.

"Mum, this is Melony," Jonathan said. "She's a good friend of ours. She saved my life many times. Both our lives."

"Not as many times as you've saved mine," Melony said with a smile. Then to Mum she said, "It's an honor to meet you."

"You as well," Mum said. "Well, let's not stand out here and catch a cold. Come inside. Tell me everything that happened." So the four of them headed inside the cottage, took their seats around the table, and began sipping on hot herbal tea, which tasted much better than anything Belnor had ever made for them.

Then, the three of them began telling their story. They told everything: leaving Silan, meeting Melony and Belnor and the druids, the storm on the river, being thrown in the dungeons, their time in Borlo and their escape, meeting the dwarves, traveling across the desert and the sea, finding Uncle Eli, the hycreni and the pirates, Jonathan's knighthood, and finally the great battle and the coronation. When Mum found out that Melony was truly the queen, she almost fainted and the boys had to help revive her. But they had all left out the part about meeting Acillion in the dungeons. *If Mum ever finds out about his crime and his fate, she'll never come to terms with it,* Jonathan thought. *It's better that she doesn't know.*

"I'm so proud of you," Mum said after the whole tale had been told. "And I missed you so much."

Later, Jonathan stood outside the cottage wrapped in a thick cloak. He watched the dark clouds pass over the starry sky, hiding and revealing the constellations. Though he was home, a weight was still pulling him down. It had been there ever since he'd met with the Creator.

Protect the young queen, the Creator's words rang through his head.

Protect Melony? Is she in danger? Jonathan heard his own words again.

All of Iyuandil is in danger, the Creator's voice had replied. It wasn't going to be easy, but Jonathan knew he had to obey the Creator. He had to protect Melony. Because if he didn't, the entire realm would be in peril. He returned to the cottage and locked the door, barring the cold and dark night from entering.

Epilogue

It had been nearly two months since the coronation. At Melony's invitation, Micah, Jonathan, their mother, and Henry had moved into the castle at Alden. Now it was nearing the end of winter. A thin layer of snow blanketed the cobblestone courtyards and frost made swirling patterns on the glass windows. Belnor had come for a visit from his clan and was talking with Micah in one of the many courtyards of the palace. He wore a long green cloak as he always had and his hair was still creeping towards his eyes. On the other hand, Micah had his hair recently trimmed, and his clothes were carefully made and lined with fur.

"Are you sure this is what you want?" Belnor gravely asked Micah.

"Yes," Micah said. "I'm sure."

"And you've talked to Jonathan about it?"

"Yes," Micah said slowly.

"What did he say?" asked Belnor.

"He wasn't happy about it," Micah said. "Not a bit. But I'm going anyway."

"Does he know that?" Belnor asked quietly.

"I'll tell him before we leave," Micah said.

"I warn you," Belnor said, "joining the Druid Order will not be easy. It comes with intense study, difficult choices, and a lot of hard work."

"This is what I'm supposed to do," Micah assured his friend. "I can feel it."

"Then you'll need to pack your things, but only what you need," Belnor said. "Then you will come with me when I leave for my clan."

"When will that be?" asked Micah.

"Not long, I promise," Belnor replied.

Meanwhile, the clanging of metal against metal filled another of the castle courtyards. Jonathan lifted his wooden shield high above his head to block a blow from Henry's broadsword. Jonathan swung his sword sideways to hit Henry in the ribs, but his friend blocked it just in time with his own shield. Suddenly, Jonathan slipped on the icy ground and fell hard on his back, the wind knocked out of him. With a quick movement of his wrist, Henry twisted his sword around Jonathan's, knocking it out of Jonathan's hand and out of his reach.

"Excellent job, Henry," Sir Marcus said as he walked into the courtyard. His breath made clouds when he spoke and he was wrapped in thick fur robes. Jonathan got to his feet with Henry's help, panting as he wiped sweat from his forehead with his sleeve. He wore a leather breastplate over his blue and white tunic and had a steel helmet on his head. In his right hand he gripped a broadsword, which had been blunted around the edges. In his left he carried a wooden shield decorated with the golden dragon of the royal crest. Henry wore something nearly identical, though his tunic was green rather than blue.

"You two are well on your way to becoming some of the greatest knights in Contaria," Sir Marcus exclaimed, a broad smile on his face.

"Tell that to my arm," Jonathan complained. His arm and every other part of his body were completely sore. They had been training in the courtyard like this for weeks. And with Sir Marcus training them, it was like being in Borlo again, though colder.

"You'll get used to it," Sir Marcus replied. "Now go again." Jonathan gripped his sword and lifted his shield. Perhaps some day he really would be the greatest knight in the kingdom. But until then, he'd have to be content with the strenuous training and hard work. And maybe, just maybe, he could save his father from his tragic fate.

A young messenger of Contaria sat in the mountains of the Kingdom of Terren, watching the magnificent sunset. That day was the third anniversary of Queen Aralyn's coronation. The messenger thought of his home back at Alden. By now, songs and dances would be starting and feasts would be prepared. But he would be sleeping in the cold of the mountains. As he thought of home, the sun sank below the horizon. Suddenly, a very old man dressed in rags scrambled around the bend behind him. His eyes were wild and wide with terror.

"What's wrong, sir?" said the messenger.

"It's coming!" wheezed the old man. "From the east. The darkness is coming!" The messenger wondered what the man could mean. Was an army coming near? Barbarians from the east? Then he saw it. On the edge of the horizon, in the farthest corner of the east, he saw it. A great, dark, unearthly cloud lurking in the far east.

"What is that?" the messenger asked the old man.

"That is death," the old man cried. "The death of all the kingdoms. And the rise of an empire of darkness!" A new wave of panic rushed though the messenger. If what the old man was saying was true, the queen had to be warned.

The messenger jumped to his feet and lifted his horse's saddle from the ground. He heaved it onto his quick-footed steed's back and hurriedly tightened the straps. As he went to mount, the old man grabbed his arm with surprising force and with his other hand he forced a small piece of parchment into his hand.

"The darkness is coming," said the man slowly. "All Iyuandil shall suffer and perish. And all shall die." Then he fell to the ground, still as stone and cold as ice.

The messenger was shocked. He looked at the place where the old man had grabbed him. On his arm was a black smudge, which he tried to wipe off. But he quickly discovered it was no smudge. It was his skin, now diseased and decomposing. And it was slowly spreading. Then he looked down at the parchment. Three words were written on the paper in dark red blood: *Ceizhar is coming*.

He took one last look at the old man, covered in blackened, diseased skin with some sort of black liquid oozing from his mouth. The messenger jumped onto his horse and snapped the reins. The horse ran down the mountainside, the messenger barely holding on. He had to get to the queen, but he knew he didn't have much time. He knew Iyuandil didn't have much time.

Our heroes will return in

The
Blood Key

Learn more about Iyuandil and Lynde Leatherwood at
lyndeleatherwood.wordpress.com

Acknowledgements

Thanks to Ross Funderburk for designing the beautiful cover for *The Lost Queen*. It was more amazing than I could have ever imagined or hoped for.

Thanks to Hillary Buchanan, my editor, for reviewing and editing this novel. Your reviews and suggestions were invaluable in this process.

Thanks to my parents, Dan and Dee Dee Leatherwood for supporting me in all my ventures and crazy ideas.

Made in the USA
Middletown, DE
10 March 2024

51213133R00208